Charles Henry Churchill

The Life of Abdel Kader, Ex-Sultan of the Arabs of Algeria

Charles Henry Churchill

The Life of Abdel Kader, Ex-Sultan of the Arabs of Algeria

ISBN/EAN: 9783744751124

Printed in Europe, USA, Canada, Australia, Japan

Cover: Foto ©Raphael Reischuk / pixelio.de

More available books at **www.hansebooks.com**

THE

LIFE OF ABDEL KADER,

Ex-Sultan of the Arabs of Algeria;

WRITTEN FROM HIS OWN DICTATION, AND COMPILED
FROM OTHER AUTHENTIC SOURCES.

BY

COLONEL CHURCHILL,

AUTHOR OF "TEN YEARS' RESIDENCE IN MOUNT LEBANON," "DRUZES AND
MARONITES UNDER TURKISH RULE," ETC., ETC.

LONDON:

CHAPMAN AND HALL, 193, PICCADILLY.

1867.

DEDICATION.

———•———

NAPOLEON III.,

EMPEROR OF THE FRENCH.

SIRE,

OTHERS may claim for themselves the glorious privilege of recording the courage, the sagacity, and the skill with which you wield the destinies of Imperial France.

I have claimed, and am proud to have procured at your hands, the humbler but scarcely less glorious privilege of dedicating to you a work which, while it celebrates the great actions, and portrays the magnanimous character of one of the most remarkable men whom the Arab race has ever produced, records at the the same time, though feebly and inadequately, the loftiness of principle, the chivalry of sentiment, and the sensitive jealousy of French honour which induced you to release him, spontaneously and unconditionally, from treacherous detention on French soil.

That act was a worthy inauguration of your splendid reign. That act alone would suffice to give it imperishable lustre.

CHARLES HENRY CHURCHILL.

PREFACE.

If I should unfortunately be mistaken in the belief and expectation that some interest may yet be excited in the public mind by a narrative of the deeds and exploits of the illustrious Arab whose extraordinary career I have selected as my theme, I shall willingly impute my disappointment, not to any want of judgment and discrimination on the part of the reading public, but to my own involuntary and sincere enthusiasm for all that is grand, ennobling, and romantic.

That these characteristics attach largely, and in their most inspiring and soul-stirring sense, to the life I here depict, the following pages amply corroborate.

Having thus exhibited the feeling which induced me to approach a subject, to me fraught with peculiar and almost irresistible attractions, I proceed to state the circumstances under which my present work was commenced and matured.

I was at Constantinople in the month of September, 1853. Abdel Kader was living, an exile, at Broussa. To have been within such an easy distance of one who had for so many years been invested in my mind with all the attributes of heroic greatness, without gratifying myself with a sight of his person, would have been doing treason to my warmest and most deeply cherished feelings.

I went accordingly and saw him. The acquaintance thus formed has been, through a course of wholly unexpected events, gradually cemented into permanent and unalterable friendship. In 1855 he came to Syria, his place of exile having been changed from Broussa to Damascus. On his way to the latter, from Beyrout, he passed a short time with me in the Lebanon.

Our long conversations turned almost exclusively on his proceedings in Algeria—his campaigns, his mode of administration, his plans of reform, and his principles of government. He expatiated on all these topics not only without reserve, but with exuberance. The stirring recital, delivered at times in a tone of martial energy and enthusiasm, at others with an air of melancholy which touchingly told of glowing hopes cruelly frustrated, of lofty and patriotic inspirations rudely crushed, was more than simply interesting and exciting. It had the grandeur and sublimity of a tragic epos.

What, I thought to myself, shall all this wealth of incident, these marvels of adventure, these varieties of good, and great, and glorious deeds be suffered to become "alms for oblivion,"* without even a feeble attempt at rescue? Shall no one ever have an opportunity afforded him of being urged to greater self-discipline, to the attainment of more mental hardihood, to the practice of more severe abnegation, by having placed before him the record of a life marked and distinguished by such absorbing devotion to a sense of duty, such fixity and concentration of purpose, such unflinching and indomitable perseverance?

Filled with these reflections, I one morning asked Abdel Kader if he had never kept any written me-

---

* " Time hath, my lord, a wallet at his back,
  Wherein he puts alms for oblivion."
  TROILUS AND CRESSIDA.

morial of the transactions in which he had been engaged. He smiled, and said, "I was far too much and constantly occupied for that. I did my duty. That was quite occupation enough for me." "But," I added, "if I were to endeavour to draw up an account of your various doings, would you assist me?" "With the greatest pleasure," was his reply; "I will gladly answer any questions you may wish to put me." That day I resolved to write the biography of Abdel Kader.

I resided at Damascus during the winter of 1859—60, expressly for the purpose of carrying my resolution into effect. Abdel Kader, though a perfect miser of his time, courteously consented to give me an audience of one hour every day. The mine was before me. I had to extract the ore. I laboured at it for five months. Some French works assisted me in my course of inquiry, such as " Annales Algériennes," by M. Pellissier de Reynaud ; " Histoire de la Conquête d'Alger," by M. Alfred Nottement, and others of less note. At a later period I also profited by a publication more exclusively devoted to my subject, entitled " Abdel Kader, sa vie Politique et Militaire," by M. Bellemare.

Abdel Kader was most ample in his remarks and commentaries on these authors. He thus supplied me with many useful rectifications, as well as a vast amount of valuable and important original information from himself.

Little did I contemplate, on leaving Damascus in the spring of 1860, that another chapter was so soon about to be added to his strange and eventful history; or that his glorious star, apparently for ever set, was destined shortly to burst forth again with meteoric splendour. Of his magnanimous and exemplary conduct during the fearful massacre of the Christians in that city, through the shameless and heartless complicity of the Turkish authorities, I obtained the most extensive and correct details from eye-witnesses.

Such, then, were my materials. It remained for me to compile and embody them. I have done so. With all diffidence and humility I invite my readers to pronounce their verdict on the performance.

CONTENTS.

Contents.

LETTER OF ABDEL KADER TO THE AUTHOR.

PRAISE BE TO GOD ALONE!

To the amiable, the honourable, the all-accomplished and virtuous Colonel Churchill.

After offering you our salutations, and inquiring after your noble pleasure, we have to acknowledge your valued letter, showing your high regard for us.

May God recompense you with His highest rewards, and make your portion exceedingly rich and full in everlasting felicity.

We have now to state that we were hindered from replying to you sooner by an illness, which prevented us even for several days from going to the house of prayer. But now it is the most imperative of our imperative duties to thank you, in reply, for your great kindness. We never cease inquiring about all that may concern, or be connected with your Excellency; and we pray God to smooth and prosper our affairs in common, and to establish us in all rectitude and good works. With best wishes for your peace and happiness,

ABDEL KADER IBN MEHI-ED-DEEN.

1 *Jumadi*, 1273.
25th December, 1856.

LIFE OF ABDEL KADER.

CHAPTER I.

1807—1828.

ABDEL KADER NUSR-ED-DEEN, fourth son of Abdel Kader Mehi-ed-deen, was born in the month of May, 1807, at the paternal *ketna*, or family village, on the banks of the river Hammam. This locality lies in the district of Eghrees, appertaining to the province of Oran, in Algeria.

From his infancy Abdel Kader was the especial object of his father's fondest affections. Even when at the breast, the doting parent would constantly insist on taking the child in his arms; and he reluctantly permitted anyone but himself to do the duties of a nurse. Some secret and undefined impulse, as it seemed, impelled him to devote more than ordinary care and attention to the child, whose future career was to be so indelibly and gloriously associated with his country's weal.

The physical constitution of the boy early exhibited a robust development; whilst, by a strange contrast, his disposition displayed a great natural timidity. The term "frightened at a shadow" might have been taken in its most literal

B

sense in his case. In after years, and when in the pride and vigour of manhood, he shone forth as the bravest of the brave —ever foremost to lead the charge, or cover the retreat—his father would often rally him on his boyish frailty, and wonder at the extraordinary contrast.

The mental powers of the boy were more than usually precocious. At the age of five he could read and write; at twelve he was a Taleb, or an approved proficient in the Koran, the Hadeeth (traditional sayings of the prophet Mohammed), and all the most esteemed religious expositions. Two years later he attained the highly-prized distinction of being a Hafiz, or one who knows the entire Koran by heart. In this position he had a class in the family mosque, where he explained the most difficult and recondite passages of the commentators. The extent of his youthful ambition was to be a great Marabout, like his father, whom he loved and regarded with an enthusiasm amounting to adoration.

In his seventeenth year the youth was conspicuous amongst his associates for his remarkable strength and agility. The perfect symmetry and compactness of his figure—his height being about five feet six inches—his bony make, his broad, deep chest, all betokened a frame formed for untiring activity, and capable of enduring the utmost fatigue.

As an equestrian, none approached him. Not only was he a graceful rider, but his marvellous superiority in all those feats of horsemanship which require the nicest eye, the steadiest hand, and the greatest efforts of muscular power, was the theme of all who knew him. Touching his horse's shoulder with his breast, he would place one hand on its back, and vault over to the other side; or, putting the animal to its full speed, he would disengage his feet from the stirrups, stand up in the saddle, and fire at a mark with the utmost precision. Under his light and skilful touch, his well-trained Arab would kneel down, or walk for yards on his hind legs, its fore ones pawing the air, or spring and jump like a gazelle.

But it was on the race-course that the youth more particularly shone. That exciting pastime, into which the Algerian nobles enter with a passion not exceeded by our most devoted amateurs of the turf, was his peculiar element. Mounted on a jet-black steed—a colour he especially affected, as generally accompanied by superior equine qualities, and as throwing into relief the whiteness of his burnous—he was the cynosure of every eye.

His apparel was plain and simple. His arms alone displayed ornament. His long Tunisian musket was inlaid with silver; his pistols were encrusted with mother-of-pearl and coral; and his Damascus blade encased in a sheath of silver gilt. These brilliant appurtenances, combined with the partial gifts which Nature had lavished on his person, threw an inexpressible charm around his appearance.

His countenance, of the purest classic mould, was singularly attractive from its expressive and yet almost feminine beauty. His nose—middling-sized and delicately shaped—a pleasing mean between the Grecian and the Roman type; his lips, finely chiseled and slightly compressed, bespoke dignified reserve and firmness of purpose; while large, lustrous hazel eyes beamed from beneath a massive forehead of marble whiteness with subdued and melancholy softness, or flashed with the rays of genius and intelligence.

Once the race engaged, his whole bearing and demeanour exhibited the most perfect coolness and self-possession. Distancing his numerous competitors, he would often reach the goal alone, amidst shouts of applause, clapping of hands, and the exhilarating shouts of hundreds of female voices bursting out into the *zulagheel*—that shrill and piercing cry of joy and welcome amongst the Arabs, which is so cheering to the triumphant warrior.

Thus, when at a later period of his life he performed those marvellous courses which astonished and confounded his enemies—never sleeping for weeks together under cover, and rarely ungirdling his sword—it was truly said of him that "his saddle was his throne."

In Algeria, the nobility is divided into two distinct classes—the Marabouts and the Djouads. The former derive their position from religion; the other from the sword. These respective representatives of moral influence and physical strength regard each other with mutual scorn and jealousy. The Djouads accuse the Marabouts of ill-disguised ambition, and of a greedy covetousness after wealth and power, veiled under the specious pretext that every fresh acquisition they make was solely for the service of religion. The Marabouts taunt the Djouads with their violence, licentiousness, and love of rapine.

The Djied devotes himself entirely to the chase. He delights in all the bracing recreations which call forth skill and courage. His pride is to excel in falconry, in hunting the gazelle, the ostrich, the panther, and the wild boar. These violent pursuits, the thrilling excitement of which calls forth all the energies of body and mind, prepare him for the more serious encounters of war. The chase is the school for the razzia.

Abdel Kader, although he certainly never contemplated the possibility of ever being engaged in a razzia, and altogether repudiated such a mode of warfare (based as it generally was on the mere love of plunder), as equally contrary to his principles and his inclination, yet engaged ardently in field sports. His favourite diversion was to hunt the wild boar. Carefully avoiding the ostentatious display of the Djouads, as they sallied forth with their long train of adherents, their falcons, and their greyhounds, he privately mounted his horse, and taking only two or three domestics, plunged into the depths of the forest. On his return from his sporting excursions, he betook himself to his studies with renewed ardour.

It is not surprising that one so highly gifted by nature, and so earnest in the task of self-culture and improvement, should have gradually obtained a considerable ascendancy over all around him. Abdel Kader, indeed, already shared the unbounded respect, confidence, and affection which the Arabs of Oran had so long extended to his father. The latter, overjoyed to see his fondest hopes thus realised, could not perform a duty, or enjoy a social pleasure, without the presence of his favourite son. In his public audiences, his plans and projects, his lesser journeyings, or his more distant visits to the Turkish beys in the town, and the Arab tribes in the Tell or Sahara, Abdel Kader was his unfailing confidant and companion.

According to Moslem usage, and the law of the Koran, Abdel Kader married young. "Marry young," says the Prophet, "marriage subdues the man's look and regulates the maiden's conduct." At that period of life when the passions first agitate the breast, Abdel Kader was, in an especial manner, the object of his father's solicitude. Faithful and trustworthy servants accompanied him wherever he went. He was never allowed to be alone. Temptations were thus avoided which might have endangered the purity of his morals. At the age of fifteen he married his cousin, Leila Heira, who was alike remarkable for her beauty and her moral attractions.

The time at length arrived when Mehi-ed-deen, now in his fiftieth year, felt it his duty to perform a pilgrimage to Mecca. Large preparations were made for the solemn event. Many were the entreaties on the part of his sons and retainers to be allowed the boon of sharing the dangers and the honours of the journey. None could endure the thought of being left behind. Mehi-ed-deen, embarrassed by such applications, declared his intention of going alone. The next day an exception was made in favour of Abdel Kader. All, though with mournful hearts, were obliged to submit to the final mandate ; and father and son left the ketna, in October, 1823.

The rumour of Mehi-ed-deen's movement soon spread through the province of Oran. Suddenly, a sympathetic impulse seemed to inspire the Arabs in all directions. All remembered they had a pilgrimage to perform. "To Mecca, to Mecca!" resounded on every side. Parties were made, mules procured, tents prepared.

On his first day's halt, Mehi-ed-deen saw his place of encampment invaded by hundreds of Arabs claiming the privilege of joining him on his pious errand. On the second day they increased to thousands. On the fourth, a sea of tents surged around him. Gentle remonstrance and stern refusal were equally unavailing. Mehi-ed-deen was their Marabout, their chief, their saint, and doubly blessed would those be who under such auspices should kiss the Holy Shrine. On the sixth evening the vast pilgrimage had assembled on the banks of the Ejdowia, in the valley of the Cheliff.

At dead of night a Turkish horseman rode up at full gallop, and dismounted at the tent of Mehi-ed-deen. He was the bearer of a dispatch from Hussein Bey, the governor of Oran. The missive was hastily opened by Abdel Kader, and found to contain a courteous summons to his father to repair to that seat of government. Before daybreak Mehi-ed-deen had finished his arrangements for a return to Oran, in obedience to his chief's commands.

Great was the consternation which seized the Arabs when the news of this unexpected summons got abroad; not only were all their hopes damped and frustrated, but their liveliest fears were awakened for their beloved leader. Numbers thronged around him. Some clung to his person, others seized his horse; others again flung themselves despairingly across the horse's path—all entreating and imploring him not to heed the message. To all these ardent demonstrations of attachment Mehi-ed-deen, with that sense of loyalty which never forsook him, calmly replied, "My children, it is my duty to obey, and I go, though it cost me my head."

Having thus spoken, and bidden the friends around him farewell, he took his course with Abdel Kader to the spot to which he was summoned.

The reception given them by Hussein Bey was apparently frank and cordial. Addressing himself to Mehi-ed-deen, he said, " You know, my friend, how high you stand in my favour and esteem. Deeply has it grieved me to hear the malicious reports which have been spread about you. Your enemies are numerous. I dreaded lest you should fall into the hands of the Dey of Algiers, whose territory you have just entered in a way which, I know, has excited his suspicions. I sent for you, to save you from impending danger. My heart was filled with anxiety on your account."

" And it was to save you anxiety," mildly and sarcastically replied Mehi-ed-deen, " that I obeyed your summons."

There is no doubt, in fact, that Hussein Bey was himself actuated by those very feelings of jealousy and suspicion which he had described as peculiar to his colleague at Algiers. The strange and unusual gathering of the Arabs around Mehi-ed-deen had alarmed him. He knew and hated the great Marabout's popularity. He dreaded lest it might one day raise him into the position of a rival power. Any overt acts of hostility against the man he feared, he was well aware, were dangerous, if not fruitless. But now he had succeeded, under the garb of friendship, in getting this very man into his power. His subsequent proceedings soon revealed his real intentions. Scarcely had Mehi-ed-deen and Abdel Kader gone to their lodgings ere a Turkish guard was placed over them. Wherever they went they were escorted by soldiers. Soldiers entered with them into the houses of their friends. Soldiers stood by them in the mosque. They were prisoners of state.

This irksome position of things continued with unabated

rigour for two years. Mehi-ed-deen never made a remonstrance. Profiting by their forced seclusion, he and Abdel
Kader ardently pursued their favourite studies. They awaited
with stoic resignation the issue of their tyrant's caprice. At
last Hussein Bey, awakened to the folly of his fears, sent
for Mehi-ed-deen and gave him permission to resume his
pilgrimage.

Resolving not to return to the ketna, even to bid adieu
once more to his family, lest such steps should produce a
similar manifestation to that which had previously caused
them so much embarrassment, Mehi-ed-deen and Abdel
Kader left Oran with the greatest privacy, in November,
1825. Passing through Medea and Constantine, they reached
Tunis, where they joined a company of 2,000 pilgrims who
were awaiting a favourable occasion to proceed by sea to
Alexandria. The whole party shortly afterwards embarked
in a vessel bound for that port. But they were overtaken by
a violent storm, and were obliged to put back. A more
prosperous result attended their next essay; and after beating
about for a fortnight they reached their destination.

After stopping a few days at Alexandria, Mehi-ed-deen
and Abdel Kader went on to Cairo, and pitched their tents
near the town. Here for the first and only time Abdel
Kader saw Mohammed Ali. Little did the youthful pilgrim
imagine, while gazing on that successful soldier, that he
himself was already destined to outrival him, before many
more years had past, in military prowess, in administrative
ability, and in deeds of wide-world renown.

The usual route to Mecca, by Suez and Djedda, was performed without any incident worthy of notice. Having

performed their devotions at the Caaba, Mehi-ed-deen and
Abdel Kader separated from their companions and went to
Damascus. In that city they remained for some months.
They there made the acquaintance of the principal Ulemahs,
and spent most of their time in the great mosque, engaged
in religious readings.

They now set out on another pilgrimage, scarcely less
sacred in their eyes than the one to Mecca,—that to the tomb
of the famous Abdel Kader il Djellali, the patron saint of
Algeria. They reached Bagdad in thirty days, by the
Palmyra route. Belonging as they did to a family well
known for the costly presents which many of its members
had laid upon the sacred tomb, they received a most hospitable reception from the cadi of the city, Mohammed il
Zachariah, who was himself a descendant of the great saint.
Mehi-ed-deen contributed a bag full of gold. To doubt the
miraculous powers of Abdel Kader il Djellali would have
been as great a sin in the eyes of the Marabout as to have
doubted the apostolic mission.

His father Mustapha had thrice performed the pilgrimage
to Bagdad, and had at each time been favoured with peculiar
manifestations. Once when returning, and while yet eight
days from Damascus, he got separated from the caravan and
lost his way. Bewildered and benighted, he found himself
alone in the desert. Suddenly a negro appeared by his side,
and offered to conduct him to the city. At break of day he
saw the minarets. The muezzin's call to prayer struck
upon his ears. In a few hours, time and space had been
annihilated.

At another time, when at Cairo, he was desirous of buying

a book, but he had no money for the purchase. A stranger all at once advanced towards him, placed some coins in his hand, and disappeared. Such, according to the belief of Mehi-ed-deen, were the rewards of a firm and unshaken faith in Abdel Kader il Djellali.

This Moslem saint flourished in the twelfth century. There are cenotaphs to his memory all over the East. In Algeria the operations of the physical world are believed to be under his control. No journey is ever undertaken without prayers for his protection; none are terminated without a festival in his honour. The Arabs attribute the success and good fortune of Abdel Kader to the patronage of his mighty namesake. But whenever Abdel Kader was questioned as to his own belief in such a superstition, he invariably replied, with finger pointed up to heaven, "My trust was in God alone."

Many stories have been circulated about mysterious indications given to Abdel Kader, while at Bagdad, of his future greatness. They are all without foundation. It is true Mehi-ed-deen had a dream. An angelic being appeared to him, and putting a key into his hand, told him to hasten back to Oran. On demanding what he was to do with the key, the spirit replied to him, "God will direct you." The dream made an impression at the time on the two pilgrims, for it was noted down, and long remembered; but it only excited curiosity, without fostering delusion.

After spending three months at Bagdad, father and son returned to Mecca. Their funds were exhausted. For the remainder of their journey, they depended on the resources of their fellow-travellers, pilgrims like themselves, who were

going back to Algeria. They took the land route the entire
way, and reached home early in 1828, after an absence of
more than two years.

Great were the rejoicings which celebrated their safe
arrival at the ketna. The first and most prominent in the
round of festivities was a great banquet in honour of Abdel
Kader il Djellali. Fifteen oxen and eighty sheep were sacrificed. Guests of every rank and class hourly arrived from
all parts, spontaneously and uninvited. Some were superbly
mounted and splendidly attired, followed by trains of slaves
and domestics ; others of the middle classes came riding on
mules and donkeys, whilst hundreds of the lower orders kept
pouring in, eagerly anticipating the princely fare of their
revered Marabout.

Mehi-ed-deen, whose hospitality was proverbial, would
hear of no limits to this costly profusion ; and thus week
after week rolled on, and still fresh guests were perpetually
arriving to swell the general tide of festivity. Nor was it
till nearly all the Arabs of the province of Oran, and
numerous deputations from the tribes of the Sahara, had paid
their tribute of homage and congratulation to the respected
chief of the Hashem, that the Wady Hammam resumed its
wonted aspect of quiet and repose.

Abdel Kader was now once more a peaceful dweller at the
paternal ketna. He made a vow of religious seclusion. No
visions of human greatness rose before him. No worldly
aspirations agitated his breast. He scorned the allurements
of ambition. His whole time was given up to close and unremitting study. No cloistered monk ever shunned more
carefully all contact with his fellow-men. From sunrise to

sunset he rarely left his room. His only interruptions were his meals and the sacred intervals of prayer.

The works of Plato, Pythagoras, Aristotle, treatises by the most famous authors of the Arabian Caliphates, on ancient and modern history, philosophy, philology, astronomy, geography, and even works on medicine, were eagerly perused by the enthusiastic student. His library accumulated. The master-spirits were around him. He would not have exchanged his communion with them for all the thrones in the universe. But a change was about to come.

The mysterious power which regulates the human will, and makes every mortal career subservient to its all-wise, all-comprehensive and resistless fiat, was exercising its invisible influence. Abdel Kader had renounced the world. He was ere long to appear one of its foremost actors. He hated battle—yet was he soon to shine mightiest in the battle's front.

CHAPTER II.

1830—1832.

THE taking of Algiers by the French in 1830 did not at first inspire the Arabs with any unusual feelings of dread or anxiety. The Franks had often descended on their coasts, and even occupied some of their maritime towns. The standards of Spain and England had waved triumphantly on the ramparts of Oran and Tangiers. Bona and Algiers had been compelled at different times to yield a sullen deference to the requirements of European civilisation; but the military occupation and the political pressure had alike ceased. Thus the Arabs had never as yet seen any reason to regard a hostile incursion on their soil, by the Franks, as pregnant with danger to their national existence.

.The proceedings of the French, however, in Algeria, soon convinced them that the presence of these invaders was no ordinary visitation. General Bourmont, indeed, from the outset, declared in a public proclamation, that France took possession, not only of the town of Algiers, but of the whole Regency. This announcement, closely followed as it was by the exile of the Dey, the removal of every trace and vestige of Turkish power, the deportation of the Turkish population, the issuing of laws and ordinances in the name of the King of the French, the enlarging and beautifying of the town of

Algiers, the seizure of all the towns along the coast, and the advances of military reconnaissance towards the Atlas, revealed designs which neither the Arabs of the actual generation, nor their ancestors, had ever been called upon to counteract.

Before the French began to move beyond the walls of Algiers, the disposition of the Arabs towards them had been apparently friendly. Provisions had been brought in abundantly. Some of their chiefs had made overtures of submission. The Bey of Tittery had even accepted French investiture. So promising, indeed, was the aspect of affairs, that the French fancied they were about to be hailed as deliverers, and considered that the Arabs, overjoyed at being emancipated from the hated Turkish yoke, would thankfully accept French domination. The first movement of the French into the interior rapidly dispelled this pleasing illusion.

An expedition, commanded by the French general in person, to Blidah, a town situated at the foot of the Lower Atlas (July 24th, 1830), at once revealed the rising feeling of the Arabs. Lulled into security by the apparent heartiness of their reception among the inhabitants of Blidah, the leading men of which town came out to meet them, the French threw off their knapsacks, and wandered joyously amidst its delicious gardens. Suddenly, bands of Arabs and Kabyles rushed down upon them from the mountains above, and with wild cries commenced a vigorous attack. The French rapidly collected, bravely held their ground, and the next day retreated in good order to Algiers.

The Arabs took this temporary advantage as an earnest of

future successes. From that moment, the spirit of defiance and resistance assumed a decided form. The Marabouts, leading and directing the national mind, proclaimed
the Djehad, or Holy War. The Bey of Tittery, anxious to
atone for his recent defection, wrote to Bourmont, fixing the
day when at the head of 20,000 men, he would drive him
and his Frenchmen into the sea.

On the other hand, French garrisons were quietly being
stationed in all the seaport towns. At Oran, Hussein Bey
became anxious to be delivered from a position which had
become dangerous to his person. He was closely blockaded
by the Arabs, burning to revenge themselves on his tyranny.
His Turkish militia was utterly powerless for his defence.
The Arabs in Turkish employ, the *Maghzen*, as they were
called, were flying before the tribes so long oppressed, who
now considered that their hour of retaliation was come.

In this dilemma, Hussein, unwilling to fly, and yet unable to hold his post, determined on adopting a course which,
though humiliating to his pride, was dictated by the sternest
necessity. He sent for Mehi-ed-deen, and craved his protection. Mehi-ed-deen, astonished at such an application,
and fearing to compromise himself with his own countrymen
by a hasty consent, asked leave to return home to consult
the Hashems.

On his arrival at the ketna, he assembled a family council,
and called on each member to give his opinion on the subject.
The prevailing opinion was to the effect that it would be
ungenerous to refuse the Bey's request. It was true, as was
on every hand admitted, that the injuries done by him to
their beloved chief had been wanton and malicious; but it

was urged, that it would be a stain upon Arab character to refuse an asylum to the fallen.

Abdel Kader spoke. He begged the indulgence of his relatives, and particularly of his father, if he ventured to differ from them. In the state of anarchy which now existed in the province of Oran, he argued, it was by no means certain that they could protect the Bey from the effects of the universal feelings of hatred and indignation which prevailed against him. Whatever steps they might take, the Bey would still run the risk of being insulted, assaulted, perhaps murdered. Who could avert an outburst of popular fury, or be answerable for its consequences? In such an event, how great would be the disgrace of those who had given him a safe-conduct, and had been unable to make it respected!

"Another and equally important reason," pursued Abdel Kader, "militates against the reception of the Bey in our ketna. An asylum given by our family to that detested representative of Turkish tyranny, would be looked upon by the Arabs as a kind of tacit forgetfulness of all his past conduct. Consequently we should make to ourselves enemies of all the tribes to whom the Bey is obnoxious; in other words, of all the Arabs of Oran."

Mehi-ed-deen at once declared himself a convert to his son's reasoning; and in this step he was shortly followed by every member of the council. A messenger was sent to inform the Bey that his request could not be granted, as Mehi-ed-deen would not become responsible for his safety. On the 4th of January, 1831, General Damremont entered the port of Oran. The Bey at once surrendered, and he was allowed to embark for Alexandria.

C

The disorder and anarchy which had already broken out in the interior was now constantly on the increase. The Mohammedans of the sea-coast towns, who had fled from the French, were roaming about the country with their families in terror and despair. The Arabs waylaid them, and robbed them without mercy. Mehi-ed-deen, who had hitherto been a passive observer of events, felt that the time had now arrived for action. By his orders Abdel Kader and his brothers, with effective escorts, scoured the plains in all directions, protecting the unfortunate fugitives, rescuing many from the hands of the marauders, and conducting all to places of safety.

But whatever good Mehi-ed-deen effected by this humane and timely interposition, it was evident that a far more potent arm than his was requisite to establish anything like a semblance of order and government. Not only on the plains, but in the towns, strife and contention were raging unchecked. Party feuds, which had been long suspended, broke out afresh with redoubled acrimony. The Arabs were everywhere giving the reins to their innate propensities for unbridled licence and lawlessness.

Long and anxious were the consultations held by the Marabouts on this frightful state of affairs. At length, with one accord, they determined to go to Mehi-ed-deen for counsel. Mehi-ed-deen thus appealed to, addressed the applicants for his advice in the following terms :—

" For many months, as you all know, I have been trying to preserve some degree of order amidst the general confusion which prevails ; but my utmost endeavours have only been able to rescue a few of the weak and unprotected from the brutality of violent men.

"The tyranny of the Turks cramped and crushed our energies; but the present state of things, if allowed to continue, will destroy them utterly. The bonds of society are dissolved. Every man's hand is raised against his neighbour. Our people, given up to their vile passions, are daily outraging the laws of God and man. At the same time, the evils which menace us from without are not less formidable than those which consume us from within. Shall we call in the French? Impossible. To submit to them, much more to invite them, would be to betray our duty to our God, our country, and our faith.

"Yet the French are a warlike nation, strong in numbers, abounding in riches, and burning with a love of conquest. And what have we to oppose to them? Tribes at variance with each other; designing and rapacious chiefs striving for personal aggrandisement; a commonalty which has thrown off all restraint, some enriching themselves by plunder, others precariously holding their own. The parties are too unequal. With such materials, to imagine even a successful struggle with the infidel would be folly, to attempt it, madness.

"No. The French king, powerful as he is, can only be effectually opposed by a king like himself at the head of a well-regulated state, disposing of a well-filled treasury, commanding a disciplined army. Nor need we go far to find such a one. The Sultan of Morocco already sympathises with us. He must know full well that the external danger which threatens us may ultimately menace him. His presence amongst us will at once encourage and embolden the good, and awe the wicked. Order will be enforced.

Fighting under him, we shall march to assured victory ; for his standards are the standards of God and the Prophet."

A few days afterwards, an embassy, comprising ten of the most influential Marabouts and Sheiks, with an escort of fifty horsemen, and mules laden with presents, took its departure for Fez. Sultan Abderahman received the embassy with every appearance of cordiality, and promised to consider its demands. Six months elapsed without any reply. At last the Arab chiefs were sent for. Movements in the palace, and the assemblage of the troops, showed that the petition of the Arabs of Algeria had been granted. In six weeks, the Sultan's son Ali, at the head of 5,000 cavalry and two parks of artillery, established his headquarters at Tlemsen, in the province of Oran.

Mehi-ed-deen and Abdel Kader, with all the chiefs of the Hashem, chiefs from the Beni Mejaher, the Beni Amer, and other tribes, hastened to pay their homage to the son and representative of their new Sultan. His authority was speedily recognised in all parts of the regency. The *khotba*, or public prayer for the Mohammedan Sultan, was pronounced in all the mosques for the Sultan of Morocco. Everything conspired to confirm the belief that Algeria had peaceably passed under the Moorish sceptre. But the French Government, seasonably apprised of these newly-formed relations between the Arabs and the Sultan Abderahman, at once sent the latter an ultimatum of immediate withdrawal from Algeria, or war.

Abderahman, compelled to choose one or other of these alternatives, and being totally unprepared to commence hostilities, immediately sent orders to his son to return. In a few days, although the Moors had been warmly welcomed, even in the provinces of Tittery and Constantine, not one was to be seen in the whole country. The Marabouts and chiefs now resolved to offer the dignity of Sultan to Mehi-ed-deen, and went in a body for that purpose to the ketna. He modestly declined the offer; but at the same time he recommended a second appeal to Morocco.

Another embassy was accordingly sent to Fez, to implore the Moorish Sultan to lend his name, at least, if he could not give material aid and assistance, to the movement which was being made in his favour. Unable to act overtly, yet hoping to profit by events, Abderahman so far complied with their request, that he sent a confidential agent to Mascara. This clandestine proceeding, however, produced no effect. The Arabs scorned a power which dared not openly display itself; and in a short time the Moorish agent was withdrawn.

Again all eyes were turned to Mehi-ed-deen. Again the Arabs entreated him to be their Sultan. "No," he replied. "I am not adequate to perform the duties of such a post; but what religion imposes upon me, that will I do. I will go with you to the Djehad." The Arabs had for some time been making approaches to Oran, now strongly occupied by the French. Abdel Kader had taken the field, and his father served under him.

The Arabs had recently been attacking Fort Philip, a strong citadel to the south of the town. Abdel Kader had both proposed and superintended the operation. Conspicuous in a scarlet burnous, he led on a mixed body of cavalry and infantry to the very walls of the fort. Ordering the latter to descend into the ditch and keep up a constant fire on the ramparts, he placed the former in such a position as to be ready to resist any sortie which might be made from the place. The fire of shot and shell which the French opened on the Arabs was such as might have staggered the best disciplined troops. But Abdel Kader, careering to and fro, and cheering his comrades by his voice and gestures, kept them together, and taught them to despise the tremendous missiles which were so wont to fill them with terror and amazement.

Word was sent him that the Arabs he had placed in the ditch had expended their ammunition, and that no one would expose himself to supply them. "Cowards!" he exclaimed, "give me the cartridges." Wrapping them up in the folds of his burnous, he dashed singly across the plain, rode up to the fort, threw them into the ditch, and urging his men to be firm and go on with their work, returned, to the surprise of all, without being touched.

On this and many similar occasions of peril and enterprise, in which he fleshed his maiden sword, Abdel Kader's courage and bravery drew forth not only praises, but rapturous admiration. The Arabs began to look with superstitious reverence on one, who as with a charmed life, rode fearlessly and harmlessly wherever danger menaced; now breaking through the line of the enemy's skirmishers; now charging up to a square, and sweeping the bayonets with his sabre; now standing unmoved and pointing contemptuously at the cannon balls as they whizzed by his head, or at the shells as they exploded at his feet.

Nevertheless, however confident the Arabs might feel in their young chief, however they might acknowledge that in him a master-spirit had arisen to conduct them in their struggle against the infidels, they felt that this desultory mode of attack was not war. They saw full well that without a responsible head to organise, to raise revenues by regular imposts, to husband resources, and to form and carry out a clearly defined plan of campaign, all their efforts would be abortive, all their sacrifices useless. At a grand meeting held at Mascara, these topics were earnestly discussed.

Mehi-ed-deen, who was enjoying a short repose at the ketna, was invited to attend. Scarcely had he arrived and dismounted, when an excited throng surrounded him. A tumult of voices was raised. On all sides he was thus apostrophised, —"How long, O Mehi-ed-deen, are we to be left without a leader? How long will you remain a callous spectator of our distractions; you, whose name alone would suffice to rally all hearts, to encourage the desponding, to curb the malignant, to give strength and cohesion to the common cause? Already many of our bravest have fallen off in weariness and disgust. Who, they say, is to repair our losses, to replace our horses killed, our arms broken and useless? You, O Mehi-ed-deen, are answerable for all this." Then, placing their swords at his breast, the chiefs exclaimed:—"Choose between being our Sultan or instant death."

Mehi-ed-deen, violently agitated, but still preserving his presence of mind, demanded to be heard. "You all know," he said, "that I am a man of peace, devoting myself to the worship of God. The task of ruling involves the use of brute force and the shedding of blood. But since you insist on my being your Sultan, I consent; and abdicate in favour of my son, Abdel Kader."

This sudden and unexpected solution of the question was received with loud acclamations of approval. The name of Abdel Kader was repeated with enthusiasm. The character, the personal appearance, the manly bearing, the tried gallantry of the favourite son of Mehi-ed-deen, became the general topic of discourse. A horseman was forthwith despatched to bring him from the ketna.

Early on the next morning, November 21st, 1832, Abdel Kader entered Mascara. All the streets and avenues leading to the town were thronged. Men, women, and children vied with each other in joyful demonstrations of welcome to their future Sultan. Ushered into the large court where the council was assembled, Abdel Kader was informed of all that had passed. Calm, self-collected, and unelated, he simply said, "It is my duty to obey the commands of my father." A burst of applause followed this simple avowal of filial obedience and patriotic devotion.

Placed in an antique chair of state, which had formerly belonged to some Spanish grandee, and which had been dragged forth from its musty recess for the occasion, the young Sultan, of twenty-five years of age, received the allegiance of the nobles and chiefs congregated around him. Loud shouts of " Long life and victory to our Sultan, Abdel Kader!" burst from the whole assembly. They were caught up and reiterated by the people from without, and thus heralded the inauguration of an Arabian Caliphate.

In the afternoon Abdel Kader went to the Mosque, which was already crowded to suffocation. After performing his devotions, he stood up. A Koran was put into his hands. He read and expounded. By degrees his countenance became more animated, his voice more resonant, his manner more impressive, and his action more emphatic, as, leaving the language of disquisition, he passed to more noble and exalted themes.

Not for minutes, but for hours, and until the sun had sunk below the horizon, did the soldier orator pour forth one continued stream of burning and impassioned eloquence. He expatiated, in heart-rending tones, on the sins, the iniquities, the crimes, the horrors which polluted the land. In vivid terms he depicted Heaven's judgments overtaking a godless and vice-abandoned people ; and now, again, he conjured up before the minds of his audience, in characters of flame, the appalling picture of their country ravaged by the infidel, their domestic hearths violated, their temples desecrated.

The sensation of wonder and astonishment which had at first filled the breasts of his hearers, now rapidly changed into conscience-stricken feelings of shame, contrition, and remorse. But when, with outstretched arm and lightning glance, he called on his countrymen, in words which glowed with the fire of inspiration, to stand boldly forward in the sacred cause of God and the Prophet, to rally round the standard of the "Djehad," and to emulate the glorious martyrs of the true faith ; and then painted in vivid colours the liberated spirits of the slain entering the blissful mansions, they sprang to their feet, they shook their spears, they clashed their swords, they wept aloud, and with frantic cries yelled out, "Il Djehad! Il Djehad!"

Exulting in his prowess, again and again did the consummate artist strike the chord, whose vibrations had thrilled every heart and enkindled every soul, and, as the frenzied voices rose louder and louder around him, his voice yet surged above them all. Gathering fresh impulse from the responsive acclamations of his hearers, he swayed to and fro. He smote his breast. Big drops of sweat suffused his brow. His eyes glistened and flashed. He flung his hands aloft, as though appealing to celestial witnesses. At last, so crushing and overpowering became his excitement, that Reason might have succumbed, had not Nature, by a copious flood of tears, relieved the fearful tension.

The next day (November 22nd, 1832) Abdel Kader proceeded in state to the valley of Ersibia, ten minutes' distance from Mascara. Ten thousand Arab cavalry were there in waiting to receive and welcome their newly-elected sovereign. They were arranged, according to their tribes, in one continuous crescent, around a splendid tent, which had been erected in the centre of the plain. The entire population of Mascara occupied the intervening ground.

Just as the sun's slanting rays peered over the heights of Djebel Nusmut, lighting up this scene as if by magic brightness, the shrill cries of the women, the shouts of the men, and incessant crashes of musketry, announced the approach of the royal cavalcade. First came a chosen band, escorting the standard of the Djehad. Then followed the chiefs of the Beni Amer, the Beni Mejaher, the Beni Yacoub, the Beni Abbas, on their high-mettled steeds, with their brilliant equipments, and well-burnished arms. Now appeared Abdel Kader—a plain, unornamented, red burnous flung over his shoulders, riding his favourite black charger. The chiefs of the Beni Hashem, his own tribe, brought up the rear of the splendid *cortège.*

Passing on, as quickly as the crowd would permit—for some thronged round to kiss his hand, some the hem of his burnous, others even his horse's feet—Abdel Kader reached the tent and dismounted. For some minutes he was lost to view: At length Mehi-ed-deen came forth, leading him, by the hand, in order to present him to the people. "Behold the Sultan announced by prophecy!" he exclaimed. "Behold the son of Zohra! Obey him as you would have obeyed me. God protect the Sultan!" "Our lives, our properties, all that we have, are his!" shouted the people. "We will obey no law but that of our Sultan Abdel Kader."

"I, in my turn," replied Abdel Kader, "will know no law but the Koran. By the precepts of the Koran, and the Koran alone, will I be guided. If my own brother forfeits his life by the Koran, he shall die."

Amidst the acclamations which saluted this short but pregnant speech, Abdel Kader vaulted into his saddle, and, followed by all his chiefs, swept at full speed along the Arab lines. At intervals he reined up, briefly ejaculating, "Il Djehad! Il Djehad! Liberty and independence are only in the Djehad. Paradise is in the shade of sabres. Rally round the standard of the Djehad!"

The banners waved, the drums and trumpets sent forth their martial sounds, and the mighty mass, breaking ground, circled round their Sultan in successive squadrons, and then escorted him back to Mascara. After snatching a hasty meal, Abdel Kader shut himself up in a small room, and, summoning his secretaries, dictated the following proclamation:—

" Praise be to God alone, and blessings and salutation from on high on him,* after whom there is no prophet.

" To (such and such a tribe), and in particular to its nobles, sheiks, notables, and alemahs.

" May God enlighten you, guide and direct your counsels, and give success to your deeds and actions. The citizens of the districts, Mascara, the Eastern and Western Gharees, and their neighbours and allies, the Beni Sokrân, El Borgiés, the Beni Abbas, the Yacoubiés, the Beni Amer, the Beni Mejaher, and others, have agreed unanimously to appoint me, and have accordingly appointed me, to the government of our country; pledging themselves to obey me in success and in distress, in prosperity and in adversity; and to consecrate their persons, their sons, and their properties to the great and holy cause.

" We have, therefore, assumed this important charge (though with extreme reluctance), hoping it may be the means of uniting the great body of Moslems, of preventing dissensions amongst them, of affording general security to all dwellers in the land, of checking all acts of lawlessness on the part of the disorderly against the well-disposed, and of driving back and overcoming the enemy who has invaded our country with a view of placing their yoke upon our necks.

" As a condition of our acceptance, we have imposed on those who have delegated to us the supreme power, the duty of always conforming, in all their actions, to the holy precepts and teaching of the book of God, and of administrating justice in their various spheres, according to the law of the

* Mohammed.

Prophet; loyally and impartially, to the strong and the weak, the noble and the respectable. This condition has been accepted by them.

" We hereby invite you to be partakers in this pledge, or compact, between ourselves and them. Hasten, therefore, to make manifest your allegiance and obedience; and may God prosper you in this world and in the world to come. My great object is to reform, and to do good as much as in me lies. My trust is in God; and from Him, and Him only, I expect reward and success.

" By order of the Defender of Religion, our sovereign lord, the Prince of the Faithful, Abdel Kader-ibn-Mehi-ed-deen. May God give him the victory. Amen. Dated from Mascara, November 22, 1832."

CHAPTER III

1833.

THE appeal thus made by Abdel Kader was variously entertained by the different tribes to which it was addressed. The religious party was inclined to give its strenuous support to one who summoned them to fight for the faith. The men of worldly views and individual ambition looked with jealousy on such an assumption of sovereignty. Chiefs, who even under the Turkish rule had struggled to maintain an independent existence, felt little disposed to accept the mandates of a compeer, whose claims to an extended sway were in their eyes no better than their own.

Even in the province of Oran, the imposing circumstances under which Abdel Kader had been installed, had excited party feelings rather than disarmed them. Sidi-il-Aribi, a powerful chieftain, whose influence was supreme over the tribe of the Flittas, in the valley of the Cheliff, spoke of the new power with undisguised contempt. El Ghomari, chief of the Beni Engad, held sternly aloof. Noona, who affected to hold Tlemsen for the Sultan of Morocco, felt it beneath him to give his adhesion. Mustapha-ibn-Ismail, an old and experienced warrior, grown grey in the Turkish service as leader of the *Maghzen*, scornfully disdained to kiss the hands, as he expressed it, of a beardless boy.

As a contrast to these selfish views and circumscribed ambitions, Abdel Kader presented to his countrymen the one simple and majestic idea of an Arab nationality. Little as it might be at first comprehended and appreciated by a race accustomed for centuries to bow their necks to a foreign yoke, and in whom all principles of patriotism had long been extinguished, he trusted that amongst the hundreds of tribes which occupied Algeria there would be some, at least, in whom it would awake a responsive echo.

On the other hand, though not a fanatic himself, Abdel Kader well knew the latent fires of fanaticism which slumber in every Moslem breast. What love of country would not effect, zeal for religion might surely accomplish. He determined, consequently, to make this latter feeling the key-stone to the mighty superstructure his genius alone had dared to imagine. In this unity of design consisted the grandeur of the drama he proposed to exhibit to the civilised world.

He now issued invitations for a general rendezvous of forces at Mascara, in the spring of 1833. Many important tribes from the Tell and the Sahara responded cordially to the summons. Of the *Maghzen* tribes, who had been so long the instruments of the Turks for the enslavement and oppression of their brethren, some sent evasive, some insulting answers. Anarchy was better suited to their sordid dispositions. They were ready, if occasion presented itself, to offer their mercenary swords to the French.

On the day appointed—May 18th, 1833—an imposing array of 8,000 cavalry and 1,000 infantry assembled on the plains of Ersibia. Abdel Kader's own standard, a large white flag, with an open hand in the centre, was unfurled before the multitude with great pomp and ceremony. After riding through the ranks, and apostrophising the assemblage in a few short, trenchant sentences, which caused the blood to thrill through their veins, he led them off to take the field in the direction of Oran.

On this expedition he inaugurated that system, so conspicuous alike for its simplicity and its regularity, which he afterwards maintained under all changes and vicissitudes throughout his whole career. His tent was large and commodious, and displayed hangings adorned with red, blue, yellow, and green crescents. A woollen curtain divided it into two compartments. The largest of these was the *menzoul,* or general reception-room, open to all comers, and in which he heard appeals and administered justice. The smaller he used as his bedroom and library; and here he spent more time in reading than in sleeping.

On alighting at the end of the day's march, which was generally over by mid-day, he dismissed all his attendants, and retired into the strictest privacy, scrupulously devoting an hour to prayer. He then went into the *menzoul,* where his principal officers and secretaries were in waiting to receive him. The movements of the enemy and his own plans were now discussed, or orders and dispatches were dictated by himself. On these occasions he frequently supported his commands by appropriate quotations from the Koran. His ordinary military council consisted of four chiefs, a kehié, and his treasurer; but other chiefs were called in, if thought advisable. He listened to the suggestions of all with the greatest patience and urbanity.

At sunset, Abdel Kader stood at the door of his tent, and

preached. None were compelled to attend ; but none, if possible, absented themselves from these discourses. Thence, as from a central source of light and heat, all daily received that warmth of warlike and religious zeal whic'; glowed within their breasts. For Abdel Kader pre-eminently possessed the art of attracting the love and admiration of his followers ; and he wielded with an almost magical power that talisman which is the gift, as it is the sign, of noble and exalted natures.

For some weeks previous to Abdel Kader's present advance on Oran, the Hashem Gharabas, his family tribe, had been engaged in a series of encounters with the French, under General Boyers. This general had lately been replaced by General Desmichels ; and Abdel Kader came up just in time to assist his allies in resisting a vigorous attack made on them by the latter. Dividing his force into two portions, he sent one to fall on the enemy's left flank,. whilst, at the head of the other, he marched directly up to a fort which the French general had erected at a place called Figuier. The defence of this fort was supported by a battalion of infantry, a squadron of Chasseurs d'Afrique, and two pieces of artillery.

On approaching the fort, the Arab infantry wavered. Abdel Kader at once sprang from his horse, and taking the lead on foot, attempted an escalade. Twice repulsed in his endeavours to take the fort, he remounted, and drawing off his men, rejoined his cavalry in the plain. There the French were utterly unable to resist the onset made upon them. Their lines of skirmishers were swept away, their squares broken. The engagement was prolonged till night, when

D

Desmichels retreated under cover of the fire from his artillery. For some days there was a suspension of hostilities.

Abdel Kader, impatient of inaction, proceeded one night with a hundred picked horsemen, and placed himself in ambush in a copse, a short distance from Oran, through which the French were accustomed to send their reliefs of cavalry to the outposts. At the ordinary hour, a squadron of Chasseurs made their appearance. Abdel Kader led on the charge, routed and dispersed them, slaying several, and taking thirty prisoners. One Chasseur made a thrust at him with his spear. The weapon passed under his left arm. He held it firmly between his left arm and side as in a vice, and with a swing of his sabre cut off the Frenchman's head.

In the *mêlée* his cousin Achmet was shot down. Abdel Kader was by the side of his wounded relative in a moment. After stanching the blood and binding up his wound, he placed the sufferer before him on his horse, and carried him out of reach of danger. Shortly afterwards, seeing that the French were not disposed again to measure their swords with his, he drew off his whole force, and returned to Mascara.

Abdel Kader had conducted this movement more with the intention of trying his men, and of inspiring them with confidence, than with the hopes of achieving any permanent result. He felt that the jealousies and rivalries which environed him could only be dispersed by the tumult of battle; and that all internal difficulties would vanish before success. His reception at Mascara fully confirmed this impression. Many chiefs who had hitherto withheld their allegiance, were there awaiting him. Hadj-ibn-Isa, a celebrated Marabout, alone brought with him deputations from twenty tribes in the Sahara.

Abdel Kader, deeply impressed with the necessity of absolute union amongst his countrymen, to enable him to complete their common independence, now determined on smiting with the sword all who questioned or attempted to resist his power. Sidi-il-Aribi had been collecting forces, which, as he never hesitated to declare, were to be directed against the aspiring son of Mehi-ed-deen.

Abdel Kader paid him an unexpected visit at the head of 5,000 men, announcing his approach by discharges of musketry and shouts of triumph. His rival was completely taken by surprise; and the defence he attempted was quickly paralysed. Tents were knocked over, prisoners made, flocks carried off. It was only by sending a written engagement of submission, and sending his son as a hostage to his conqueror, that the old chief obtained forgiveness of the past, and security for the future.

On continuing his course through the vast valley of the Cheliff and the adjoining regions, Abdel Kader received the adhesion of several important tribes. He even advanced as far as the Ouarensis, a difficult mountain range, inhabited by fierce Kabyles. These stern republicans, secure in their fastnesses, and indifferent as to the doings of the outer world, were accustomed to scorn all authority. Uncertain as to their attitude, Abdel Kader refrained from pushing his expedition further. At a later period these very tribes obeyed him like children.

Where no great feudal influences prevailed, the authority of Abdel Kader was promptly and even thankfully accepted. The small provincial towns at once opened their gates to him. His occupation of Arzew, situated two leagues from the port of that name, was marked by a circumstance which gave rise to reports reflecting both erroneously and injuriously on his character for humanity.

He had issued the most stringent orders that no communications should be opened with the French. In direct violation of this order, Sidi Achmet-ibn-il-Taher, the Cadi of that town, had supplied the French with cattle and forage, and, what was considered a far graver crime, had even sold them horses. Abdel Kader had often written to him, warning him of the consequences of his conduct, and menacing him with exemplary punishment if he persisted in his proceedings. The Cadi, unable to give up the profit he was making by his transactions, and calculating on French protection, persevered. Abdel Kader one day suddenly dashed into the town. The Cadi was seized, loaded with chains, and conveyed to the prison at Mascara.

Giving strict injunctions that nothing was for the present to be done to the delinquent, he rode off to the Beni Amers on matters which detained him several days. His private intentions were to allow the Cadi to ransom his life (justly forfeited by the law of the Koran) for 5,000 francs. On his return to Mascara he found, to his surprise, that the Cadi had been put to death. Mehi-ed-deen had had him tried. He had been condemned to capital punishment, and the sentence had been carried into immediate execution. His eyes had been put out. The responsibility of this latter act of brutality, which was the spontaneous suggestion of one of the executioners, has been spitefully thrown by some on Abdel Kader.

Fully comprehending that mere successes in the field would not be sufficient to consolidate his dominion, Abdel Kader now sought to place his sovereignty on a more solid basis, by holding places of strength, erecting arsenals, and establishing stores and magazines. With this view he attacked Tlemsen, about seventy miles to the south-west of Oran. This town is situated on an eminence at the foot of steep and lofty mountains. Its walls are remarkable for their thickness and solidity, and it had frequently withstood sieges.

The mainspring of Abdel Kader's strength at this epoch lay in the Beni Amers and the Hashems. Taking strong detachments from these tribes, he approached the town. Its population was divided into two parties, Turks and Kolouglis. The latter (descendants of Turkish and Arab parents) occupied the citadel. The Arabs were commanded by Noona, who has been already mentioned. Abdel Kader summoned the latter to surrender. He refused. The resistance which he offered was, however, quickly overcome; for while Abdel Kader assaulted him on one side, the Kolouglis opened fire on him from the citadel.

When the town of Tlemsen was won, Abdel Kader treated its inhabitants with the greatest consideration. He had hoped that the Kolouglis would acknowledge him. But, secure in their stronghold, they rejected all his overtures. They consented, however, to maintain with him a friendly intercourse. Having no artillery wherewith to reduce them, he accepted the compromise, and installing one of his lieutenants as governor of the town, returned to Mascara.

On the road he received tidings of his father's death. Mehi-ed-deen had lived long enough to see his favourite son embarked in that career which he fondly hoped would be the prelude to his country's freedom and independence. The bereaved son was deeply afflicted by the loss of a parent who had from his infancy lavished on him all the endearments of love and affection, who had always treated him as a bosom friend and companion, and to whose influence he in truth owed his high position. But, so far from having time to indulge in the temporary retirement from public affairs which his grief demanded, he was barely able to follow his father's remains to the grave.

Desmichels had just taken Arzew and Mostaganem. Abdel Kader had thus not a moment to lose. It was imperative on him to make every endeavour to nullify this extension of French dominion in the province of Oran. On the 2nd of August, 1833, he was under the walls of Mostaganem, and led an assault against it. Desmichels, leaving the garrison to defend itself, immediately returned to Oran. He hoped that the presence of Abdel Kader at Mostaganem would leave him free to carry out successfully an incursion he had long contemplated.

On the 5th of August, the day after his arrival in Oran, consequently, he sent a force of 3,000 cavalry and infantry and three field-pieces to attack the Douairs and Zmelas, two tribes who were doing the French irreparable injury by the activity with which they were enforcing the blockade established by Abdel Kader. On the 6th, at daybreak, the column came upon the Arab encampments. The artillery opened, the infantry moved on at the double, the cavalry charged.

The Arabs, surprised, bewildered and stupefied, made but a straggling and ineffectual defence. Finally they decamped, leaving their herds and their flocks, and many women and children, in the enemy's hands. Suddenly their retrograde movement appeared, to the astonishment of the French, to be stopped; their numbers, as if by enchantment, to be increased; their attitude to have become offensive. Abdel Kader had arrived.

Divining his adversary's intention in leaving Mostaganem, he had ceased to superintend the siege in person, and had rushed to the point more directly menaced. He came up at the critical moment. It cost him little to turn the tide of battle. The French infantry beat a rapid retreat, some in hastily-formed squares, some in broken file; the cavalry maintained a flying flight; the artillery alone did good service. Anticipating an easy conquest, the French had not brought provisions. They were now driven from their spoil. The pangs of hunger and thirst assailed them. The scorching sun blazed over their heads. The Arabs presently enveloped them on all sides.

"Fire the plains!" cried Abdel Kader. Instantly hundreds of horsemen galloped off, and lighted the dry herbs and brushwood extending behind the French rear. The unfortunate soldiery, retarded in their march by the wounded, whom they nobly refused to abandon, had to tread on burning cinders and wade through sheets of flame. Human nature sank beneath the trial. Many flung away their arms. Some were suffocated; others, in their despair, threw themselves frantically on the ground, eager to part with their lives, of which the Arab yataghans soon relieved them.

Desmichels had been apprised by some fugitives of the disasters which had befallen the expedition. The whole garrison of Oran was promptly turned out to rush to the rescue. The troops barely reached the ground in time to save their comrades from utter annihilation.

Abdel Kader, in the full flush of victory, returned without delay to hasten on the siege of Mostaganem. It is difficult to say whether most admiration should be bestowed on the boldness of his design, or on the courage and perseverance which so nearly accomplished it. Abdel Kader had no siege artillery; he possessed only infantry and cavalry. The infantry had already made themselves masters of the suburbs, and were attacking one of the forts close to the sea. A French brig galled them with its fire. The Arabs stripped, swam off, holding their muskets over their heads, and attempted to board it. They were driven off; but the fearless audacity thus displayed shows how much may be achieved by Arabs when commanded and inspired by a spirited leader. Abdel Kader had commenced sapping. The sap reached the foot of the walls. An explosion effected a breach. The order for a general assault was given. The Arabs, led on and animated by the voice and example of their Sultan, rolled on like a mighty wave, and like a wave, dashed and receded. The French, lining the tops of the wall on either side, poured in such a flanking fire on the assailants, that after a desperate struggle they were hurled back in confusion. Abdel Kader, finding his last resource exhausted, raised the siege and returned to Mascara.

Though Abdel Kader had already done sufficient to justify and secure the confidence of his immediate companions in arms, and (despite the jealousies of certain chiefs) to centre on himself the hopes and good wishes of all the tribes within the province of Oran, yet the force of circumstances had compelled some of the latter, however anxious to rally round his standard, to submit to the invaders.

The Douairs and Zmelas, constantly exposed, by their vicinity, to the incursions of the French, had suffered losses which the pardonable instincts of nature had induced them to repair by an apparently friendly accommodation with an enemy whom they inwardly detested. Strangers to that spirit of self-abnegation which true patriotism requires, they had consented to purchase a momentary tranquillity by accepting French protection. By a treaty with Desmichels they had established themselves under the French flag, in the valley of Miserghin, three leagues distant from Oran.

The lofty policy of Abdel Kader could ill brook such a glaring violation of the clear and unequivocal injunctions of the Koran. That sacred volume neither countenanced nor admitted the principle of expediency. To conquer or to die, sword in hand, for the Faith, was its uncompromising and inexorable dogma. Zealous interpreter and dauntless defender of that soul-inspiring mandate in all its heroic greatness, Abdel Kader made it his imperative duty to uphold it with ceaseless and untiring vigilance, and to visit its slightest infraction with unsparing rigour.

Independently of this superior and all-sufficient consideration, he well foresaw that if vicinity to the enemy was to be made the pretext for submission, and hardship and suffering the signal for treason, the views which he entertained for the working out of the salvation of his country would speedily be dissolved, his plans for its regeneration become illusory, and his utmost efforts for their realisation abortive. He knew that the edifice he was so laboriously erecting, thus breached at its very base, would crumble away like a rope of sand.

He considered, consequently, that to condone, to overlook,

or to excuse such weakness, whatever the plea advanced, would be tantamount to abandoning the trust which had been solemnly committed into his hands, and the task which he had sworn to accomplish. The alternative presented to him might be ungracious, it might be painful; but, calm and unshaken in the purity of his conscience, firm and confiding in the goodness of his cause, he accepted it.

Whilst maintaining a bold front to the enemy, it might become incumbent on him so to act as to become an object of terror rather than of love, to hundreds, perhaps thousands, of his own countrymen. His severity might be called oppression, his exactions and punishments might be stigmatised as tyranny. But at whatever cost to the sufferers, at whatever detriment to his own popularity, he determined to make it understood and felt throughout the tribes, as a policy indispensable to the common welfare, that in him alone was vested the prerogatives of making peace, or signing conditions ; he resolved, therefore, to impress on the minds of all the tribes, that if any accepted terms from the French on their own account, their last and heaviest account would be with him. The Douairs and Zmelas in due time experienced this correcting discipline.

CHAPTER IV.

1833.

THE enthusiasm excited in France by the taking of Algiers was of short duration. A revolution had overthrown the dynasty of the elder branch of the House of Bourbon, under whose auspices the conquest had been achieved. The dark cloud of hatred and execration which enveloped the departed tyranny, threw its ominous shadow over the glories of that brilliant feat of arms.

Willingness to abandon the fruits of a triumph obtained under such circumstances became the prevalent feeling. In the French Chambers a large party denounced the contemplated occupation of Algeria as costly and useless. Some suggested that the sea-coast towns should be held, not so much with views of aggrandisement, as from a desire of saving the national honour.

None understood, and few troubled themselves to investigate, the nature of the country which was the subject of debate. All knew that Algeria was a nest of pirates, that the governors were barbarous Turks, and that the government were degraded Arabs. But what was the condition of the interior, what were the manners, customs, and social characteristics of the people, what kind of government would best replace the one which had been overthrown, what system of administration should be adopted, no one attempted duly to consider. On all these points the ignorance and indifference was complete.

Fluctuating in its plans, and unwilling to release its grasp, the French ministry, at an early period, reduced its army in Algeria to 10,000 men. For a long time afterwards, all its measures were marked by weakness and indecision. In the space of six years, no less than ten governor-generals were sent over to experimentalise on new theories of legislation. The thread of official experience was constantly broken by the arrival of successive neophytes in the art of governing. Each new actor appeared on the stage with his peculiar crotchets, which he crudely endeavoured to carry into execution.

In the autumn of 1830, Marshal Clausel, the Governor-General, proposed to entrust the provinces of Oran and Tittery to princes of the family of the Bey of Tunis, on the condition of their becoming vassals of France. He gave Oran, accordingly, to Prince Sidi Achmet, for an annual tribute of one million francs. The prince, uncertain as to his reception by the Arabs of that province, prudently sent before him a deputy, named Heir-ed-deen, to feel the way. This functionary, on his arrival, found the city nearly deserted, and the magazines void of provisions.

Nevertheless, he proceeded to feel his ground. He issued a proclamation to the Arabs, giving them the most flattering assurances of his future intentions. They were told that the French had not the slightest desire to interfere with their established usages and customs; that they would confine themselves to the occupation of the sea-coast towns; and that the tribes in the interior should be governed by native chiefs of their own selection. Some Arab sheiks, seduced by these promises, came in, and received pelisses, and other marks of honour. They returned to their tribes, but to become objects of ridicule. The plan proved utterly abortive. It neither awakened hopes, nor dispelled fears. After a few weeks, the agent of the prince withdrew.

To the immense advantages which accrued to him from the fluctuations and failures which embarrassed the councils of the French government, Abdel Kader was daily adding those solid results which arose from his own energy and courage. The fruits of the impulse which he had imparted to his countrymen were becoming more apparent. Confidence, if not victory, followed everywhere in his train. The Arab character was developing long-concealed virtues from its inmost depths. Patience, constancy, perseverance, concentration of purpose, and a spirit of union, had all been summoned to the surface under the presiding genius of Abdel Kader.

His principal care was to get rid of all the causes likely to endanger the common weal, or to disturb his general line of action. The edict which he had issued, forbidding all commercial transactions with the French, had borne heavily on some of the tribes, who had long been accustomed to trade with the towns now in French possession. The fruits of a traffic exercised from generation to generation, and the enormous profits actually reaped, were advantages not easily foregone. But, by the influence of certain Marabouts, who, by the order of Abdel Kader, were moving constantly amongst them, more patriotic feelings were made to prevail. The Arabs ceased to frequent the French markets.

The system of blockade enforced by Abdel Kader had a telling effect on the French garrisons. They depended almost entirely on the Arabs for the necessaries of life. The sea brought them little or nothing, and only at rare intervals. Hence the nervous anxiety, leading to acts of violence, with which, like birds of prey, they scented and pounced upon their food in the interior. Whilst Desmichels was revolving in his mind in what manner he could, without lowering his dignity, bring about negotiations with Abdel Kader, and relieve him from his pressing wants and necessities, there occurred an event which opened the door to a transaction.

Towards the end of October, 1833, an Arab, named Kudoor, of the Borgia tribe, came to Arzew and sold some cattle. On his departure he asked the French commanding officer to give him an escort, as he dreaded the Sultan's scouts, whom he knew to be on the look-out. An escort of four horsemen was given him. At the distance of about a league from the town the escort was attacked by a large force of Arabs. One man was killed; the three others were taken prisoners and carried to Mascara.

Desmichels, only too happy to have a plausible pretext for writing to Abdel Kader, now addressed him the following letter :—

"I do not hesitate to make the first advances to you. My position, strictly speaking, does not allow me to do so, but humanity compels me. I reclaim the liberty of those Frenchmen who, while engaged in escorting an Arab, fell into an ambuscade. I cannot suppose that you will make their release dependent on conditions, since, when by the fate of war some of the Zmelas and Gharabas were not long since brought in to me, as prisoners, I at once sent them back to their tribes, without any stipulation, and treated them, moreover, with the greatest kindness.

" If, therefore, you wish to be considered a great man, I hope you will not be behind me in generosity, and that you will immediately release the Frenchmen who are now in your power."

Abdel Kader returned the following reply :—

" I have received the letter, in which you express your hope that the prisoners to whom you allude will be liberated. I understand its contents. You tell me that, notwithstanding your position, you have consented to make me the first advances. It was your duty to do so, according to the rules of war. Between enemies, each has his turn : one day the chances are for you, another for me. The mill turns for both, and always crushing new victims.

" As for myself, when you have taken prisoners, I never troubled you with reclamations in their behalf. I was pained, as a man, for their unhappy fate ; but, a a Mussulman, I looked upon their death, if it occurred, as a new life. You tell me that your Frenchmen were employed to protect an Arab. That is no reason with me. Protectors and protected were alike my enemies ; and all Arabs who are found with you are bad believers, ignorant of their duty.

" You boast that you gratuitously liberated some of the Gharabas and Zmelas. That is true. But you surprised men who were living under your protection, and who were actually supplying your own markets. Your troops robbed them of all they had. If, instead of falling on those who were doing you a service, you had advanced beyond your lines ; if you had attacked men who were anxiously waiting for you, such as the Beni Amers and the Hashems, then you might, with justice, talk of your generosity, had you taken prisoners from them, and set them free.

"Then you would have deserved the praises you claim for yourself for having pillaged the Zmelas, and setting about the report that I had fallen into your hands. When you march two days beyond the walls of Oran I hope we shall behold each other; and then it will be seen which of us will remain master of the field."

This haughty challenge would, under other circumstances, have aroused in the breast of the French general the loftiest feelings of chivalry. The drums would have been beat, the trumpets sounded, the standards fluttered, and the Arab champion would have been swiftly summoned to the test. Desmichels retorted by again attacking and plundering the Douairs and Zmelas. Abdel Kader was amongst the Beni Amers when he heard of the incursion.

He was instantly at the head of 5,000 cavalry, and rushed to the rescue. With slackened reins and thundering hoofs, the Arab horse traversed a distance of fifty miles in less than three hours. Not more than one-half of the men, on his arrival, were fit for duty. But with these troops Abdel Kader charged. The French, utterly confounded by this un-expected apparition, hastily retreated, abandoning the women and children, whom they had taken with them, as hostages. Fresh troops come up to their relief, with more pieces of artillery; but, despite the galling fire to which he was exposed, Abdel Kader followed up the enemy, and hovered round them, to the very outskirts of Oran.

On his return to the Arab encampment he ordered the Douairs and Zmelas to prepare for immediate departure from a spot where temptations to transgress his edict were constantly held out to them, and where they were as continually exposed to vile and cruel assaults. He marched them off, with all their flocks and herds, and located them on a large plain behind Tlemsen.

Desmichels, paralysed by the boldness and ubiquity of his redoubtable foe, and finding his resources failing, his supplies cut off, and famine ready to swoop down on his men, saw no alternative before him but evacuation or peace. In this dire necessity he thus appealed to Abdel Kader :—

"You will never find me deaf to any sentiments of generosity, and if it would be convenient to you to grant me an interview, I am quite ready to consent, in the hope that we may be able, by the most sacred and solemn treaties, to stop the effusion of blood between two peoples destined by Providence to live under the same dominion."

Abdel Kader seeing his adversary in the attitude of a suppliant, affected indifference. He left the letter unanswered. At the same time he employed a Jew, named Mordecai Amar, his agent at Oran, to pacify the French general with excuses, if any complaint were made as to his silence, and to suggest the advisability of more explicit and categorical propositions. After a month had transpired, Desmichels penned a third dispatch :—

"Not having received any answer to the letter I lately wrote to you, I prefer supposing that it has never reached you, to imagining that you have not chosen to give it your attention."

E

The general terminated his reasonings by imploring for peace as follows:—" If you wish to maintain the exalted position to which circumstances have raised you, in my opinion you could not do better than accept my invitation, in order that the tribes may devote themselves to the cultivation of their lands, and enjoy the fruits and the blessings of peace, under the shadow of treaties binding us firmly together."

The young and victorious Sultan, with this document in his hand, could now show his subjects that the enemy had been the first to crave for a suspension of hostilities. There was no occasion for any further delay, and he sent the following answer :—

" I have received your letter, and fully understand its contents. It gives me great satisfaction to find that your sentiments agree with mine. I feel quite assured of your loyal intentions ; and you may feel assured that any engagements into which we may enter shall be faithfully observed on my part. I send you two superior officers of my army— Milond ibn Arasch and Ould Mahmoud. They will confer, outside Oran, with Mordecai Amar, and will make known to him any proposition. If you accept them, you can send him on to me, and then we will draw up a treaty, which shall obliterate the hatred and enmity now severing us from each other, and replace them by an indissoluble friendship. You may count upon me, for I have never been unfaithful to my word."

The proposed interview took place February 4, 1834. The Jew Amar was accompanied by the whole of the French staff. A long discussion ensued on various propositions made by Desmichels. The Sultan's agent, Ibn Arasch, then left, saying he would report what had passed to his master, and return. He took with him a paper containing a draft of the propositions, but without the general's signature.

On the 25th, Ibn Arasch returned to Oran, bearing this draft, approved and sealed by Abdel Kader, with another paper, containing the propositions of Abdel Kader. He was instructed not to deliver the former until the latter had been signed and sealed by Desmichels. Abdel Kader conceived that these documents, mutually exchanged, would constitute the Treaty. Their substance was as follows :—

CONDITIONS OF GENERAL DESMICHELS.

" 1. Hostilities shall cease between the French and the Arabs from this day.

" 2. The religion and usages of the Mussulmans shall be respected.

" 3. French prisoners shall be given up.

" 4. The markets shall be free.

" 5. Every French deserter shall be given up by the Arabs.

" 6. Every Christian travelling in the interior shall be furnished with a passport sealed with the seal of Abdel Kader's consul, and that of the General."

CONDITIONS OF THE SULTAN ABDEL KADER.

" 1. The Arabs shall be at liberty to buy and sell powder, arms, sulphur ; in a word, everything necessary for war.

" 2. The commerce of the port of Arzew shall be under the jurisdiction of the Prince of the Faithful. No cargoes shall be shipped except in that port. Mostaganem and Oran

shall merely receive such articles of merchandise as are necessary for the wants of their inhabitants. To this there shall
be no opposition. Those who wish to ship goods must repair
to Arzew.

"3. The General shall give us up all deserters in chains.
He shall not harbour criminals. The general commanding at
Algiers shall have no power over Arabs who may come to
him with the consent of their chiefs.

"4. No Mussulman shall be prevented returning home
when he wishes."

To the paper containing these conditions of Abdel Kader,
Desmichels, who dreaded nothing so much as the breaking off
of the negotiation, at once affixed his seal and signature.
The former naturally thought that, by virtue of the 2nd
Article, he had secured a monopoly of commerce.

On the 26th February, 1834, Desmichels proposed to Ibn
Arasch, that a homogeneous treaty should be drawn up, embodying the substance of both documents, but stating the
French conditions more at large. Ibn Arasch made no difficulty, never conceiving for a moment that such a document
could be intended to abrogate the conditions already conceded
to his master, in the paper which had just been signed and
sealed by the general. Hence arose the "Treaty of Desmichels," which afterwards gave rise to so many difficulties and
complications.

TREATY OF GENERAL DESMICHELS, *February* 26, 1834.

" The General commanding the French troops in the town
of Oran, and the Prince of the Faithful, Sidi-il-Hadj Abdel

Kader-ibn-Mehi-ed-deen, have decided on the following conditions :—

"Art. 1.—Hostilities shall cease between the French and the Arabs from this day. The General commanding the French troops and the Emir Abdel Kader will neglect nothing to maintain that union and friendship which ought to exist between two peoples, destined by God to live under the same dominion. To this end, representatives on the part of the Emir shall reside at Oran, Mostaganem, and Arzew ; and, to prevent collisions between the French and the Arabs, French officers shall reside at Mascara.

"Art. 2.—The religion and usages of the Arabs shall be respected.

"Art. 3.—All prisoners shall be immediately given up, both on one side and the other.

"Art. 4.—Freedom of commerce shall be complete and entire.

"Art. 5.—Military men belonging to the French army, who desert their colours, shall be brought back by the Arabs. In like manner, all Arab malefactors, who, to avoid punishment, fly from their tribes and seek refuge with the French, shall be immediately seized and delivered over to the Emir's representative, in the three maritime towns occupied by the French.

"Art. 6.—Every European, having occasion to travel in the interior, shall be furnished with a passport countersigned by the representatives of the Emir, and approved by the General in command, in order that they may find assistance and protection throughout the province."

These conditions, written in parallel columns of Arab and

French, were signed and sealed by both parties. Nothing is said in this treaty of a monopoly of commerce. But Abdel Kader had his bond, and was content. Desmichels, proud of what he considered a diplomatic triumph, hastened to send the grateful tidings of a peace to the French ministry, and allowed himself to indulge in the following strain :—

"I have to announce to you the *submission* of the province of Oran, the most considerable and warlike of the regency. This great event is the result of the advantages which have been obtained by the troops of my division."

Abdel Kader might well repose on his laurels. He had compelled his enemy to sue for peace ; he had made his own terms ; he paid no tribute ; his territory was not limited ; the French general had acknowledged his independence by offering him the power to appoint and receive consuls. The French were to load at one port alone, and were to submit to his tariff.

In virtue of the monopoly secured to him by his own terms, Abdel Kader now issued orders, prohibiting the Arabs from selling corn, or barley, or agricultural produce, of any kind whatever, to Christians, whether native or foreign. His agents were declared to be the sole authorised buyers and sellers, and by them the prices in the markets were to be fixed.

The French merchants at Arzew complained loudly to Desmichels of the restriction. Abdel Kader appealed to his bond. Desmichels affected to ignore it. He adhered to his homogeneous treaty, in which commerce was declared free. Abdel Kader agreed to the test, but contended that though the market *places* (or *sook*) were free, he had the sole right of supplying them.

One of the French merchants, acting upon the view of the question, as put forward by the French general, bought a large quantity of corn and barley from an Arab of the tribe of Hamian. The agent of Abdel Kader went over and seized it. The merchant complained to the French local authorities, but he was told that no interference could be tolerated with the regulations of the Emir.

Desmichels, embarrassed with fresh complaints, and pressed for explanation by General Voirol, the governor-general, to whom all this misunderstanding was utterly incomprehensible, adopted a middle course. He declared that the authorisation given to the Emir to make a monopoly of grain, extended only to the grain raised on his own private property. Abdel Kader ridiculed the subterfuge. He knew nothing of the exclusive interpretation which Desmichels chose to put upon his treaty; he only knew that he had the General's seal and signature to a document granting him a monopoly; and this monopoly he was determined to enact. The French were not in a position to dispute his verdict; and he carried his point.

Abdel Kader, free at length from external molestation, devoted his earnest attention to the internal affairs of his kingdom. Difficulties and trials were yet before him. Jealousy of his successes on the part of some, envy at the eminence he had attained on the part of others, insinuations malevolently propagated by his rivals, and readily entertained by the fanatical party, that he had betrayed the sacred cause by making peace with the infidels—all combined, as disturbing elements, to affect, more or less, the stability of his government.

But his retort was ready. To the taunting demand, "Where is now the leader of the Djehad—where the lofty tone which breathed nothing but battle and defiance, and invoked death rather than submission?" he replied by calmly pointing to the French garrisons, confined to the walls on which their cannon was planted; to the plains freed from infidel marauders; to the cities unmolested by Frank invaders; and, more than all, to a treaty, dictated at his sword's point, which now, for the first time in the lapse of ages, gave good warranty for hopes of Arab freedom, and which promised to be the basis of Arab independence.

CHAPTER V.

ABDEL KADER now entered on the task of organisation. He trusted but little to the pacific professions of the French, and looked on the present cessation of hostilities merely as an armed truce. He resolved, consequently, to make use of the breathing time thus afforded, in maturing his plans, husbanding his resources, and preparing for future battles. Declaring the Djehad to be only suspended, not abandoned, he issued his usual edict for the collection of the war-tribute, consisting of the *ashur*, or tenth of all agricultural produce, and the *zekka*, or tax on cattle.

To his astonishment, the most faithful of all his tribes, his most zealous adherents, the very men who had been the guardians and supporters of his nascent power, and by whose aid he had been enabled to inflict his most deadly blows, refused obedience. The Beni Amers asserted that cessation of impost was, in their eyes, the legitimate consequence of cessation of war.

Abdel Kader hesitated not a moment. The Beni Amers must be attacked. Writing to Mustapha-ibn-Ismail at Tlemsen, he ordered him to prepare the Douairs and Zmelas for instant action. That old and wily leader of the Turkish *Maghzen*, desiring nothing better than to have an opportunity of falling on his old and mortal enemies, and rejoicing in the prospect of plunder, joyfully accepted the summons, and boastfully enlarged on the loyalty of his tribes.   An unexpected incident turned the tide of events.

As Abdel Kader was preaching one Friday, as was his wont, in the mosque of Mascara, his eye lighted on some of the Beni Amer Sheiks.   Suddenly turning the stream of his eloquence, he thus apostrophised them :—" Were not you, O Beni Amers, the first to call me to the post I now hold ? Were not you the first to implore me to establish a regular government, which should inspire the good with confidence, and the wicked with terror ?

" Did you not solemnly pledge your lives, your properties, and all that you held most dear and sacred, to assist and strengthen me in the arduous task ?   And will you be the first to abandon the common cause, the first, by your example, to countenance and encourage conspiracies against the very government you invoked ?   How can any government be carried on without taxes, how maintained without the cordial union and support of all ?

" Think you that the smallest coin of the tribute which I demand, will ever be appropriated to my personal or family expenses ?   You all know that my paternal property suffices for my own needs.   What I demand is what the law of the Prophet renders it imperative on you, as good Mussulmans, to give ; and in my hands, I solemnly swear, it will be held as a sacred trust, for the triumph of the faith ! "

Moved by this frank appeal, the Beni Amer Sheiks demanded a conference.   The throng pressed around them. All ranks and ages joined their entreaties to effect an accommodation. Thus surrounded, the Sheiks advanced towards their young Sultan, and kissed his hand. In the name of their tribe, they promised to pay the tribute. Orders were forthwith despatched to Mustapha to suspend his march on the Beni Amers.

Three days afterwards, a horseman came riding in at full speed, to say that Mustapha had, notwithstanding, commenced an attack. Abdel Kader, hastily gathering together such horsemen as were within reach, galloped off to the scene of action.

On arriving, he sent word to Mustapha to withdraw. On his refusal to obey the order, Abdel Kader advanced to charge his recalcitrant chief. A few only of the Beni Amers followed. After a desperate skirmish, Abdel Kader had the mortification to see his men dispersed, and flying before superior numbers. A handful of men alone remained to rally round his person. Animated by the example of their chief, they fought with desperation. Nearly all were killed, or dismounted. At last, after performing prodigies of valour, Abdel Kader, his burnous riddled with bullets, and his horse covered with wounds, cut his way through the hostile ranks which closed him in, and galloped back to Mascara. He reached it late at night—alone.

Abdel Kader defeated by the Arabs! The news spread like wildfire. In an instant all slumbering rivalries were aroused. Sidi-il-Aribi raised the standard of revolt. El Gomari, and the Beni Engad, prepared to join Sidi Hamadi, the Governor of Tlemsen, who entered into correspondence with Mustapha.

The tidings of these defections, so far from oppressing the soul of Abdel Kader with despondency, only nerved him

with fresh vigour.   The Hashem Gharabas, the Mejahers,
the Beni Abbas, were staunch.   The Beni Amers had confirmed the adhesion given in by their Sheiks, at Mascara.
He could wield a force of 15,000 cavalry.   With a large
proportion of these he at once took the field.

Mustapha had led off the Douairs and Zmelas to their old
campaigning ground near Oran, in the hopes of propitiating
the French, and getting their support.   To his disgust, he was
warned by the latter of the consequences which would ensue if
he persisted in rebelling against Abdel Kader, the ally of France.

Desmichels had found out by bitter experience, the impossibility of conquering the province of Oran, with such
forces as his government had placed at his disposal.   The plan
of raising up a native power to supply this deficiency, and
to assist in extending the French dominions, either as vassals
or allies, seemed to him to afford the easiest method for
escaping from a serious dilemma.   He was dazzled by the
great and commanding qualities displayed by Abdel Kader,
and always took a pleasure in extolling his heroism, his
prowess, and even his generalship.   He seemed almost to
envy and covet his glory.

Desmichels was known to have frequently declared that
he would make the young Arab Emir all powerful, from the
frontiers of Morocco to the frontiers of Tunis.   No doubt
this declaration was made with the mental reserve that the
gallant chief should only be so as the vassal of France.
Abdel Kader, fully understanding the profitable tendency to
himself of this exuberant admiration, cared not to dispel
an illusion which marvellously promoted his own designs.
He was secretly bent, however, on preserving a perfectly

independent position, and on confining his allies to their counting-houses on the sea-coast.

Mustapha having been thus kept in check, Abdel Kader fell with his whole force upon Sidi-il-Aribi, enveloped him in a crushing defeat, and took him prisoner. At the same time he inflicted on the rebellious tribes a signal chastisement, and collected all the arrears of tribute. Flushed by this victory, he now sought out Mustapha. He met him on the plains of Mahraz, July 13, 1834. The battle between the hostile chiefs raged for some hours with alternate success. At last, both sides, worn out with fatigue, and fainting with the heat, drew breath.

Abdel Kader seized the moment to send some Marabouts through the enemy's ranks, to offer terms. Mustapha, fearing an attack from the French, who had advanced as far as the camp of Miserghin, and were in observation, was nothing loath to listen to any propositions which might relieve him from his perilous situation. Though declining a personal meeting with Abdel Kader, he sent him his charger in token of reconciliation.

Abdel Kader now marched upon Tlemsen. His appearance before that town, with all the prestige of victory, at once annihilated the intrigues of which that place had been the focus. His faithless lieutenant, Sidi Hamadi, was seized and imprisoned, but afterwards generously pardoned, although not allowed to retain his post. This was conferred on Noona, who after his late defeat had fled to Morocco, and had returned, bearing letters of recommendation from the Moorish Sultan.

Abdel Kader entered Mascara in triumph. Two events

had occurred during his absence, which materially aided him. El Gomari, chief of the Beni Engad, had been tried before a tribunal, and shot; and Sidi-il-Aribi had died in prison. Freed from these rivals, and unimpeded by internal faction, he was again at liberty to carry out his measures of general administration.

The province of Oran was divided into two great districts, and placed under khalifas, or lieutenants. That of the east, subdivided into seven agalicks, and having Mascara as the seat of government, was placed under the command of the Sultan's brother-in-law, Mustapha-ibn-Tamy. That of the west, with Tlemsen for its capital, was entrusted to Bou Hamadi. Every tribe was held responsible for the peace and good order of its locality. Weekly reports were required, as to the amount of cattle, beasts of burden, and horses fit for service in each agalick. A Cadi, appointed by the Sultan, and paid out of the public treasury, was sent to each of the tribes, to administer justice.

A body of regulars was raised, consisting both of cavalry and infantry. The latter were drilled and instructed by French non-commissioned officers, who had been allowed to offer their services for that purpose. Cannon-foundries, powder-mills, and manufactories of small arms, were established and superintended by European artisans. The Arabs wondered at these strange and novel proceedings. They felt that a new order of things had suddenly fallen on them.

This, together with the vigilance with which crimes were detected, and the certainty and severity of its punishment, soon had its effect on the community. The entire province, which eighteen months previously had been a prey to every kind of anarchy and confusion, now enjoyed the most thorough tranquillity. So complete was the feeling of security which existed in all parts, that, to use the favourite Arab illustration of the perfection of good government, "A girl might have travelled the length and breadth of the land with a casket of diamonds on her head, without fear of molestation."

Abdel Kader's fame had now spread through Algeria. It was generally felt that a man had arisen who had not only shown himself capable of preserving order within, but who, by his skill and daring, had succeeded in imposing conditions on the infidels from without. The eyes of all the well-disposed naturally turned towards one who had achieved such signal results.

The inhabitants of Medea and Miliana, the principal towns in the province of Tittery, sent deputations to Abdel Kader, begging him to do for their province what he had already done for the province of Oran. Had he been free to act on his own inspirations, forty-eight hours would not have elapsed before he had been on the march in compliance with their request. The invitation was not only flattering to his pride, as showing the influence his name exercised over parties utterly unknown to him, but offered—what in his eyes was its strongest inducement—a further opening for the prosecution of the great object he had in view, the establishment of a widely-extended Arab nationality.

The Treaty of Desmichels in no way precluded him from entering Tittery; for that treaty had not confined him within any prescribed limits. Still he was not disposed to undertake the enterprise without first ascertaining how such a step would be viewed by the French authorities. Contenting himself, therefore, for the present, with replying to the deputations, that he required time to consider their demands, he proceeded to fathom the thoughts of Count D'Erlon, the new Governor-General, on the momentous topic. The recent arrival of that personage gave him an opportunity of broaching the delicate question without appearing to make it a special subject of negotiation.

Under the garb of a letter of felicitation to the general on his appointment, the following feeler was adroitly put forward : — " The Kaid, Miloud ibn Arasch, will give you every particular about us. I have instructed him to ascertain your views as to the best manner of establishing tranquillity in all the districts, whether maritime or in the interior, along the coasts between Algiers and Oran, and in the plains and the mountains, from Tlemsen and Mascara, *up to Medea and Miliana.*"

Count D'Erlon had come to assume the arduous and responsible duties which now devolved upon him, without any clear instructions, and without any additional force. The French government, still uncertain as to its European relations, had neither money nor troops to spare for the prosecution of an Algerian war on a great scale. A vague idea possessed it that Abdel Kader was the ladder by which the French were to scale the heights of the Atlas. To keep on good terms with this influential chief was, consequently, at this period, a cardinal point of French policy.

Accordingly, the reply of Count D'Erlon to Abdel Kader consisted of vague generalities, and was altogether couched in such terms, that the latter had every ground to believe no measures would be taken to oppose his proposed step if he only had the boldness to take it. Still he felt the necessity of having his actual rights confirmed by the new Governor-General before assuming new ones; and to this end he sent the document containing his own terms, which had been duly signed and sealed by Desmichels, as above related, to the Count, for his perusal.

D'Erlon, to whom even the existence of such a document was unknown, as it had never been notified to the French Government, was thunder-struck. Here was a French general, who had taken upon himself to sign a secret treaty, giving solid and exclusive advantages to an enemy whose hostility had not been disarmed, and whose friendship was doubtful. His representations to the French ministry relative to this extraordinary procedure were such, that they were speedily followed by the recall of Desmichels from Oran.

At the same time he thus gave his opinion to Abdel Kader on the subject :—" I would wish you to observe, that General Desmichels had no power or jurisdiction, except in the province of Oran, and that he could in nowise make any stipulations as regards any other part of the regency. Even by giving the widest interpretation to the Treaty made between you and him, in February, 1834, you can have no pretensions beyond the province of Oran, limited as it has been by the sovereign power of France.

" My desire for the present is, that you should not cross the lower Cheliff, towards the east. If you govern the territory you now possess according to Mohammedan laws, and with strict justice, we shall be friends ; but we cannot allow you to enter the province of Tittery. What passes there is

F

my concern. I am not at war with its inhabitants ; I have no fixed project of making establishments at Blidah and Bouffarick, but whenever I think it for the interest of France to do so, I shall allow no one to embarrass me."

Abdel Kader paused for the present before such an interdict. Besides, disturbances amongst the Flittas, in the valley of the Cheliff, excited against him by the sons of Sidi-il-Aribi, called for his immediate presence in that direction.

While engaged in appeasing these troubles, he was surprised by the information that a certain Hadj Mousa, a shereef from the Sahara, had entered Medea, and had been warmly received by a large portion of the population. After waiting for a time to see what steps would be taken by the French Governor-General, and finding that no opposition to the assumptions of this adventurer was offered on the part of Count D'Erlon, Abdel Kader determined to exercise full liberty of action. If a shereef from the desert might snatch a province, why not he ? Fortune is the friend of the bold, and the world is for him who will seize it. He dashed across the Cheliff, and marched on Medea, followed by all the cavalry contingents of Oran, two battalions of regular infantry, and four pieces of cannon. Cæsar had crossed the Rubicon.

Hadj Mousa came out to meet him, prophesying that God would give him the victory, and that the cannon of Abdel Kader would not go off. Abdel Kader replied that if, indeed, his cannon did not go off, he would acknowledge a divine interposition, and withdraw. The battle was gained, and the prophet and pretender was completely defeated. Abdel

Kader took possession, amidst general exultation, of the province of Tittery, and appointed Khalifas at Medea and Miliana.

General Trezel, who had replaced Desmichels at Oran, proposed to reply to this movement of Abdel Kader by seizing Mascara. D'Erlon temporised. He was neither authorised nor prepared to commence hostilities. He even condescended to treat with Abdel Kader in the very town he had occupied in direct violation of his prohibition. Captain St. Hippolyte was sent to him, bearer of the following draft of a treaty :—

1. Acknowledgment of the sovereignty of France.

2. Precise definition of the power of the Emir, which is to be exercised in the province of Oran alone, bounded on the east by the Cheliff, from its mouth to its confluence with the Wady Riou, and by the river of that name up to Godjidah.

3. Right of French and all Europeans to travel in the province of Oran.

4. Entire freedom of commerce in the interior.

5. Engagement on the part of the Emir not to export, except in ports occupied by the French.

6. Tribute to be paid by Abdel Kader, and hostages to be given by him. The tribute to be considered a mark of his acknowledgment of French sovereignty.

A treaty which thus abrogated, by a stroke of the pen, all the rights and privileges his own good sword had obtained, might apparently have been regarded by Abdel Kader as an insult or a defiance. But, in reality, it was the result of his own diplomacy. He had learned to appreciate the value and importance of the power to make treaties. He knew that this power implied an independent position, whether for proposing or accepting terms. Already a French general had, by treaty, acknowledged and confirmed his right to an independent sway, had saluted him as Emir, and Prince of the Faithful, or Sultan.

Negotiations once opened with the new Governor-General might lead to similar concessions. What the nature of the propositions, presented to him in the first instance, might be, was to him a matter of supreme indifference. What he wanted, and what he earnestly urged his agent at Algiers to obtain from D'Erlon, was a treaty. He trusted to the chapter of accidents to mould any fresh negotiation to his own wishes.

The employment of well-paid spies introduced him into the most secret councils of the French authorities. Able and crafty agents, accredited to the responsible heads of the French administration, in its various centres of action, were made the means of promoting his views and advancing his interests. These agents were instructed to gain the confidence of all important personages; to be always about them on some pretence or other; to be constantly extolling their master's merits, and enlarging on his talents for administration; to speak loudly of his extraordinary influence in the country; and, finally, to insinuate the immense advantages which would accrue to France by having such a pioneer in the path of conquest.

A Jew, of the name of Durand, had performed all these functions, at Algiers, with rare ability. He had easily contrived to get the ear of D'Erlon. He was consulted by him in all affairs of moment connected with the internal government of the regency. He had gradually impressed him with a favourable opinion of his master; and he succeeded, finally, in drawing him into the current of credulous expectation with regard to the conduct of Abdel Kader, which had carried away more than one of his predecessors. In the meantime, he had wormed out of him the foregoing treaty, and was commissioned to accompany the bearer of it to Medea.

There, though the treaty met with very little ceremony or attention, the bearer of the treaty received the most striking marks of friendship and hospitality. A grand review was held; and the French envoy gazed with dubious admiration on the nucleus of an Arab army. He was invited to accompany the Sultan on a tour of inspection about to be made through the provinces of Tittery and Oran. The offer was accepted; and Captain St. Hippolyte and the Jew Durand figured conspicuously in the royal suite.

Abdel Kader made the most of his time. Purposely going into those districts which had recently shown symptoms of disaffection, or were wavering in their allegiance to him, he secretly enjoyed the impression made on the tribes by the French uniform. What, they thought, must be the power of a chief who had made the infidels his vassals, and who could, no doubt, at any moment summon their armies to march to the support of his throne? Any resistance to such a potentate would be mere madness. Unqualified submission was their best and only alternative.

On reaching Mascara, fresh tokens of politeness and cordiality awaited the distinguished guests. On the third day after their arrival, Abdel Kader put his own treaty into their hands. It was to this effect :—

1. The provinces which are under the dominion of the Prince of the Faithful, and which are in submission, shall remain dependent on him. In like manner the country which the Governor-General actually holds shall remain under his dominion.

2. Whenever the Emir shall think fit to appoint or to remove the Governors of Medea and Miliana, he will inform the Governor-General, that he may take note of the fact; and also make those functionaries the medium of any dispatch or communication he may have to convey to him.

3. Freedom of commerce for all. The Arabs shall be respected in the markets by the French, and the French by the Arabs, in all the provinces under the dominion of the Emir.

4. The Prince of the Faithful shall buy at Algiers, through his agent, everything he requires in the shape of mortars, muskets, powder, and sulphur.

5. The Emir shall give up to the French all deserters; and the Governor-General will act similarly towards the Emir.

6. If the Emir projects a tour towards Constantine or elsewhere, he will inform the Governor-General of his intention and of his motive for doing so.

A treaty so ridiculously contrasting with the one sent for his acceptance by the French Governor-General, and which, so far from limiting his power, proposed to allow him to leap at one bound, from the gates of Oran to those of Constantine, and to make the French themselves the complaisant approvers of this encroachment, was certainly one which the Prince of the Faithful never expected to see accepted.

Perfectly comprehending, however, the exaggerated importance attached to his friendship and support by the French Government, and relying on the efficacy of those secret influences he had hitherto so successfully employed, Abdel Kader was not without hopes that by a strenuous and even overstrained assumption of right, and a bold avowal of design, dimly suggestive of reserved strength, he might at all events procure such a treaty as should enhance the advantages he actually possessed, strengthen his position, enlarge his sphere of action, and still further dispel the clouds which yet obscured the brilliant vista of glory lying before him.

Up to this time he had succeeded in almost all he had undertaken. His faith in his mission, always strong and unshaken, now possessed his mind with the strength of a religious conviction. By inspiring all around him with a like confidence and belief, this faith became to him an instrument of power. His past success was accepted as a sure omen of future triumphs. A French officer, about this time, advised him, out of honest sympathy and regard, not to be presumptuously confident. " What ! " replied Abdel Kader, " it is but three years since I was simply one of my father's five sons, and obliged to mount and equip myself from the enemy's spoils. You see what I am now ; and you tell me not to have confidence in myself ! "

CHAPTER VI.

1835.

COUNT D'ERLON visited Oran in the month of June, 1835. Abdel Kader wrote to compliment him on his arrival, and anxiously awaited overtures. The Governor-General was desirous of inviting him to a personal interview. Trezel firmly and successfully pointed out the impolicy of such a step. He maintained that, so far from Abdel Kader being willing to see, much more to aid in, the extension of French dominion in Algeria, he was, in fact, adroitly making the French Government the instrument for his own exaltation, and that to enter into closer relations with him would be tantamount to an approval of his late conduct.

Such, indeed, was the indignation of that uncompromising soldier at the facility with which Abdel Kader was achieving his own ends at the expense, as he conceived, of French honour, and to the great scandal of French common sense and discrimination, that he had more than once been tempted to march against him on his own responsibility. D'Erlon, on the contrary, strongly impressed by this time with the importance and necessity of Abdel Kader's support, would not hear of any steps being taken that might possibly lead to a rupture; and on returning to Algiers, ordered Trezel carefully to cultivate his friendship and alliance.

Such, however, in a short time, became the state of affairs in the province of Oran, that Trezel had only before him the choice of two courses—either to submit to Abdel Kader's dictation, and await his sovereign pleasure in all things connected with the interior, or to place himself in such a position as to be enabled to act independently.

The Douairs and Zmelas had resumed a friendly intercourse with the French. Abdel Kader threatened to take them back forcibly to Tlemsen. Those tribes, rather than abandon their crops and be deprived of a profitable traffic, at once demanded French protection. Trezel granted their request; and, hearing that Abdel Kader's officers were engaged in harassing them with forcible measures—seizing their cattle and carrying off some of their Sheiks—he sent a brigade to their camping ground near Miserghin. On the 16th June, 1835, a treaty, containing eleven articles, was signed by both parties, in which the Douairs and Zmelas were declared French subjects.

Abdel Kader was still desirous to avert hostilities, and even so anxious to avoid any pretext which might lead to them, that he had issued strict orders that no Arab was, under any circumstances, to fire on a Frenchman except in self-defence. He therefore simply wrote to Trezel, strongly protesting against a step which he looked on as a glaring infraction of the treaty of Desmichels, by which the French engaged not to harbour refugees from the tribes, and to send back Arab deserters.

Trezel answered him that he was quite willing to abide by that treaty; but argued that the word "deserter" applied only to individuals, and could never have been intended to extend to whole tribes who preferred French rule to his. Viewing the sense of the treaty in that light, he said, he could never deprive the Douairs and Zmelas of the rights they had obtained.

This notification drew from Abdel Kader the following letter :—

" You know the conditions which Desmichels made with me before you came to Oran, and to which you yourself promised to adhere. By those conditions, every Arab who commits a misdemeanour or crime, and flies to you for refuge and protection, is to be sent back to me, even when it is a question of more than one individual. How much stronger becomes my claim on this point, when it is a question of whole tribes deserting and going over to you!

" The Douairs and Zmelas are my subjects; and according to our law, I have a right to do with them as I please. If you withdraw your protection from them, and let them obey me, as heretofore, it is well. If, on the contrary, you persist in breaking your engagements, recall at once your consul from Mascara ; for even should the Douairs and Zmelas enter within the walls of Oran, I will not withdraw my hand from them until they repent and atone for their fault. Moreover, my religion prohibits me from allowing a Mussulman to be under the dominion of a Christian. See what suits you best; otherwise the God of Battles must decide between us."

Trezel could only reply to such a tone by the sound of cannon. Indeed, hostilities had, in some degree, already begun. A few days previously, the French cavalry, being short of forage, had cut down the crops of the Hashem

Gharabas. Abdel Kader, on hearing of this irruption on his family tribe, had moved up 2,000 horse and 800 foot to their vicinity, near the river Sig. Trezel now determined to attack this force before it assumed any greater development. On the 26th of June, 1835, he led out a column for that purpose, consisting of 5,000 infantry, a regiment of Chasseurs d'Afrique, 4 mountain pieces, and 20 waggons for provisions, besides the ordinary ambulance.

Shortly after entering the wood of Muley Ismail, the leading companies opened fire on what they conceived to be a straggling party of the Arabs. The fire was vigorously returned. Presently cavalry appeared. It was Abdel Kader's advanced guard, coming from the Sig. In a few minutes the French were furiously attacked in front and on their flanks.

The suddenness of the onset, the thickness of the wood, and the undulating nature of the ground, which tended to conceal the real number of the enemy, combined with the shouts and cries by which the Arabs sought to magnify their number, all contributed to shake the steadiness of the French column. In vain were certain changes in its formation attempted : the rear battalions ordered to close up, the centre compacted, and the cavalry thrown out. In a short time the whole body was thrown into confusion, the cavalry was driven in, and the infantry and artillery were only able to fire their discharges at random.

For a while the Arab attack seemed to relent. The French now broke from their ranks. The provision waggons were seized and emptied; the wine casks were staved in. All eat and drank ravenously. At length, by the greatest exertions on the part of the officers, some sort of order was restored, and an onward movement was effected. The banks of the Sig were reached about sunset; and there the French column encamped in solid square.

Fortunately for the French, the main body of Abdel Kader's army, approaching by forced marches from Tlemsen, had been obliged to halt for a short repose some two leagues higher up the stream. The French, for that night, had a respite. At dawn of day, Trezel commenced a retreat; but Abdel Kader had not been inactive. By a rapid night march he had succeeded in placing himself on the enemy's line of communication with Oran. Trezel was in no condition to fight his way, and took the direction of the seaport town of Arzew. Knowing the difficulties of a direct movement in that point—part of the intervening country being almost impassable to waggons and artillery carriages—he determined to turn the Hamian Mountains, and to emerge on the plain of Arzew by the defile of the Habra, where that river Habra changes its name to that of the Macta.

Abdel Kader, seeing the direction the French were taking, at once devised their object. If he could only occupy the defile of the Habra before they reached it, he knew they would be at his mercy. But the distance was too great for infantry to accomplish in time to effect his object. Selecting a thousand horsemen, he ordered each rider to mount a foot soldier behind him, and gallop to the spot. This lucky inspiration was crowned with complete success. The French, after patiently toiling across the plain of Ceirat, harassed all the way by the Arab cavalry, entered the defile about midday.

To their surprise they found the slopes on either side of them bristling with arms. As they proceeded, huge pieces of

rock were hurled down upon them. While the French skirmishers were occupied during two hours in bravely but
slowly opening a way, Abdel Kader with his whole army
closed in upon them from behind. Their rear guard, fearing
to be cut off, pushed on confusedly to the front.

Part of the ambulance and artillery took ground to the
right, and got swamped in a marsh. The artillerymen cut
their traces and fled. Regiments got intermingled. Companies and sections of companies rushed here and there for
places of shelter or escape. Luckily for them, the Arabs
were too much occupied in plundering and stripping and
slaying the wounded, to follow them into the nooks and
corners in which they had sought for refuge. Many, trying
to swim the river, were carried away by the stream and
drowned. Night came on. The crushed and mutilated
mass dropped away towards Arzew in disjointed fragments of
helpless and bewildered fugitives.

The Arabs knew no bounds to their exultation. Shouts of
joy resounded, and the glare of torches flashed to and fro in
the defile all through the night. An aerial spectator might
have seen one part of it occupied with busy architects. Drawing near, he would have seen something growing up from the
ground, like a pyramid. Bending down and listening, he
would have heard frantic cries of "more heads, more heads!"
A closer inspection of this work of art would have revealed
to the astonished gaze hundreds of French heads, piled up
promiscuously.

Abdel Kader rode towards the place about midnight. He
reined up, and paused for awhile in silent and painful con-
templation. His soul revolted at the ghastly trophy. For
the moment he was powerless; but as he passed on, he

resolved in his mind that this should be the last of such barbarities.

Such was the terrible episode of the Macta. France was electrified at the news of the disaster. The nation, with one accord, demanded investigation, punishment, and vengeance. D'Erlon was recalled ; the brave but unfortunate Trezel was replaced by General D'Arlanges. Marshal Clausel was sent to inaugurate a new era in what was now called the African colony of France ; but his new weapons were destined to break in his hands.

In the session of 1835, M. Thiers spoke powerfully in the French Chambers on the subject of the system which had, up to that time, been pursued in Algeria. "It is not colonisation," he said. "It is not occupation on a large scale ; it is not occupation on a small scale. It is not peace ; it is not war. It is war badly made." Roused by this taunt, so bitterly justified by the late deplorable event on the Macta, the French Government at last threw some energy into its mode of action, augmented the army in Algeria, ordered the vigorous prosecution of the war with Abdel Kader, and decreed the occupation of Mascara. It was thought that the seizure of his capital would bring the aspiring young Sultan to terms.

Marshal Clausel arrived at Algiers August 10th, 1835. A pompous proclamation which he issued boastfully announced the speedy submission of the whole regency. A map was at the same time published, showing the colony divided into beylicks, with the names of the native beys appointed to govern them. Abdel Kader was held to be a thing of the past, or, if existing, to be easily disposed of.

This highly satisfactory arrangement, however, never

extended beyond the domain of imagination. The marshal's
military deeds were destined to contrast awkwardly with his
military dreams. Expeditions to Medea, to Miliana, to Cher-
chell, all returned with sad tales of humiliation and reverse.
"In two months," he had ostentatiously declared, "the
Hadjouts shall cease to be." The marshal theorised; Abdel
Kader performed.

His Khalifa at Miliana descended, by his orders, into the
Metija with 5,000 cavalry and infantry, rallied these very
Hadjouts, swept the plains of Algiers of all the French
colonists, and blockaded Algiers itself. On the other hand,
D'Arlanges and the garrison of Oran were reduced to the
greatest straits. They were little more than prisoners of war.
Abdel Kader had almost realised his threat that not a bird
should fly over the towns occupied by the infidels without his
leave.

The French everywhere writhed in their fetters. The
army breathed fury and indignation, and almost mutinied.
From the general to the drummer, all loudly demanded to
be led out against the daring and successful Arab who was
thus setting them at defiance and enveloping them in the
toils of his fearless and enterprising genius. On the 21st of
November, 1835, Clausel went to Oran, and prepared to take
the field with 12,000 men.

Abdel Kader was already on the alert. His available force,
to meet the coming shock, was 8,000 cavalry, 2,000 infantry,
and four pieces of cannon. With these he proposed to check,
harass, and perhaps scatter, the French army on its line of
march. To defend Mascara never entered into his plan; his
was not a siege power.

Clausel quitted Oran November 27th. The wood of Muley

Ismael was passed, and the fording of the Sig effected without opposition. As the column drew near to the Habra, the Arabs were seen moving in a parallel direction along the adjacent heights. Abdel Kader was watching the moment when a break in the French lines would offer him a favourable point of attack. Clausel, penetrating this intention, halted, closed up, and, making face to his right, advanced against the Arabs, in *échelons* of battalions from his left.

Abdel Kader refused battle. Leaving his adversary to enjoy the barren fruits of his change of front, he pushed on rapidly, and placed himself across the main road leading to Mascara. His left was posted on an eminence, where he placed his artillery; his right was protected by a wood. His selection of ground would have done honour to a European general.

An able commander may seize a strategical point in such a manner as to decide the fate of a campaign. He may over-bear, and even turn to a good account, obstacles apparently insuperable, by tactical skill; he may make time and space subservient to his designs; but he cannot give irregulars the firmness requisite to hold the part assigned to them in a regular order of battle. It was the fate of Abdel Kader to discover now, that, in attempting to realise the theories of European military science in the open field, and on a given ground, with the levies under his command, the elements he wielded were below the requirements of his genius.

Four chapels, dedicated to Sidi Embarek, were occupied by his advanced posts. These the French quickly drove in. The Arab cavalry charged in various places; but they were broken and dispersed by shells and rockets. Abdel Kader directed in person the fire of his artillery. Some well-directed shots had thrown a French brigade into confusion. Immediately he led on his infantry against it. Animated by his presence, his Arabs and Kabyles went in valiantly. But they measured themselves in vain against the courage and obstinacy of French infantry. The struggle on their part was desperate but fruitless, and they retreated in confusion.

The French had in the meantime, and after some hours' hard fighting, possessed themselves of the wood on the right of the Arab position, whilst their artillery had pushed well up the main road. The Arabs abandoned the field at all points. Abdel Kader vainly endeavoured to preserve some order in the retreat. That night, his regular infantry disbanded. Of the cavalry of the tribes, some went to their homes; others hurried off to Mascara, and began to plunder the place. He himself withdrew to Cachero, his family property, about two leagues beyond that town.

The army of Abdel Kader had melted away like a wreath of snow. It was evident that the French would soon be in Mascara. Tlemsen might even fall into their hands in a brief space of time. Whole tribes, as a probable consequence, would seek safety by submission. Some of his chiefs, on whom Abdel Kader most relied, had already deserted him. His case seemed to be hopeless. But he calmly awaited the time when the panic should subside; he felt assured that it would be only transient. He was mortified and indignant at the stain which had been put upon his fame and reputation by the weakness and pusillanimity of some, and the treason of others. Yet he never uttered an invective or a reproach.

The few followers who remained with Abdel Kader anxiously endeavoured to read his thoughts. The alarmists he re-assured; the faint-hearted he encouraged; to his mother, who, with womanly tenderness and compassion, now approached him to pour words of comfort and consolation in his ear, he calmly replied, taking her hand in his, "Women, mother, have need of pity, not men."

Clausel entered Mascara December 6, 1835. A miserable crowd of Jews was all that remained of its population. They came out of their dens to crouch at the feet of the victorious French. All masters were alike to these exiles from the Land of Promise. The Mohammedans had disdained to allow them to accompany them in their flight. On the 7th, flames burst forth in various parts of the town, but were soon extinguished. The French were just beginning to repose from their fatigues, and were contemplating a permanent occupation, when, to their surprise and disgust, they got orders to prepare for leaving. On the 8th December, Mascara was evacuated.

The next day, a horseman appeared before its gates. It was Abdel Kader. Rumours of his presence spread rapidly. Some Arabs made their appearance before him; they looked abashed and mistrustful. El Aoura, Aga of the Hashems, was amongst the number. In the flight, he had carried off the royal parasol. He now produced it. "Keep it for yourself," said Abdel Kader, with a sarcastic smile; "you may, one of these days, be Sultan."

As the day wore on, some of the fugitive chiefs came dropping in. Abdel Kader eyed them contemptuously. At last, one ventured to ask him, if he had any orders to give them. "My orders!" he exclaimed. "Yes, my orders are, that you instantly relieve me from the burden you imposed upon me, and which the interests of religion alone have enabled me to support, up to this hour. Let the tribes make choice of my successor, and inform Il Hadj Djellali of the result. I am going with my family to Morocco."

By a common impulse, chiefs and men prostrated themselves before him, kissed his hands, his feet, his burnous, imploring pardon and forgiveness for the past, and promising fidelity and constancy for the future. "He was their father, their Sultan, the chosen of God to lead on the Djehad; their lives were his; if he left them, they had nought to do but surrender to the infidels." At these last words, Abdel Kader turned round abruptly. The blood mantled to his cheeks. They had struck the only chord to which his heart responded—the sense of duty. "God's will be done," he exclaimed; "but remember, I swear never to enter Mascara except to go to the Mosque, until you have avenged your ignominious defeat. I see traitors amongst you; Mamoor yonder is one; let him be hung." The unfortunate culprit was seized and executed forthwith.

The master spirit had prevailed; confidence was restored. That night, from the royal tent, dispatches went forth to all the tribes, summoning them to renewed action. On the morrow, Abdel Kader, buoyant and cheerful as ever, towering above misfortune, mighty in disaster, dauntless where all desponded, arresting victory in her flight from the very depths of humiliation and defeat, sallied forth, sword in hand, at the head of 6,000 cavalry, to attack and harass the French column, as, wrapped in tempest, drenched with rain, and benumbed with cold, it pursued its incomprehensible retreat on Mostaganem.

CHAPTER VII

1836.

Notwithstanding Clausel's temporary occupation of Mascara, Abdel Kader had already regained his ascendancy. Everywhere he was in possession of the field. Several tribes who had shown an inclination to accept the rule of the French were punished, either by money levied, or cattle distrained. Moreover Clausel sued for peace.

To the proposition that he should acknowledge the sovereignty of France, Abdel Kader replied, that before acknowledging a suzerain he should like to know precisely the extent of power and territory which he was to hold, as well as the obligations he should be called on to fulfil. Milond ibn Arasch was invited to come to Oran to discuss the negotiation. Clausel was, at this time, meditating an expedition against Tlemsen.

The presence of the French in the interim had encouraged their partisans. Mustapha ibn Ismail had promised Clausel the co-operation of more than one Arab tribe, if he advanced upon Tlemsen. The Beni Engad declared themselves his friends, and they were already drawing near the town in large force with the view of assisting him, and aiding the escape of the Kolouglis from the citadel, in which the latter were still blockaded.

Abdel Kader hearing of this combination, made a rapid descent on both parties. He caught Mustapha and the Kolouglis in the very act of making a sortie, and drove them back. Turning round on the Beni Engad, he completely routed them. The action was scarcely over, when Clausel and his column, 8,000 strong, were seen marching on the town. Abdel Kader had barely time to complete its evacuation. He withdrew with the whole population, unmolested, to Ouchda, on the frontiers of Morocco. Clausel entered Tlemsen January 13th, 1836.

Mustapha and the Kolouglis, followed by a miserable crowd of Jews, presented themselves before the Governor-General and his staff, overwhelming him with exuberant professions of loyalty and submission, and calling him their saviour and benefactor. He demanded from them 100,000 francs as a proof of their sincerity. In vain the astonished dupes pleaded their utter inability to raise such a sum, Clausel was inexorable. The screw was mercilessly applied. Threats and blows, and even torture, were used, and the contribution was finally paid, partly in coin, partly in diamonds and articles of jewellery.

This mode of treatment pursued by the French was as great an advantage to the cause of Abdel Kader as any victory would have been.

"If that is the way," he exclaimed, "the French treat their friends, what are their enemies to expect?"

It was diligently spread abroad that a Jew had presided at the tying up and castigation of the Kolouglis. The Arabs were furious. Such an indignity put upon Mussulmans had never been heard of. The Beni Engad opened a correspondence with Abdel Kader. The Kolouglis sent him word privately that they only awaited the departure of the French to give him up the citadel.

It was the intention of Clausel, however, to occupy the town, as he was extremely anxious to establish a direct communication between Tlemsen and the sea-coast. The mouth of the Tafna was the nearest available point for this purpose, but the intervening ground was mountainous. He set out to accomplish his object, January 23rd. He soon found himself in presence of Abdel Kader, with his whole army.

For ten successive days the battle raged between them. The Arabs, burning to avenge their late defeat, were obstinately tenacious. Abdel Kader, moreover, had not attempted a regular formation. Hills, ravines, rocks, and rivers were seized and defended, according to the exigencies of the moment. Against such tactics, and in an unknown country, French courage and discipline were at fault. Clausel was defeated and driven back to Tlemsen with considerable loss. After placing a garrison in the citadel under the command of Captain Cavaignac, he returned with his column to Oran, harassed by Abdel Kader to its very gates.

On his arrival at Algiers, he consoled himself for all his futile expeditions by issuing a proclamation declaring the war to be finished. " Abdel Kader," it stated, " utterly beaten and discomfited, has fled to the Sahara, there to conceal his treason and revolt." In April, the Marshal embarked for France, leaving instructions to General d'Arlanges at Oran, to make a fortified camp on the Tafna, with the view of opening from thence the desired line of communication with Tlemsen.

General Perregaux about this time made an incursion on the tribes located in the valley of the Cheliff. Influenced by their chiefs, the sons of Sidi il Aribi, these tribes had continued, despite their repeated corrections, to waver in their obedience to the Sultan. They had not paid the tribute without considerable reluctance and complaints, and they had furnished their contingent of cavalry to his army with manifest repugnance. They now, under pretence of superior pressure, again entered into an alliance with the French.

Abdel Kader was too much occupied, for the moment, with the blockade of Tlemsen and the proceedings of D'Arlanges on the Tafna, to interrupt the military promenade of Perregaux. But the recreant Arabs, who had welcomed the French general, were soon made to feel the weight of the Sultan's indignation. No sooner had the French withdrawn than he came down on them like an avalanche. Eighteen tribes were heavily fined, and their cattle distrained. The Borgia tribe, singled out to serve as a terrible example, was decimated, and then driven out of the district to find shelter where it could.

D'Arlanges had reached the Tafna, with great difficulty, on the 16th of April, with 3,000 infantry and eight pieces of artillery. Having completed an entrenched camp on the banks of the river, he marched out on the 21st, in conformity with his instructions, to open the road to Tlemsen. Abdel Kader, who from the central position of Nedroma, which commanded equally the road from the Tafna to Tlemsen and to Oran, was able to watch his enemy's movements in either direction, rapidly descended to the encounter, enveloped the French column with masses of Kabyles and Arabs, and obliged it to retrace its steps.

He owed this success to his own unwearied exertions and commanding influence. So long as he could keep each separate French garrison in a state of isolation, the game was his own. But to effect so comprehensive a plan, he was obliged to keep the whole country constantly on the alert. With this view he had for weeks past been traversing the mountains of the Kabyles which spread around the Tafna. Through toilsome days and sleepless nights he had been summoning, preaching, and haranguing. His fiery eloquence had raised the enthusiasm of those fierce and ungovernable mountaineers to a pitch of frenzy. When the time for action came, and Abdel Kader once more led them in person against the foe, they rushed to the combat more like wild beasts than men, came at once to close quarters with the French infantry, grappled with them in single combat, swept through their ranks, and rushed up to the cannon's mouth.

The French government, irritated by such prolonged and unexpected resistance, continued to pour in reinforcements. On the 6th of June, 1836, General Bugeaud landed at the mouth of the Tafna with three fresh regiments. The attempt to force a passage to Tlemsen was immediately renewed, and, at last, the point was carried with success. Abdel Kader fought a long and desperate battle with the invading force on the banks of the Sikkak, but on this occasion he was completely defeated.

This reverse had its usual effect on the tribes. Many of the cavalry contingents rode off and returned to their homes. The sudden abandonment to which Abdel Kader was sometimes exposed, after a defeat, would have prostrated the energies of a weaker mind, and paralysed a less iron-moulded will. But such oscillations had long ceased to affect him. He well knew that whenever Fortune smiled, a wave of his sword would at any hour bring both waverers and rebels crouching to his feet.

But when he was informed that a certain Sidi Ibrahim had so far calculated on his present emergency as to excite a revolt against him, and even to assume the title of sultan, he drew his sword from its scabbard, hung it to his saddle bow, and vowed never to sheathe it or descend from his horse till he had the traitor's head. Appearing almost singly in the midst of the tribe Beni Amers, among whom he knew the traitor to be, he demanded his instant delivery. The tribe, startled and subdued by this act of bold decision, and dreading the charge of complicity, gave up the rebel Sidi Ibrahim. His head was at once taken off.

Abdel Kader, by the ceaseless activity of his movements in all directions, and by the untiring vigilance with which he superintended his system of blockade, had again reduced the French to the greatest extremities. They had established posts in the interior, but they could neither reach them nor communicate with them. Their letters were intercepted. The bearers of them, when seized, were invariably decapitated. No friendly tribes brought the French provisions.

Whether at Oran, or at the Tafna, they could only move out in large bodies, and on such occasions large supplies, beasts of burden, and means of transport were required. The Douairs and Zmelas, seeking shelter under the walls of Oran, lived upon the rations scantily doled out to them by their protectors. At Tlemsen, Cavaignac was buying cats for his table at 40 francs a head.

In the month of November, 1836, Clausel, who had re-turned to his post, undertook the siege of Constantine, the stronghold of Achmet Bey, the last representative of the Turkish power in Algeria. Abdel Kader abstained from taking any steps which might thwart the complete develop-ment of that design. Whether the French were successful in their design or not, he flattered himself that he should be the gainer in the end. He felt that if the Bey were van-quished, he should be delivered, without cost or trouble to himself, from a dangerous rival, and that the Arab tribes of the province of Constantine would then be free to join his standard. If he were triumphant, the French, wearied out by the difficulties of their general position in the country, might abandon it; in which case, a struggle between himself and the Bey for the mastery would neither be doubtful as to its issue, nor of long duration.

But when the expedition failed, he felt his hour was come. From his head-quarters at Medea, he issued orders for a simultaneous advance against all the French possessions between the Atlas and the sea-coast. In the province of Oran little remained to be effected. But the plain of the Metija was at his mercy. Thousands of Arabs and Kabyles, supported by the tribes of Tittery, descended like a torrent from the mountains, sacking and burning the French colonial establishments, slaying and capturing the colonists, and carrying terror and dismay into Algiers itself.

The state to which the French garrisons were now reduced was pitiable. The utmost ingenuity of their commissariat was daily and hourly taxed to avert the horrors of famine. Fortunately for the French, they were relieved from their painful predicament by the speculative genius of a Jew.

Durand, the Sultan's wily and influential agent at Algiers, had long been feasting his imagination with the splendid harvest he should gather, could he only be constituted sole conductor of commercial transactions between the contending parties. To this end he had for months been labouring to convince Abdel Kader that the advantages, even in a military point of view, to be gained by feeding the French would far outweigh the value of any glory which might be gained by starving them.

Authorised to drive the best bargain he could, Durand hurried off to Oran, and opened a negotiation with General Broussard, who, at that period, was in command of the garrison.

"The French," he said, "have need of corn and meat. The Sultan wants iron, lead, and sulphur. Let each party sell the other what it wants, and all will be satisfied. You need not fear that you will be in any degree compromised with the Sultan by such an arrangement. He will not appear in the matter at all. I will sell you corn and cattle; and you will sell me iron and sulphur. The Sultan will merely know, indirectly, that the former articles are for you, and the latter for him. The Sultan will even go so far as to allow you to re-victual Tlemsen; but as such a concession would undoubtedly exasperate and disgust the Arabs, to whom the presence of the French in that town is hateful, he can only take on himself the odium and responsibility of granting it, on the condition that all the prisoners taken at the battle of the Sikkak are set free and sent back to him."

Broussard at once accepted the proposal. The French again enjoyed the long unaccustomed luxury of abundance. Abdel Kader, on his side quietly obtained from his enemies, reduced to assume the garb of friends, the materials of war, which were hereafter to be wielded against them.

Not only did this singular contract, as it turned out, give him the means of increasing his aggressive power, but, at the same time, it also raised his *prestige*. To the sneers of fanatics, who reproached him with his defeats, and the complaints of whole families, constantly demanding their lost ones, languishing in the prisons of the infidel, he could now reply by triumphantly pointing to prisoners arrested from the victor's hands, restored to their homes, and able again to take part in the holy war. Such was the state of affairs when General Bugeaud arrived from France at Oran, with instructions either to make peace with Abdel Kader, or to conquer him.

Wishing to try, in the first place, to effect a negotiation, he sent him the following propositions as a basis of accommodation :—

1. Acknowledgment of the sovereignty of France.

2. Limitation of his territory to the river Cheliff.

3. Payment of tribute.

4. Delivery of hostages, as guarantee for, and the due execution of, any future treaty which might be agreed on.

Abdel Kader replied, through his agent Durand, that having never experienced any fatal check, and having amply compensated himself for any disasters which had temporarily befallen him, he could never consent to be placed in a position inferior to that which he enjoyed by the treaty of Desmichels ; that Arabs would never hear of living under even the nominal dominion of Christians ; and that if France endeavoured to place them under it by force she would be embarking in an endless war. He declared, moreover, that he had not entered the province of Tittery from any design of his own, but had been summoned thither by the voice of its inhabitants, and that neither his honour nor his religion would allow him to abandon those who had thrown themselves on his protection. He added, that in his opinion the real interest of France was not to seek an extension of sway over populations irreconcilably hostile to her, but rather to confine herself to commercial enterprise in the towns on the sea-coast.

By the voice of his agent, Abdel Kader admitted, however, that he would consent to allow the French to occupy the Metija, or Plain of Algiers, with the exception of Blidah, which belonged properly to the mountains, and that he was willing to yield them all the territory near Oran, comprised between the Bridia and the Macta. He was ready, moreover, as he declared, to renounce the monopoly granted him by Desmichels, to allow complete freedom of commerce, and to guarantee the security, and repair the losses, if any occurred, of all Frenchmen who chose to settle in the interior. He would pledge himself, finally, never to give up any sea-port which was ceded to him to a foreign power.

Bold and dictatorial as such language appeared to the General, he preferred, under all circumstances, to continue in the path of concession, rather than to make any resistance which might have precipitated hostilities. His Government had expressly warned him against granting Abdel Kader any further extension of territory. The latter had firmly stated that he would not give up an inch of what he held. The General yielded, and on his own responsibility, offered to give up to Abdel Kader the province of Tittery, with the stipulation, however, that he should consent to be the vassal of France.

The following ultimatum, embodying the terms of this important compromise, was now drawn up, and forwarded to Abdel Kader. The circumscribed limits, within which the military representative of the French Government therein offered to confine his countrymen in Algeria, constituted a point which was in itself a glorious testimony to the successful prowess of the great leader who had hitherto rendered barren all the expeditions which the French had directed against him, and thwarted all their schemes of conquest.

1. The Emir will recognise the sovereignty of France.

2. France reserves, in the province of Oran, a belt, from ten to twelve leagues in breadth, beginning at the Rio Salado, and terminating at the Cheliff. In the province of Algiers, he reserves Algiers, and all the province of that name. She cedes to the Emir the province of Tittery and that of Oran, excepting the belt afore-mentioned.

3. The Emir will pay an annual tribute in corn and cattle.

4. There shall be perfect freedom of commerce.

5. All the goods which the French have acquired, or may acquire, in the country will be guaranteed.

This ultimatum reached Abdel Kader at Medea, where he had already opened negotiations with General Damremont, the new Governor-General of Algeria, not without sanguine hopes of a satisfactory result. He now found himself engaged with two negotiators, both willing to treat with him on terms highly favourable to his views and expectations. Their zeal to conclude with him, indeed, amounted to rivalry.

Bugeaud had requested, as a particular favour from his Government, that to him alone should be reserved the glory of dealing with Abdel Kader. When, therefore, he learned that Damremont had entered into diplomatic relations with the Arab Sultan, his jealousy was aroused. He taxed his superior with exercising an unauthorised and unwarrantable intervention in a complication, the adjustment of which depended entirely on himself. A recriminating correspondence took place. Reference was made to the Minister of War, who decided that Bugeaud was to be left full liberty of action, without interference or supervision.

As soon as Abdel Kader heard of this decision, he returned to the province of Oran, and on the 12th of May sent the following propositions in reply to Bugeaud's ultimatum :—

1. The Emir acknowledges the sovereignty of France.

2. All the Mussulmans who live outside the towns shall be under his jurisdiction.

3. The territory of the French to the west of Oran shall be confined to the country between Bridia and the sea, and extend as far as the Macta. On the side of Algiers, they will be allowed to hold the country between that town and the river Beni-Azza.

4. The Emir will give, for this year only, 20,000 measures of corn, 20,000 measures of barley, and 3,000 head of cattle.

5. The Emir shall be empowered to buy, in France, powder, sulphur, and arms.

6. The Kolouglis who choose to remain in Tlemsen, shall keep their properties, be under our power, and conform themselves to our land.

7. Those who leave the French territory, or the territory of the Emir, shall be reciprocally given up on the requisition of the one or the other party.

8. France cedes to the Emir, Rachgoun, Tlemsen, its citadel, and the mortars and cannons which anciently be-

longed to it. The Emir undertakes to transport the effects of the French garrison to Oran.

9. Commerce shall be free between the Arabs and the French.

10. The French shall be respected amongst the Arabs, as the Arabs amongst the French.

11. The farms and properties which the French may have acquired in the Metija shall be guaranteed. They shall enjoy them freely.

In the preceding stipulations, Abdel Kader made no allusion to the cession of Tittery and Oran. He looked on it as a matter of course, inasmuch as in the former province the French had not even the shadow of power; whilst in the latter they only traversed as birds of passage, flitting from town to town. But, bent on the consolidation of his power, and the strengthening of his lines of communication, he boldly insisted on the evacuation, by the French, of Tlemsen, and on their yielding up the port of Rachgoun.

But he went even still further. Feeling well his vantage-ground, and seeing the straits to which the French were reduced, he did not hesitate to require that all Mussulman residing on French territory should be under his exclusive jurisdiction. In this demand he endeavoured to carry out and enforce a principle which, in his eyes, was paramount to every earthly consideration, as based on the very essence of the Koran—the principle, that under no circumstances, if possible, should any Mussulman voluntarily acknowledge or submit to Christian rule.

At this period, Abdel Kader approached the zenith of his career.

CHAPTER VIII.

1837.

NOTHING more loudly testifies to the immense superiority enjoyed by Abdel Kader, at this period, than the fact of his being in a position to advance such pretensions, and make such demands. Their real and evident meaning was, that he should be acknowledged Sultan of Algeria, whilst the French lived, as it were, under sufferance, on the outskirts of his empire, simply enjoying the advantage of trading with his subjects.

It must be borne in mind, at the same time, that Abdel Kader was perfectly aware of the state of public opinion in France. He subscribed regularly to the French journals. The debates in the Chambers, and the leading articles on Algerian affairs, were interpreted to him. He saw the liberal party cordially approving and supporting the principle laid down by their chief orator, M. Dupin, who denounced Algiers as a fatal legacy, bequeathed by the Restoration, which ought to be abandoned, "if," as he exclaimed, "we would not see our last man, and our last sons, swallowed up."

He gathered, from the general tenor of the passages which were read .to him, that many of the principal politicians in France looked upon colonisation in Africa as a dream; that they considered all warlike operations there carried on as so

H

much blood and treasure thrown away; and that they maintained the true policy of France to be, merely to hold a few places along the coast for the purpose of preventing piracy, and cultivating peaceable and honourable relations with the natives.

When, in addition to this, Abdel Kader saw the French Chambers making a practical comment on such sentiments, by refusing to vote more than 30,000 men for the colony, and learned, that after the disastrous retreat from Constantine, the opinion in favour of an immediate evacuation of the country began to prevail more than ever, it is not to be wondered at if he thought that, by a little pertinacity, and a little more perseverance, he should succeed in obtaining such terms as would enable him to realise his cherished idea of founding an independent Arab kingdom.

The propositions sent in by Abdel Kader seemed, to Bugeaud, so utterly incompatible with French interests, that he determined to carry out the second part of his programme, —an appeal to arms. In the beginning of May, 1837, he assembled his whole force, consisting of 12,000 men, in the camp of the Tafna, preparatory to offensive operations. When he came to review his resources, he found the transport service so utterly inadequate to the occasion, that he was obliged to suspend his march.

To procure animals from the interior was impossible. A supply from France was not expected. The summer heats, so fatal to soldiers in the field, were fast approaching. The time fixed for the second siege of Constantine was at hand, and he had engaged that a large portion of his little army should be sent round to take part in it. The home govern-

ment had made its arrangements in full reliance on the fulfilment of this pledge. Peace with Abdel Kader, however
humiliating, became a necessity. The latter was informed
that the door was still open for negotiation. He asked leave
for a few days' consideration.

Various reasons conspired to make Abdel Kader anxious to
base his action, in a measure of such importance as that of
again making peace with the French, on an appeal to the
wishes of the tribes at large. The fanatical party accused
him of personal ambition, and of sacrificing the uncompromising principles of the Faith to his own selfish views of
aggrandisement. The restless, the lawless—all, in fact, who
preferred unbridled liberty to the solid advantages springing
from a well-established central power, and who felt that the
return of peace would hand them over unreservedly, and
without the power of resistance, to the master-hand which
would soon reduce them to implicit obedience—only wanted
a pretext to assume the cloak of religion, and join the
fanatics in their senseless cry.

With well-timed skill and foresight, Abdel Kader now resolved to cut the ground from under the feet of both these
parties. The demand for peace, or, rather, the willingness
to accept it, ought, he opined, to be looked on as a national
act. A general assembly was summoned to meet on the
banks of the Habra, May 25, 1837 ; and thither, according to
invitation, came all the great Sheiks, the leaders of cavalry
contingents, the venerable Marabouts, and the most distinguished warriors of the province of Oran.

The Sultan opened the deliberations in the following
words : — " Let no one amongst you ever accuse me of wanting

to make peace with the Christians. It is for you to decide the question of peace or war." He then proceeded to explain the nature of the correspondence, which had taken place between himself and Bugeaud; the propositions and overtures which had been made to him, and those he had made in return. In conclusion, he commented carefully on each of the articles of his own ultimatum, sent in to the French general on the 12th May.

A long and stormy discussion ensued. The fanatics, and those secretly indisposed towards the Sultan, were violent in their cries for war. The Marabouts silenced them by the nicely-drawn discrimination between peace accepted and peace demanded. The Koran, they said, nowhere inculcated a useless shedding of blood, when the infidel had submitted, and craved that the sword might be sheathed. The French had submitted. They begged for peace. The Sultan had dictated his own terms.

This reasoning prevailed. It was decided by a large majority that the benefits which would accrue to the commonalty from a state of peace, justified the giving up of Blidah, and the plain of Algiers, to the French. A slight extension of the limits to which the Sultan originally intended to confine them would be no inconvenience to the Arabs, inasmuch as every Mussulman would be free to emigrate from the French possessions to the Sultan's territory. The demand, however, of the French Government for tribute, was declared to be inadmissible.

Sidi Sekkal was shortly afterwards sent to the French head-quarters on the Tafna, with the following concessions:—

" 1. Blidah abandoned.

" 2 Renunciation of all authority over Mussulmans residing on French territory.

" 3. A certain extension of the French boundaries."

Sidi Sekkal was commissioned, at the same time, to enter into the nature of the limits proposed, and to give other necessary explanations. Bugeaud, convinced that further delay would not procure him better conditions, agreed to everything. Thereupon the following treaty, celebrated as the " Treaty of the Tafna," was drawn up and signed by both parties, May 20th, 1837.

"THE FOLLOWING TREATY HAS BEEN AGREED UPON, BETWEEN LIEUTENANT-GENERAL BUGEAUD, COMMANDING THE FRENCH TROOPS IN THE PROVINCE OF ORAN, AND THE EMIR ABDEL KADER.

" Art. 1. The Emir Abdel Kader acknowledges the sovereignty of France.

" Art. 2. France reserves to herself, in the province of Oran, Mostaganem, Mazagnan, and their territories, Oran, Arzew, and a territory limited in the following manner :—On the east, by the river Macta, and the marsh from whence it flows ; on the south, by a line starting from the said marsh, passing by the shore on the south of the lake, and continuing its prolongation up the Wady Maleh, in the direction of Sidi Said ; and from this river down to the sea, shall belong to the French. In the province of Algiers, Algiers, the Sahel, the plain of the Metija, bounded on the east by the Wady Khuddra, onwards ; on the south, by the crest of the first chain of the lesser Atlas, as far as the Chiffa, including Blidah and its territory ; on the west, by the Chiffa as far as the Mount of Mazagnan, and from thence, in a direct line to the sea, enclosing Coleah and its territory, shall be French territory.

" Art. 3. The Emir shall have the administration of the province of Oran, that of Tittery, and that part of the province of Algiers which is not comprised on the east, within the limits indicated by Article 2. He cannot enter any other part of the Regency.

" Art. 4. The Emir shall have no authority over Mussulmans who wish to reside on the territory reserved to France; but these shall be at liberty to go and reside on the territory under the Emir's administration; in the same manner the inhabitants living under the Emir's administration may establish themselves on French territory.

" Art. 5. The Arabs dwelling on French territory shall enjoy the free exercise of their religion. They may build mosques, and follow their religious discipline in every particular, under the authority of their spiritual chiefs.

" Art. 6. The Emir will give to the French army 30,000 measures of corn; 30,000 measures of barley; 5,000 head of oxen. The delivery of these provisions will be made at Oran, in three instalments; the first, on the 15th September, 1837, and the two others every successive two months.

" Art. 7. The Emir shall be empowered to buy in France, powder, sulphur, and the arms he requires.

" Art. 8. The Kolouglis who wish to remain in Tlemsen, or elsewhere, shall have free possession of their properties there, and shall be treated as citizens. Those who wish to withdraw to French territory, may sell or rent their properties freely.

"Art. 9. France cedes to the Emir, Rachgoun, Tlemsen, its citadel, and all the cannons which were anciently in it. The Emir engages to convey to Oran all the effects, as well as munitions of war, belonging to the garrison of Tlemsen.

"Art. 10. Commerce shall be free between the Arabs and the French. They may establish themselves reciprocally, on each other's territory.

"Art. 11. The French shall be respected amongst the Arabs, as the Arabs amongst the French. The farms and properties which the French have acquired, or may acquire, on the Arab territory, shall be guaranteed them: they shall enjoy them freely, and the Emir engages to indemnify them for any damages the Arabs may cause them.

"Art. 12. The criminals on both territories shall be reciprocally given up.

"Art. 13. The Emir engages not to give up any part of the coast to any foreign power whatever, without the authorisation of France.

"Art. 14. The commerce of the Regency shall only be carried on in French ports.

"Art. 15. France shall maintain agents near the Emir, and in the towns under his jurisdiction, to act as intermediaries for French subjects, in any commercial disputes they may have with the Arabs.

"The Emir will have the same privilege in French towns and seaports.

"Tafna, May 30, 1837.

"The Lieutenant-General commanding at Oran."

(The Emir's seal under   (Bugeaud the General's seal
     the Arab text.)   under the French text.)

Bugeaud had been strictly enjoined by his Government to confine Abdel Kader to the province of Oran ; on no account to cede him the province of Tittery, and to insist on his paying tribute.

In a letter to the Minister of War, he thus excused himself for having signed a treaty which violated such orders :—

" You may well suppose that it pained me greatly to be obliged to make up my mind not to follow your instructions, as regards the limits to be assigned to the Emir. But that was impossible. Be assured that the peace I have concluded is better, and is likely to be more durable than any I could have made by confining Abdel Kader between the Cheliff and Morocco."

By this treaty, nevertheless, the French were substantially confined to a few towns on the sea-coast, with very circum-scribed adjacent territories; whilst all the fortresses and strongholds in the interior were left in the hands of their triumphant and victorious adversary. In a word, Abdel Kader thereby possessed two-thirds of Algeria ; and in addi-tion to the immense accession which this splendid triumph had added to his influence and power, he now carried along with him the advantage of appearing before the world as the friend and ally of France.

The French generals, who had hitherto followed each other in rapid succession through the various phases of the war, had sought in vain for an interview with the illustrious Arab chief, who, whilst he sorely taxed their military talents, had excited in their breasts feelings of soldierly admiration. This favour was now vouchsafed to General Bugeaud.

On the 31st of May, 1837, the General, followed by six battalions, with all his artillery and cavalry, reached the appointed place of rendezvous. Abdel Kader had not yet arrived. Five hours were passed in expectation; still nobody appeared. At last, about two o'clock, several Arabs came up, one after another, bearing various kinds of excuses. The Sultan had been indisposed. He had set out late. He was thinking of asking to have the interview postponed till next day. He was not far off. He was close at hand.

A horseman now came up and begged the General to move on a little; he would soon meet the Sultan. It was getting late, and the General, who wished to get his troops back to their camp before dark, advanced. After marching for more than an hour, he at length came upon the Arab army, consisting of more than 15,000 cavalry, drawn up in tolerable order, on an undulating plain. At this moment, Bou Hamedi rode up to him, and pointed to the spot where the Sultan was surrounded by a large escort, on a hillock not far off.

In a few minutes more, Abdel Kader and his escort were seen advancing towards the General. It was an imposing sight. Nearly two hundred Arab chiefs, on prancing steeds, closed around their Sultan, whose simple apparel offered a striking contrast to their splendid appointments, glittering with highly-burnished arms, which flashed and sparkled in the noon-day sun. Abdel Kader rode a few paces in front, mounted on a magnificent black charger, which he handled with extraordinary dexterity, sometimes making it spring with all fours in the air, sometimes making it walk for several yards on its hind legs, and evidently seeking to make an impression by his superior horsemanship. Several Arabs ran by his side, holding his stirrups, and the ends of his burnous.

General Bugeaud now dashed forward at full gallop, and on reaching the Emir, shook hands with him. Both alighted, and seating themselves on the grass, entered into the following conversation.

Bugeaud.—"Do you know that there are very few generals who would have dared to make the treaty I have concluded with you? But I have not been afraid of aggrandising you, and adding to your power, because I felt assured that you would only employ the great existence which we give you in ameliorating the condition of the Arab nation, and in maintaining peace and a good understanding with France."

Abdel Kader.—"I thank you for your good sentiments towards me. Please God, I will make the Arabs happy; and if the peace is ever broken, it will be no fault of mine."

B.—"On this point, I am your security with the King of the French."

A.—"You risk nothing in so doing: we have a religion which obliges us to keep our word. I have never been faithless to mine."

B.—"I count on it; and it is in this conviction I offer you my personal friendship."

A.—"I accept your friendship, but let the French beware of listening to intriguers."

B.—"The French are never led by individuals, and it is not the acts of individuals which can break the peace: it is only the non-execution of the treaty, or some great act of hostility. As to the culpable acts of individuals, we will be on our guard against them, or punish them reciprocally."

A.—"Very good. You have only to give me notice, and the guilty shall be punished.".

B.—"I recommend to your good offices the Kolouglis who may remain at Tlemsen."

A.—" Be easy on that score; they shall be treated like citizens."

B.—" You have promised me that you will locate the Douairs amongst the Hafras: the country will, perhaps, not be sufficient for them."

A.—" They shall be located in such a manner as not to endanger the maintenance of peace."

B.—" Have you ordered commercial relations at Algiers, and around the towns, to be resumed ?"

A.—" Not yet; but I mean to do so, when you have put me in possession of Tlemsen."

B.—" You must know, I cannot do so until the treaty has been approved of by the King."

A.—" What, then, have not you the power to treat ?"

B.—" Yes; but the treaty must be approved. That is necessary for you, as a guarantee; for if it was only made by me, any general who might replace me would be able to undo it; whereas, once approved by the King, my successor would be obliged to abide by it."

A.—" If you do not give me back Tlemsen, in accordance with the stipulation in the treaty, I do not see the necessity of making peace: we shall only have a truce."

B.—" That is true. But it is you who will be the gainer by the truce; for, while it lasts, I shall not destroy the crops."

A.—" Destroy them, if you like: it will be all the same to me. I will give you my full permission, in writing, to destroy all you can. It will only be a very small quantity you can get at, and the Arabs will still have abundance of grain."

B.—" I don't think the Arabs are of the same opinion."

Abdel Kadir now asked how long it would be before the confirmation of the treaty arrived from France.

B.—"About three weeks."

A.—"That is rather long. At all events, we cannot reestablish our commercial relations until after the King's approbation shall have arrived. Then the peace will be definitive."

B.—"It is only your co-religionists who will be the sufferers; for you will be depriving them of a commerce of which they stand in need. As for us, we can get all we want by sea."

The General, not wishing to prolong the interview, as it was getting late, rose to take leave. Abdel Kader remained sitting, and affected to be engaged with his interpreter, who was standing beside him. Bugeaud, suspecting his motive, took him familiarly by the hand, and pulled him up, saying at the same time, "*Parbleu,* when a French General rises, you may as well rise too—you!"

Thus ended this singular meeting, at which the French General had merely gratified an idle, though pardonable, curiosity; but which, from the premeditated delays and misunderstandings that immediately preceded it, gave Abdel Kader the immense advantage of appearing in the eyes of his countrymen as a grand personage, who kept even the leaders of the infidels awaiting his good pleasure and convenience. Abdel Kader, after shaking the General again by the hands, now vaulted into his saddle; and both armies moved off the ground to the strains of martial music, the Arabs shouting enthusiastically—"Long live our Sultan, Abdel Kader! may God ever make him victorious!"

CHAPTER IX.

1838.

THE Treaty of the Tafna was warmly applauded by the French Government, who regarded it as a master-stroke of policy. The French people looked on it as a humiliation. The former boasted that Abdel Kader from being an enemy had been transformed into an ally. The latter saw in it the criminal surrender of a French province to a rival power. To Abdel Kader it was the corner-stone of the edifice he had so long been laboriously and perseveringly constructing.

For years a double duty had been imposed on him—on the one hand, that of moulding into shape and consistency the discordant materials which lay scattered around him, appeasing feuds, allaying discords, and quelling insurrections; on the other, that of boldly confronting the formidable attacks of an enemy, immeasurably his superior in all the means and appliances which raise war to the dignity of a science. Relieved from external pressure, he was enabled to grapple with his whole and undivided strength against internal difficulties.

He now stood face to face with a people who looked on their emancipation from a foreign yoke as the signal for unbounded licence, whose only idea of liberty was freedom from restraint, and who, while they recognised and even obeyed the genius which had risen up amongst them, when directed against their foes, shunned and dreaded it when brought to bear upon themselves. Whole tribes of Arabs, now freed from the harassing excitement, the heavy demands, the constant liabilities, the ever-recurring hazards and uncertainties of a state of war, seemed bent on resuming, each in its little sphere, a separate and independent existence.

Thinking only of their selfish and individual interests, and unable to comprehend that a continuance of their newly-acquired independence could only be upheld by a continuation of those sacrifices which had enabled them to achieve it, these little democracies could see no use or occasion for a central government, and grudged contributing towards the expenses necessary to support it.

The extensive organisation which Abdel Kader contemplated, which he was already carrying out, and which could alone consolidate a power capable of permanently resisting external attacks—and in his keen foresight he felt that they were only temporarily suspended—manifestly required the enforcement of certain imports throughout the vast extent of country now committed to his charge.

The short-sightedness and avarice of the Arabs prevented them from seeing any such necessity, and although Abdel Kader never in his life exacted from his subjects more than the *ashur* and the *zekka* (all other imports, including custom-house duties, being held in abomination by the Koran), yet the recusants had a line of argument always ready to exonerate themselves from the obligation of paying taxes.

"They wanted," they said, "no legislature; they could manage their own concerns. If the war should break out again, then it would be time enough for the Sultan to call on them to pay their contributions, but why were they to pay them in time of peace ? That the Turks should have been always craving for money was natural and comprehensible. The Turks had harems of a hundred women each, dancing girls, hybrid boys, and all sorts of combinations of profligate expenditure to maintain."

" The name of a Turk," they argued, " was, and is, and ever will be, as long as the pest exists, the synonym for villainy and corruption. But what did Abdel Kader want with money ? He had only one wife. His days and nights, when not at war, were spent in study and prayer. His gardens at Cachero were more than enough to defray all his expenses."

Abdel Kader made short work with such of these reasoners as were within his reach. Their doctrine of resistance was never permitted to be more than a grumbling theory. But in the distant provinces, which had lately been consigned to him, and over which he had hitherto only exercised the influence inherent to his great deeds, that doctrine had in many parts assumed shape and substance.

In the southern parts of the provinces of Tittery, his demands for the usual contributions were peremptorily rejected, and a league was formed to resist their payment, headed by one Ibn Mochtar, a chief from the Sahara, near Boghar ; the Beni Mochtar, the Beni Nail, the Beni Mousa, the Beni Abid, the Zenekara, presented a formidable confederacy. Abdel Kader saw that he had not a moment to lose. He felt that he must at once crush the opposition, or resign his sceptre.

Summoning contingents from his faithful tribes in the province of Oran, so as to form an effective force of 8,000 cavalry and 1,000 infantry, he ordered Ibn Allal, his Khalifa at Miliana, to meet him in the country of the Zenakera, with all the regulars and irregulars under his command. The whole force when assembled constituted an array of 12,000 cavalry and 2,000 infantry, with some pieces of cannon.

On his way to the place of rendezvous, he passed by Mascara. His wife, who had not seen him for many months, sent messengers begging him to turn aside, though only for a day. He stoically replied, he was wedded to his country, and went on. Such was the intensity of his purpose and the all-absorbing influence of his devotion to his duty, that more than two years at one time elapsed without his allowing himself time to go and see his family.

Before resorting to force, Abdel Kader attempted persuasion. He wrote a letter to the disaffected tribes, in which he conjured them, in the name of the Prophet, to obey the law ; to imitate the tribes of the north and west in their obedience, and to beware of the pernicious counsels of designing men. In the same document he promised to overlook the past, if, returning to better sentiments, they came and presented themselves before him with "horses of submission." "Do not trust in the number of your warriors," he concluded, "for were the number double I should overcome them ; God is with me, and Him I obey. Do not flatter yourselves you can escape me. I swear you are no more to me than a glass of water in the hands of a thirsty man."

The letter had no effect, and Abdel Kader advanced to the attack. The battle lasted for three days. Finally the rebels gave way, and dispersed. The Beni Antar held out for some days behind entrenchments which they had thrown up, over what they conceived to be impregnable heights, in the fastnesses near Boghar; but they also were ultimately reduced.

Ibn Mochtar surrendered, and, coming in person, craved the Sultan's mercy. Not only did he obtain grace, but, to his surprise, he was named the Sultan's Khalifa over the subdued tribes. He was ever afterwards one of Abdel Kader's most faithful adherents.

Success, as usual, was followed by fresh submissions. All the tribes along the southern frontiers of the province of Constantine sent deputies to the Sultan, inviting him to come amongst them. His moderation and good faith, as well as his loyal adhesion to the treaty of the Tafna, alone prevented him carrying his standards to the walls of Constantine itself.

Abdel Kader now returned to Medea. His entry was triumphal. For miles ere he reached the gates, the road was thronged with thousands who had flocked from all the villages round about to feast their eyes on the mighty chief whose fame had long been made familiar to their imaginations. Shouts of "Long live our victorious Sultan Abdel Kader!" resounded in the distance, and heralded from afar his approach to the city. There fresh tokens of enthusiasm awaited him. Garlands of flowers were strewn on his path, and perfumed waters sprinkled on his head. He rode straight to the mosque, entered, prayed, and preached. For weeks presents and offerings poured in from all parts. The great Sheiks, the Marabouts, the Cadis of Tittery, and several even from Oran, headed by the Khalifas of districts, came in state to offer their congratulations to the victorious Sultan. It was now considered by many that Abdel Kader had reached the pinnacle of greatness. He himself was seriously contemplating a retirement into private life. But much remained to be done before he could conscientiously resign the task he had sworn to accomplish.

I

His whole attention was now turned towards an obstacle which had long chafed and ruffled his soaring spirit. Far away to the south of the great Sahara, in the province of Laghouat; about two hundred miles from Oran, ranged ten powerful and numerous tribes, called the Beni Arasch. They had hitherto, amidst all the battle and turmoil which had been raging in the north, kept coolly aloof from the exciting contest in which their countrymen had been engaged. Abdel Kader had frequently summoned them to send their cavalry contingents, but in vain.

Their principal chief and Marabout, El Hadj Mohammed ibn Salem il Tejini, refused altogether to entertain the idea that there was to be an Arab Sultan in the land. He accordingly left all Abdel Kader's letters unanswered, and disdained even to receive his orders for the delivery, to his agent, of the legal contributions; secure, as he thought, in his distance, his fortress, and his sands, he set Abdel Kader at defiance. His confidence, at the same time, was increased by his possession of a town, strongly fortified after the fashion of the Arabs, called Ain Maadi.

This place had been repeatedly besieged by the Turks, and with repeated failures. In 1826, the brother of Tejini had even attacked the Turks in their turn, and had menaced Mascara. Already had he gained a footing in the town, when Hassan Bey, of Oran, came to its relief. Tejini drew off his forces to the plain of Eghrees, and there gave his adversary battle, but was defeated and slain. Hassan advanced on Ain Maadi; but Hadj Mohammed, who had succeeded his brother in the command of the tribes, compelled him to retire. From that day, Mohammed Tejini had comported himself as a small independent sovereign.

Ain Maadi contained only three hundred houses; but it had its kasbah, or serail, and was surrounded by thick walls, flanked with towers. Gardens spread around it; and these, also, were capable of defence. The spring of Ain Maadi, from which the town took its name, though at some distance, poured its limpid stream, by means of a canal, into the kasbah. Wells of rain water supplied the wants of the inhabitants.

Abdel Kader was still at Medea, when a certain Hadj Aissa, of Laghouat, came, accompanied by several chiefs of the Beni Arasch, to offer him presents, and " horses of submission." The Hadj announced, that owing to the influence he exercised over the majority of those tribes, they most of them desired to acknowledge Abdel Kader as their Sultan, and that he had only to show himself amongst them to be joyfully received. Abdel Kader, flattered by an adhesion which gave so satisfactory a testimony to the influence of his name in the province of Laghouat, appointed the Hadj his Khalifa over that oasis of the south, gave him proclamations for distribution, in which he called on the Beni Arasch to obey his lieutenants, and dismissed him with the assurance that he would shortly come in person to receive the proffered allegiance.

The time had now come when he could strike a blow at Tejini. On the 12th of June, 1838, he advanced towards Ain Maadi at the head of 6,000 cavalry, 3,000 infantry, six mortars, and three field-pieces. The place was reached after a tedious march of ten days over large sandy wastes. Tejini, taken by surprise, and having made no preparations for sustaining a siege, had barely time to shut the gates and, organise, as well as he could, the 600 Arabs who were at the moment within its walls.

For some time he attempted to defend the gardens with skirmishers led out at night, and able, by their knowledge of the localities, to harass the enemy in his approaches. These endeavours gradually failed. The besieged were confined within their ramparts. The Sultan ordered all the trees to be cut down. Batteries were erected in the spaces thus obtained; and the fire commenced. On the fourth day, the European engineer, who commanded this operation, declared the breach that had been made to be practicable. A storming party was told off; but on the morrow, the breach was found to have been repaired. Again and again the process of breaching and repairing was mutually effected.

On the fifteenth day, Abdel Kader challenged Tejini to come out and fight him in presence of both armies drawn up to witness the encounter; and proposed that the fate of the place should depend on the result. Tejini, though young and brave, prudently declined the test. Abdel Kader now commenced mining. The mine in due time reached the walls. Tejini made a countermine; and in these mines several serious encounters took place.

In this manner the siege was prolonged for months; the brave defenders, the while, were eking out their existence from their small stores of corn and barley, which now barely sufficed to keep them from starvation. The besiegers, on their side, were dependent for their supplies on the arrival of convoys from the north; and these convoys, even, were liable to be intercepted. More than 2,000 cavalry were constantly employed for their protection through the Sahara.

Hadj Aissa was of no use whatever. He turned out to be an impostor.

Both sides were at last perishing from sheer exhaustion. Their ammunition was all but expended. The anxiety of Abdel Kader was intense. He had often before been in straits and difficulties; but never had he been engaged in a struggle which involved more important consequences. He well knew that if he acknowledged himself baffled by raising the siege, he should have all the Sahara on his hands; and he declared he would die on the spot, rather than give in.

At this critical juncture, Abdel Kader had the unexpected satisfaction of receiving some fresh supplies of ammunition, and three siege pieces, from his French allies. A diplomatic difficulty had arisen as to the right interpretation of a certain article in the treaty of the Tafna; and the Governor-General hoped to gain the Sultan's compliance with his version of the disputed passage, by thus generously aiding him in his extremity. This opportune assistance turned the scales, which were still trembling in the balance.

Tejini surrendered. On the 17th of November, 1838, a treaty was signed between him and Mustapha ibn Taamy, the Sultan's brother-in-law. By this treaty, the former engaged to evacuate the Ain Maadi in eight days, and to retire thence with his family and his immediate followers to Laghouat. His eldest son was to remain as a hostage in the Sultan's camp. Abdel Kader, at the expiration of the term, rased the town to the ground. Two tribes of the Beni Arasch, in the immediate vicinity, at once sent in the *ashur* and the *zekka*. The other tribes still refused. A terrible retribution awaited them.

The following dispatch, announcing the success of Abdel Kader, was forwarded to Hadj il Taib, his agent at Oran :—

"God having given us the mission to watch over the welfare of Mussulmans, and to take on us the direction of all the people in this land, submissive to the law of our Lord Mohammed (prayer and salutation be to him), we marched into the Sahara—not to harm the true believers, not to humble and destroy them—but to awaken their faith, to consolidate them into a common bond of union, and to establish order.

"All listened to our voice, and obeyed as much as circumstances would permit. El Tejini alone refused. We found ourselves face to face with those who had been seduced by him. They were preparing to fight us. We conjured them, for the love of God and the Prophet, to come over to us. To this effect, we recalled to their minds several passages of the sacred writings. All was in vain. We despaired of their conversion. Yet we feared that if we were indulgent to them, we should miss the object we have solely in view. This object is, to rally all the Arabs round one common centre, to instruct the ignorant in the law of the Prophet, to prevent the spread of evil examples amongst them, to preserve them from the corrupting influences of certain towns, and to enable them, their wives, and children, to live in peace and security.

"Therefore, exercising our sovereign right, and moreover being the injured party, we ordered our victorious soldiers to fight them. Religion ordained it. They fled before our troops. Again we entreated them to listen to us. Again they refused. Tejini declared that he counted on the strength of his ramparts and the courage of his followers. Then the place was closely besieged. Our miners having reached the foot of the walls, the inhabitants, in consternation, prayed for pardon and deliverance. Although they had deceived us more than once, both were accorded them; for the Most High has said, 'Pardon and forget.' We hope that he will remember our conduct on this occasion, and have mercy upon us for the sake of the blood we have spared, and the women whose chastity we have protected.

" Pardon was granted to all the inhabitants on condition that they should leave the town and go and reside elsewhere, wherever they chose. All have left. Tejini, with his harem and children, have gone to Laghouat, but his eldest son remains a hostage in our hands. May God ever grant us the victory, and preserve us from misfortune.

" Oh Mussulmans, pray to God for your Sultan. He only labours for your welfare. Rejoice, and call on God to strengthen and confirm him. Trust in the Divine mercy. Read the chapter of the Koran, 'Amran,' and say, 'Oh Thou that rulest the universes, Thou givest and takest away according to Thy will, and Thou choosest and Thou raisest up, at Thy good pleasure. In Thy hands is all good. Thou alone art all powerful. Thou changest the night into day, and the day into night. Thou bringest forth life from the midst of death. Without any effort, Thou prosperest whomsoever Thou wilt.' Oh Mussulmans, seek not protectors from among the Infidel, only look for them amongst the true believers."

Abdel Kader returned to Mascara. But the defiant attitude and hostile demonstrations of the Beni Arasch, who had already had the audacity to attack his convoys, preyed upon his mind. He had, moreover, indubitable proofs that they had been in correspondence with the French. By the rules of the Koran, they deserved death. After allowing his troops a few weeks' repose, he announced an expedition; 5,000 cavalry, and cavalry alone, were ordered to hold themselves in readiness.

On the day appointed, they assembled on the plain of Eghrees. None knew or guessed what was to be the nature or direction of the expedition. It was the depth of winter. Each man had been ordered to supply himself with a bag of corn and a bag of barley, and no more. No mules nor tents were required. At sunset Abdel Kader appeared, mounted his horse, and led his forces at a brisk trot towards the north-west.

It soon became dark. Four men in advance carried lanterns affixed to the points of their spears. The lanterns were lighted, and muffled in front, but their rays streamed far away to the rear, over the cavalcade.

Suddenly a countermarch was directed, and the party bore off towards the south-east. The previous direction had been a feint. At midnight the troops of the expedition reached a rivulet. All dismounted. The horses were fed. Abdel Kader and his men ground their corn as well as they could, between stones, and making a paste of flour and water, partook of food. After a rest of three hours the troops were directed to remount. Again they rode on at a brisk trot, which occasionally broke into a canter, till mid-day. Then another short halt was made, and then again the expedition rode on as before till near midnight, and then only were food and rest once more taken. Thus they pursued their way for four days and nights.

As dawn broke on the morning of the fifth day, the vast encampments of the Beni Arasch burst upon their view, spreading away to the horizon. More than ten thousand tents covered the plains. The Arabs were sleeping. A wild and prolonged shout roused them from their slumbers. They rushed out to learn the cause, and saw to their dismay a crowd of cavalry swooping down upon them like a whirlwind.

Frantic cries of "Abdel Kader, Abdel Kader!" now filled the air. The women and children ran about screaming. The men, amazed and bewildered, appeared to have lost their senses. Some flew instinctively to their arms, others took to their horses. But before they could collect, form, or rally, the storm was on them. "Spare the harems," cried Abdel Kader, as he led on the onslaught, "but as for those dogs, treat them as they deserve."

Driving the Beni Arasch before them like a flock of sheep, charging and chasing them in all directions, Abdel Kader and his cavalry soon succeeded in securing the principal Sheiks. Moved by their piteous entreaties and solemn assurances of future good conduct, Abdel Kader mercifully refrained from inflicting capital punishment. The tribes, however, were compelled to pay up, on the spot, five years' arrears of the *ashur* and the *zekka*, and to furnish a contribution of 4,000 camels and 30,000 sheep. Warned by this example, the Beni Arasch became ever after Abdel Kader's most faithful adherents, and remained constant to him to the last.

CHAPTER X

1838.

THE facility with which the French had taken possession of Mascara and Tlemsen, convinced Abdel Kader of the necessity of having strongholds beyond the easy reach of their incursions. The plan which he projected and carried into effect had the double object of resisting the French invasion, and of cementing his own authority over the Arabs. It bears the highest testimony to his military genius. No better explanation of this design can be given than in the words which Abdel Kader addressed in after times to General Daumas, who had for three years resided at his head-quarters in the capacity of consul.

"With the twofold view of imposing on the turbulent tribes of the Sahara, and keeping myself beyond the reach of your attacks, I had constructed on the limits of the Tell, at great expense and amidst innumerable difficulties, a certain number of forts, which you afterwards destroyed. They were situated, in setting out from the west, at Sebdou; to the south of Tlemsen, at Saida; to the south of Mascara, at Tekedemt; to the south-east of the same town, at Taza; to the south of Miliana, at Boghar; to the south of Medea, at Bel Kherout, south-east of Algiers; and, lastly, at Biskra, to the south of Constantine.

"I was convinced, in fact, that whenever the war re-commenced, I should be obliged to abandon to you all the towns of the central line of the Atlas; but that it would be impossible for you, at least for a long time, to reach the Sahara; because the transports which encumber your armies would be a great obstacle in your way. Marshal Bugeaud proved to me that I was mistaken; but at the time I had only the experience of my action with his predecessors.

"Nevertheless, even in face of the system pursued by Marshal Bugeaud, you would have found almost insurmountable difficulties in trying to reach my true line of defence, if the Arabs had only agreed to my proposition of rasing to the ground, and utterly destroying, the towns of Medea, Miliana, Mascara, and Tlemsen: that is to say, the steps of the ladder by which you gradually mounted so high.

"Some argued that the French would soon re-build what I had destroyed; others, that it would be cruel to throw down, merely in view of an eventuality, what it had cost so much to erect. Both sides were wrong: I ought to have followed out my own inspiration.

"Tekedemt, according to my project, was to have become a large town—a binding centre of commerce—between the Tell and the Sahara. The Arabs were pleased with its situation. They came there with much pleasure, because it afforded them great advantages. It was also a thorn I had placed in the eye of the independent tribes of the desert. They could neither escape me, nor incommode me. I held them by their bodily wants. The Sahara producing no crops, they would have been obliged to come to me for food. I had built Tekedemt over their heads. They felt it, and hastened to make their submission.

" In fact, from this time, I could always come upon them
unexpectedly with my *goums* (irregular cavalry), and at least
carry off their flocks and herds, if I did not stop to take their
tents.   The severe examples I made of some of the most distant tribes soon made them give up all hopes of being able to
elude me.   Thus all had finished by submitting to my authority, and regularly paying the *ashur* and the *zekka*.   I used
even to send and count their flocks, and they said not a word.

" There are only four points in the desert which my
authority had not reached : Mzab, Ourgla, Tougourt, and the
Souf. The Benis Sidi Cheikh, however, had all acknowledged
me.   It is true I had granted them certain privileges, and I
allowed them to pay a reduced impost ; but they were a tribe
of Marabouts, and it was my duty to pay them a certain
degree of deference.   As to the *ksours* (entrenched villages in
the Sahara), they paid me little ; nor did I care to be strict
with them.   They looked on my forbearance as a concession
to their poverty.   At a later period, however, I should have
made them amenable to my orders, and have brought them
into complete subjection."

Tekedemt, the town which Abdel Kader raised from its
ruins, intending to make it the capital of his kingdom, had
been built by the Romans.   It is situated sixty miles to the
south-east of Oran.   Judging from the remains of its walls,
it must have been ten miles in circumference.   It contained
two large temples.   During the prosperous days of Arab
dominion in Algeria, it was a seat of government, had a college, and produced its doctors and poets.   The wars between
the Caliphs of Kerouan and Fez, towards the close of the
tenth century, doomed it to final destruction and oblivion.

The first stone of the new fortress was laid by Abdel Kader in May, 1836. He himself supplied the plans for the fortifications which were to surround it. He remitted the payment of tribute to all the tribes within a certain distance, on the condition of their sending labourers to assist in the construction of the ramparts. The people of Mascara brought baskets, shovels, and pickaxes. Medea and Miliana sent supplies of cheese and fruits of all kinds, which, with excellent white bread, and occasionally meat rations, formed the food and wages of the workmen. Soon houses and streets arose. A population poured in. Families of Arabs, of Moors, of Kolouglis, from Mascara, Mazagnan, and Mostaganem, came and settled. Old Roman vaults were turned into stores for ammunition, sulphur, saltpetre, brass, lead, and iron; and for all the machines, implements, and utensils which Miloud-ibn-Arasch had bought in France for the sum of £4,000. A musket manufactory turned out eight muskets a day, the work of French mechanics procured from Paris at liberal salaries.

A mint struck off silver and copper coins, ranging in value from five shillings to twopence, and bearing on one side the inscription, " It is the will of God : I have appointed him my agent ; " on the other, " Struck at Tekedemt, by the Sultan Abdel Kader." Finally, twelve pieces of cannon and six mortars frowned from the ramparts; and the defences were complete.

Abdel Kader superintended all the works by constant personal inspection. M. de France, who was one of his prisoners during the time that these works were in their highest activity, thus describes what he saw :—" After having visited the ruins, we came to a redoubt which Abdel Kader was erecting at about two hundred paces from his citadel. We approached the Sultan, who was reclining, in company with Ibn About, his secretary, and Miloud-ibn-Arasch, on the ground recently thrown up from a ditch which some men were busily digging.

"His costume is so simple, that one can hardly distinguish him from the labourers. He wore a large straw hat, plaited with palm leaves. The brim, tied up to the body of the hat with woollen cords and tassels, must have been three feet in circumference. The hat itself was at least a foot and a half in height, and looked like a tunnel terminating in a peak.

"As I passed the Sultan, he saluted me with that incomparable grace and fascinating smile for which he is so remarkable, and waved his hand for me to be seated. 'To judge by the ruins,' I remarked, 'the town which was formerly here must have been large and flourishing.' 'Yes, it was very fine and very powerful,' he answered. 'Does the epoch of its foundation remount to a very ancient date?' 'Tekedemt is a very ancient town.' 'Do you think I shall be able to discover any stones with inscriptions?' 'You will find none. This town was never Christian. It was one of the first cities built by the Arabs. The sultans, my ancestors, who had their residence at Tekedemt, ruled from Tunis to Morocco.'

"The Sultan then asked me what I thought of the construction of the fortifications. I replied that they appeared to me to be well proportioned and ably laid out, and that it was evident he had profited by a critical examination of our block-houses. He seemed quite pleased with my answer.

" ' Yes,' he resumed, ' with animation, ' I hope yet to restore Tekedemt to its ancient splendour. I will gather the tribes in this place, where we shall be secure from the attacks of the French; and when all my forces are collected, I will descend from this steep rock, like a vulture from his nest, and drive the Christians out of Algiers, Bona, and Oran.

" ' If, indeed, you were content with those cities, I would suffer you to remain there; for the sea is not mine, and I have no ships. But you want our plains and our inland cities, and our mountains. Nay, you even covet our horses, our tents, our camels, and our women; and you leave your own country to come and take that in which Mohammed has placed his people. But your sultan is not a horseman or a saint; and your horses will stumble and fall on our mountains, for they are not surefooted like our horses; and your soldiers will die of sickness; and those whom the pestilence spares, will fall by our bullets.' "

Had Abdel Kader been allowed time to complete his intentions, it was his design to have made Tekedemt not merely a place of strength, but a seat of learning; to have established a library and founded a college. " But," to use his own expression, " God did not so will it. The books which I had brought from all parts of the east for this institution, were taken when the king's son seized my smala; and to my other misfortunes was added that of being able to mark the traces of the French column, on their return to Medea, by the torn and scattered leaves of the books which it had cost me so much time and pains to collect."

During the years 1838 and 1839 Abdel Kader pushed on his plans of reform and improvement with wonderful rapidity.

His army, his police, his schools, his local tribunals of justice, were all fully constituted. His projected fortresses were completed. Manufactories conducted by Europeans were in full operation in all his principal towns. At Tlemsen, a Spaniard superintended a cannon foundry, which turned out twelve and six pounders.

In Miliana, an eminent French mineralogist, M. de Casse, established a musket manufactory and powder-mills. Iron was procured from a mine in the neighbourhood. Cloth of superior quality was also manufactured. Mines of saltpetre, sulphur, iron, and brass, were diligently worked. Europeans were invited to come and settle in the country, with the right of holding freehold property. The land seemed to be waking up from a long slumber. The spirit of European civilisation everywhere percolated the torpid mass, lighting up the dark places, and piercing its way into the strongholds of ignorance and superstition.

The irregular force at Abdel Kader's disposal, during the early part of his career, amounted nominally to nearly 60,000 men. This included all the contingents which the tribes could, on emergency, supply. But rarely more than a third of that number ever assembled at one time, for the purpose of carrying out a military operation. A finer irregular cavalry did not exist.

But Abdel Kader soon discovered the incompetency of such warriors to compete with the disciplined legions of the great military power he confronted. But to raise regular troops amongst a people who, even in the days of Turkish rule, had never been harassed by a conscription, and whose nature revolted at the very idea, was a hazardous experiment, requiring great tact and circumspection. Such a design could only be hinted at as a suggestion, not promulgated as a command.

Accordingly, the following friendly invitation was posted up in all the towns and douairs :—" Whoever wishes to be clothed in fine cloth, and to become the son of the Sultan, let him come and engage himself: he shall be well paid, and indulged in everything." . Several young men were tempted by the inducement thus held out to present themselves for enlistment; and the formation of a regular army almost imperceptibly began.

Abdel Kader thus describes his military organisation :— " Besides the contingents of tribes who rallied at my call, or that of my Khalifas, and which constituted a powerful auxiliary force, although merely temporary, inasmuch as I was never able to keep them away from their tribes for any great length of time, I had latterly a regular army of 8,000 infantry, 2,000 cavalry or spahis, and 240 artillerymen. I had twenty field-pieces, without reckoning a large store of cannons both in iron and brass left by the Turks, many of which, however, it is true, were unfit for service.

" I could thus afford to give each of my Khalifas 1,000 infantry, 250 horsemen, two or three pieces of cannon, and thirty artillerymen. My infantry was recruited only by volunteers ; but they were sufficient, considering my pecuniary means and the arms at my disposal. Later, if time had been afforded me, I should have used the French mode of raising soldiers. My religion would not have prevented me, for a Sultan may have recourse to enrolments to sustain the honour of his flag, and to save his country from Christian invasion. K

" The instructors of my regular infantry were soldiers of the *nizam*, from Tunis and Tripoli, and French deserters. The latter became so numerous at last as to form a battalion of themselves, and fought against their own countrymen with a fury and desperation which was hardly rivalled by my own Mussulmans. I distributed them amongst my Khalifas.

"As for my regular cavalry, they refused to be placed under instructors. In their style of war they were led by an independent pride which disdained to acknowledge a master. They knew they were worth nothing for a shock ; but they thought themselves unrivalled in single combat, in ambuscade, surprise, and light skirmishing. It was no dishonour to them to fly before even inferior forces ; their flight being often a mere feint. To do as much injury as possible to the enemy without exposing themselves to loss—that was the principle I inculcated on them.

"All my regulars were armed with French or English muskets. I got them in battles, from deserters, or by purchase from Morocco. Every Arab found with a French musket in his possession, was obliged to sell it to me for a sum amounting to two English pounds sterling. He then provided himself with a *fusil* as best he could, either in the bazaars, or, when the tribe of the desert, coming to the Tell, inundated the country with arms from Tunis, from Tougourt, from the Mzab, and the Oulad-Sidi-Cheikh. I made my own powder at Tlemsen, Mascara, Miliana, Medea, and Tekedemt. I bought a good deal, also, from Morocco, where I also procured flints, of which our own country was completely destitute. Sulphur came from France. Saltpetre I found everywhere.

" During the peace, the French sea-coast towns supplied me with lead ; Morocco yielded me a considerable quantity ; and I worked a lead mine in the Ouarsenis. But all this was very costly ; so I was very sparing in my distribution of the stores of the Beylik amongst the Arabs, who squander away their powder without reflection, in their festivities and games. I only deviated from this principle in favour of those who were employed in blockading the French garrisons, or when, on the field of battle, the ammunition ran short. I then distributed cartridges on the spot.

" At the seat of government of each of my Khalifas, I had placed tailors, armourers, and saddlers, to make the clothing of my troops, repair their arms, and keep up their horse-equipments. I had also distributed many such workmen amongst the tribe, so as to make them also ready and efficient at a moment's call. To meet the expenses of my administration, where everything had to be created, and though confining myself to what was strictly necessary, heavy imposts were indispensable.

" I ordered my Khalifas to watch, personally, over everything connected with such an important matter. They made their tours twice a-year ; once in the spring to collect the *zekka*, and during the harvest to gather the *ashur*. During these tours, they were expected to inspect and regulate the administration of the Aghas, to report to me any complaints made against them, and to superintend the working of the properties of the Beylik.

" My Khalifas were followed by a regular battalion, their Spahis, and their irregular cavalry. The Arab people are so constituted, that if they had not seen a display of force, they would have refused to pay the impost. After a temporary defeat, what difficulty have I not often experienced to raise again the proper return of contributions! 'The Sultan,' they would say, ' is occupied with the Christians; he cannot compel us. Do not let us pay; let us see what will happen.' What invariably happened was, that they had eventually to pay up everything, with arrears; but nothing corrected them. The Arabs only look to the present moment.

"At the same time that I demanded from the tribes what was necessary to support the Beylik, I endeavoured, as much as possible, to reconcile their interests with those of the State. My Khalifas were instructed to accept, in lieu of the impost or of fines, articles for consumption, mules, camels, and especially horses. With the horses I remounted my cavalry; the mules and camels gave me means of transport; with the provisions, I supplied my troops, or filled my magazines.

"My resources were also augmented by *razzias*, which I made whenever the tribes appealed to arms to fight out their differences. I was resolved to be the sole arbiter of these differences, and I had laid it down as a rule, that not a shot should be fired without my permission. The horses, mules, or camels which I did not immediately require were distributed amongst the tribes, under the charge of agents, who, while they were liberally paid, were so checked, as to be unable to defraud.

"It was well I looked to the future; for the number of horses I had to replace in my regular cavalry was immense. There is not a man amongst these troops who had not had

seven or eight horses killed under him, or rendered unservice-
able. Indeed, it was not uncommon to find men who had
lost from twelve to sixteen. Ibn Yahia—that noble soldier
who, rather than survive my misfortunes, threw himself on
certain death, in my last battle with the Maroccians (Dec.,
1847)—had had eighteen horses killed under him. The emu-
lation in this point was such, that any horseman who passed
a year without being wounded or having a horse killed under
him, was looked on with contempt.

"As far as lay in my power, I also replaced the horses
which my *goums*, or irregular cavalry contingents, lost in
battle. They have had from me more than six thousand.
But latterly, when I could no longer give them horses, I
allowed them, in lieu of a horse, two camels, or thirty sheep,
or a good mule. They sold those animals, and then with the
price remounted themselves at their leisure. But, at last, I
became so straitened as not even to be able to give them this
indemnity.

"To form an idea of the consumption of horses—in one
year alone I gave 500 to the Gharabas of Oran, and nearly
as many to the Hagouts in the plains of Algiers. At the
same time, there were many which I never attempted to
replace, either because their proprietors were rich, or because
I had no longer the means.

"The flocks and cattle which came from the *zekka* were
entrusted to the tribe, under the superintendence of their
Kaids. It was the duty of these officials to take account of
them and appoint them shepherds, as well as to feed and take
care of them. These animals, in the government of each
Khalifa, served to defray the cost of guests, to support the

poor, to assist the *tholbas* (men of letters), and to supply my
army, who had meat twice a-week.   By these means, I had
begun to establish complete order in the administration of the
revenues of each Beylik.   But when the war broke out again,
I was often defrauded, and the Arabs on every side took advantage of my preoccupations.   The only two Khalifas who
maintained order to the last were Abon Hamadi and Ibn
Hallal ; they were dreaded from their severity.

" The precautions which I have mentioned did not always
suffice for the nourishment of my army, at all the points on
which it was called on by the necessities of war to act.
Therefore, as I did not wish to burden the population with
extra expenses, that might have indisposed them towards me,
I ordered *silos* (underground vaults for corn) to be made in
the territory of each Beylik.   These *silos*, placed under the
responsibility of the Kaid of each tribe, and so disposed as
to escape the researches of the enemy, contained the grain
of the *ashur*, or of the state lands, which were cultivated
partly by forced, partly by paid, labour.

I thus proved to the Arabs, who, from their nature, were
always suspicious, that I took nothing for my personal wants
from the imposts.   I obliged them to pay for the general welfare, and they rendered me justice for it.   The *silos*, in
fact, postponed my fall.   Their discovery and destruction
by the French columns decided it.   When once deprived
of my stores of provisions, I was obliged to exhaust the
resources of the tribe.   When they felt the pressure from
both sides fall heavy upon them, their ardour for the holy
war relaxed.

" As to me, what occasion was there for me to resort to

the public treasury to defray my expenses? Never, up to the moment when my private property fell into the hands of the French, did I touch the smallest fraction of what the Arabs gave me for the public expenses; and since that, I have only taken what was absolutely necessary. My clothes were made by the women of my household; my little income sufficed for the wants of my family. Even the small surplus which was left me, I spent in assisting the poor, the traveller, and more especially the needy among my brave companions-in-arms who had been wounded in the holy war.

"By acting thus, I could consistently call on the Arabs to make great sacrifices; for I showed them that the *zekka*, the *ashur*, fines, contributions—all my resources, in fact—were scrupulously devoted to the maintenance of the public welfare. In 1839, when the war recommenced, I called upon the Arabs for an extraordinary loan; but they contributed very slowly. I immediately sold all my family jewels by auction in the bazaars of Mascara, proclaiming publicly that the proceeds were to be sent to the public treasury. The loan was then very soon advanced; and it seemed only to be a question who should pay first."

As soon as Abdel Kader began to form a regular army, he drew up and published a military code, containing the most minute regulations for the discipline, pay, and clothing of his troops. This code was read out to the different regiments twice a month. It was interspersed with injunctions, and promises of reward for good behaviour, of which the following may be taken as an example:—

"It is indispensably necessary that a chief should be personally brave and courageous; that he should be of a good family, irreproachable in his morals, strictly religious, patient, enduring, prudent, prompt, and intelligent in the hour of difficulty and danger ; for the officer is to his men what the heart is to the body ; if the heart is not sound, the body is worthless.

" A soldier who throws himself dashingly on the enemy's ranks, disables and disarms his foe, or, by rallying the men when on the point of retreating, prevents a panic by his example and presence of mind, shall be decorated by the Sultan himself before the whole army ; and his heroism shall be proclaimed by beat of drum."

The decoration thus conferred varied in appearance, according to the bearer's merits. It consisted of a silver or silver-gilt hand with extended fingers. The number of fingers extended notified the number of acts of bravery performed. Each finger extended entitled the bearer to extra pay, amounting to a shilling a month. In the centre of the decoration was inscribed the words *Nusr-ed-deen*, or "the triumph of religion." It was worn, not on the breast, but affixed to one side of the hood of the burnous. It was sometimes also given to civilians who had rendered great administrative services.

The uniform of the foot soldier was dark blue, with scarlet pantaloons, a brown capote, and a small cap and turban. His pay amounted to nine francs a month. On the right sleeve of each commanding officer were embroidered the words, " Patience and perseverance are the key to victory ; " on the left, " There is no god but God, and Mohammed is his Prophet." Embroidered on his right shoulder of the Aga, in place of an epaulette, were marked the words, " Nothing profits like piety and courage;" on the left, "Nothing is so injurious as discussion and want of obedience."

All the officers throughout the army had inscriptions of a like tendency embroidered on their uniforms. The spahis, or regular cavalry, were clothed in scarlet exclusively. Their colonels wore the device, "Trust in God and the Prophet—charge and conquer;" those of the artillery, "I can effect nothing: it is God who directs the shot." Thus was religion, its duties and its efficacy, placed ever prominently forward by Abdel Kader, not only in his army, but in his whole administration, as the indispensable foundation and support of human exertion.

The following allusion to himself, with which his military code closes, placed him before his officers and men as a model to be copied and emulated. Nor was there any exaggeration in its expressions.

"Il Hadj Abdel Kader cares not for this world, and withdraws from it as much as his avocations will permit. He despises wealth and riches. He lives with the greatest plainness and sobriety. He is always simply clad. He rises in the middle of the night to recommend his own soul and the souls of his followers to God. His chief pleasure is in praying to God with fasting, that his sins may be forgiven.

"He is incorruptible. He never takes anything out of the public funds for himself. All the presents which are brought to him he sends to the public treasury; for he serves the State, not himself. He neither eats, nor drinks, nor dresses, but as religion ordains. When he administers justice, he hears complaints with the greatest patience. A smile is always on his face for the encouragement of those

who approach him. His decisions are conformable to the
words of the sacred book. He hates the man who does not
act uprightly; but honours him who strictly observes the
precepts and practises the duties of religion.

"From his boyhood he learned to mount the most fiery
horse without a teacher. He never turns before an enemy;
but awaits him firmly. In a retreat he fights like a common
soldier, rallying his men by his words and example, and
sharing in all their dangers. Thus, brave, disinterested, and
pious, when he preaches, his words bring tears into all eyes,
and melt the hardest hearts. All who hear him become good
Mussulmans.

"He explains the most difficult passages of the Koran and
of the Hadeeth (Traditions) without referring to books or
Ulemahs. The most learned Arabs and the greatest Talebs
acknowledge him as their master and teacher. May God
increase his nobleness of character, his wisdom, his learning,
his understanding, his honour, glory, and success, a thousand-
fold!"

CHAPTER XI

ABDEL KADER now saw himself the founder of an empire. The strength and versatility of his genius had given cohesion and compactness to elements the most adverse and discordant. Hundreds of tribes bowed beneath his warlike sceptre. On all sides were seen the good results of order and good government. His external relations attested the magic of his power, and the splendour of his fame. Sovereigns and Viceroys, from the Emperor of Morocco to those of Egypt, Tunis, and Tripoli, vied with each other in tendering him marks of respect and admiration. The Ulemahs of Mecca and Alexandria watched with holy joy and expectation the career of one who seemed destined to revive the pristine glories of Islam.

Burning to accomplish his secret mission in its fullest extent, Abdel Kader lost not an hour, by day or by night, in planning, arranging, and executing new schemes of progress and improvement. To make the Arabs of Algeria one people, to recall them to the strict observance of their religious duties, to inspire them with patriotism, to call forth all their dormant capabilities, whether for war, for commerce, for agriculture, or for mental improvement; and then to crown the whole with the impress of European civilisation— such was his mighty and comprehensive ideal.

His amazing activity, vigour, and enterprise, had overcome difficulties' apparently insuperable.   His victorious sword, whether striking down the enemy from without, or his rivals from within, had proved the indomitable energy of a will which had but to conceive in order to accomplish.   He was now to show that he could achieve victories without soldiers, and reap laurels unstained by blood.

Warrior, orator, diplomatist, statesman, and legislator, the secret of his force lay in his intellectual grandeur. His letters, his speeches, his conversations, all bear the stamp of their own peculiar freshness and originality.   His natural eloquence, enriched by study, matured by meditation, and enhanced by the singular charms and graces of his manner, operated like a spell.

The provinces of Oran and Tittery, the plains of the Sahara, had been won by his military prowess.   The grand Kabylia, that superb range of the Djurjura, extending towards the east, from Algiers to Borigia, was now to be the scene of a nobler triumph, one gained by the exhibition of moral power. The hardy Kabyles inhabiting those regions had defied every attempt to subjugate them.   As independent republics, bound together by the most exalted spirit of freedom, they had preserved their usages, their customs, their laws, intact amidst the changing governments which had risen and fallen around them.

It was clear that this nursery of soldiers, if once brought under his control, would give Abdel Kader a never-failing element of support, and if necessary, of aggression.   Alone, he determined to effect by persuasion what others had failed to achieve by the force of arms.   In September, 1839, he suddenly appeared at Borj Hamze, followed by only 50 cavalry. His faithful Khalifa, Ben Salem, was by his side. To the question, what the Sultan proposed to do, the answer was, "To conquer the Djurjura!" The expedition set forth.

The first slopes were rapidly passed. The appearance of the little cavalcade, as it plunged into the deepest ravines and gorges, or ascended almost perpendicular heights, spread surprise and astonishment amongst the mountaineers, gazing from their huts and precipices at the unwonted spectacle.

Presently the rumour spread that Abdel Kader was there. The magic name resounded from rock to rock. From their valleys, their dells, their fastnesses, the Kabyles came streaming forth to hail their famous guest. Thousands at length gathered about his tent. The press of Sheiks and Marabouts blocked up the entrance. The people crowded round, some rudely intruding themselves, by lifting up the folds of the tent to gratify their curiosity. The escort pushed them aside with the words, "Back with you! you are going to smother our master." Abdel Kader saw their disappointment. "Let them approach," he mildly said, "let them approach; they are rough and wild like their mountains. Excuse them, you cannot change their natures in a day."

Abdel Kader now demanded to see the chiefs who commanded them. "We obey our *Ameens* and our *Marabouts*," was the reply. The *Ameens* came forward to pay their respects. "Which of them represents the whole?" "We have no single chief," responded the jealous republicans, "to whom we delegate our power. Our *Ameens*, chosen by the popular voice, express the general will." Abdel Kader

ordered a space to be cleared, and bade the throng sit down.
A large circle was formed. He stood in the midst, with a
string of beads in his hand.

And now, in one of those stirring harangues which convinced the understanding, and melted the hearts of all who
heard him, Abdel Kader adjured them them to rally round
his standard. He came not, he said, amongst them, like the
Turks, with the emblems of brute force; he came amongst
them as a simple pilgrim, relying on the cause he upheld,
the cause of God and his Prophet. In a hundred glorious
combats, glorious for Islamism, he had defeated the infidels,
who strove to subdue their land. All the west obeyed his
laws, and if he chose, it would be as easy for him to roll the
west on the east, as to roll up the carpet on which he stood.

"If you tell me that the east is stronger than the west,"
he continued, "I reply, God sends me victory, on account of
the purity of the motives which guide and direct me. You
know, besides, what is written in the Koran, 'Elephants are
subdued by flies; lions have been killed by mice.'

"Be assured, that if I had not firmly opposed the invasions
of the French, if I had not shown them their weakness and
impotency, they would have dashed over you before this, like
a raging sea, and then you would have seen what neither
times past nor times present has ever witnessed. They
have left their own country merely to conquer and enslave
ours. But I am the thorn that God has planted in their eyes,
and if you will assist me I will drive them into the sea.

"Otherwise they will subjugate and humiliate you. Be
grateful to me, then, that I am their mortal enemy. Rouse
yourselves, O Kabyles! Awake from your apathy. Believe

me, I have at heart no other wish than that of the happiness, welfare, and prosperity of Mussulmans. All I exact
from you this day is, obedience and concord, and the strict
observance of our sacred law, that we may triumph over
the infidel. And to support our armies, I only demand from
you what is specified and ordained by God, the Master of the
universe.

" I wish not to change your customs, or alter your laws
and usages; but the conducting of warlike operations demands
a chief. I summon you to join the Holy War. Choose a
chief. I recommend you Ben Salem. If you choose him, he
will be like a compass for you in the hour of danger and
trial. I call God to witness the truth and sincerity of my
words. If they do not find their way to your hearts, you
will yet repent one day; but that repentance will be too
late. It is by reason and not by force that I seek to convince
you. I pray God to direct and enlighten you."

A general shout arose : " Give us Ben Salem, give us Ben
Salem. Take the *zekka;* take the *ashur*. Lead us against
the infidels. We are your children, your soldiers, your
slaves ! "

After installing Ben Salem as his Khalifa in the Djurjura,
amidst much pomp and rejoicing, Abdel Kader continued his
peaceful tour throughout that hospitable land. For thirty
days his progress was one continued scene of rejoicing.
Whenever it was known that he had halted, the simple-
minded and enthusiastic mountaineers poured in with their
diffas, or enormous plates of rice, sprinkled over with bits of
meat : each one placing his *diffa* before the Sultan's tent, and
insisting on his partaking—"Eat, it is my *diffa.*" To avoid

giving offence, Abdel Kader was obliged to taste each plate successively.

This short excursion had been sufficient to make him known and appreciated. The courtesy and affability of his manners, his well-known piety, his fame as an Ulemah, the venerated title of Hadj and Marabout, his brilliant renown as a warrior, his eloquence as a preacher, all combined to make his appeal irresistible. Not one of those fierce and indomitable mountaineers who saw and heard him could escape the influence of this extraordinary combination of advantages. Their poets made him the topic of their songs. Abdel Kader bade them adieu. With difficulty he escaped from their friendly and hospitable importunities ; but at length he departed. The Djurjura had been conquered; and Abdel Kader could say, like Cæsar, " *Veni, vidi, vici.*"

Unwearied in his exertions to elevate, as well as to mould and direct, the national character of the Arabs, Abdel Kader had early established a system of public education amongst all the tribes. " My duty," he afterwards said, " as sovereign and as Mussulman was to support and exalt science and religion. In the towns and throughout the tribes I opened schools, where children were taught their prayers, where the first and most important precepts of the Koran were inculcated, and where reading, writing, and arithmetic were fully taught.

" Those who desired to push their education further were sent, free of expense, to the *zouias* and mosques. There they found *tolbas* ready to instruct them in history and theology. I appointed the *tolbas* a salary according to their learning and deserts. So important did it appear in my eyes to give encouragement to learning, that more than once I have remitted sentence of death to a criminal from the mere fact of his being a *tolba*. It requires such a long time in our country to become well instructed, that I had not the courage to destroy in one day the fruit of years of laborious study.

"The occupant of a cot may cut down a palm-tree which incommodes him; but how many years must he wait before he can taste the fruit of one that he plants!

"In order to assist the studies of the *tolbas*, I took the greatest pains to prevent the destruction of books and manuscripts. I had the more reason for being so anxious in this respect, as with us it takes months to make a single copy. I therefore gave strict orders throughout the towns and tribes that the greatest care should be taken of all manuscripts, and that if any person were found destroying or defacing one, he should be severely punished.

"Knowing my wishes on this point, my soldiers even were in the habit of carefully bringing in to me any manuscripts which fell into their hands in a *razzia;* and in order to stimulate their zeal in this respect, I always gave them a handsome reward. By degrees I made a large collection of such manuscripts, and had them safely deposited in the *souias* and mosques, and entrusted to the care of *tolbas* in whom I had confidence.

"In the same way as I provided for a system of public instruction, I established the administration of justice. The *kadis* had a monthly salary, besides perquisites, for the performance of certain duties. I desired that the representatives of justice should be seen everywhere, and even that they should follow my army on its march. The Turks put to death by caprice and cruelty : I allowed no execution to take place except by virtue of a sentence given according to the law of God, of which I merely considered myself the executor.

" Thus, wherever my columns went, they were accompanied by a *kadi* and two assistants, one of whom (the chief of the police) carried the judgments into execution. He was not looked upon with aversion on that account, since it is not the executioner who kills, but the law. No doubt many have suffered by my order, but never without a legal sentence. All had committed crimes of some sort, or betrayed their religion. Now, according to our books, whoever aids the enemy with his goods, forfeits his goods; and whoever aids him with his arms, forfeits his head.

" Thanks to the vigilance of my khalifas, of the agas and the kaids, and to the responsibility which I had attached to the tribes for all crimes or thefts committed on their territory, the roads had become perfectly secure. The vigilance of the police left nothing to be desired. In a word, amongst a people living under tents, and consequently difficult to manage and control, owing to the vast spaces over which they were dispersed, I had arrived at such a point that horse-stealing by night was no more known; and a woman could go about alone without fear of being insulted. When comments were made on this great result, and the reason asked, the Arabs replied, ' The Sultan's nets are there, we need not use our own.'

" The public morals were equally stimulated by my reforms. Prostitution was severely repressed, and if God had willed it, I should have ended by restoring the Arabs to the path of the Koran, from which they had so widely deviated.

" I had totally forbidden the use of gold and silver on the clothes of the men, for I abhorred the prodigality and luxury which enervates. I only tolerated such ornaments on weapons and on harness. Should we not cherish and adorn what so much contributes to our safety ? The women were not included in this prohibition. The weaker sex requires compensation, when man has all the excitements he can desire— war, the chase, mental occupation, government, religion, science.

" I was the first to set an example, by wearing clothes as simple as the meanest of my servants. If I did this, it was certainly not in the fear of being a mark for the balls of the enemy, but because I wished to be able to exact from the Arabs nothing but what I practised myself, and to show them that in the eyes of God it was better to buy arms, ammunition, and horses to make war, than to be covered with fine and expensive, but useless, ornaments.

" Wine and gambling were severely interdicted. Tobacco was likewise prohibited. Not that the use of tobacco is forbidden by our religion, but my soldiers were poor, and I was anxious to keep them from a habit which has a tendency to increase, and which sometimes reaches such a pitch that men have been known to leave their families in misery, and to sell even their clothes, to gratify their passion for it. There was smoking still, but it was only occasionally, and even then in secret. This was already a great step gained. As to the Marabouts, the *tolbas*, and all who were attached to the government, they renounced the practice of smoking completely. This fact shows, at all events, in what a measure I had succeeded in being obeyed.

"Such was already the extent and success of my organisation; and considering the short space of time which had as
yet been allowed me, the reforms were not inconsiderable.
They proved, at all events, what I should have ultimately
effected. But the son of the French king came with an army
from Constantine, and without giving me the slightest notice,
traversed the territory which was incontestably mine by the
Treaty of the Tafna, fought with .the contingents of my
Khalifa Ben Salem, at Ben-Hinny, and was thus the cause of
the renewal of hostilities."

It was only by his own constant and unremitting personal
supervision that Abdel Kader was enabled to carry forward
and complete his extensive plans of reform and amelioration.
Ever on the move, reviewing his troops, visiting his arsenals,
examining his schools, administering justice, the young Sultan
of the Arabs seemed to embody the principle of progress, and,
like a beneficent genius, to scatter the blessings of knowledge,
security, and contentment through the land.

As soon as it was known that he had arrived in a district,
the tribe all hastened to pay their visits of ceremony and
respect, vying with each other in their profuse and generous
hospitality. Each tribe was preceded by its Kaid on horseback. Then came the men, women, and children, walking
two and two, bearing on their heads plates of the national
dish—the *conscoussia*. The more wealthy Arabs formed a
procession apart, carrying whole sheep, spitted and roasted on
a stake.

On reaching the Sultan's tent, before which thirty negroes
always stood in attendance, the plates were ranged along the
ground, and the stakes stuck in a row, until the Sultan had

signified his acceptance of the offering, when they at once became the perquisite of his train and escort. The sheiks then entered and kissed hands. Each brought the tribute of his tribe, or produced receipts for its payment, from the khalifa within whose jurisdiction his tribe resided. The commonalty were then admitted and did obeisance. If the day was a Friday, Abdel Kader came forth and preached.

As long as the Sultan remained in any place, he was the sole dispenser of justice. The tent door was the "King's gate." There he heard complaints and redressed grievances. In criminal cases he decided without appeal. The Koran always lay open before him. His condemnations were motioned rather than delivered. If he elevated his hand, the prisoner was carried back to prison. If he held it out horizontally, he was led out to execution. If he pointed to the ground, he received the bastinado. Civil cases were referred to the Ulemahs. All decisions were made according to the Koran, to the text and spirit of which Abdel Kader bowed with undeviating reverence and submission. The Koran, in fact, was the guiding star of his public and private life.

At last, Abdel Kadir had succeeded in establishing a machinery of government, which, by the harmonious relationship of its various parts, gave fair promise of success and durability. The simple hierarchy he had created was exactly conformable to the administrative wants and hereditary sentiments of his people. The public functionaries were few, their salaries moderate, their spheres of action well defined. If their power was absolute, and their sway over the public revenues extensive, the lynx-eyed vigilance of the Chief of the State precluded the possibility of tyranny, corruption, or abuse.

With a just appreciation of the beneficial effects resulting from a due regard to the natural gradations of society, and with a thorough knowledge of the instinctive deference paid by the Arabs to blood and descent, he filled all his more important posts with men of noble birth. But those thus selected were, at the same time, men of good character and spotless reputation—examples to be followed, as well as rulers to be obeyed. A high and lofty sense of duty and self-respect thus came to pervade all ranks, from the apex to the basis of the social pyramid; and religion, virtue, honour, and morality, which had been blighted by the withering dominion of the Turks, revived.

Abdel Kader had now performed his task. He had beaten the French. He had signed a glorious peace. His kingdom was a model of order and regularity. He trusted he might now be allowed to lay down the sceptre. He had come forward at his country's call. He had vindicated its choice. He now sought permission to return to that seclusion and retirement, that life of study and devotion, which he had so reluctantly abandoned. With this view, he wrote to the Sultan of Morocco.

After the usual titles due to sovereignty, the letter thus proceeded :—

"The people of Algeria are now united. The standard of the Djehad is furled. The roads are secure and practicable. The usages of barbarism have been abandoned and obliterated. A girl can traverse the land alone, by night and by day, from east to west, without fearing obstruction. A man even meeting the murderer of his brother dares not retaliate, but appeals for justice to the authorities.

"The book of Almighty God and the law of His Prophet are the only rules of adjudication. Provisions for the support of our army abound, as well as men to fill the ranks. All this must be attributed to the blessing of God, obtained through your prayers and approbation. Otherwise, we should have been the weakest of men for such achievements.

"We did not come forward and assume the task of government from ambitious motives, or a desire for exaltation and power, or a love for the vanities of this world; but (and God knows the secrets of my heart) to fight the battles of the Lord, to prevent the fratricidal effusion of the blood of Moslems, to protect their properties, and to pacify the country, as zeal for the faith and patriotism require.

"We have been ever on the alert, night and day, moving through the length and breadth of the land, in mountains and in plains; sometimes leading forth to battle, and at other times regulating affairs. We now beg your Highness to send one of your sons, grandsons, or servants, to assume the reins of government; for now there is neither trouble nor opposition from any quarter. I will be the first to serve under him, and to exert my poor abilities to the utmost, to counsel and advise him.

"I trust to that consideration and indulgence which distinguishes you, to accept this my prayer to be relieved from the charge which is weighing on me.

"I send your Highness some presents which have been sent me by the King of the French, from which I have only retained a pair of pistols. Also some of the best mules in Algeria. Their number, together with that of the other articles, are detailed in the account enclosed in this letter.

"We beg you to accept our excuses, and hope for the expression of your pleasure and approbation. The presents
will be delivered to you by my brother, whom I have deputed
in my place, to seek the honour of an interview with your
Highness, and to convey to you the dutiful regards and
assurances of devotion of your son and servant,

"ABDEL KADER IBN MEHI-ED-DEEN.

" *October*, 1838.

" *Moharrem*, 1254."

The words written by Brougham on Washington might,
indeed, have been admirably applied to Abdel Kader at this
remarkable juncture of his life:—"A triumphant warrior,
where the most sanguine had a right to despair; a successful
ruler in all the difficulties of a course wholly untried; but a
warrior whose sword only left its sheath when the first law
of our nature commanded it to be drawn; and a ruler who,
having tasted of supreme power, gently and unostentatiously
desired that the cup might pass from him, nor would suffer
more to wet his lips, than the most solemn and sacred duty
to his country and his God required."

Sultan Abderahman, in a highly complimentary reply,
refused even for a moment to hear of such self-renunciation
on the part of one who had shown himself so eminently fitted
to command, to organise, to renovate, and to save his country.
He called on Abdel Kader, in the sacred name of Islamism,
to stand forth, as ever, the champion of the Djehad, to complete his noble work, and to extend and accomplish his victorious career. Finally, he begged the young Sultan to send
him his shirt, that he might hang it up in his private
mosque as a saintly relic!

SCARCELY had the " Treaty of the Tafna" been signed, when its defects and inconsistencies became apparent. It was impossible that a measure, hurried on by General Bugeaud to a hasty and immature conclusion, solely in order to enable him to send the troops under his command in the province of Oran, that they might take part in the siege of Constantine, could have had any other result.

The General, defending his act in the French Chamber, during the session of 1838, thus expressed himself:—"Much has been said about the defects in the details of the treaty. I frankly avow there were some, but I think their importance has been exaggerated. There is only one of any consequence, and that is the expression, 'as far as the Wady Kuddra, and *beyond.*' This word may imply, as far as the province of Constantine. The expression is certainly vague; but it must be remembered that I was hard pushed for time. A steamer was waiting for my dispatch. It was absolutely necessary that I should conclude for war or for peace."

But it was precisely the doubt hanging over the proper interpretation of this word as it stood in Arabic, which kept open the door for endless disputes and misunderstandings, and ended by nullifying the treaty altogether. So hastily and inconsiderately, indeed, had it been drawn up, that a few days after the peace, when a French detachment had occasion to go from Arzew to Mostaganem, Abdel Kader, without opposing its march, sent to Bugeaud to remark that the French troops had violated his territory. The complaint was perfectly just, inasmuch as no mention had been made in the treaty of the right of passage.

The evils arising from incorrect translations are notorious. In the diplomatic relations, between Abdel Kader and the French authorities, more than one had occurred, which, had they been discovered by the latter, might have entailed serious complications. But Abdel Kader was satisfied, in general, with what he had written in Arabic, and the French authorities with what they had written in French, and no more questions were asked.

One instance may be given. The French had always placed at the head of their treaties, that Abdel Kader acknowledged the sovereignty of France. Abdel Kader never dreamed of making any such admission. It would have cost him his throne. What he had written, in Arabic, in the article he subscribed was, properly translated, "The Emir Abdel Kader acknowledges that there is a French Sultan, and that he is great." The difference is wide.

In a matter of limits of territory, moreover, such matters become of vital importance; and Abdel Kader was the last person to yield a point, when he felt he was borne out by justice and common sense in maintaining it.

By the French version of the 2nd article of the "Treaty of the Tafna," France is declared to possess, in the province of Algiers, "Algiers, the Sahel, the plain of the Metija, extending to the east as far as the Wady Kuddra, and *beyond*."

So the French chose to translate the Arabic word "*fauk*," which really means, "above." The Gordian knot which the French had made, and which they at last unscrupulously cut with the sword, was this : they had given themselves a limit, and yet wanted to have no limit. All their efforts to make Abdel Kader stultify himself, by subscribing to this solecism, were unavailing.

Because the Arab Sultan maintained the absurdity of such a proceeding, and finally threw down the gauntlet of defiance rather than sacrifice the interests of his subjects and co-religionists, he was held up to execration as a rebel, as a breaker of treaties, as a man of wild and unprincipled ambition. He was treated as if he were contending with the lawful possessors of the land; not fighting, as was truly the case, against invaders, who had come to its shores denying all schemes of aggrandisement, and pledged to achieve the single object for which they came, and then withdraw.

In presence of a treaty, which each party read and construed after its own fashion, political and commercial relations of any durable or confidential nature were clearly impossible. An attempt, at least, to come to some understanding was indispensable. The task of entering on a discussion with Abdel Kader on the subject devolved on Marshal Valée, who assumed the functions of Governor-General in Algiers, on November 30th, 1837.

The Marshal applied to the French Ministry for instructions. The reply thus simply and categorically announces the doctrine of appropriation. "By the words, 'Wady Kuddra, and *beyond*,' must be understood, all the country in the province of Algiers which is beyond the Wady Kuddra, up to the province of Constantine. The evidence of right, independent of political considerations, permits no concession on that point. Since we are masters of the province of Constantine, we cannot be without land communication with it."

The Marshal forwarded this view of the question to Abdel Kader, with his own comments, as follows:—"France has ceded to you all the province of Oran, less the reserved districts; all the ancient Beylik of Tittery, without exception; lastly, all that part of the province of Algiers situate to the west of the Chiffa. But you can have no pretension to any part of that province which lies to the east of that river. As for the Beylik of Constantine, about that there can be no misunderstanding, as it is not even spoken of in the treaty; and, moreover, it was placed under the rule of Achmet Bey when the treaty was signed."

Abdel Kader replied:—"As regards the Beylik of Constantine, there can be no difficulty: on that point we are agreed. But it is not so as regards the province of Algiers. Remember what happened at the time of the treaty. I wished to limit you to the plain of Algiers. General Bugeaud begged me to extend this limit, and I consented. I ceded the country as far as the Wady Kuddra towards the east, and as far as Blidah, inclusively, towards the south. The expression, ' as far as the Wady Kuddra and above," must have a value. If not, why was it inserted in the treaty? If it signifies anything, it must mean that you are limited to the east, as you are to the west.

" To justify your interpretation, you base your reasoning on the necessity there is for you to have a land communication between Constantine and Algiers.' But you admit, in the same breath, that Constantine was not yours when the treaty was signed. Consequently, you clearly could not have reserved for yourself a tract of country in anticipation of an event which had not yet happened. Besides, is it anything extraordinary, that you should have done towards the east, what you have done towards the west?

"Arzew and Mostaganem belong to you; yet you have not claimed or appropriated the tract of country which lies between those two towns. Do not let us fling ourselves into interpretations. Let us keep to the text; and let us frankly say, that all that portion of the province of Algiers which is not included between the Chiffa on the west, and Wady Kuddra on the east, and the first chain of mountains on the south, belongs to me."

"But," answered the Marshal, "your interpretation is erroneous; for you forget the word *beyond*, which is also in the treaty. 'As far as Wady Kuddra, and *beyond*'—which evidently meant, at the signing of the treaty, up to the very limits of the province of Algiers in that direction. But since that time we have taken Constantine. It means now, therefore, as far as the *frontiers of Tunis*."

Nowithstanding this pat of the lion's paw, Abdel Kader retorted with the coolness of a logician.

"The word *beyond*," he wrote, "signifies something; but the Arab word *fauk* translated as you translate it—*beyond*—means nothing at all. Let us make an experiment. Take any twenty Arabs you choose to select, and ask them the meaning of the word *fauk*. If they say that the natural interpretation of this word can, by any twisting of meaning, be made to signify '*beyond*,' I will accept your interpretation.

Take all the territory between Wady Kuddra and the province of Constantine. But if, on the other hand, they all decide that the word, what you translate ' *beyond,*' really and strictly means *above,* accept the proposal I make you. This proposal is to give over to you, as a limit towards the east, the first crest of mountains which rises *above* the Wady Kuddra."

The Marshal prudently declined the test. He might have declared war at once ; but war with Abdel Kader was not so enticing as to be lightly undertaken. A better mode of getting over the difficulty suggested itself. Abdel Kader was ardently engaged in the task of organisation. Peace was indispensable to him. Attentions, flatteries, cajolements—or, these failing, petty annoyances and harassing vexations—might mollify or weary out his tenacious spirit. Both were tried ; but both ineffectually.

In the mean time Abdel Kader was firmly establishing himself in all the districts to the south of Tittery. With a boldness and rapidity of movement, which paralysed and subdued, he laid his iron hand on all the tribes on the borders of the province of Constantine, who were known or even suspected of intriguing with the French. He boldly occupied the disputed territory beyond the Wady Kuddra. More than that, he made it the scene of one of those acts of uncompromising severity, with which he visited all traitors to the faith.

A colony of Kolouglis had lately settled there, trusting for their security to French protection. Their kaid, a Turk, had received French investiture. Abdel Kader summoned them to break off their treasonable connection. They refused. The French supplied them with arms and ammunition to resist.

Abdel Kader swept down on them, crushed them, and cut off the Frenchified kaid's head. All the tribes of the vast district of Sebaou instantly sent in their adhesion; and the Sultan appointed Achmet Ibn Salem to be his Khalifa over them.

In the midst of these successes, Abdel Kader was threatened with a rival. Achmet Bey, when turned out of Constantine, had taken refuge in Mount Aures. He had commenced agitating amongst the tribes of the district of Zab. Biskara, its capital, was in the possession of his most implacable enemy, Farhat-ibn-Said. This chief applied to the French for assistance to defend the country against the Bey, promising that, in case of success, it should be made to submit to French domination. The French were lukewarm; and so he turned to Abdel Kader.

Before entering the Zab country by force of arms, Abdel Kader considered it expedient to inform the French Governor at Constantine of his intention. As the friend and ally of France, he said, he was going to quell the disturbances which had arisen there, and save it from anarchy. Since agitation so near a French province might prove contagious, he considered it was in the interest of France that he undertook the expedition.

Having sent this communication, Abdel Kader ordered Ibn Berkani, his Khalifa at Miliana, to collect his forces, and march on Biskara. Farhat received him with open arms. A combined attack was made on Achmet Bey, who was defeated, and hid himself in the Sahara. Farhat expected to be named the Sultan's Khalifa over the Zab. To his disgust, the latter appointed one of his own chiefs, Ben Azouz, to that post. In revenge, he immediately began to correspond with the French. The correspondence was intercepted. Of his treason there could be no doubt. He was seized, and sent in chains to Tekedemt.

Abdel Kader was now absolute sovereign of two-thirds of Algeria. The country which he had newly occupied, to the south-east of the province of Algeria, was one of the greatest utility to the French, since the garrison of Constantine drew from it its provisions, and they could not but feel that Abdel Kader could now at any moment stop the supply.

Well aware that all those movements would awaken the jealousy, if not excite the alarm, of the French authorities in the regency, Abdel Kader made a step towards setting himself right with the French Government at home. After the treaty of the Tafna, Louis Philippe had sent him a magnificent present of costly arms. These gifts Abdel Kader had forwarded, as usual, to the Sultan of Morocco. The arms he prized but little; but they enabled him to pay a graceful tribute to one, on whose friendship and assistance he greatly relied.

Milond-ibn-Arasch and Durand, the Jew, were now sent to Paris to return the compliment. They took with them six splendid Arab horses, as a gift to the King of the French. The presentation of this complimentary peace-offering was the ostensible object of their mission. But their secret instructions were to soften down any acrimonious feeling which might exist on the part of the French Government towards their master—to explain away his recent conduct in such a manner as to leave a favourable impression—and to procure, if possible, a confirmation of his reading of the disputed article in the Treaty of the Tafna.

Marshal Valée was fully cognisant of the whole of this proceeding. In fact, he had contrived to see Ibn Arasch for a short half-hour, on his way, at Algiers; and during this interview he had immediately began to argue about the true meaning of the article. Divining the real object of the ostentatious embassy, he had written to his Government, warning it against making any concessions which might interfere with his own course of negotiation. The Arab envoys, consequently, were graciously received; their horses were admired and praised. They themselves were brilliantly entertained. All the sights of Paris were shown them; and, in the French phrase of the time, they were the "lions" of the day. But when they broached the subject of the disputed article, their mouths were stopped with an evasion or a compliment.

On their return to Algiers, after their fruitless mission, the envoys were summoned by the Marshal to an interview. He drew out of his pocket an amended version of the treaty, in which the ground contested was given over to the French, Abdel Kader receiving in exchange the districts of the Beni Djead, Hamza, and Oranougla; whilst, at the same time, the measures of corn and barley which by the treaty he had engaged to furnish, were remitted to him. Ibn Arasch declared he was not authorised to negotiate.

The envoy was still further pressed, and he at last offered to affix his own seal to the document, to show that personally he acceded to the stipulation. But he positively refused to be answerable for his master's approval. The perplexity of the affair was mitigated by a proposal on the part of the French to send a commission to the Sultan, and accordingly

M

a commission started. On reaching Miliana, the Khalifa there refused to allow the French commissioners to proceed, without instructions from the Sultan. Ibn Arasch feigned illness, and escaped to Mascara.

The Marshal was again thrown on his own resources. He propitiated the Emir by friendly offices. He sent him cannon and ammunition to assist him in the siege of Ain Maadi. These timely succours arrived there most opportunely; in fact they turned the scale of fortune, then trembling in the balance. But no concession was obtained. Abdel Kader felt himself in the right. He would not be put in the wrong.

He returned to Tekedemt, January 10th, 1839. His envoy, trembling and doubtful as to the reception he should receive, presented himself, to give an account of his late proceedings. When Abdel Kader learnt that he had affixed his seal to a document which gave away all for which he had been so long and so persistently contending, he was almost beside himself with vexation and anger. "Never," he exclaimed, "never will I ratify a convention which gives the French a land communication between Constantine and Algiers, and thus lose all the advantages I have gained by their oversight in circumscribing Algiers within a circle formed by the sea, the Chiffa, and the summits of the lesser Atlas, immediately above the Wady Kuddra."

The vacillating policy of the French Government had hitherto prevented it from taking any decisive step for the settlement of this interminable dispute. Now, it talked of confining the French occupation to Bona, Algiers, and Oran. Anon, it announced its intention of asserting its rights in the interior by force of arms. In the meantime Abdel Kader was hourly extending his dominion. Where was all this to end? The momentous question could no longer be avoided, and the French Government at last determined to act. Abdel Kader it could not reach. But his agents were within its grasp. It determined to operate on him through them.

By the treaty of the Tafna, Abdel Kader was clearly entitled to nominate what agents he pleased, to reside near the French authorities in all places occupied by French garrisons. These agents were now, under various pretences, arbitrarily ignored, or assailed with studied affronts. Some inoffensive Moors who wanted to go and settle on Abdel Kader's territory—a privilege which the treaty had secured to all Mussulmans—were rudely treated and violently detained within the French lines. A wheelwright whom Abdel Kader had long been in the habit of employing to make gun-carriages for him in Algiers, had his shop closed and was expelled the town.

By the 7th Article, Abdel Kader was entitled to be furnished with whatever arms or ammunition, or materials for war, he might require, by the French authorities, at cost price. His agent at Algiers was expressly instructed to facilitate such a transaction. He had been further useful in procuring for his master French mechanics from Paris, to superintend his various internal improvements, in strict conformity with the 10th Article. The agent was now suddenly arrested, put into chains, and sent to France. Abdel Kader appealed to Marshal Valée against such monstrous infringements of his rights. He was told the Marshal had unlimited authority, and could do what he pleased.

His consul at Algiers was a certain Italian, named Garavini, who was also consular agent for the United States of America. For nearly two years this agent had exercised this double function without molestation. He was now informed that the French Government refused to acknowledge him in the first capacity. Abdel Kader had just returned from Ain Maadi when he received this notification. He immediately penned the following letter to Marshal Valée :—

"The Prince of the Faithful, who defends by arms the cause of God, Il Hadj Abdel Kader, son of Mehi-ed-deen (whom God preserve in his holy keeping), to the Governor of Algiers. Grace be to those who conform themselves to the will of God.

"Our consul, Garavini, has informed us that he is no longer allowed to occupy himself with our affairs. You have written him a letter, of which he has sent me a copy. This letter we have read, and we have understood it. It prescribes to him to leave our service, and announces that you wish his place to be supplied by an Arab.

"In the first place, we cannot find any Arab who could perform his functions in such a manner as to give satisfaction to our two nations, and promote their reciprocal interests. Garavini is a wise and discreet man, who only upholds what may be advantageous to both parties. In the next place, France has no right to force us to take a consul against our will and inclination. It is for us to judge what is best for us to do. If you wish to name an Arab as your consul with us, do so. We shall offer no objection. Why do you interfere with our choice of agents ? Do we interfere with yours ? Your way of acting violates the sacred principles of honour which ought to animate our respective modes of proceeding.

" It would almost seem that you were desirous of seeing disorders once more prevail in the districts of Algiers and Oran. Individuals wishing to come and reside on our territory have not only been arbitrarily prevented, but have been fined, and thrown into prison. When our consul, Garavini, protested against such proceedings, you disdained to reply to him ; you would have nothing to say to him. Such conduct denotes violence of character. It shows that you desire to provoke misunderstandings between us and the French Government. We have chosen a Christian out of your own town, and you reject him !

" However, since usages are thus violated, since we are thwarted in what regards the good of our service, since there is evidently a design to lower us, we are ready for a rupture as soon as it may please you. All the world knows that we have chosen Garavini. We shall choose no other. Write to your ministry, therefore, that we mean to keep our consul Garavini. We expect an immediate answer.

" We hope France will send a more moderate man to command in Algiers, a man who will let us enjoy the fruits of peace, a man who will do what is just and reasonable. We had hoped that your mode of acting would not have been like that of some of those erring men who have preceded you. But if you choose to tread in the steps of such persons, God, be assured, will make us victorious over our enemies, over those who unjustly seek to molest us. God has said, ' Let injustice fall on the head of its author ; He has also said, ' It is better to be the oppressed than the oppressor.' As for us, we will not deviate an inch from the treaty, if you will only abide by it."

All the satisfaction Abdel Kader could obtain in reply to this able and spirited remonstrance, was that the French Government understood the 15th Article to mean that the consuls named by the Emir should be taken from amongst the Arabs, in the same way as the consuls named by the French Government were taken from amongst the French.

The extensile qualities of the Treaty of the Tafna seemed, in the eyes of the French authorities, to be as illimitable as their own powers of constructive reasoning. But they were, as yet, as far from their object as ever. Abdel Kader would neither be cajoled nor bullied. All their devices had failed. Matters had come to a dead lock.

CHAPTER XIII

MARSHAL VALÉE, notwithstanding his repeated failures, determined to make one more effort to obtain Abdel Kader's adhesion to the views taken by his Government on the disputed
article.   In the month of February, 1839, Commandant de
Salles was sent on a mission to the head-quarters of the
Sultan, who was then at Miliana.   The object of his mission
was to induce Abdel Kader to give his sanction and approval
to the supplementary treaty, which had been signed by his
enemy, Milond-ibn-Arasch.

Although a continuation of the peace was of vital importance to Abdel Kader, in order to enable him to complete his
work of organisation, yet to yield the disputed territory was
to him a moral and political impossibility.

Politically it was impossible to him, because the territory in question, once ceded to the French, would have given
them free means of communication between the provinces of
Algiers and Constantine, and would thereby have rendered
their possessions more compact, and proportionally augmented
their aggresive power.   Morally it was so also, because, not
only was it repugnant to his own sense of honour to yield up
tamely and submissively a point on which he felt himself to
be in the right, but the mainstay of his hourly-increasing
influence, gained by the almost magic success with which he
had gradually circumscribed the French to within-little more

than gunshot of their own fortresses, would have been dangerously imperilled by any such concession.

He had already repeatedly pacified many anxious inquirers, by the assurance that France would never dare to overstep the limits assigned to her in the plain of Algiers. It was on the strength of this assurance that the military and religious chiefs, convoked on the Habra, had consented to the peace. Without their consent, whatever might have been his own inclinations, he was precluded from listening to any modification of the treaty.

Already, too, sinister reports and insinuations were circulated by the fanatical party that he was secretly paying tribute to the French; that the infidels had received his permission to settle on the sacred soil of Islam, and that the tolerance of such a profanation was little consistent with his lofty boast that he would, ere long, drive them all into the sea.

Placed in this delicate position, Abdel Kader resolved on again convoking all the principal personages in his kingdom, and again calling on them to arbitrate on the differences existing between him and the French Government. The French commissioner was informed of this intention, and invited to attend the meeting, with full permission to enounce his propositions. He accepted the invitation, though with small hopes that he should be able to obtain from the Sultan's council of war, concessions which the pressure of his Government had failed to obtain from the Sultan himself.

The course of action which Abdel Kader thus adopted was, however, the only one which afforded any prospect for a peaceable adjustment of affairs. Marshal Valée had always ascribed Abdel Kader's pertinacity to his individual pride and ambition. His feelings of irritation at the manner in which all means of accommodation had been rejected, were increased by the inward conviction that the obstacles raised were the consequence of his adversary's personal caprice. Abdel Kader counted on his present proceeding to dispel the Marshal's delusion, if not to induce him to adopt a change of conduct. The Marshal would discover that it was not the sentiments of an individual, but those of a whole people, with which he was contending.

The council of war met. The French envoy spoke; but the decision was unanimous : " War, rather than give up the disputed territory." M. de Salles returned to Algiers to state the result of his mission. Abdel Kader, on his part, without waiting for further circumvolutions of policy in that direction, appealed at once to a higher quarter, and addressed the following letter to the King of the French :—

" Praise be to the One God!
"The servant of God, Il Hadj Abdel Kader, ibn Mehi-ed-
. deen, Commander of the Faithful, to H.M. Louis Philippe,
King of the French : may his reign be long, happy, and
full of glory.

" Since the foundation of Islamism, Mussulmans and Christians have been at war. For ages this was a sacred obligation on both sects ; but the Christians, neglecting their religion and its precepts, have finished by looking on war merely as a means of worldly aggrandisement.

"To the true Mussulman, on the contrary, war against the Christians is merely a religious obligation; how much more so when Christians come to invade Mussulman territory !

According to this principle, I deviated from the rules laid down in our sacred books, when, two years ago, I made with you, King of the Christians, a treaty of peace; and more especially when I endeavoured to consolidate this peace by every means in my power. You know the duties imposed by the Koran on every Mussulman prince; therefore you ought to give me credit for having taken upon myself to relax, as regards you, the rigour of its precepts.

" But you now demand a sacrifice from me which is too formally in contradiction with my religion to allow me to submit to it; and you are too just to impose it on me as a necessity. You call upon me to abandon tribes whose submission I have received; who came to me of themselves to pay me the imposts prescribed by the Koran, and who beseeched me, and still beseech me, to govern them. I have myself traversed their territory, *which, moreover, is beyond the limits of that which the treaty reserved to France;* and can you now wish, by another treaty, that I should order those tribes to submit to the yoke of the Christians?

" No. If the French are my friends, they can never desire to bring about a state of things which would lower and degrade their ally in the eyes of his people. They would not for the sake of a few miserable tribes, to govern which, themselves, or leave to others to govern, can be of very little moment to them, place me in the terrible alternative either of breaking the law, or of renouncing a peace which is so desirable for us both.

" But some may tell you that this consideration which forces me to reclaim those tribes will oblige me to reclaim the Arabs of Metija, of Oran, and of Constantine. No; for those have remained, and still remain, with the French of their own free will; and I have reserved to myself the right of giving an asylum to those amongst them who may become disgusted with Christian dominion. Whereas, the tribes in question, who are not nomad, but are attached to the soil, seek to be under my government, and are too numerous to allow of my giving them grounds in my territory equal to those they might wish to abandon.

"Great King of the French! God has appointed each of us to govern some of his creatures. You are in a position far superior to mine, by the number, power, and riches of your subjects; but on both of us he has imposed the obligation of making our people happy. Examine, then, with me our positions; and you will acknowledge that on you alone depends the happiness of both people.

"'Sign,' I am told by your agents; 'or if you do not sign, your refusal will be war.' Well, I will not sign; and yet I desire peace—nothing but peace.

"In order that a treaty should be useful to your subjects, it is necessary that I should be feared and respected by mine; for the moment they see that, according to my good pleasure, I hand them over to the administration of the Christians, they will no longer have any confidence in me, and then it will be impossible for me to make them observe the least clause in the treaty.

"How can you be compromised—you, Sultan of the French nation—by making concessions to a young Emir, whose power is now beginning to be strengthened and fortified under your shadow? Ought you not rather to protect me, to be indulgent towards me—me, who have re-established order amongst tribes which were slaying each other; who seek every day to raise in them a taste for the arts and for liberal professions? Help me, in the place of embarrassing me, and God will recompense you.

" If the war breaks out again, there will be no more commerce, which might confer such inestimable advantages on the country, and no more security for the colonists. There will be increased expenses, and diminished productions. The blood of your soldiers will be uselessly shed; it will be a partisan war to the death. . I have not the folly to suppose that I can openly make head against your troops; but I can harass them without ceasing. I shall lose ground, no doubt; but then I have on my side, knowledge of the country, the frugality and hardy temperament of my Arabs, and, more than all, the arm of God, who supports the oppressed.

" If, on the contrary, you wish for peace, our two countries will be as one; the least of your subjects will enjoy the most perfect security amongst the tribes; the two peoples will intermix more and more every day; and you will have the glory of having introduced into our countries that civilisation of which the Christians are the apostles.

" You will comprehend, I am sure, what I say; you will grant me what I ask; and what I ask is this,—that you do not see in a refusal to sign a new treaty, the desire of recommencing war, but rather the wish to consolidate the basis of the old one, and to confirm a sincere friendship between our nations.

" May God inspire you with an answer worthy of your power, and the goodness of your heart."

The almost supplicating earnestness of this simple and straightforward letter fully evinces the anxiety entertained by Abdel Kader at the aspect which affairs between himself and the French were now assuming, and his sense of the vast importance to himself of a continuation of the peace. On the 31st May, 1839, the ministry of M. Molé was overthrown. A false report had reached Algiers, that he had been replaced by M. Thiers, with Marshal Gerard as Minister of War.

Abdel Kader immediately wrote again to the king, and, at the same time, addressed two letters to the said ministers, with a power of language and a form of argument, which could only have emanated from a mind consoled and supported by the rectitude of its intention, and a firm and unshaken reliance in the justice of its cause.

LETTER TO THE KING.

" I have written you three letters, in which I gave you all my thoughts; not one of them has been honoured with an answer. They have been, doubtless, intercepted; for you are too kind and considerate not to have given me the satisfaction of knowing what were your true feelings and dispositions. May this, my last attempt, meet with better success ! May this exposition of what is passing in Africa attract and fix your attention, and lead to a system which shall conduce to the welfare and happiness of the two populations whom God has confided to your care and solicitude !

" The behaviour of your lieutenants is most unjust with regard to me; and I cannot suppose that it is known to you; I have too much confidence in your justice to suppose it. Endeavours are being made to induce you to regard me as your enemy. You are imposed on; if I were your enemy, I should already have found many causes for commencing hostilities.

" Since my refusal to sign the new treaty, presented to me by M. de Salles on the part of Marshal Valée (my motives for which I have already explained to you in one of my former letters), there is no kind of injustice with which I have not been assailed by your representatives at Algiers. My soldiers have been arrested and thrown into prison without any legal cause ; an order has been given not to allow the importation of any more iron, or brass, or lead, into my country ; my agents in Algiers have been ill-treated by the authorities ; my most important letters are answered by a simple receipt, cavalierly handed to the horseman who bears them ; letters written to me from Algiers are intercepted.

" After such treatment they tell you I am your enemy. They say that I want war at any price—I who desire, in every way, to follow the example of your industrious nation— I, who in spite of these tokens of hostility, facilitate the arrival of all the productions of my country into your markets —I who surround myself with Europeans, in order to give an impetus to industry, and who issue the most stringent orders that your merchants, and even your men of science, should not only be allowed to travel all over my country in perfect security, but be received and treated with hospitality.

" But you may be told—' The Emir has not yet fulfilled the first conditions imposed on him by the treaty of the Tafna.' To this I reply, I have only postponed the execution of these clauses, because your representative, Bugeaud, broke, in the first place, his engagements.

" Where are all the supplies of muskets, of powder, of lead, of sulphur, which were promised to me ? Why do I still see at Oran the chiefs of the Douairs and Zmelas, whose removal to France was solemnly promised me? Does Bugeaud think I have not yet in my possession the particular treaty, the only one which interests me, written out entirely in his own hand, and signed with his seal? Could I believe for an instant that written promises from the representative of the King of the French could possibly be invalid?

"I confess, I had so high an idea of the good faith of French Christians, that I was scandalised by their want of good faith, and that having had no direct communication with you, I refused to sign another treaty.

"Yes, your military deputies only wish for new combats and fresh conquests. I am certain this system is not yours. You have not descended on the shores of Africa to exterminate its inhabitants, nor to drive them from the country. You wished to bring them the benefits of civilisation. You came not to make a nation of slaves, but rather to implant amidst the people that spirit of liberty which is the most powerful lever of your own nation, and with which it has dowried so many other countries.

"Is it by the force of arms, is it by bad faith, that your agents will accomplish this end? Should the Arabs be at last convinced that you have come to attack their religion and conquer their country, their hatred will grow stronger than ever. They will break away from my control and authority, and our mutual prospects of civilisation will vanish away for ever.

"I pray and entreat you then, in the name of God, who has created us both, to try and understand a little better this young Arab, whom the Most High has placed, despite himself, at the head of a simple and ignorant people, and who is falsely represented to you as being an ambitious chief. Make him acquainted with your intentions. Above all, communicate with him directly, and his conduct will prove to you that he has been badly appreciated.

" May God grant you the light necessary to govern your people wisely."

The letter to M. Thiers was couched in the following terms:—

" I congratulate France on your return to the ministry. The important labours which formerly signalised your presence in it, apd the interest you always bear towards Algiers, make me salute you with joy.

" Your countrymen who are about me have informed me that your post is charged more especially with watching and superintending the prosperity of France. A part of Africa is become French. In speaking to you of the dangers which menace the prosperity of the two countries, I perform a duty.

" Counsellor of the King of the French, it is for your enlightenment, it is for your philanthropy, to strengthen and consolidate a peace which France and Algiers both demand.

" The despotic caprices of the agents of an honoured Government, the failures in the execution of a treaty on the one side, leading to similar failures on the other; and the greedy and unprincipled ambitions of some, who aim at new spheres of riches and emoluments, threaten to mingle French and Arab blood, when, to my belief, the real truth is, that we all long for a peace which will bring to the Arabs the precious results of progress and civilisation, and to France the glory of having conferred them.

" You are great for France—be so for Africa; and both

countries will bless you. Your influence with a king, whose minister you are, and your counsels to a young Emir— entirely ignorant of the intricacies of European politics—are the materials with which you might erect a monument of glory for your own nation, and one of happiness and gratitude for mine.

"May God assist and enlighten you, and maintain you in the high position of which you are so worthy!"

The letter to Marshal Gerard was not less admirably conceived. It ran as follows :—

"As soon as I was informed that the powerful King of the French had made you Minister of War, I had reason to be rejoiced. I felt that one who has nothing to add to his military glory, could never look to the French occupation in Africa as his sole field for military distinction. One who, like you, knows how to make war, must also know how to make peace, and to enjoy its fruits.

"This peace is menaced; and wherefore? For the sake of a few leagues of ground, and a road impracticable from its natural difficulties. Has not France sufficient military glory —has it not space enough—that it should seek to acquire more at the expense of my influence over Arabs, whom I have bound myself to keep in submission?

"My religion prevents me from violating my engagements. Why, then, seek, without any necessity, to lower me in the eyes of my co-religionists by calling on me to give over and place under French administration populations, to whom it is my duty, by the injunctions of our law, to preach the holy war? Let those who would compel me to do so try to understand my religion, and the obligations which it imposes

N

upon me; and then, perhaps, they may be inclined to give me credit for the sacrifices I am making.

" I approach you, then, to call your attention to the exactments of a local administration, which I refuse to believe can be guided in its acts by the wishes of France and of its chief. The French are too great to inspire the vexatious meannesses to which my subjects are constantly exposed in their relations with your representatives at Algiers. My dignity has obliged me to suspend these relations in part. When I saw that they were anxious enough to take the produce of our soil, but refused to supply the iron necessary for cultivating it, I said to them, ' Sell, but buy no more ; God who has given us land has also placed in our mountains all the metals which our pretended civilisers refuse us.'

" I pray to God, that your powerful influence with the king may be employed in seconding my pacific views ; and that you and his noble son may, for the sake of self-information, come and visit this country, and meet with him whom you wrongly look upon as your enemy. Then your penetration and your genius, finding in me only sincerity and the desire of doing good, will assist me in moderating, either by civilisation or by arms, the fanaticism of populations who are only just beginning to appreciate the advantages of peace and industry.

" May God make your armies victorious so long as they fight in the true cause."

These were noble words—words well worthy of being recorded. They were noble in the grandeur of their appeal—noble, as indicating the heroic struggle which rent and lacerated the breast of one conscious of his powers, burning with great designs, and painfully oscillating between a nervous anxiety to prolong a peace which would have enabled him to exhibit before the world a Mohammedan kingdom at its highest possible pitch of progress and development, and the lofty determination to abandon even this his heart's desire, and to waive the brilliant future, if such objects could only be attained by a craven submission, however temporary, to the imperious dictates of an overbearing and unprincipled ambition.

Such appeals, it may be well imagined, were entirely thrown away on a government which, finding itself entangled in a labyrinth, and thus fettered in the realisation of its secret views, was bent on adopting any measures likely to deliver it from its embarrassing position, however inconsistent they might be with good faith.

Thus, whilst Abdel Kader was still fondly dreaming over the possible fulfilment of plans and projects, meant to harmonise and combine the requirements of Mohammedanism with the advantages of European intercourse, and the fruits of European civilisation, the subtle and powerful enemy with whom he was coping was already meditating a line of action which was destined, before long, to scatter those plans and projects to the winds.

Both parties, it is true, wished for peace; but whereas the one sought for it as a temporary expedient, the other clung to it as a vital principle. Both were bound to their respective people by pledges and obligations, from which they could not recede. Abdel Kader had vowed to keep the French at his sword's point, in every case of unjustifiable aggression. His attitude was clear and unequivocal; it embodied the strength and the simplicity of truth.

The French Government, on the other hand, had officially and falsely declared to the Chambers, that the difficulties which had been raised about the Treaty of the Tafna had been explained to the advantage of France, and that the possession of the disputed territory was henceforth assured. The pen had easily traced such words, and the mouth had freely spoken them. But it required the sword to make good and establish this foregone conclusion.

The state of doubt and uncertainty had now reached its utmost limit. The period of compliments, of evasions, of hollow friendship, of hypocritical alliance, had passed away. The co-existence of **Abdel Kader** and **France** on the soil of Algeria was henceforth impossible. Freed from the entanglements of diplomatic garniture, the gladiators again stood face to face, ready to descend into the arena.

MARSHAL VALÉE, while informing his Government of the inutility of all his efforts to induce Abdel Kader to yield to his remonstrances, made proposals of his own as to the best mode of action to be pursued.

"The Government," he suggested, "might either assume a defensive attitude, protesting against the Emir's seizure of the disputed territory, and trusting to time and friendly offices to make him relax his hold; or it might attack him at once; or, again, it might place a force on the ground in question, intimating to the Emir that such a measure was not intended as a hostile demonstration, but merely as a joint occupation whilst the final arrangement was still pending."

The Government accepted the last proposition, with the modification, that, instead of the permanent occupation of Hamzé and its neighbourhood, a corps should merely traverse the country, and that if the Emir resented such a proceeding, explanations might be given.

The Duke of Orleans had lately arrived at Algiers. In order to give the projected movement a greater degree of importance, it was arranged that he should superintend its execution. An expedition was to start from Milah, in the province of Constantine, penetrate the pass of the "Iron Gates," cross the disputed territory, and thence onwards to

Algiers. All the secrecy necessary for the accomplishment of a stratagem of war was used in order to give effect to the project.

A demonstration was made towards Boujie. The Kabyles rushed to that quarter to defend their country against the threatened invasion. The Marshal and the Prince left Milah on the 18th October, 1839, and going in an opposite direction, reached Setif on the 21st. Here, also, the Kabyles presented themselves. Their sheiks demanded an interview. Admitted to an audience with the French generals, they were shown passports, bearing Abdel Kader's seal, authorising the passage of French troops, and they were satisfied. These passports were an artifice—Abdel Kader's seal had been forged!

In place of entering the Kabyle mountains, the column which had been moved towards Boujie was countermarched, and joining the Marshal, advanced with him in the direction of the " Iron Gates." The country was mountainous and intricate ; but the Kabyle chiefs, serving as guides, were all delighted to · facilitate the progress of the friends and allies of their Sultan. Under these auspicious circumstances the expedition, amounting to nearly 5,000 men, passed through the formidable defile of the " Iron Gates " without firing a shot. Had Abdel Kader been there with but 500 men, they would either never have entered it, or never emerged from it.

The next day the French passed through the Kabyle tribe, Beni Munsoor, who stared at them as if they had dropped from the clouds. On the 31st the column reached Ben Ini. There, at last, the French and Kabyles exchanged shots. Ben Salem, the Emir's Khalifa over that district, starting, as from a troubled dream, when informed of the approach of the

French, had just had sufficient time to make a tardy and useless demonstration against the invaders. On the 1st of November the Prince and the Marshal made a triumphal entry into Algiers, and were greeted with loud acclamations. The festivities to celebrate the event lasted four whole days. A splendid entertainment was given on the esplanade of the Bab-el-Oued to the heroes of the " Iron Gates." Enthusiastic toasts were drunk in their honour. A palm wreath, plucked and woven in the pass itself, was formally presented to the Prince. Algeria was supposed to be conquered. It was the triumph of Caligula over the cockle-shells of Britain.

The idea on the part of the French Marshal had been that Abdel Kader might possibly write an angry letter or two on hearing of this unexpected irruption, that explanations would be given, and that there the matter would end. He was soon undeceived. The news of the passage of the " Iron Gates " reached Abdel Kader at Tekedemt. In eight-and-forty hours, by riding night and day, he was at Medea, and on the 4th of November he sent off the following dispatch to Marshal Valée :—

" We were at peace, and the limits between your country and mine were clearly defined, when the King's son set out with a *corps d'armée* to go from Constantine to Algiers ; and this was done without giving me the slightest intimation, without even writing me a line to explain away such a violation of territory. If you had informed me that he had an intention of visiting my country, I would either have accompanied him myself, or sent one of my Khalifas to do so. But, so far from that, you have proclaimed that all the country between Algiers and Constantine is no longer under my orders.

The rupture comes from you. Nevertheless, that you may not accuse me of treachery, I give you warning that I am about to recommence the war. Prepare yourself, then ; warn all your travellers, your garrisons, your stations; in a word, take all the precautions you deem necessary."

To his Khalifa Ben Salem, who had written for instructions how he was to act, he addressed words of consolation and encouragement in the following terms :—

"The rupture comes from the Christians ! Your enemy is before you. Gather up your banners, and prepare for battle. On all sides the signal for the holy war is given. You are the man of these parts. I place you there to bar their entrance.

" Beware of being disconcerted. Tighten your waist-band, and be ready for everything. Rise to the height of events. Above all, learn patience. Let human vicissitudes find you impassible. They are trials—God sends them. Such trials are blended with the destiny of every good Mussulman who vows to die for his faith. Victory, please God, shall crown your perseverance. Salutation from Abdel Kader ibn Mehi-ed-deen."

In similar words of sterling import, his other Khalifas were summoned to instant action.

"Treason has burst upon us from the infidel," wrote Abdel Kader. "The proofs of his perfidy are glaring. He has traversed my territory without my leave. Gather up your burnous, tighten your waist-bands for battle—it is at hand. The public treasury is not rich; you yourselves have not sufficient money to hand to make war. Levy, therefore, as soon as you get the orders, an extraordinary impost. Be quick in action, and hasten to join me at Medea, where I am awaiting you."

Valée was loth to believe that all hopes of accommodation were irrecoverably gone, and still more loth to enter into a struggle for which he was wholly unprepared. The French colonists in the plain of Algiers were utterly defenceless. No precautions whatever had been taken for their safety and protection; as if Abdel Kader's terrible daring, promptness, and activity were things hitherto unfelt and unknown. Even whilst the storm was hourly gathering on the mountains before his eyes, Valée contented himself with reporting home, and sending the Jew Durand on a mission to Medea, with a letter to Abdel Kader. This missive concluded with these words :—

"Have a little patience; I expect orders from Paris; the affair will yet be satisfactorily arranged."

On the very day that Durand arrived at Medea, Nov. 14th, 1839, the Khalifas, assembled together according to orders, were holding a grand military council, presided over by the Sultan himself. Durand was introduced, and the Marshal's letter was read aloud. An agitated discussion ensued, ending in an unanimous cry for war.

"You are wrong," said Durand. "France is a powerful country. You have had experience of her armies. You know how great is her strength, and how vast are her resources. You will be defeated."

"Then how long," exclaimed Abdel Kader, "are we still to endure the insults of the Christians? They have given us proofs upon proofs of their bad faith."

"I assure you," said Durand, "you do wrong to get angry

about a trifle. The French have no wish to deceive you, or to quarrel with you; and if the King's son has passed through your country, it was only on a journey of pleasure."

The council adjourned till the following day. Abdel Kader and Durand remained together alone.

The latter now endeavoured to convince his sovereign of the risks and dangers he would incur by involving himself in another war. He expatiated on the rawness of the troops which Abdel Kader had at his command, his feeble resources, and the internal agitations which, more or less, at all times fettered his actions, as opposed to the military strength and discipline, and the unity and concentration of purpose, which enabled the French to triumph over every obstacle.

"All that I know," said Abdel Kader. "But my Khalifas loudly call for war. My people already look upon me as an infidel because I have not yet commenced it. I do not desire war. It is the French who are urging me into it."

The council met again; and again there was but one voice, and that was for war—the holy war.

"Be it so," said Abdel Kader, "since such is your desire. But I accede to your wishes on one condition alone. You are going to be exposed to fatigues, to hardships, to trials and reverses. You may despond, grow weary of the contest, repent. Swear to me, then, on the sacred book of God, that so long as I wave the standard of the Djehad, you will never desert me."

The chiefs and Khalifas all swore.

On the 18th November, 1839, Abdel formally declared war against the French, in the following letter to Marshal Valée:—

" Il Hadj Abdel Kader, Prince of the Faithful, to Marshal Valée.

" Peace and happiness on those who follow the path of truth.

" Your first and your last letters have reached us. We have read and understood them. I have already informed you that all the Arabs, from Ouelassa as far as Kef, are unanimous for the holy war. I have done all in my power to appease them, but in vain. There is not a voice for peace. All are preparing for war. I must conform to the general opinion, in obedience to our sacred law. I am acting loyally by you in thus informing you of what is passing. Send me back my consul who is in Oran, that he may return to his family. Be prepared. All the Mussulmans declare the holy war. Whatever may happen, you cannot accuse me of treachery. My heart is pure, and never will you find me acting contrary to justice.

" Written this Monday evening, at Medea, 11 Ramadan, 1255 (18th Nov., 1839).

" P.S.—When I wrote to the king, he replied that you had the direction of all affairs, both for peace and war. I choose war, as well as all the Mussulmans. Consider yourself hereby warned, and answer as you think proper. It is for you to speak, and no other."

The lightning had darted from the cloud, and the storm burst. Such was the admirable concert which pervaded the measures of Abdel Kader, that in a few hours, from the heights of Beni Sala he saw his Arabs and Kabyles spreading themselves all over the plains of Algiers. Fresh relays came pouring down from the mountains on every side. The defiles and gorges of the Atlas bristled with horse and foot. They came rolling onwards like a mighty avalanche bursting its barriers and rushing on the plains below.

The Khalifas of Medea and Miliana at the head of their bands crossed the Cheliff. Ben Salem and his Kabyles closed in on the devoted French stations and colonies from the east; the Hadjouts came raging on from the west. The French cantonments, their agricultural establishments, their model farms, their scattered outposts, were presently overwhelmed and destroyed by the resistless and relentless cataclysm. The smoke of blazing villages darkened the air. In many, the colonists were massacred. Flying from others, the wretched fugitives were pursued to the very gates of Algiers.

There the consternation surged and swelled like a tornado. The native population menaced insurrection. Rumours, magnified into imagined realities, filled every breast with alarm and terror. The wildest and most impossible suggestions were received and treated as facts. Abdel Kader was said to be advancing at the head of 30,000 men, preceded by 5,000 pioneers to sap the walls. The houses in the suburbs were evacuated. The Marshal's house, in the quarter of Mustapha Pacha, was dismantled. The barracks bearing the same name were loopholed. For weeks the terror and dismay went on increasing. Officers swept the horizon with their telescopes, and were obliged to remain helpless spectators of the scenes of devastation which spread before them. Provisions at length fell short. Famine aggravated the horrors of distress and fear.

Now, like an eagle soaring from his eyrie, Abdel Kader hovered over the field of carnage. Hordes of Kabyles followed in his train. These hardy warriors, electrified by his appeals, had sworn to carry him triumphantly into the heart of Algiers. Relying on their prowess and devotion, he had solemnly fixed the day when his horse should drink at the waters of Bab-el-Oued. But before leading them against the redoubtable ramparts of the town itself, he resolved to essay their firmness and resolution against the fort Boudourou.

The Kabyles rushed impetuously to the attack, but the cannon balls which mowed down their ranks filled them with unaccustomed terror. They vacillated, broke, retreated, and dispersed. Abdel Kader felt his prey had eluded his grasp, and, in a paroxysm of grief and indignation, exclaimed, as he looked at their broken ranks, " These, then, are the proud Kabyles! May their vows be ever confounded. May their prayers be never heard. May they live in misery and contempt. May they fall to that degree of wretchedness, that a miserable Jew may have them at his feet." And he returned to his heights.

Marshal Valée had at last awakened to a sense of his situation. Blidah and Bouffarick, at the foot of the Atlas, were hastily strengthened and reinforced. A few thousand troops were sent out in detachments to protect what remained of the ravaged colonial settlements. Urgent dispatches to the Home Government fully stated the extent of the recent disasters. The ministry ostentatiously declared their adoption of a firm and irrevocable policy. Algeria was announced to be " henceforth and for ever a French province."

Reinforcements rapidly arrived at Algiers, and the effective force of Marshal Valée was soon raised to 30,000 combatants. It was for him so to handle them as to make a permanent impression on his restless and indefatigable enemy. The system adopted by his predecessors—of sudden incursions, followed by as sudden retreats—was abandoned. His plan of attack comprised three elements of action. These were—to seize and destroy the strongholds which Abdel Kader had erected, and with them his arsenals, his magazines, his stores; to attack and annihilate his regulars, the mainstay of his power; and to occupy permanently the districts inhabited by the principal Arab tribes, and by thus showing them how wholly unable their Sultan was to defend or protect them, to destroy his influence and power.

Abdel Kader was at this moment virtually the sovereign of all Algeria with the exception of the towns on the sea-coast. Oran and Tittery were his by treaty. The tribes stretching along the south of the province of Constantine acknowledged his sway. The Sahara, for the most part, obeyed his mandates. Nominally, 70,000 cavalry were at his beck; although in reality he could only depend on the Arab contingents who were directly controlled by his Khalifas, or who were within the sweep of his arm. His fighting force was about 30,000 cavalry, regular and irregular, and 6,000 regular infantry.

Concentrating his force at Blidah, at the foot of the lesser Atlas, Valée prepared to carry his first offensive movement into effect, by marching on Medea and Miliana. The river Chiffa was passed on the 27th April, 1840. The Sultan's cavalry now appeared in considerable numbers. The right wing of the French army extended towards a lake, but without reaching it. Abdel Kader threw his squadrons into the intermediate space, passed on, and disappeared. The plain of Algiers thus became exposed to his blows; and for some time it was thought that he was advancing, in that direction, sweeping everything before him. But the movement had only been a feint. The object of Abdel Kader was to force Valée to abandon his march along the valley of the Cheliff, and to oblige him to enter the mountains by the gorges of the Mouzaia. In this purpose he succeeded.

He had been for months labouring night and day to render these formidable passes still more formidable by all the appliances of art. It was here, he declared, the French army should find its grave. Every available height and eminence had been cut into entrenchments. A redoubt with heavy batteries crowned the highest peak. In its immediate vicinity were placed his regular infantry—the battalions of Medea, Miliana, Mascara, Sebaou, and Tekedemt, officered by French deserters. Arabs and Kabyles swarmed in all directions, and, crouched in nooks and crevices, stood ready to open a dropping fire on the French column, as it wound its way with staid and heavy tread along the narrow causeway which hung midway on the mountain slopes.

Valée divided his force into three columns. These were led by Duvivier, Lamoricière, and D'Hautpoul. To the astonishment of the Arabs, the French, leaving the road, came vaulting over the steeps. Ravines, woods, and rocks were all equally mastered by them. Slowly but surely they were reaching the entrenchments. Suddenly a thick mist enveloped the scene. The firing was incessant. It flashed and sparkled through the vapoury panoply like the coruscations of a phosphorescent sea. The mist rolled away. The combatants had met. They fought hand to hand. The Arabs and Kabyles clung with desperation to their hiding-places. The French clambered up, grasping at shrubs, branches, and sprigs. They appeared able to surmount every difficulty before them.

There still remained the grand redoubt. Abdel Kader here made a last stand in person. His regulars and masses of the Kabyles rallied round him. The converging columns of the French came creeping on. The roll of drums and the clang of trumpets resounded on every side. The Arabs were bewildered by the ubiquity of their foes. Alike attacked in front and menaced in rear, they wavered, broke, and fled. Lamoricière and his Zouaves, Changarnier and the 2nd Light Infantry burst over the entrenchments. The tricolour waved on the highest summit of the Atlas.

Abdel Kader retreated on Miliana. On arriving there he found the inhabitants in the very act of deserting the town. Placing himself in the gateway, he drew his sword, and threatened to cut down the first that crossed his path. The panic ceased. The people returned. ·Valée, in the meantime, entered Medea, and found it abandoned and half burnt.

Abdel Kader had made his last attempt to fight the French on the principles of European warfare. It had failed. He never repeated the experiment. All his Khalifas and chiefs received orders never again to encounter the French in masses, but to confine themselves to harassing them, hanging on their flanks and rear, cutting off their communications, falling on their baggage and transports, and, by feigned retreats, by ambuscades, by sudden and unexpected sallies, perplexing, wearying, and bewildering them.

Valée, after leaving a garrison in Medea, under Duvivier, prepared to return to the plains. He advanced on Miliana, which Abdel Kader at once evacuated. But when the French column took its departure and entered the mountain passes, Abdel Kader quickly resumed his ascendancy, and by unceasing attacks, day and night, compelled it to emerge from its perilous position at the sacrifice of whole companies annihilated, baggage captured, and wounded abandoned.

It now became necessary for the French to re-victual their garrisons in Medea and Miliana. This dangerous task was entrusted to Changarnier, who accomplished it with consummate skill and daring, whilst his troops were running a gauntlet of fire. Closely blockaded by Abdel Kader, these garrisons had led a life of privation and suffering difficult to portray. The Arabs and Kabyles occupied all the surrounding country. They attacked the French foraging parties. The most daring and vigorous sorties, though scaring them for the moment, made no permanent impression on their vulture-like tenacity. In the month of October, 1840, the garrison of Miliana had nearly disappeared under the complicated effects of famine, fever, and nostalgia. Out of 1,500 men, 750 were dead, 500 were in the hospital, and the remainder, poor crawling skeletons, could hardly hold their muskets.

Not only in the mountains of Tittery did Abdel Kader hold the French in his iron grasp. From the frontiers of Morocco to those of Tunis he kept them constantly at bay, counteracting or nullifying their operations by his almost superhuman efforts. Ever in the saddle, sudden and mysterious in his movements, to-day engaged with the French, on the morrow a hundred miles off, rallying and inspiriting a flagging tribe of Arabs—he seemed, with his constitution of iron, to dispense with rest or repose; as though his body had become in a manner etherealised by the fiery soul within.

CHAPTER XV.

1841—1842.

WITH the year 1841 commenced the real and decisive struggle. The French, with too exclusive reliance on their superiority in discipline and resources, calculated that it would terminate in a few months. Owing to the unimagined means of resistance evoked and wielded by the great chief who defied them, it was destined yet to last, with alternate vicissitudes of success, for six years.

On the 22nd of February, 1841, General Bugeaud assumed the functions of Governor-General of Algeria. Abdel Kader regarded the appointment as a hopeful presage. He would have little difficulty, he conceived, in coming to a good understanding with one who had already sanctioned and confirmed his claims to regal power. One of his most famous predecessors, Ouchba-ibn-Naifé, lieutenant of the Caliph Mouaiah, towards the close of the seventh century, after having led his victorious Arabs from Alexandria to Morocco, had signed a treaty with the Christian Emperor of Constantinople, by which he was to be paramount ruler in the interior, while the latter was to be content with holding the towns along the coast.

Such was the arrangement which Abdel Kader had always fondly hoped to see established between himself and the

French Government. He thought it not impossible that the new Governor-General might be induced to support and promote such a solution of existing difficulties. Bugeaud's first proclamation quickly undeceived him. The General therein declared that his opinions on Algerian affairs were completely changed. So far from the French occupation being limited, it was to be extended. Every rival power was to be crushed.

In truth, the French Government had at length taken the measure of their formidable adversary, and had placed 85,000 men at Bugeaud's disposal. With such an imposing force it was anticipated that Abdel Kader would soon be beaten and driven out of the field.

But the great difficulty was not so much to defeat Abdel Kader as to overtake him. The French were stronger; but he was lighter. The former moved along beaten routes in long columns, encumbered with artillery, ambulances, and baggage. The latter seeing his enemy's point of attack, evaded him for the moment, and then fell on him when at fault, entangled in ravines and lost amidst precipices. With the Romans, the French might truly say, " Nostros asperitas et insolentiæ loci retinebant.".

Bugeaud altered the tactics of his predecessors. Movable columns winding in various directions obliged Abdel Kader to disseminate his forces, and kept him dubious and uncertain. Heavy baggage and heavy ordnance were abandoned. Recesses hitherto unapproachable, became accessible. Even the commissariat was dispensed with.

The Arabs had one immense advantage over the French. Wherever they went they found provisions. The *silos* scattered over the land afforded them a never-failing resource. The French had to carry their provisions with them. The difference was serious and important. Lamoricière solved the problem. " The Arabs carry no provisions," said that General, " why should we ? " And he forthwith took the field for a month.

His men carried a few portable hand-mills. On reaching a given tract of country, they spread themselves out in skirmishing order, sometimes a league in extent. They probed the ground before them, as they advanced, with their swords and bayonets. The stones concealing the underground granaries were struck. They had been but loosely and scantily covered with earth. The *silos* were discovered. Razzias procured sheep. The hand-mills converted corn into flour ; and thus the French troops found themselves provisioned on the very spot where they stood.

Bugeaud's military operations were based on the double principle of conservation and aggression. The main objects of his tactics consisted in re-victualling his garrisons, which barely held their own amidst the ever-active foes surrounding them on every side ; in keeping in subjection the Arab tribes who had already surrendered to his arms, by giving them an efficient organisation under French officers,—in overawing others by inexorable razzias and ruthless burning of their crops ; and, lastly, in striking, without pause or cessation, at Abdel Kader's power in all its vital parts, by occupying his strong positions, destroying his arsenals, rasing his fortresses, with the hope of forcing him back, by continual pressure, into the wilds of the Sahara.

The campaign of 1841 opened with a second re-victualling

of Medea and Miliana. The losses of the French, before they effected that object, were immense. Abdel Kader disputed every inch of the ground. Bugeaud had gone to the province of Oran. From Mostaganem he led in person an expedition against Tekedemt. On reaching it, May 25th, he found it deserted and partly in flames. Boghar, Saida, and Taza, were successively destroyed.

Abdel Kader, faithful to his lately-adopted system, had determined not to waste his forces in vain attempts to defend his fortresses. He abandoned them all. His regular army was more usefully and successfully employed in harassing the French on their lines of march, or in keeping wavering tribes to their allegiance. In the new style of warfare which he was now called upon to confront, walled towns were an encumbrance to him—impediments, in fact, of which he felt glad to be relieved.

The following characteristic letter, addressed by him about this time to General Bugeaud, admirably portrays the buoyancy of spirit which animated him at a period when everything seemed to indicate his hopeless and irretrievable ruin :—

" What is that craving thus urging France, which calls itself a strong and peaceful nation, to come and make war against us? Has she not sufficient territory? What harm can all she has taken do us, compared with what still remains to us? She will advance, we will retire ; but she, in her turn, will be obliged to retire ; and then we shall return.

" And you, the Governor-General, what injury can you do us? In battle you lose as many men as we do. Your army is yearly decimated by disease. What compensation do you think you can offer your king and your country for your enormous losses in men and money ?   A tract of ground, and the stones of Mascara!

"You burn, you ravage our crops, you pillage our *silos*. But what signifies to us the loss of the plain of Eghrees, of which you have not ravaged even a twentieth part, when we possess so many others ?   The ground you take from us is but as a drop of water taken from the sea. We will fight you just when we think proper ; and you know we are not cowards.

" As to our opposing the forces you drag after you, it would be folly.   But we will harass them ; we will wear them out ; we will cut them up in detail ; the climate will do the rest. Does the wave cease to rise and swell when a bird skims it ?   That is the image of your passage in Africa."

The French had, indeed, already reason to shrink from the task before them.   What with the losses entailed upon them by marches and counter-marches, by incessant fighting, by blasting heats, their army had nearly vanished away. Bugeaud, at the close of the year 1841, had to report, that of 60,000 men, he had only 4,000 fit for duty.

The French Government again sought relief in projects of peace.   If the Emir would raise the blockade of the French garrisons, and nominally lay down his arms (it being understood, at the same time, that 30,000 stand should be secretly paid for), all his former rights would be confirmed, it said, all the territory taken from him restored.   Abdel Kader laughed at the proposition.   "Let the French keep the towns," he replied.   "Will the towns give them food ? So long as I hold the country, and can attack and intercept their convoys, my position will still be superior to theirs."

The very fact, that a proposal for peace had been first

broached by the French themselves, confirmed Abdel Kader in his resolution to try the extremities of war. He had already twice reduced them to terms, before his fortresses and arsenals existed. The elements he then wielded still remained to him, even after the loss of these strongholds, and, in truth, were even more effective than before. The Arab tribes had been organised; they moved by a common impulse; they expanded and contracted by word of command; when least dreaded, they attacked; when pursued, they disappeared. Such was henceforth to be the formidable but ever fluctuating principle of Abdel Kader's operations.

To break the links of this well-compacted chain, and destroy the influence which held it together, by establishing permanent centres of action in the very heart of the Arab confederation, and by rapidly consecutive expeditions radiating from these centres, to give his troops the ubiquity of the Arabs, became Bugeaud's main object.

It was determined that the province of Oran, as the chief seat of Abdel Kader's power, should henceforward be regarded as the principal scene of operations. Lamoricière occupied Mascara; Bedeau held Tlemsen; Changarnier watched the western frontier of the plain of Algiers; D'Aumale menaced Tittery. All these were men of promise, able, bold, enterprising, successful; but destined, at a later period, to experience the fickleness of fortune.

Three columns moving from Oran and Mostaganem were despatched to act upon the tribes occupying the vast extent of territory between the sea and the Atlas, as well as those extending towards the Sahara. The first, headed by Bugeaud in person, advanced along the valley of the Cheliff, and then made its junction with the second column under Changarnier, which had started from Blidah. The third column, commanded by Lamoricière, aimed at pushing Abdel Kader back to the south, with the view of isolating him from the tribes attacked by Bugeaud and Changarnier.

Now commenced those wonderful episodes, thrilling in their effect, sublime in their grandeur, as marvels of daring and genius, by which Abdel Kader stamped this glorious struggle in which he was engaged with the impress of his own extraordinary individuality.

Lamoricière, zealously acting up to the instructions given him, to pursue and overtake the Sultan, was always fancying himself on the traces of his object. Suddenly he heard that Abdel Kader was before Mascara. When he had contrived to arrive by forced marches at that place, he was told that Abdel Kader had passed by the rear of his column, and was making a razzia on the Borgia tribes.

Again came the pursuit, and again Abdel Kader, by a bold and rapid manœuvre, leaving his bewildered foes behind him, dashed across the Cheliff, placed himself between Bugeaud and the sea, recovered his ascendancy over the tribes who had deserted him in that direction, made another sweeping razzia to the south of Miliana, and then, rushing back to the Sahara, showed himself there in full force, just as the French had returned, in despair of finding him, to their cantonments.

By ever-recurring evolutions of this nature, slipping between the enemy's columns, flitting in their front, hovering on their flank, falling on their rear, never at fault, never discouraged, sometimes in the mountains, sometimes in the plains, disconcerting and rendering abortive the most scientific military combinations, Abdel Kader amply compensated for the disparity of his means, and counterbalanced the manifold disadvantages under which he laboured.

Leaving to his Khalifas in Oran the duty of carrying on the desultory kind of warfare which he had so rigidly prescribed, Abdel Kader now repaired to the Traara Mountains on the frontiers of Morocco. The military skill and diplomatic aptitude of Bedeau had imposed obedience on many of the frontier tribes. Abdel Kader saw his communications with Morocco menaced, and it was from Morocco that he drew, for the most part, his arms, his clothing, his ammunition, not, as has been erroneously stated, by splendid and gratuitous grants from Sultan Abderahman, but by the ordinary course of commercial transactions.

The Kabyles of Nedrouma, once his most devoted partisans, had, amongst others, submitted to the French general. The sight of Abdel Kader amongst them at once rekindled all their former loyalty and enthusiasm. They prayed for forgiveness ; they asked to be allowed to wipe out their shame on the field of glory. The Beni Snassen, and other frontier tribes, followed their example, and rallied again around his standard. These, in addition to his own regulars, gave him about 3,000 cavalry and 5,000 infantry,—a force sufficient to confront the enemy.

During the months of March and April, 1842, the hills and valleys of the Traara and Nedrouma Mountains, the banks of the Tafna and the Sickak, became the scenes of constant encounters between him and General Bedeau. The fate of the campaign still hung doubtfully in the balance, when Abdel Kader was summoned to the environs of Mascara.

Despite the precautions of his brother-in-law, Mustapha-ibn-Tamy, of Il Berkani, and of Sidi Embarak, his most illustrious chiefs, Lamoricière was gaining ground. Several tribes had gone over; a large portion even of the Hashems, his own tribe, had been carried away by the contagious example. Lamoricière, imagining Abdel Kader to be sufficiently occupied by Bedeau, had extended his excursions towards the Sahara. Abdel Kader seized the opportune occasion to re-assert and enforce his power amongst the tribes who had deserted him around Mascara. But, with due discrimination, he drew a line between wilful treason and unavoidable secession. Wherever there were proofs of collusion with the French, of treasonable correspondence, of active participation, his punishments were severe and unsparing. Terrible, indeed, were, at times, the examples he made of tribes who, by their premeditated alliance with the infidel, had justly drawn down upon themselves the fearful punishment awarded by the Koran upon traitors to their religion and their God.

Lamoricière hurried back in all haste on hearing of the Sultan's re-appearance on his own field of operations. But he had to re-conquer all the territory he had lately gained. To his surprise, tribes, which had but recently joined him, now stood coalesced against him. Fighting his way galiantly through all obstacles, he eagerly sought to measure his sword with the moving genius of this unexpected revival. He heard that Abdel Kader was in force at Tekedemt, and on Tekedemt he forthwith marched.

He arrived there, indeed, but just in time to learn that Abdel Kader had fallen on Changarnier in the direction of Miliana. That general, counting on the absence of his redoubtable foe, was there engaged in the comparatively easy task of subduing some refractory tribes. One day he found himself enveloped with an overwhelming force of Arabs and Kabyles, horse and foot, regulars and irregulars, led on by Abdel Kader in person, and rushing furiously to the combat.

For two days and nights the battle raged incessantly. The combatants engaged in deadly strife, hand to hand and foot to foot with pistols, swords, yataghans, or bayonets. Suddenly the combat ceased. Abdel Kader drew off his army and disappeared. The French had suffered too severely and were too exhausted to follow him up. Two days afterwards news reached them to the effect that Abdel Kader had dashed into the Metija, was ravaging the plains, and carrying terror to the very gates of Algiers.

Bearing away to his right, after performing this exploit, Abdel Kader ascended the Atlas, penetrated to the Ouarensis, beyond Tittery, and reached the Sahara. Everywhere he occupied himself in arousing populations, inspiriting tribes, and organising contingents. After sweeping over a space of some three hundred leagues, he returned, with recruited forces and increased energy, to press upon the garrison of Mascara, under Lamoricière, with all the rigours of a winter blockade.

Notwithstanding all these incredible and in some measure successful efforts, which were now, more than ever, necessary to sustain him in his arduous and double task of thwarting the designs of his formidable enemies from without, and of curbing the fast-spreading spirit of defection within, Abdel Kader began to feel that he was struggling with adverse fortune. All his fixed establishments had been invaded and destroyed. The ketna, his ancestral abode, had been ravaged and laid waste. The members of his own family were outcasts. More than all, the families of his most faithful adherents were constantly exposed, despite all his vigilance, to rude visits from detested strangers, clothed in uncouth garb, the soldiers of the infidel, who violated the sanctity of the harem with heartless mockery and vindictive malice.

Feelings of religion and humanity urgently compelled him to take measures to meet the exigencies of such a painful and trying emergency. He determined to remove altogether from the scene of war those whom it was impossible for him to desert, and whom in the hour of need he might be unable to rescue. He formed his *Smala*.

This new and singular organisation was simply an agglomeration of private hearths. To the *Smala* as to a common asylum and place of security, the Arab tribes sent their treasures, their herds, their women, their children, their aged and their sick. It became an immense moving capital, amounting to more than 20,000 souls. It followed the Sultan's movements, advancing to the more cultivated districts, or retreating to the Sahara, according to the fluctuations of his fortunes.

When in the Sahara, the numerous tents of the *Smala* were lost in the distant horizon. When in the Tell, they filled up the valley, and covered the slopes of the mountains. It was arranged with military regularity. The *deiras*, or households, with their tents varying in number according to the respective strength of each, were distributed into four large encampments. Each *deira* knew its place. Each chief had his station marked and his functions appointed, according to his importance or the confidence he inspired.

Abdel Kader spared no pains to encourage and popularise a system of emigration, which daily increased from the strongest of human impulses, and thus gradually and imperceptibly bound the Arab tribes to him by the strongest of human ties. Four tribes were set apart to watch, protect, and guide the *Smala* in its wanderings. A body of regulars kept guard over it. Jews were expresely commissioned to advance sums of money to the needy.

Ultimately, indeed, the *Smala* became a powerful check on the disaffection of the tribes. For when the French, alluring them with fair promises, said to them, " Come over to us, we will protect you," an invisible voice whispered in their ears, " I have your women, your children, your flocks, beware ! " Thus, an establishment, which was at first constituted by Abdel Kader as a measure of domestic arrangement, became in his hands a vast and widely extended political engine.

CHAPTER XVI

IT was the month of March, 1841 ; the night was cold, dark, and tempestuous. More than a thousand fires glimmered in house, and tent, and bivouac. Men were anxiously discussing the past stages and future prospects of the war. Generals were conning their maps ; soldiers were drinking the old accustomed toasts to love and glory ; priests were reading their breviaries ; the Bishop of Algiers had just finished midnight mass. Suddenly a young woman, holding a little girl by the hand, rushed into his apartment, threw herself at his feet, and in accents of wild despair exclaimed :—" My husband ; the father of my child ! " Her husband had disappeared in the frightful hurricane of war which had devastated the plain of Algiers. But he was safe ; he was with Abdel Kader.

The good bishop had long deplored, though unavailingly, the melancholy fate of French prisoners in the hands of the Arabs. He had often suggested measures for their relief, but French national pride and dignity had hitherto opposed an impassable barrier to his benevolent designs. Now, however, touched and excited by the scene before him, he determined to break the restraints imposed on him, and, confident of finding a response in the breast of the magnanimous chief to whom he was about to appeal, he wrote to Abdel Kader.

" You do not know me," he said, " but my profession is, to serve God, and in Him to love all men, his children and my brethren. If I was able to mount on horseback I should dread neither the blackness of the night nor the roaring of the tempest. I would present myself at the door of your tent, and would cry out in a voice which, if my idea of you deceives me not, you would be unable to resist, ' Restore to me my unfortunate brother, fallen into your warlike hands.' But I cannot come myself.

" Let me then send you one of my followers, and let the letter which he will present to you, and which I have written in haste, supply the place of that verbal appeal which God would have blessed, for it would have proceeded from the bottom of my heart.

" I have neither gold nor silver to offer you. Your only recompense will be the sincere prayers and the deep-felt gratitude of the family on whose behalf I write. ' Blessed are the merciful, for they shall obtain mercy.' "

Abdel Kader at once replied in the following terms:—
" I have received your letter and comprehended it. It has not surprised me, after all I had heard of your sacred cha-racter. Nevertheless, permit me to observe that in the double title you assume of servant of God and friend of men, your brethren, you ought to have demanded from me not merely the liberty of one, but of all the Christians who have been made prisoners of war since the resumption of hostilities.

" Nay more. Would you not be, in a twofold manner, worthy of the mission of which you speak, if, not content with procuring such a boon for two or three hundred Christians, you were to endeavour to extend it to an equal number of Mussulmans who languish in your prisons ? "

The celebrated exchange of prisoners at Sidi Khalifa, May 21st, 1841, was the glorious fruits of this touching fusion of two noble hearts.

The bishop had reserved some Arab orphans whose parents had died in French captivity. He expected a protest. To his surprise and astonishment he received a present and a recommendation. "I send you a flock of goats," wrote the catholic-minded Sultan of the Arabs, "with their young who are still sucking. With these you will be able for some time longer to nourish the little children you have adopted, and who have lost their mothers. Pray excuse this gift, for it is very trifling."

The generous care, the tender sympathy exhibited by Abdel Kader towards his prisoners is almost unparalleled in the annals of warfare. Christian generals might sit at his feet in this respect and blush for their degeneracy. No doubt the prisoners taken by the Arabs were often exposed to the insults of their barbarous captors, especially when falling amongst tribes exasperated by the sufferings inflicted on them by the French. Effectually, however, though slowly, the spirit inculcated by the Sultan at length gained ground. Barbarism recoiled before it, mercy prevailed, humanity triumphed.

Wherever Abdel Kader was present, indeed, the French in his power were treated more like guests than prisoners. He frequently sent them, in secret, sums of money, varying from five to twenty dollars, out of his privy purse. They were sure to be well clothed and well fed. Abdel Kader even went so far as to desire that their spiritual wants should receive due attention.

It is thus the uncompromising champion of Islamism writes on the subject, in words that deserve to be printed in letters of gold, to the Bishop of Algiers:—"Send a priest to my camp. He shall want for nothing. I will take care he shall be honoured and respected as becomes his double character of a man of God, and your representative.

"He shall pray with the prisoners daily, he shall console them, and he shall correspond with their families. He may thus be the means of procuring them money, clothes, books, in a word, everything they may desire or want, to soften the rigours of their captivity. Only, on his arriving here, he must solemnly promise, once for all, never to allude in his letters to my encampments or military movements."

The very sight of a prisoner seemed to touch a chord within the breast of Abdel Kader, which called forth all the more lofty sentiments and magnanimous feelings ennobling to human nature. His heart, so stern and dauntless when confronted with danger, expanded and softened with all a woman's tenderness before the captive's dark and dreary fate, like flowers which only exhale their fragrance to the shades of night.

"Sultan," said two French prisoners who were brought before him, "we wish to become Mussulmans; we are ready to make profession of your religion."

"If you do so in good faith," replied Abdel Kader, "well and good. But if you are needlessly alarmed at your present situation, you will do wrong. Though you are, and remain Christians, not a hair of your heads shall be touched. Con-

P

sider rather what will happen to you should you return to your countrymen after having renounced your faith. Would you not be treated as the most criminal of deserters? How can you hope to benefit by the occasion should an exchange of prisoners take place?"

A French prisoner, kindling with indignation at the bare mention of apostacy, exclaimed, in presence of Abdel Kader, "As for me, I will never renounce my religion. You may cut off my head, but make me a renegade, never!"

"Be perfectly easy, your life is sacred with me," was the reply of Abdel Kader. "I like to hear such language. You are a brave and loyal man, and merit my esteem. I honour courage in religion more than courage in war."

A celebrated Moroccan chief asked to see the French prisoners. Having remarked a trumpeter, he asked him to play a tune. The trumpeter sounded the charge. "What does that mean?" said the chief. "Tell the Sultan," said the trumpeter, "that when he hears that sound, the sooner he gives his horse the reins and gallops off, the better." The chief, feeling himself insulted, demanded that the offender should have the bastinado. "No, no," said Abdel Kader, "we must be generous and forbearing to our prisoners."

Abdel Kader's repugnance to see female prisoners was extreme. The thought that women should become victims of war was a source of constant anxiety to him. One day, the cavalry of one of his Khalifas brought him in four young women, as a brilliant capture. He turned away in disgust. "Lions," he said, sarcastically, "attack strong animals; jackals fall upon the weak."

Once he and his followers were reduced to the greatest

straits. Subsistence could hardly be procured. In this extremity, he bethought him of ninety-four French prisoners lying in his camp in the greatest misery. He released them all without ransom or exchange. He even had them escorted to the advanced posts, where they were delivered over to their comrades, astounded by such an act of generosity.

Numberless acts of magnanimity, known only to the French superior officers whom he encountered, or with whom he corresponded, testified to the elevation of his soul. One general officer has since said, "We were obliged to conceal these things as much as we could from our soldiers; for if they suspected them, we should never have got them to fight with the due ardour against Abdel Kader."

Some French artisans had, by permission of the Governor-General, entered into a contract with Abdel Kader to execute certain works in four of the towns he was rebuilding. They were to receive 3,000 francs each. The war broke out before their contract was completed; nearly half of their work had yet to be completed. They petitioned for leave to return.

Not only did Abdel Kader at once consent, but he gave them a safe-conduct and an escort through tribes who were all in arms, and crying out for French blood. At the frontier the entire sum which had been agreed upon was counted down to the French artisans, who were thus paid by the Sultan for works which they had actually not finished.

Converted, animated, inspired by such an example, the Sultan's chiefs and delegates, throughout the provinces and districts under their control, for the most part engaged willingly and cordially in acts of sympathy, kindness, and hospitality to their fallen foes. Such were Ibn Salem and

Ben Hamedi; such a one, also, was Sidi Embarak, that brilliant reflex of his master's mind, whose prisoners, when released, subscribed to present him with pistols of honour.

But, in all those tender offices which soothe and assuage the unutterable sufferings of the estranged and forlorn, none exceeded the Sultan's mother, the mild, the gentle Leila Zohra. She assumed, as by inherent right, the guardianship of all the female prisoners. The care and solicitude she lavished on them was as extraordinary as it was exemplary. They occupied a tent close to hers. Two of her negro slaves guarded the entrances. No one was allowed to approach them without an order. Every morning they received from her own hands presents of oil, butter, meat, and other articles, for their repast. Did sickness overtake any of them, she would bring them, with maternal anxiety, tea, sugar, coffee—anything she thought would contribute to their ease and comfort.

One day, a batch of French prisoners was brought in and placed temporarily near her tent. She came out to see them. "What have you come to do in our country?" she observed, looking on them with compassion; "it was calm and prosperous, and you have covered it with the desolation of war. No doubt, it is the will of God which is being accomplished; but that God is all-powerful, His designs are impenetrable. Perhaps, one of these days, in the hour of reconciliation, we may restore you to your homes and families." Such words of hope, which thrilled through the breasts, and cheered the wounded spirits of the unhappy prisoners, and seemed to them like distant gleams of future freedom already beaming on their captivity, revealed, in one glorious trait, the mother of Abdel Kader.

By his humanity, Abdel Kader had done much more than only inaugurate a new era in the treatment of prisoners amongst the Arabs; it was due to him that soldiers had ever been spared on the field to be taken prisoners at all. The very word "prisoner" had been hitherto unknown amongst their savage tribes. To show no quarter, to massacre all who came in their way and fell into their hands, to count their vanquished enemies by the number of bloody heads dangling on their horses' flanks, and to receive prizes for them, had been their custom, until custom had almost grown into an instinct.

Who was the first to abolish such atrocious practices? Who prohibited, with all the severity which circumstances would allow, the custom of adding to the heads of those who had been slain in open fight, the heads of prisoners taken alive, wounded or not? Who, in place of the sum of money heretofore given for each of these sanguinary trophies, gave double and triple the sum for every prisoner brought in safe and sound?—Again and again, let Christendom and the whole civilised world be told, that it was Abdel Kader.

Nor was it without the risk of a general insurrection that Abdel Kader insisted and persevered in the new course he had marked out. Undeterred, however, by threats, unshaken by menaces, he went steadily on till he had achieved the moral revolution dictated to him by religion and humanity. One of his soldiers, at the commencement of this reform, insolently demanded of him—

" How much will you give for a prisoner? "

" Eight dollars."

" And how much for a head cut off? "

" Twenty-five blows on the soles of the feet."

One day, Abdel Kader desired that five prisoners, already some weeks in custody, should be brought before him. Three were immediately summoned by the Khalifa, to whose charge they had been given. The latter, dreading the Sultan's queries, turned to the prisoners and said—

"There, take these burnouses, throw them over your shoulders; the Sultan calls for you. If he asks you any questions, mind you say that you have been well treated, and that you have wanted for nothing."

"Very good; but if we are asked if those burnouses are our own?"

"Say that you have had them a long time."

"Agreed."

"Woe to you if you make any complaint. Now follow me to the Sultan."

After having given these warnings, the Khalifa proceeded with his prisoners to the tent of the Sultan. Abdel Kader was seated in one corner, surrounded by his principal chiefs and Marabouts. The reception of the prisoners was designedly solemn. The Arabs and their Sultan preserved a mysterious silence. The three prisoners advanced, preceded by Hadj Mustapha, the Sultan's brother-in-law.

" Which of you is the trumpeter?" said the Sultan.

"I am."

"Take that letter, it is for you."

As the prisoner read the letter, his cheeks became flushed; tears rushed into his eyes; his limbs trembled with excitement. It was a letter from his General, informing him that the Legion of Honour had been conferred on him, for his bravery in devoting himself for the safety of his colonel, in the affair of Sept. 22nd, 1843.

" Step forward," said the Sultan.

The trumpeter advanced a few paces.

Abdel Kader, with his own hands, fixed the Cross of the Legion of Honour on his breast.

Then, turning to his brother-in-law, he said :—

" I only see three prisoners. There were five: where are the other two ?"

" They are dead."

" Since when ?"

" A long time ago."

" Did they die of sickness ?"

" We shot them."

" Shot them !" exclaimed the Sultan, looking sternly at his brother-in-law.

" They tried to escape."

" Is that a reason for killing them ? This is wicked, unjust, infamous. If the French were to kill my Arabs who are their prisoners, what would you say ?"

" Dogs of Christians."

" Enough; for shame ! I will have no more of these doings. Do you understand me ? This shall and must be the last. Give the prisoners thirty francs a-piece, place them in my camp, and mind they are well provided for."

From this moment, Abdel Kader determined to procure a national edict as regarded the treatment of prisoners; for notwithstanding all his vigilance, isolated instances of barbarity still continued to occur. He convoked a grand council of all the Khalifas, the Agas, the Kaids, and chiefs of tribes.

Three hundred assembled. Standing up before them, he took for the text of his oration, an article in the Koran, where Mohammed blames his brother-in-law Ali for having slain five hundred infidels after they had surrendered.

Applying this passage to the case of French soldiers taken prisoners, Abdel Kader vehemently insisted that they should no more be wantonly killed or mutilated. After eloquently showing, to the conviction of his audience, the inhumanity, the disgrace, the inutility of such actions, he demanded a decree to the effect, that every Frenchman, whether taken in action or otherwise, should be looked upon as a prisoner, and be treated with every consideration, until an opportunity presented itself for effecting his exchange.

The proposition of the Sultan received the approval of the majority of the council. The following decree was at once drawn up; and hundreds of copies were made, and forthwith distributed throughout all the towns, villages, and tents, in the Sultan's dominions :—

"Be it ordained, that every Arab who shall bring in a French soldier, or a Christian, safe and sound, shall receive a reward, amounting to eight dollars for a male, and ten dollars for a female.

"Every Arab who has a Frenchman or a Christian in his possession, is held responsible for his good treatment. He is hereby commanded, on pain of the severest punishment, to conduct his prisoner, without delay, either to the nearest Khalifa, or before the Sultan himself. On doing this, he shall receive the promised reward.

"In the case of any prisoner complaining of the slightest ill-treatment, the Arab, his captor, shall lose all claims for reward."

Once—and once only—after the publication of this order, it was reported to Abdel Kader that one of his regulars had been taken up with a Frenchman's head in his hands. Starting with indignation, he instantly wrote to the Khalifa of the district where the case had occurred, commanding him to bring the culprit forthwith to head-quarters. He resolved to make a severe example. His regular regiments, both infantry and cavalry, and the contingents of irregular cavalry, of the tribes nearest by, were all convoked to a grand parade.

On the day, and at the hour fixed, all were under arms. Abdel Kader stood surrounded by his civil and military chiefs. The culprit was led forth; the head was placed before the Sultan.

"Prisoner," said Abdel Kader, "was the man to whom this head belonged dead or alive, before you cut it off?"

"Dead."

"Then you shall receive two hundred and fifty blows, for having disobeyed my orders. This punishment shall teach you that, as a dead man can be no man's enemy, it is cowardly and brutal to mutilate him."

The soldier was laid down, and received his award. He rose, and thinking his punishment over, was moving off.

"Stay a little," said the Sultan, "I have another question to ask you. While you were cutting off the man's head, where was your musket?"

"I had laid it on the ground."

"Two hundred and fifty blows more, then, for having abandoned your arms on the field."

After this second punishment, the unhappy regular could hardly stand on his feet. Some men stepped forth to carry him away.

"Not in such a hurry," said the Sultan, again; "I have another question yet to ask. After you had cut off the man's head, how did you manage to carry your musket and the head at the same time?"

"I held my musket in one hand, and the head in the other."

"That is to say, you carried your musket in such a manner that you could not have made use of it. Give him two hundred and fifty blows more."

Such unbending severity had its due effect. The French had no longer occasion to dread falling alive into the hands of the Arabs. When taken they were regularly and carefully conducted to the station of the nearest Khalifa. On arriving there, they were subjected to a strict but mild examination, and were simply asked to what corps they had belonged, when and how they had been taken, and whether they had been well treated by their captors.

After their declarations had been duly taken down and registered, they were forwarded to certain *depôts* appointed for the reception of prisoners. The men were generally sent to Taza, or Tekedemt. The women, invariably to the Smala, to be cared for and superintended by the Sultan's mother.

Not satisfied with ameliorating the condition of his own prisoners of war, Abdel Kader was extremely desirous of pushing the principle of humanity still further, by establishing a regular exchange of prisoners on both sides. Often and earnestly did he plead with the French generals, that the precedent so auspiciously established and carried into effect at Sidi Khalifa, might be extended and confirmed as a system. But he pleaded in vain.

CHAPTER XVII

At this period of his fortunes, Abdel Kader was almost as much engaged in subduing his own subjects and keeping them to their allegiance, as in fighting with the French. The latter, by promises, by bribes, by threats, by measures of the utmost severity, tried to gain over the Arab tribes as allies and auxiliaries. A razzia on the part of the French was sure to be followed by a razzia on the part of the Sultan. Both parties endeavoured to establish their power by terror. But, whilst the one was actuated by the thirst for conquest, the other was influenced by the desire of rescuing his country from its evils, and rendering it eventually great and powerful.

The French had learned to appreciate the importance of the Smala. They saw in it the real nucleus of Abdel Kader's influence. They ascertained that it was the depository of immense wealth. It now became the chief object of their research. From generals of *corps d'armée* to colonels of detachments, all displayed an eager and zealous activity to snatch the splendid prize.

In the spring of 1843, Lamoricière opened the campaign by occupying Tekedemt. Abdel Kader, with 1,500 cavalry, watched his further movements from the neighbouring woods of Scrisso. He had learned by spies that the general's object was the Smala. For twenty days he remained in ambush.

All communication with him was strictly prohibited, lest his presence should be discovered. He and his men lived on acorns. The horses were fed with leaves. To add to the intenseness of his abnegation, this trial came on them during the period of the fast of Ramadan.

One day the chiefs of Abdel Kader came to him radiant with joy. They had found a stray sheep. The Sultan at least might have a repast. "Take it to my starving soldiers," said Abdel Kader, and he turned to his meal of acorns. Unconsciously, he was following the example of David, when he looked on the waters from the well of Bethlehem, and said, "Is not this the blood of the men who went in jeopardy of their lives? and he would not drink it;" of Alexander, when he refused the helmet of water—"If I alone drink, my men will be dispirited;" of Sidney, who on the field of Zutphen resigned the cooling draught to his wounded comrade, with the touching remark, "This man's necessity is greater than mine."

Twice Lamoricière led forth his troops in search of the Smala, and twice Abdel Kader drove him back. But treason was at work. Sheik Omar ibn Ferrath, of the Beni Aiad, offered to point out the exact spot on which the Smala was encamped. Immediately the plan was laid. From Abdel Kader no obstruction was feared. He was occupied with Lamoricière. The column stationed at Medea was selected for the enterprise. The execution was entrusted to the Duc D'Aumale.

On the 10th of May, 1843, D'Aumale left Boghar with 1,300 infantry, 600 cavalry, and 2 field pieces. Sheik Omar had announced the Smala to be at Gojilat. The French reached that place on the 14th. But the Smala was gone. Its new locality was unknown. The column wandered about weary and uncertain. A fierce simoon sweeping over it reduced the men to utter exhaustion. They halted and piled arms. D'Aumale rode on for some miles in front, merely accompanied by his cavalry.

At break of day on the 16th, the traitor Sheik rode up to say that the Smala was at the spring of Taguin. D'Aumale at once gave orders to march on the point indicated. The Sheik expostulated. To attack the Smala with 600 cavalry appeared to him to be madness.. He entreated the Duke either to return to his column or to wait till it came up. "No prince of my race ever receded," was the gallant reply ; and the trumpets sounded the advance.

The Smala was reached. The French cavalry, spreading out like a fan, went dashing through that sea of tents, and quickly scattered a bewildered and panic-striken population of old men, women, and children. The small guard of 500 regulars fired a volley and fled. A handful of the Hashems bravely attempted to stem the torrent, but were swept away. In less than an hour the victory was complete.

The scenes of confusion and despair which were crowded into that brief interval—the frantic efforts at escape, the terror of the flying, the dismay of the abandoned—the careering and plunging of a promiscuous mass of camels, dromedaries, horses, mules, oxen, sheep, tossing about like the waves of a raging sea, have been immortalised by the genius of Horace Vernet. The painter's art alone could do adequate justice to that unparalleled and almost inconceivable scene of tumult.

The bloodshed had been comparatively trifling. The trophies consisted chiefly of the families of Abdel Kader's most influential chiefs. His own family had escaped. The booty was immense. It comprised thousands of animals of all kinds, Abdel Kader's library, consisting of the rarest Arabian manuscripts, richly bound, and valued at £5,000; his military chest, containing millions of francs; the chests of his Khalifas and Kaids, all deposited in the Smala for security, and filled with gold and silver coins, and costly jewellery.

The French soldiers baled out dollars and doubloons in their shakos; they filled their haversacks with pearls and diamonds. In the general disorder, the voice of command was unheeded; and each seized the prize, which a more or less happy chance threw into his hands.

Abdel Kader received the news of the taking of the Smala, in the woods of Scrisso. The blow for a moment overwhelmed him. He measured at once the extent of his misfortune, and saw in that severe decree of fate the presage of a dark and calamitous future. Dismissing the messengers who brought him the intelligence, he retired from some hours to his tent, engaged in meditation and prayer.

His chiefs, his officers and men, had, in the meantime, assembled in groups outside. Some were silent and downcast, others gave way to the wildest imprecations. Many had lost their all; their wives and their children had been taken captive—they might be separated for years, perhaps for ever; disordered imaginations filled up this dark shadow of the unknown with exaggerated horrors; the distracted sufferers saw no prospect of relief. One only feeling gave them a shadow of consolation—their Sultan was still amongst them.

Abdel Kader came forth. They crowded to his presence. They watched his looks. Some essayed to address him, but the words faltered on their lips; none ventured to fathom the secret workings of that profound prostration. But the cloud had passed over; a smile played on his countenance. "Praise be to God," he said; "all those objects which I so highly prized, which were so dear to my heart, and occupied my mind so much, only impeded my movements, and turned me aside from the right way. For the future, I shall be free to fight the infidels."

Then, speaking of those who had fallen, he added, "Why should we mourn and complain? Are not all those whom we loved and have lost, now blessed in Paradise?" The next day he wrote to his Khalifas:—"The French have made a razzia on my Smala; but let us not be discouraged, we shall henceforth be lighter and better disposed for war."

Thus, rising superior to events, Abdel Kader stilled the troubled waters which rose around him; from the deepest of his misfortunes he gathered hope and encouragement for the future.

When alluding afterwards to this disastrous period, Abdel Kader thus expressed himself:—"When my Smala was attacked by the Duc D'Aumale, its population could not have comprised less than 60,000 souls. He did not carry off a tenth part; it extended from Taguin as far as Djebel Amour. When an Arab lost sight of his family in it, he was sometimes two days in finding it. Wherever it was encamped, the wells and rivulets were dried up. I had established a police force expressly to prevent the waters from being muddled or wasted by the flocks. In spite of all my precautions, many perished from thirst.

"My Smala contained armourers, saddlers, tailors—every trade, in fact, necessary to its organisation. An immense fair was held in it, which was much frequented by the Arabs of the Tell. As to our grain, corn, and barley, it was either brought to us, or we sent to procure it from the tribes of the north.

"The order of the encampment was perfectly regulated. When I had pitched my tent, every one knew the place he was to occupy. I had around me three or four hundred of my regular infantry, and the irregular cavalry of the Hashems of Eghrees, who were especially devoted to me. It was no easy task to reach me. Not that I took these measures for my own personal security; I felt I was necessary to accomplish the work of God, and trusted in Him to strengthen and protect the arm that carried his standard.

"At the time of the surprise, I was near Tekedemt, observing the division of Oran, which was in the neighbourhood, and from which I thought I had most to dread. I had with me 1,500 or 1,600 cavalry. Ben Kharoub was with the Flittas, Ben Allal in the Ouarensis, Mustapha-ibn-Taamy amongst the Beni Ouragh. But I never thought there was occasion for me to fear so terrible a mischance in the direction of Medea; and none of my Khalifas were watching the movements of the king's son.

"Despite all that, however, we should not have been surprised if God had not blinded our people. On seeing the Spahis coming on, with their red burnouses, it was thought in the Smala that they were my irregulars returning. The women even raised the usual cries of welcome and rejoicing to their honour. Nor were they undeceived until the first shots were fired. Then ensued a scene of inexpressible confusion, which baffled all the efforts of those who sought to defend themselves.

" If I had been there, we should have fought for our wives and children, and the French would have seen a grand day. But God decreed it otherwise. I only heard of the misfortune three days afterwards; it was too late."

The smallness of their force prevented the French from taking more than 3,000 prisoners; but amongst them were the families of several of the Sultan's Khalifas. The rest of the Smala dispersed in all directions. Some fell among Arab tribes, who plundered them. Others were overtaken by Lamoricière.

Foremost in the pursuit was Mutapha-ibn-Ismail, who throughout the war had made himself conspicuous by the malicious zeal with which he had ever aided and directed the movements of the French against the distinguished chief whom a base jealousy urged him to thwart and oppose. But the traitor now met a merited doom. Crossing the district of the Flittas, he was attacked, shot down, and decapitated. His head was taken to the Sultan's head-quarters. Abdel Kader gazed upon it for some moments with pardonable satisfaction, and then contemptuously ordered it to be thrown to the dogs.

To recover his influence and restore the general confidence by the re-establishment of his Smala, was now to Abdel Kader a matter of vital importance. But all his efforts were vain. The moral effects of its defeat and capture were irremediable. Every day brought Abdel Kader information of the defection of large and influential tribes. Arab contingents now swelled the ranks of his enemies, and marched openly against him.

Yet deeper misfortunes followed. At the very moment when his ablest Khalifas were most needed, a remorseless fate removed them. Their career was cut short by captivity, or terminated by a glorious death. Deprived of these connecting links, his empire lost cohesion. His distant provinces fell an easy prey to the French, who everywhere displayed their triumphant standards. But the lion heart and iron will still bore up, and defied fortune to do its worst.

The province of Oran became the scene of an almost superhuman struggle. Followed by a chosen and devoted band of some 5,000 followers, Abdel Kader made his presence felt at all points; now he fell on recreant tribes; now he made head against the French columns. Ever in the van, leading on the charge, plunging into the thickest of the fight, by his heroic example he encouraged, animated, and inspired his small band. His bravest followers fell around him; his horses were killed under him; his burnous was riddled with bullets; but still he fought on, desperately braving and sustaining the battle's brunt.

Once he was taken unawares. On the 23rd September, 1843, he was encamped near the Marabouts (or sacred edifices) of Sidi Yoosuf, with a battalion of infantry and 500 irregular horse. A spy betrayed his position to Lamoricière. A distance of six leagues was between them. The general at once led out in person the 2nd Chasseurs d'Afriques. All were elate and confident. The space was rapidly traversed by a night's march. In the grey of dawn the spot was reached.

Abdel Kader was aroused from sleep by cries of "The French! the French!" He had barely time to mount. He might have escaped, but death in his eyes was preferable to the double stain of surprise and flight. His infantry sprung to their arms, and by his orders advanced and fired a volley. His cavalry rallied at his voice. Then, as the smoke slowly rolled away, he dashed into the French chasseurs, overwhelmed and dispersed them by the suddenness of the shock, and after a few minutes' hard fighting drew off his whole force in perfect order.

The Beni Amers had gone over to the French—those same Beni Amers whose 4,000 sabres had waved in exultation around the young hero of the Djehad; whose brilliant courage had opened before him the path of glory and of empire. Abdel Kader determined to attack them. Descending suddenly upon them with all his available levies, he swept through their encampments, slew numbers, and carried off a large booty. A French battalion stationed amongst them struggled vainly to arrest his progress. But an Arab chief, one of his old followers, boldly singled him out, rode up to him, and fired at him point blank. The ball missed. Abdel Kader turned round and shot the traitor dead with his pistol.

Notwithstanding the temporary success of these desperate efforts, Abdel Kader well knew that unless some more stable and permanent form were given to his energy and perseverance, all attempts to regain his former ascendancy, and repair the crumbling edifice of his fortunes, would be vain and illusory. Algeria, he now clearly saw, was closed to him, as a battle-field likely to be productive of any solid advantages to his position, notwithstanding his endless raids and triumphant razzias. Without external aid, he felt the game was lost.

The magnificent Smala was now reduced to his own Deira, barely amounting to 1,000 souls, wandering about in miserable uncertainty. By fixing it in a place of security, he would be ready for fresh efforts. While escorting it to a more favourable spot, Lamoricière again crossed his path. A desperate engagement ensued. The women animated the combatants with their voices. Abdel Kader and his followers, fighting in the presence of their wives and children, performed prodigies of valour. Again the Sultan's formidable antagonist was foiled. The Deira was safely established at Bouka Cheha, on the territory of Morocco.

The political relations between England and France were at this time threatening. Abdel Kader thought the moment propitious. He sent an embassy to the Queen of England. In a letter addressed to her Majesty, he opened to her the prospect of possessions in Algeria. All the sea-coast towns should be ceded to her in full and undivided sovereignty. On the other hand, the Arabs required at her hands the acknowledgment of their national independence. A glorious alliance between the English and the Arabs would present an impassible barrier, he urged, to French aggrandisement in Africa. The letter was placed in the hands of the Prime Minister. An interview with the Queen was sought by his agent, and refused. An answer was promised, but it was never sent.

The embassy was at the same time entrusted with a letter

from Abdel Kader to the Turkish Sultan, to be transmitted through the British Foreign Office. In return for succour promptly sent, the Sultan of the Arabs offered to acknowledge the descendant of Othman as his suzerain. The letter was forwarded to its destination, but no results ensued.

Whatever were his expectations from the quarters he thus addressed, Abdel Kader's main reliance was in the support and co-operation of the Sultan of Morocco. For years, Sultan Abderahman had shown him every mark of unbounded cordiality and esteem, had loaded him with presents, and offered him the sweet incense of flattery and adulation. But there his friendship stopped. Throughout the whole career of Abdel Kader, he had never offered to supply him gratuitously with material aid of any kind; and Abdel Kader had never condescended to demand it.

Now, however, stern necessity and a solemn sense of religious duty compelled him to make the appeal. In the most urgent and pressing terms, he adjured the Moorish Sultan to come forward with the whole strength and resources of his empire in behalf of the common cause. He pointed out the common danger. If all Algeria were to be subdued, where, he asked, could be the security for Morocco? Pretexts would not be wanting for invading the latter, as pretexts had been found for invading the former. The Arab tribes, momentarily dispirited, would revive at the sight of the Moorish armies, and, with re-enkindled enthusiasm, range themselves round the Moorish standards.

Not content with challenging the political and religious sympathies of the Sultan of Morocco, Abdel Kader resolved to win his patron's adhesion, if not to extort his alliance, by

an act of personal devotion. Several of the frontier Morocco
tribes had long been in open revolt against their sovereign.
He marched against them, subdued them, and sent the leaders
of the rebellion in chains to Ouchda, forwarding at the same
time a letter from himself to Sultan Abderahman, stating his
services.

The reply of the Moorish monarch was complimentary, but
reserved. It held out to him no encouragement. Abdel
Kader, finding the fruitlessness of his advances in that quarter,
now summoned around him a few faithful adherents, and,
relying on his own efforts to retrieve his fortunes, disappeared
for some months in the Sahara.

The French, relieved of Abdel Kader's presence, imagined
that their work was done. His withdrawal from the scene of
action was to them the grateful symbol of his abdication and
defeat. Marshal Bugeaud thus congratulated his Government
on the glorious result :—" After the campaign of the spring
(1843), I might have proclaimed Algeria to be conquered and
subdued. I preferred stating less than the truth. But now,
after the battle of the 11th of this month, in which the remains
of the Emir's infantry were destroyed, and in which his first
and most distinguished Khalifa was killed, I will boldly
declare that all serious warfare is finished. Abdel Kader
may, indeed, with the handful of cavalry he still has about
him, make some isolated *coup de main* on the frontier, but he
can never again attempt anything important."

CHAPTER XVIII.

1844—1845.

THE erection of an Arab kingdom in Algeria had been viewed by the Sultan of Morocco, not only with feelings of religious sympathy and approval, but with a cordial appreciation of its commercial advantages. The government of the young Sultan of the Arabs, based on a strict and undeviating adherence to the principles of the Koran, had largely increased both the trade and the revenues of his empire.

Formerly the rich caravans which plied between Fez and the southern parts of Africa, passed through Algeria as through an enemy's country. Large guards were necessary to save them from spoliation. They were frequently attacked and plundered, with serious loss of life. They had to run the gauntlet both of Arabs and Turks. If they escaped from the open hostility of the one, they were devoured by the grasping avarice and unblushing extortion of the other. Now they traversed the whole extent of Algeria in perfect safety. In the interior they paid no tolls; at the frontiers they paid no duties. In Abdel Kader's eyes a custom-house was an anomaly and an abomination. The legal *zekka* and *ashur*, and, in case of urgent necessity, the *marouna*, an extraordinary war-contribution, were all that his conscience allowed him to demand from his subjects. Industry fructified in its natural channels; the reciprocity of exchange was unfettered.

When to all these considerations were added the personal esteem and regard, the admiration little short of idolatry with which the Moorish Sultan reverenced the once triumphant leader of the Djehad, it was fully expected throughout the Moorish population, who secretly longed to be led on, in alliance with the Arabs, against the infidels, that a loud and strenuous appeal to arms would sooner or later have signalised the adhesion of Morocco to the common cause, and imparted fresh strength and vigour to Abdel Kader's noble, though waning, efforts of constancy and heroism.

But, however sensitive Sultan Abderahman might have been to the instincts of his faith, he was not the less tenacious of the stability of his own throne. The invading element had swept triumphantly over the barriers raised alike by Turkish and Arab desperation. The power which had planted its victorious standards in Algiers and Mascara, might well carry them to Fez. A demonstration in favour of Abdel Kader on the part of Sultan Abderahman, would probably involve them both in a common ruin. Balancing between his personal predilections and his political fears, the Moorish Sultan hoped to save his conscience and his crown, by doing nothing.

Unfortunately for the astuteness of these calculations on the part of the Moorish Sultan, the position of Abdel Kader was of such a nature as to render a hostile collision between France and Morocco inevitable. The sympathies of the Moorish population were gradually burning more and more strongly towards the indomitable hero who had honoured their soil by making it the sanctuary of his accumulated glories, his sanctified misfortunes, and his unflagging hopes. It required but a spark to raise a widely-spreading and inextinguishable conflagration.

Abdel Kader had for some time made the Morocco frontier the basis of his forays into Algeria. He could retire within the Morocco territory without molestation. The French, in order not to be thus baffled, had at last advanced a strong division to that part of the frontier from whence he made his sallies. But the frontier lines were ill defined. There was a portion of the territory which might be considered as debateable ground, and this debateable ground was boldly occupied by the French.

The name of the place on which Lamoricière and Bedeau fixed on for their encampment was Leila Maghnia, so called after the name of a celebrated and highly venerated female saint, whose remains lay deposited in a stately tomb, erected on the spot. Here the French dug entrenchments, hung up their accoutrements, smoked their pipes, and sung songs.

The profanation was too glaring to be overlooked, too monstrous to be endured. A shout of indignation rolled through the Moorish empire. It roused the vacillating monarch from his ignominious repose, and compelled him either to see himself engulphed amidst the tempestuous waves of an irrepressible fanaticism, or at once to send an army to the scene of outrage, for the purpose of asserting the national dignity, and avenging the foul insult offered to the national faith.

On the 22nd May, 1844, El Ghenaoui, commander of the Moorish garrison at Ouchda, summoned the French to evacuate

Leila Maghnia. The summons was treated with contempt. On the 30th, some Moorish troops approached the French position, and encouraged by their leader, a fanatic Shereef, allied by birth to the Sultan's family, gave way to their impetuous zeal. With menacing shouts and gestures they reached the French lines. They fired into the French entrenchments. Lamoricière and Bedeau displayed the French standards and marched against them. Quickly defeated and dispersed, the enemy fell back upon Ouchda.

On the 11th of June, Marshal Bugeaud arrived at the camp. He proposed an interview between himself and El Ghenaoui, and the arrangement was accepted. The interview was fixed for June 11th. Distrust prevailed on either side. Each party came towards the ground with a large body of troops. In presence of both armies, the chiefs advanced towards each other, accompanied by a small escort.

Scarcely had the conference begun when the Moorish cavalry were observed to be breaking ground and closing in upon the scene of parley. With cries of insult and defiance they brandished their sabres and discharged their pistols. Bedeau withdrew with dignity, disdaining to attempt reprisals. The main body of the enemy, mistaking this moderation for weakness, rushed on tumultuously. The French drew up in order of battle, waited a short time for reinforcements, and then, headed by Bugeaud, retorted the challenge. A general engagement ensued. Again the Moors were routed and put to flight.

Bugeaud, astounded at these acts of treachery, determined to take and occupy Ouchda itself. He wrote to El Ghenaoui demanding an explanation. The latter only replied in a spirit of prevarication and evasion. The French general then sent his ultimatum. In this despatch Abdel Kader was declared to be the sole obstacle to a renewal of peace and friendship between France and Morocco. The genius of one man thus held the reciprocal positions of two empires in suspense. "We wish," wrote General Bugeaud, "to have the same frontier limits which the Turks, and Abdel Kader after them, possessed. We want nothing which belongs to you. But we must insist on your no longer receiving Abdel Kader, granting him aid and support, reviving him when he is nearly dead, and launching him forth afresh upon us. This is not good friendship; it is war; and such war you have been making on us in this manner for two years.

"We desire that you confine to the west of the empire both Abdel Kader's Deira and his principal chiefs, and that you disperse his regular troops, both infantry and cavalry. We require also that you no longer countenance the emigration of our tribes to your territory, and that you immediately send back those who are already located there.

"We will bind ourselves reciprocally towards you, in the same sense, should the occasion present itself. This is what may justly be called the practical observance of the principle of good friendship between two nations. On these conditions, we will be your friends, we will encourage your commerce, and favour the government of Muley Abderahman as much as lies in our power. If you act otherwise we shall be your enemies. Answer at once and without evasions, for I do not understand them."

This despatch led to no results. The Moorish army retired into the interior; and Bugeaud occupied Ouchda, although but temporarily. The dispute, thus commenced on the frontier, soon spread into the higher regions of diplomacy. The French Government, in the month of June, 1844, sent a squadron under Prince de Joinville to the coast of Morocco to support its official reclamations. Marshal Bugeaud received instructions to commence offensive operations by land. The bombardment of Tangiers and Mogador, and the battle of Isly, compelled the Moorish Sultan to carry out the views of the conquering power. France claimed no territory, no indemnity, not even the expenses of the war. It merely begged Sultan Abderahman, *to deliver it from Abdel Kader.* By the 4th article of the treaty of peace which was drawn up, and signed by both parties, it was stipulated, that "Hadj Abdel Kader is placed beyond the pale of the law throughout the entire extent of the empire of Morocco, as well as in Algeria. He will, consequently, be pursued by main force, by the French on the territory of Algeria, and by the Moroccans on their own territory, till he is expelled therefrom, or falls into the power of one or other nation. In the event of Abdel Kader falling into the hands of the French troops, the Government of his Majesty the King of the French engages itself to treat him with respect and generosity. In the event of his falling into the hands of the Moorish troops, his Majesty the Emperor of Morocco engages himself to restrict his abode, for the future, to one of the towns on the western coast of his empire, until the two Governments shall have concerted such measures as will prevent the possibility of his resuming arms, and troubling the tranquillity of Algeria and Morocco."

Abdel Kader, on the breaking out of hostilities between

France and Morocco, had returned to the Deira, there to watch the course of events. Sultan Abderahman went through the formality of summoning him to Fez. But another summons reached Abdel Kader from the Moorish capital, of a far different nature. The defeat of their armies, the humiliating dictation of the French, the bitter reversal of all their ardent hopes, had filled the Moorish population with fury and resentment. All ranks inveighed against the incapacity, and the craven weakness of their sovereign. All demanded Abdel Kader.

Letters from the first grandees of the state, from military and civil functionaries, from the commercial classes, informed Abdel Kader of the general wish, implored him to rescue the empire from impending degradation and ruin, and invited him to ascend the throne of his ancestors.

Had Abdel Kader been a vulgar usurper, he had now only to put out his hand to seize the sceptre of Morocco. But patriotism, not ambition, was his ruling motive. He had taken the field for the freedom and independence of Algeria. His thoughts, his vows, his prayers, all his concentrated energies of body and mind, were devoted to his native land. No offer of greatness could seduce him beyond that legitimate sphere of action. He disdained to wear a borrowed crown.

" I refused the tempting offer so unanimously made to me," he afterwards said, " not only because my religion forbade me to injure a sovereign chosen and appointed by God, but because, knowing Morocco as I did, with its discordant races, I felt it would have cost me at least twelve or fifteen years, not, indeed, to govern like Muley Abderahman, but to enable me in any way to enforce submission to the law, and to make my government respected."

During the spring of 1844, in the hopes of embarrassing the concentration of the French army on the frontiers of Morocco, Abdel Kader had made a rapid incursion into the regions of the Tell, penetrating even as far as Tiaret. Everywhere he appealed to the tribes, convoked their chiefs, and called for contingents. But the presence of French detachments in all directions had overawed and stupefied the national spirit. His summons met with a feeble response. He returned to his Deira in the deepest despondency.

In long and anxious reveries, he now examined his position; he weighed his prospects; he questioned his conscience. Had he done all, he asked himself, that love of country and devotion to his faith demanded? Was it too soon to abandon all hope? Was despair criminal? He looked around on his Deira, composed of his family and a few hundreds of devoted followers, dependent on chance supplies for the bare means of existence, and acknowledged that the closing scene had come.

Again his mental horizon cleared up. A grand idea presented itself to his imagination. He would rally all the tribes of Algeria, unable to endure the yoke of the infidels, and lead them forth in a body towards Mecca. In this expedition he would live on terms of friendship with all who, on their route, welcomed them as friends; and pass over the bodies of those who opposed them as enemies.

What Arab, he argued to himself, could resist such a mighty impulse, or fail to be electrified by such a magnificent proposal? What a glorious spectacle would be presented by a whole people voluntarily abandoning a land which their forefathers, twelve centuries before, had won by their swords, rather than share it with the mortal enemies of their faith;

and bearing back the standards of the Prophet in solemn pomp and grandeur, unsullied and uncontaminated, to the scenes and regions of their pristine glories!

But while pondering over this gigantic scheme, fresh circumstances again aroused him to renewed exertions. Old memories rose up before him. The touching appeals of his devoted Khalifas still occasionally reached him; renewed assurances of adhesion came in from time to time. His heart vibrated and responded to the innate conviction that his name still possessed its talismanic influence, and that his presence might yet re-animate and inspire the breasts of thousands, now sunk in apathy and despair. All combined in urging him to undertake the hazards of another campaign, in spite of the fearful odds opposed to him.

From the gorges of the Djurjura, the loyal and chivalrous Ben Salem had thus addressed his long-absent sovereign:—"How is it that you no longer write to us? The sight of your seal, as you well know, revives all our hopes. I assure you, your very existence is called in question; and it is generally given out that your mother writes in your name. The French are preparing to march upon me, and I cannot answer for the Kabyles; I am almost inclined to believe, they are secretly of the religion of the conqueror. If you delay coming amongst us, the misfortunes of Berkani will be nothing compared to those with which I shall be overwhelmed. Answer me in your own handwriting, I conjure you."

Abdel Kader replied,—"I have received your letter, informing me, that the news of my death is spread abroad in the east. No one can escape death; such is the decree of the Most High. However, God be praised, my hour is not yet come. I am yet full of force and vigour, and I still hope to attack with energy the enemies of our religion. It is by such proofs that men are known. Be always the same, calm, patient, unshaken, and God will recompense you. I will come to you as soon as my affairs in the west are settled."

His absence being still prolonged, and disasters rapidly succeeding each other in every quarter, his three Khalifas in the east held a consultation as to the best measures to be adopted in such a desperate state of affairs. Their master was not there to cheer and animate their drooping spirits ; and as they separated, Ben Allal, embracing his colleagues, exclaimed, "May God re-unite us in another world, for I have small hope that we shall meet again in this." "Despair not," said Ben Salem, newly consoled and supported by a letter he had just received from Abdel Kader, "I trust we shall yet all three of us meet in Algeria." "Perhaps so," added Ben Allal, dejectedly, " if we submit to the Christians, which God forbid."

Soon after, all communication having been cut off by the French troops, the Khalifas to the east were again without any news from Abdel Kader. Ben Salem dispatched several chiefs of tribes to gather intelligence of his movements. By an unexpected piece of good fortune, they found out Abdel Kader himself. He received them with affectionate sympathy. Calm and cheerful in the midst of his reverses, he listened eagerly to their accounts of the embarrassments of his faithful lieutenants, and their still untiring zeal. He consoled them with words of comfort and assurance ; and, on their taking leave, he gave them a horse richly caparisoned, as a present to Ben Salem, with the following letter :—

" Be patient in adversity; it is that which is the touch-stone of great minds. Encourage your officials; aid and assist them; bear with their faults of judgment; measure the extent of their capacities with charity and consideration. This state of affairs cannot last long. I hope to be with you speedily, and then we will come to an understanding as to the proper course to be adopted. In the meantime, I beg you to accept the horse which I send you : it was a present to me from Mouley Abderahman. It may perhaps be pro-pitious to you."

The Arab tribes had, in some degree, viewed with satis-faction the state of comparative repose which had succeeded to those years of constant conflicts, in which, whoever conquered, they were sure to be the sufferers. But the gradual establish-ment of French regulations amongst them, and especially the haughtiness and severity with which they were enforced, as well as the constant presence of French officials, too often dis-tinguished by that superciliousness and contemptuous display of superiority which intimate intercourse with the eastern races generally engenders in the breasts of Europeans, failed not again to awaken their slumbering feelings of hatred and fanaticism.

To minds thus prepared for renewed action, the emissaries of certain secret religious societies which existed amongst the tribes, found ready access. The arm of the Lord, they were assured, was about to be visibly revealed. The *Mouley Saa*, or " Master of the hour," so long expected by all true and fervent believers, had appeared, as they were told, and was already in the field. "Woe be to those who hung back in doubt or fear," was the rallying cry of these fanatics.

R

The sect of the "Derkaouas," famous above all others for their furious and infatuated zeal, had found a tool, and boldly put him forward. In March, 1845, Mohammed-ibn-Abdallah, surnamed Bou Maza, raised the sacred standard in the Dahra and the valley of the Cheliff. This newly-installed prophet preached from place to place, exclaiming, " I am the destined one who is to appear at the hour predicted in the prophecies, the hour of deliverance." He pledged himself to rid Algeria of the French within the year.

This impostor had his goat (which suggested his nickname, Bou Maza, or " father of the goat "), as Sertorius had his bitch, through which he pretended to receive celestial communications. He promised to all who believed in his mission, not only the plunder of the Christians, but also of all recreant Mussulmans. By these means he collected around him several hundred followers, and surprised and attacked some French posts. His successes aroused competitors. Whenever the French advanced, they were met by Bou Maza. The fermentation was temporarily, but only temporarily, appeased by the French. A greater personage than Bou Maza was about to re-appear on the scene.

Abdel Kader, though not a participator in the agitation which had been lately set on foot to excite the tribes, saw the ground prepared for him. He resolved to reap the harvest which had been sown. He descended into the valley of the Tafna, and routed and cut to pieces a French detachment at Sidi Ibrahim. In this action the lower part of his right ear was carried away by a musket ball. This wound was the only serious one that he ever received.

Another detachment laid down its arms to him without

firing a shot, at Ain Temouchen. The collective prisoners amounted to six hundred. They were brought before him. He consoled them in their misfortune. "Never despair of the future," he said; "no harm shall come to you. God has decreed that you should fall into my power; He may yet decree your liberation."

The news of these successes spread rapidly abroad. Rumour magnified their importance. All hearts beat high with expectation. Soon letters from Abdel Kader were read and handed about with transport. In these letters the Arabs were told to be of good cheer, since their Sultan would soon be amongst them, and implored not to permit any partial and ill-judged rising to defeat the common aim. The Khalifas of Abdel Kader had received their instructions. "Let all patiently await the signal," it was written, "and then rush with fury on the foe before them."

The French felt the coming storm; they recognised the genius of Abdel Kader; the danger was imminent. Lamoricière, Cavaignac, Bedeau, pressed the government for reinforcements. They urged the immediate return of Bugeaud. The Marshal left France accordingly, and reached Algeria October 15, 1845. He brought new legions. Within a week he took the field at the head of 120,000 men. He determined, by a timely display of unrelenting rigour, to forestall the menaced blow.

Fourteen divisions, each complete in infantry, cavalry, and artillery, scoured the devoted land in every direction, some acting in concert, others independently, but all crushing out resistance, wherever it appeared, with fire and sword. Men were pitilessly slain, habitations ruthlessly burnt, crops given over to conflagration, fugitives smothered alive in caves. St. Arnaud led on "The Infernal Column." Algeria once more felt all the strength of European civilisation, but now untempered by that mercy which ought to be its attribute.

CHAPTER XIX

FLUSHED with his recent triumph, and anxious to realise the hopes it had awakened in every quarter to which the news of it had reached, Abdel Kader, in the month of October 1845, carried his standards to the plains of Mascara. Here he was again hailed with as much enthusiasm as at the outset of his career. All the tribes which had submitted to the French rallied round him. The garrison of Mascara came out against him, but was driven back with loss. The French entrenched camps of Saida and Tàza were strictly blockaded.

But other portions of the country required his presence. It was his policy not so much to adopt a system of combined attack against the French, which, from his want of regular infantry and artillery, was next to impossible, as to foment the spirit of insurrection in all parts of the Regency, to keep the French perpetually on the alert by his meteor-like appearance in districts apparently subdued, to revive hostilities ostensibly extinguished, and then, by the rapidity of his movements, to baffle all the measures directed against him.

He now advanced to Tekedemt with 6,000 cavalry, and prepared to descend into the valley of the Cheliff. The Beni Shaib, a large and important tribe, one hundred and fifty miles away to the south, were reported to him as about to go over to the French. The contemplated movement into the valley of the Cheliff was instantly suspended. The wavering tribe suddenly found itself attacked by Abdel Kader at the head of 5,000 cavalry. Their chiefs were seized, their flocks carried off, their coffers emptied.

The movements of the French had, in the meantime, compelled him to alter his plans. No sooner was it known that Abdel Kader was in the Tell, than all their efforts were concentrated in that direction. The columns of Lamoricière, Bedeau, Yoosuf, and Marcey, were all set in motion. Orders were given, that whichever column found itself in presence of Abdel Kader, was to fire a signal gun, on which the other columns were immediately to converge and lend their aid.

Lamoricière was the first to come up with him, near Tiaret, December 1, 1845. He was protecting the emigration of several tribes, who, under his direction, were withdrawing into the desert. The signal gun was fired. Bedeau, Yoosuf, and Bugeaud, rapidly emerged on the scene. But Abdel Kader, always admirably served by spies, frustrated this combination, and within forty-eight hours had removed the seat of his operations to the Ouarensis.

Bugeaud, Lamoricière, Yoosuf, and St. Arnaud, followed in breathless haste, and were again on the Sultan's traces ; but their ubiquitous foe everywhere gave them the slip, and for weeks led them a fruitless dance through the valleys of the Cheliff.

On one occasion he nearly succeeded in annihilating the third-named general. On encountering Yoosuf in person on 23rd December, near Temela, he pretended to fly. Yoosuf, falling into the snare, followed him up with 2,000 cavalry.

After thus drawing the French on for some time, Abdel Kader suddenly faced about and charged them with 500 irregulars. The rain fell in torrents. The firearms of the French would not go off. Their horses were dead beat. They got lost in the intricacies of the ground, and were on the point of surrendering, when the unexpected advance of a column of infantry averted their fate.

That very night Abdel Kader slipped between the columns of Bugeaud and Lamoricière, made a sweeping razzia on the Beni Esdama, between Tekedemt and Mascara, carried off all their cattle, with abundance of corn and barley, and retired unmolested into the Sahara. Several tribes here brought him the usual tribute.

He now conceived the daring project of visiting the Djurjura, rallying the Kabyles, and making a dash into the Metija. Ben Salem, duly informed, prepared to second this movement.

Abdel Kader left the Sahara in February, 1846, followed by part of the Beni Hassan, passed, unobserved, through the Wady Isser to the east of Medea, and, making a razzia by the way on the Beni Hadoura, who served the French, reached the Djurjura, where the Kabyles stood ready to await his bidding. With a force of 5,000 warriors, accumulated as if by magic, he now swept down into the plains, ravaged and destroyed the French colonies, and advanced to within four hours of Algiers itself. The French generals were all the while searching about for him in the high ground of the Tell.

On the 7th February, he was encamped at the foot of the Djurjura. While engaged in midnight prayer, he heard the French order to charge. In another moment, the French were upon him. He sprang on his horse and called on his men to rally. The Chasseurs closed around him. He fought with them single-handed. Two horses were shot under him. He fought on foot. He became undistinguishable in the confusion of the skirmish, and aided by the darkness of the night effected his escape.

On the 28th Abdel Kader held a grand council of war at Burj bou Keni. Deputies from all the Kabyle tribes were present. The question of war was warmly mooted. For a time the majority were in favour of a continuation of hostilities. At this moment news was brought in that Bugeaud was advancing against them with superior forces. The moderate party immediately gained the ascendancy. Attack and defence were declared to be alike hazardous. Prudence was preferable to a fruitless enthusiasm. In that would be the best guarantee for the preservation of their liberties.

Abdel Kader left the Djurjura. In a few hours he was in the vicinity of Bayhan. There, on the 7th of March, he surprised, routed, and plundered the French Douairs, with his body guard of 2,000 cavalry. The booty was immense. All the mules and camels of the tribes scarcely sufficed to remove it. The long train and its escort entered the passes of the Djebel Amour, seeking by rapid stages the districts of the Beni Nail, in the Sahara.

On the 13th, while bringing up the rear guard with seventy men, Abdel Kader was again attacked by General Yoosuf, who, finding out the direction he had taken, had followed him up by forced marches. An open space of ground gave the French unusual advantages. Abdel Kader was conspicuous on a white charger. Alternately firing and charging, he kept the enemy at bay. His men fought with desperation. Forty were killed. At length, after two hours' hard fighting, and after performing prodigies of valour, Abdel Kader was lost to view in a defile.

The French were amazed at his gallantry. When, at a later period, he was in Paris, the object of universal curiosity and admiration, the French general who commanded on this memorable day recalled to Abdel Kader the impression made on all who witnessed his chivalrous demeanour at a moment when to all appearances he was irrecoverably lost, "If one of our officers had displayed such extraordinary heroism," said General Yoosuf, "the Emperor would have sent him the decoration of the Legion of Honour."

Abdel Kader had hoped to recruit his forces amongst the tribes of the Sahara. But the French had forestalled him. Everywhere their columns and detachments made themselves felt. The Beni Nail, the Beni Shaib, the Beni Hassan, from whose resources he had long been accustomed to supply his wants, and with whom he had often found shelter in the hour of need, all submitted successively to the persevering foe. Wherever Abdel Kader presented himself he found lassitude and despondency. Indeed his presence began to be looked upon as an omen of misfortune, and a prelude to ruin.

He visited the Oulad-Sidi-Chirk, a large and powerful tribe at the southern extremity of the Sahara. Their chiefs and marabouts thronged about him. They condoled with him. They assured him of their warmest sympathies. They offered him a temporary hospitality. But they adjured him not to entail upon them the horrors of war, and so to expose the venerated tombs of their saints to the profanation of the infidel. Abdel Kader received the intimation with composure and resignation. Accompanied by his faithful escort, he now returned to his Deira, on the Melouia, in Morocco.

He arrived there July 18th, 1846. A terrible episode had just occurred. The French prisoners taken in the affairs of Sidi Ibrahim and Ain Temouchen, in September, 1845, had been sent to the Deira. They had been presented to the Sultan's mother, had met with a most assuring reception, and had been well treated. Nothing was withheld that could mitigate the painfulness of their situation. Abdel Kader had more than once written to Bugeaud, offering an exchange of prisoners, but his offer had been treated with contempt. Such was the position of the prisoners when he had left the Deira, on his late expedition.

The Deira, to which was always attached a small body of regulars, was under the charge of Ben Hamedi. On the 10th of April, 1846, Mustapha-ibn-Thamy, the Sultan's brother-in-law, arrived from the Sahara and took the command. He had left Abdel Kader three days after his brilliant action with General Yoosuf, in the Djebel Amour, and brought with him several wounded and invalids. He found the Deira greatly reduced in numbers, by desertion, by suffering, by privation. Provisions had become scarce. The Moorish tribes in the vicinity would only furnish supplies for ready money; and of money there was little or none. Two hundred and eighty prisoners had become an embarrassment.

In this crisis a report reached Mustapha-ibn-Thamy that the Moorish troops, who were not far distant, were about to advance and rescue the prisoners. He had no force sufficient to resist such an enterprise if it was attempted. The idea of such a stain upon his honour preyed upon his mind. If he made his small band of regulars fight to keep them, Moslem blood would be shed, and probably fruitlessly shed, for the sake of infidels. If he tamely surrendered them, how could he look Abdel Kader in the face? He determined to make away with them. On the night of the 24th of April they were massacred. Ten officers alone were spared.

The first step taken by Abdel Kader on his arrival at the Deira, July 18th, was to endeavour to get the survivors exchanged. His efforts, as usual in such matters, failed. They were, however, finally ransomed for 30,000 francs. Abdel Kader felt it due to his own reputation, utterly guiltless as he was of this deed of blood, to address the following letter to the King of the French :—

"Praise be to God, the merciful and compassionate. Glory to our lord and master Mohammed.

"On the part of the Prince of the Faithful, Sid-il Hadj Abdel Kader-ibn Mehi-ed-deen, may God vouchsafe unto him his favour both in this and another world; to the Sultan of the Christians, the commander-in-chief of the French armies, King Louis Philippe, may God constantly promote the increase of his power, and the execution of his projects in all that relates to the happiness of his people, and especially enable him to exalt those who follow the good path, and to confound all who do otherwise.

"I would call to your recollection that we have ever been ready to accept conditions of peace. We have even accepted conditions which you thought proper to impose upon us. We rejoiced to be on a good understanding with you. Our alliance was cemented by good faith. Our treaties had your personal approbation. By an exchange of presents we likewise confirmed our mutual feelings of friendship.

" Such was our position up to the moment when certain influential persons in Algeria gave a too willing ear to perfidious insinuations tending to interrupt the harmony which existed between us, and represented us as being culpable and blameworthy, whereas it was we, on the contrary, who had every reason to complain of their injustice committed towards us.

" I have written to you many times, both officially and confidentially, and invariably my intentions were misconstrued to such an extent that the evil consequences spread themselves unchecked all over Algeria.

" During our late expedition in the East, and in the numerous battles we fought, God permitted many prisoners to fall into our hands. We rejoiced at the circumstance, because it gave us power to offer an exchange. Last year we were unable to treat for the deliverance of the Mussulman prisoners in your hands, because we were not prepared to offer you a proposition which would have suited you. In previous years, however, we have sent back to Marshal Bugeaud more than a hundred prisoners without exchange.

" Lately, when we had a certain number of your subjects in our power, we wrote more than once to those who represent you to propose an exchange of prisoners. We received no answer. All the bearers of our letters were imprisoned. That was a treachery foreign to French usage. Besides, a message between hostile sides is always considered neutral.

" Shortly afterwards it was rumoured amongst the Arabs that the French prisoners were to be rescued by force. It was known that French agents had offered large sums of money to any who would conduct the prisoners to the French outposts. It was, moreover, openly declared that the Emperor of Morocco had undertaken to rescue the prisoners in spite of us. Your own agents thus became the chief cause of the deplorable event which has occurred, by their persistence in refusing to treat of an exchange of prisoners.

" We have never made any difference between the prisoners and our own men as regards their food and lodging. As soon as we saw there were amongst them men of rank and honour, who scorned to seek for means of escape, we gave them a marked preference over the others. We found them grateful. We proposed to set them at liberty. Their chief (Cognord) knows all the arrangements which were being made for their liberation. He knows that we never received any reply to our letters, and that this contemptuous silence was the cause of the cessation of the good understanding between you and us."

Abdel Kader concluded with an urgent appeal for the release of some Mussulman prisoners, and a warm exculpation of himself from all knowledge or connivance at any measures whatever which were contrary to justice and religion. This letter, like all the preceding, remained unanswered.

During Abdel Kader's late absence from the Deira, several Arab tribes had been gradually crossing the frontier, and fixing themselves on Moorish territory. The Moorish Sultan had given them lands to occupy. The jealousy of the French was awakened. They feared that the emigrants might eventually become the nucleus of an invading force. The late massacre added to their impatience. They called upon Sultan

Abderahman to show at once by his deeds the sincerity of his professions. They demanded the immediate expulsion of Abdel Kader from his empire.

Abdel Kader, meanwhile, only anxious for freedom from molestation, had already commenced sowing the grounds near the Melouia for the subsistence of his Deira. Bou Maza wrote to him inviting him to join him in renewing the struggle. He rejected the instigation. With whatever the future might be pregnant, for the present he sought only repose and tranquillity. But these blessings he was not allowed to obtain. Mouley Abderahman sent him a letter to the effect that he must immediately withdraw, with his Deira, from Moorish territory.

Abdel Kader assembled his followers, and read them the letter. They unanimously declared it would be ignominious to yield to the demand of a recreant who had betrayed his faith and signed a humiliating treaty with the infidel. "We have pledged ourselves by oath," they said, "to fight with you to the death. We are ready to follow you wherever you choose. But into Algeria we will not follow you. Abdel Kader conveyed these sentiments to Abderahman, promising at the same time not to attack the French. In his Deira he would resignedly await the decrees of God.

The Moorish tribes were now secretly instructed to molest the Deira. They refused to sell it provisions. Its foraging parties were attacked and robbed. Abdel Kader wrote a strong appeal to Abderahman against such conduct. He got neither answer nor redress. He endured this treatment patiently for six months. Again he addressed the Moorish Sultan, and warned him that if such annoyances were continued he should vindicate his own rights.

In self-defence he now re-assumed a hostile attitude. His body-guard of 1,200 cavalry and 800 infantry patrolled the country on all sides. The Moorish aggressors were chased to their very tents; they were brought to the Deira and chastised. By a few such acts of vigour his position was improved; provisions flowed in. More than one Moorish tribe offered to join the Deira. Wherever Abdel Kader showed his person he was welcomed with professions of submission and allegiance; his material strength increased hourly. The large and influential tribe of the Beni Hamian sent in their adhesion.

One night, while the Deira was still at Ain Zohra, an assassin glided, unperceived by the guards, into the tent of Abdel Kader. The Sultan was reading. Hearing a footstep, he raised his head, and saw standing before him a tall, powerful negro, with a dagger in his hand. Suddenly the man dashed the weapon to the ground, and threw himself at his feet. "I was going to strike you," he exclaimed, "but the sight of you disarmed me. I thought I saw the halo of the Prophet around your head."

Abdel Kader, rising slowly from his seat, and without betraying the least emotion, placed his hand on the negro's head and said, "You came into my tent as an assassin. God, who moved you to repent of your wicked intention, has ordained that you should leave it an innocent man. Go, then, and remember that the servant of God has pardoned you."

In the month of July, 1847, the Deira was encamped in Wady Aslaf, on the territory of the Kabyles of the Rif. While in this position it was suddenly menaced by a large Moorish force led by Mouley Hashem, the Sultan's nephew, and the Kaid El Hamra. The Prince began by sending out a strong reconnaissance, which was immediately repulsed by the Deira's outposts. Abdel Kader sent to the Prince to demand an explanation as to the cause of this hostile proceeding in the midst of peace. He received a haughty and disdainful answer. That very night he fell upon the Moorish camp by surprise, and completely routed and dispersed it. The Kaid El Hamra was slain, and Mouley Hashem barely escaped with his life.

A great quantity of baggage was taken, and specie to the amount of £2,000 English money. Abdel Kader and his chiefs viewed with mingled feelings of scorn and triumph the splendid cloaks and burnouses which the Moorish Prince had packed up in cases, for the purpose of distributing them amongst the Sheiks of the Rif tribes, and inducing them by such gifts to join him. On his return to the Deira Abdel Kader found that the Beni Kullayieh, availing themselves of his absence, had made an irruption into his camp and carried off all the camels. Without a moment's repose he pursued the marauders, slew upwards of a hundred of them, and captured all their Sheiks.

The rumour of Abdel Kader's renewed activity, and of the momentary gleam of success which shone upon his efforts, was quickly bruited throughout the Moorish empire. It created a sensation amongst its fanatic population which thrilled to the very capital. The emigrant Algerian tribes, which had been located by order of the Moorish Sultan within three days of Fez, longed to regain their adored chief. The Beni Amer entered into correspondence with him, and begged him to assist them in effecting a junction.

Sultan Abderahman got notice of the design. In his terror he fancied Abdel Kader thundering at his palace and hurling him from his throne. Not a moment was to be lost; a force of 15,000 men was at once despatched against Beni Amer. The tribe, taken unawares, was cut to pieces, while the women and children were carried away into slavery.

Such persevering and even barbarous acts of hostility filled Abdel Kader with despair and indignation. But what could his handful of men effect against the combined armies of France and Morocco, amounting to 100,000 men? He determined to make a last appeal to his old friend, patron, and admirer. He sent his Khalifa, Bou Hamedi, on a mission to Fez. In the most solemn manner he invoked the glorious recollections of the past. He claimed the sacred rites of hospitality in the name of every tie of friendship and religion.

But the days of country, of fraternity, of holy sympathy, were irrevocably past. Mouley Abderahman saw himself daily environed with fresh difficulties. The French Government hourly demanded the literal execution of its treaty. Bou Hamedi was thrown into prison, where he shortly afterwards died. Abdel Kader at length received the following imperial mandate : — "Abdel Kader must either surrender himself in person to Sultan Abderahman, or return to the Algerian desert. In case of refusal or delay, the imperial armies will march against him." The last link was thus broken between him and his only hope. He stood at bay, alone.

Calm and undismayed, he now saw the toils closing around him. In the Deira all was grief and despondency. His own brothers had left him. Ben Salem—the faithful, long-tried,

S

and devoted Ben Salem—was a voluntary prisoner in the French camp. His whole available force barely amounted to 2,000 men, but among these there were 1,200 horsemen, the flower of the Algerian cavalry. Most of these men, also, had been the Sultan's inseparable companions, partakers in all his hardships and dangers throughout the whole of his heroic career.

During the short period of rest which Abdel Kader now enjoyed, he daily summoned them around him. He was incessant in vocal prayer and exhortation. The bronzed old warriors hung with rapture on his accents. Fired with martial enthusiasm, they prepared for the final act.

At other times Abdel Kader retired to his tent, and kept long and lonely vigils. One night he stood up for seven successive hours while he repeated off by heart the whole of the Koran, from beginning to end. In such religious exercises he renewed his soul's strength. Ever worthy of his destiny, he now towered above it.

CHAPTER XX

1847.

On the 9th of December, 1847, the Deira was stationed at Agueddin, on the left bank of the Melouia. It comprised in all about 5,000 souls. Rumours had long been afloat that the Moroccan army was advancing towards it in great strength. On the 10th Abdel Kader got positive information that Muley Mohammed and Muley Soliman, the two sons of Sultan Abderahman, were at only three hours' distance, at the head of upwards of 50,000 men. This force, he learned, was divided into three grand divisions, with intervals of half a mile between each. The first division, consisting mostly of Arab auxiliaries, such as the tribes of the Riff, the Beni Snassen, and others, had taken up its ground, it was reported, around the ruined castle of Selwan.

Abdel Kader saw at once that if this imposing array was permitted to move forwards unmolested, his Deira would inevitably be captured. On the other hand, to attack it with his small force seemed to him like to rushing on certain destruction. Feelings of honour, of chivalry, of revenge, however, all conspired to make him determine on essaying a desperate effort.

On the 11th he collected together his 1,200 cavalry and 800 infantry. After a spirited harangue, he informed them that they must prepare that very night to follow him to battle. To such a command, amongst such followers, there could be but one reply. They all departed in silence to accoutre themselves for the approaching struggle.

At dead of night they moved on. Two camels, covered entirely with *halfa,* a kind of brushwood, and which had been dipped in tar and pitch, were driven in front of the little column. After a march of two hours the first division of the enemy was reached; the *halfa* around the camels was set fire to, and the maddened animals plunged furiously on; the infantry fired; the cavalry, led on by Abdel Kader, charged.

The amazement and bewilderment of the Moroccans and the Arabs upon whom this sudden tempest fell was immeasurable. Slumbering in fancied security during the calm silence of the night, they suddenly saw the thick darkness illumined by flashes of light, the glistening of sabres, and the glare of two incomprehensible meteors sweeping above and around them with unearthly coruscations. The terrors of superstition were superadded to those of fright and consternation. The men rushed off in all directions, as though the gates of hell had been opened and its demons let loose against them, abandoning arms, tents, and baggage.

In the meantime Abdel Kader and his cavalry had passed on, and were in deadly collision with the second division, which in like manner was surprised, defeated, and dispersed. In less than half an hour the third division was reached. There, warned by the noise and tumult in their front, the Moroccan princes had just had time to draw up some regulars to defend their persons. The intention of Abdel Kader was to make straight for their tent and make them prisoners.

Checked by a heavy fire of infantry and artillery, he now withdrew; and, as the day dawned, slowly and steadily he took up a position on an adjoining eminence, and thence enjoyed the sight of his discomfited and broken foe.

At mid-day, 5,000 Moroccan cavalry moved out against him. He calmly awaited their approach, and when they had arrived at a charging distance led on his men to the attack, ploughing through and through their clustering files, and shaking them off like dew-drops from the lion's mane. By a skilful combination of assault and retreat, Abdel Kader and his illustrious cavalcade regained the Melouia towards sunset.

Many were the brilliant passages of arms performed by those giant warriors, who, in that memorable. struggle, crowned their long career of glory by deeds of superhuman valour. Memorable also was that struggle, as having furnished the closing scene to the stirring and eventful career of Ibn Yahyié, the favourite and far-famed Aga of Abdel Kader. Ibn Yahyié was the stalwart champion of countless combats. He was surnamed "El Sheitan" from his wondrous exploits and marvellous escapes. In his day he had had seventeen horses killed under him. It was now his destiny to earn his last laurels in a martyr's death.

The Deira had nearly effected its passage across the river. The baggage and the spoils taken from the enemy were still traversing it when Abdel Kader arrived. The Moroccan army advanced, but cautiously. Their cavalry now only fired long shots, unenvious of renewing their lately-earned bitter experience.

Nevertheless, the situation of Abdel Kader was full of peril. Never had the Deira been in such imminent danger.

The ammunition was expended. The large quantities of ammunition which Abdel Kader's followers had captured and were now bringing in proved useless—it was unsuited to their muskets. The infantry, therefore, could be turned to no account. But Abdel Kader still saw his Old Guard around him, and looked and felt triumphant. Their presence was, in his mind, the Deira's safeguard.

The Melouia was at length passed. Though the foe kept pressing on, Abdel Kader refused to leave its banks until his Deira was a full hour in advance, on the plain of Triffa. At last it reached the river Kis, crossed it about midnight, and ceased to be molested. It was on French territory.

Of all that tumultuous crowd of men, women, children, and animals, not a life had been sacrificed, not a beast of burden had been lost. Abdel Kader, by his coolness, skill, and intrepidity, had been its guardian genius. Many a sad blank, however, had been made in the ranks of that heroic band, which with such unflinching devotion had answered to the voice of its chief and emulated his example, throughout the unparalleled foray in which under his guidance they had been so unequally engaged. Upwards of 200 had been slain. All were more or less bleeding from wounds. Abdel Kader himself had had three horses shot under him.

Leaving his Deira in momentary security, he now turned towards the hills of the Beni Snassen—a tribe which yet adhered to him in part. His indomitable cavalry followed in anxious silence, suffering, wearied, and exhausted. The rain fell in torrents. Heavy and conflicting thoughts preyed on the mind of the wandering chief. Though the French were seen in the distance, occupying the principal pass of the Kerbous, there were yet narrow defiles through which he could emerge into the Sahara. He might yet try his fortunes. But to what end? he thought despairingly. How was he to persevere in a bootless struggle? What force had he at command? On what assistance could he calculate? Then his thoughts reverted to his aged mother, his wife and children, his helpless followers, who were within three hours of the French camp, and might probably enter it ere long a mounted train, as prisoners of war. In no extremity had Abdel Kader ever found himself so hopelessly pressed. He felt the crisis of his fate had come. What he meant to determine, he knew he must determine quickly.

He sounded a halt. He ordered his men to close up. When they had surrounded him, he thus commenced a conference which he had that moment resolved to open :—

"Do you remember the oath you took at Medea eight years ago, at the renewal of the war," he said—"the oath that you would never forsake or abandon me, whatever might be your dangers or sufferings?"

"We all remember it, and are ready still to adhere to it."

"That oath," pursued Abdel Kader, "I have ever considered to be binding on me towards you, as well as on you towards me. It is this feeling alone which has made me persevere in our struggle up to this hour, even against hope. I was resolved that no Mussulman, of whatever rank or degree, should ever be able to accuse me of binding you to any engagement which I on my part was not equally prepared to fulfil; or to say that I had not done all in my power to insure the triumph of the cause of God. If you think I can yet do anything, tell me. If not, I ask you to release me from the oath I made you mentally, when I solemnly demanded yours."

"We all bear witness before God, that you have done all that it was in your power to do for his cause. At the day of judgment God will do you justice."

"If that is your opinion, we have now only three courses open before us—either to return for the Deira, and with it be prepared to encounter every obstacle; or to seek out a path for ourselves into the Sahara, in which case, the women, children, and wounded would not be able to follow us, and must fall into the hands of the enemy; or, lastly, to submit."

"Perish women and children, both ours and yours, so long as you are safe and able to renew the battles of God. You are our head, our Sultan; fight or surrender, as you will, we will follow you wherever you choose to lead."

Abdel Kader paused for a few moments, and then with deep emotion resumed :—

"Believe me, the struggle is over. Let us be resigned. God is witness that we have fought as long as we have been able. If He has not given us the victory, it is because He has deemed that this land should belong to the Christians. It signifies very little whether I remain in the country or not. What more can I do for the cause we have so long defended together? Can I renew the war? I shall be defeated; and the Arabs would only be exposed to renewed sufferings.

"Besides, the tribes are tired of the war. They would no longer obey me. We must submit. The only question is, whether we shall deliver ourselves into the hands of the Christians, or into those of Mouley Abderahman. In this respect you can do as you judge best. As for myself, I would prefer a thousand times to trust in those who have fought against me, than in the man who has betrayed me. Our situation is difficult; and our demands must consequently be modest. I shall confine myself to asking for a safe conduct for myself and my family, and those of you who choose to follow me to another Mussulman country."

A doubt was now raised by some of the members of the conference as to the probability of such a stipulation being faithfully carried into execution. To this doubt Abdel Kader replied, " Do not be afraid. The word of the French is one. Either they will not pledge their word to its fulfilment, and then we can see what is best to be done; or if they pledge their word, they will keep it." "Sultan," was the universal reply, " let your will be done."

The rain was still falling so incessantly that it was impossible for Abdel Kader to write down his demands. Taking a piece of paper, he affixed his seal to it, and immediately dispatched it with two horsemen, who were commissioned to show the seal to the French General, as a sign of authorisation on his part for demands which they were to make in his name verbally.

During the night of the 21st December, Lamoricière had been informed both of the arrival of the Deira within the French frontier, and of the direction which Abdel Kader and his little force had taken. To the Deira he at once sent assurances of safety. The prize was important. But the concentration of any amount of men against the camp of Abdel Kader would have been of little permanent avail, if the redoubtable chief himself were yet at large. Without a moment's delay, therefore, Lamoricière started in his pursuit, at the head of a small column of infantry and cavalry.

He had scarcely marched three hours when he was unexpectedly joined by Ben Khouia, a lieutenant of his Arab Spahis, accompanied by the two emissaries of Abdel Kader. The latter showed him their master's seal and stated his demands. Lamoricière was overjoyed. He granted everything. But, as in the case of Abdel Kader, the rain prevented him from stating his consent in writing, and his seal was not in his possession. In this emergency he gave his sword, and the seal of Commandant Bazaine, to the emissaries, to be presented to Abdel Kader in token of the acceptance of his conditions.

At a later period, when taunted in the Chamber of Deputies with having allowed Abdel Kader to escape, when by a little energy he could have taken him prisoner, and with having committed a grave error in so unreservedly granting him the privilege of unrestricted liberty, Lamoricière thus defended his conduct, defined his position, and stated the motives which had induced him to sign the treaty thus attacked :—

" It has been brought as a charge against me that I entered into a negotiation in place of marching on. Do you know what I should have taken if I had marched on ? I should have taken his convoy; I should have made one razzia the more; I should have been able to report that I had taken the tent of Abdel Kader, his carpet, his harem, perhaps one of his Khalifas; but he, with his cavalry, would have gone into the desert.

" The Emir made a voluntary abdication; and France,

after having thrown the whole weight of its brave armies upon Algeria, saw the chief who had preached, excited, and conducted the Holy War, come in the end, and voluntarily deposit his arms in the hands of the Governor-General. For France, this was at once a military, a political, and a moral triumph. The effect produced by it among the natives was immense, and its consequences have yet to be developed.

" Abdel Kader is the incarnation of a principle—of a great religious sentiment; and in Algeria this is the only political sentiment which unites the population. This principle manifested itself in the Holy War. It had the same force which legitimacy formerly possessed amongst us. When a man by the prestige of the past, by his belief, by his eloquence, by the battles he has fought, and by the successes he has gained, has become the living representative of an idea profoundly agitating the masses, an immense danger is incurred as long as he is left in his country."

Abdel Kader had moved on to the village of Triaret. His emissaries returned. He convoked his men to deliberate on the answer which he had received. It was remarked that the promise given by the French general was merely verbal; and, although the value of the answer was acknowledged, supported as it was by the transmission of the general's sword and the seal of one of his officers, yet it was considered only prudent, when a decision of such vital importance to all was to be taken, that a further guarantee should be claimed.

The rain having ceased, Abdel Kader now wrote a letter to Lamoricière, stating his demands, and again dispatched his emissaries to seek him out. The general had already communicated the important transaction to the Duc

D'Aumale, the new Governor-General, who happened to be in the immediate neighbourhood. On receiving Abdel Kader's letter, he had addressed his Royal Highness as follows :—

" I have been obliged to make engagements; I have made them, and I have done so with the fullest confidence that your Royal Highness and the Government will ratify them if the Emir relies on my word.

" I am this instant mounting my horse to go to the Deira. I have no time to send you a copy of the letter which I have received from the Emir, or of my reply to it. Suffice it for me to state, that I have only *promised and stipulated* that the Emir and his family shall be conducted to St. Jean d'Acre or Alexandria. These are the only two places which I have mentioned. They are those which he designated in his demand, and which I have accepted."

With a written stipulation in his possession, in entire compliance with his own terms, Abdel Kader had no further cause for hesitation or delay. On the morning of the 23rd of December he proceeded, accompanied by such of his chiefs and followers as had decided on sharing his fortunes in a foreign land, to the marabout (or temple) of Sidi Ibrahim. There he was received by Colonel Montauban, at the head of 500 cavalry, with all the respect, sympathy, and consideration due to his exalted rank, to the recollection of his past glorious deeds, and to the spectacle of his present heavy and severe misfortune.

Abdel Kader begged for permission to be allowed to enter the sacred edifice. On this request being granted, he dismounted, and, on reaching the door, took off his sword, and gave it to one of his attendants. His military career had ended. Hitherto his life had been devoted to God and his country. Henceforth it was to be devoted to God alone. After having been an hour engaged in prayer, he came forth, and the whole cavalcade at once moved on.

At six o'clock in the evening it reached Djemma Ghazouat, the head-quarters of the Duc D'Aumale. A few minutes afterwards Abdel Kader, accompanied by General de Lamoricière, General Cavaignac, and Colonel Beaufort, was presented to his Royal Highness. After a moment's pause he pronounced the following words:—" I had wished to have done what I am doing this day at an earlier period. I awaited the hour destined by God. The general has given me a word on which I fully rely. I am not afraid that it will be broken by the son of a great king like the King of the French."

The Prince, in a few clear and explicit words, pledged himself that the general's word and engagements should be strictly observed. Abdel Kader then withdrew and went to his Deira, which had recently joined the French encampment.

The next morning the Duc D'Aumale held a review. Abdel Kader, riding a magnificent black charger of the purest Arab breed, and surrounded by his chiefs, awaited his return from the field. On his Royal Highness approaching he dismounted, and advancing to his side, said, "I offer you this horse, the last which I have mounted. It has been a great favourite, but now we must part. It is a testimony of my gratitude, and I hope it may always carry you in safety and happiness." "I accept it," replied the Prince, "as a homage rendered to France, the protection of which country will henceforth be ever extended towards you; and as a sign that the past is forgotten."

On the 25th December, 1847, Abdel Kader, his family and followers, embarked in the *Asmodeus* frigate for Toulon. All his personal effects, his baggage, his tents, his horses, mules, and camels, had previously been sold by the French authorities for 6,000 francs. But even this paltry sum was afterwards only doled out to him in instalments, and a strict investigation was even instituted as to the manner in which each instalment was disbursed. General de Lamoricière accompanied him on board, and generously made him a present of 4,000 francs. Abdel Kader, in return, gave him his sword.

The sensations of joy and triumph excited in France at the news of Abdel Kader's surrender were unbounded. Algeria could at last and with truth be styled "a French colony." The *Moniteur* of January 3rd, 1848, thus alludes to the welcome intelligence:—" The subjugation of Abdel Kader is an event of immense importance to France. It assures the tranquillity of our conquest. It permits us sensibly to reduce the quota of men and money which we have been sending for so many years to Africa. It contributes, from this fact alone, to augment the force of France in Europe. *To-day, France can, if necessary, transport to other quarters the hundred thousand men which held the conquered populations under her yoke.*"

What a tribute are these words to the genius and ascendancy of one man!

CHAPTER XXI.

1847—1848.

ABDEL KADER arrived at Toulon the last week in December, 1847. A few hours, or days at most, he thought, would suffice for any arrangement which might still be necessary to facilitate his departure for the East. He was invited to disembark, though no preparations whatever had been made to receive him.

To his surprise, he and his family, and followers, eighty-eight in all, were marched up to a fortress—the Fortress of Lamalgue. He remonstrated. He was told not to be alarmed; and it was explained to him that a certain time was necessary for the requisite correspondence, either with the Turkish Government, if he was to be sent to St. Jean d'Acre, or with the Egyptian Government, if he was to be sent to Alexandria; and that then he could be allowed to proceed to his place of destination.

The day after his imprisonment a French officer demanded an interview. General Daumas came, officially charged by the King of the French, to make him the most brilliant offers, if he would only consent to forego the solemn word which had been given him by General Lamoricière and the Duc D'Aumale when he surrendered. He was offered a splendid position in France—a royal château, a guard of honour, and all the pomp and appurtenances of a prince.

Abdel Kader listened to the shameful proposal in contemptuous silence. Being pressed for a reply, his countenance flashed up, and fixing his eagle eye on his old friend, he said with warmth, "Have you ceased to know me? What! is it you who thus speaks to me? Your diplomatic talents, I have no doubt, are very useful to France; but I intreat you not to expend them thus uselessly on me."

Then, taking up a corner of his burnous with both hands, and leaning towards the window, he exclaimed, "If you were to bring me, on the part of your King, all the wealth of France in millions and in diamonds, and it were possible to place them all in the fold of my burnous, I would throw them on the instant into the sea which washes my prison walls, rather than give you back the word which has been so solemnly given me. That word I will carry with me to my grave. I am your guest. Make me your prisoner if you will; but the shame and ignominy will be with you, not with me."

He was asked if he would like to go to Paris. "I know," he replied, "that Ibrahim Pacha lately visited it, and admired its wonders. But France was to him a land of hospitality. He was free! As for me, as long as I remain a prisoner, all France is but a dungeon. I have no wish to be a victim crowned with garlands."

Patient and resigned himself, Abdel Kader infused his followers with the same spirit. They had hitherto been his subjects, accustomed to approach him with all the deference and respect due to royalty. They were now his companions.

A common calamity had levelled all barriers. He placed his little means at their disposal, too happy if he could in any way contribute to their wants and alleviate their sufferings. "In the position in which I am now placed," he said, "I must do as my ancestors have done. I can no longer say, 'My horse, my burnous, my goods;' but 'Our horse, our burnous, our goods.'"

One day General Daumas came to visit him. It was in the depth of winter. Abdel Kader was without a fire. The general expressed his surprise. "My wood," he replied, "was finished yesterday, and I could not bring myself to ask any of my companions to spare me some of theirs. Poor fellows! in place of taking from them, I wish it were always in my power to bestow." "You are not, then, like those great chiefs who seem to take a pleasure in exhausting their people," remarked General Daumas. "If I had resembled such rulers," was the reply of Abdel Kader, "would the Arabs have sustained the struggle with you so long as they did, and sacrificed everything to uphold me?"

Day after day passed, and still there came no orders for his release. A painful uncertainty agitated his mind. At one time Colonel Beaufort, the Duc D'Aumale's aide-de-camp, assured him, on the part of the Prince, that the King had resolved that the stipulation made with him should be fulfilled. At another time he was told that the Chamber of Deputies had called its validity in question.

On the 28th of February, 1848, Abdel Kader got the news of the revolution, of the abdication of the king, of the proclamation of the Republic. He saw at once the immense import of that event to his own prospects, and felt himself to be the sport of a capricious fortune. With the new Government he had no bond. He could no longer plead for the sanctity of treaties, of honour, of good faith. He could not expect an act of generosity, he felt, when he had failed to obtain common justice.

The sudden crash of a monarchy, hitherto supposed to be fixed on a solid and enduring basis, was to him an apposite spectacle. He moralised to those around him on the worthlessness and instability of human grandeur. "Behold," he said to General Daumas, "behold a Sultan who was everywhere esteemed great and powerful, who had contracted alliances with other sovereigns, who had a numerous family to perpetuate his line, who was renowned for his wisdom and experience! A day has sufficed to overthrow him. Am I not right in my conviction that there is no other real force, no truth and no reality, but in the will of God? Believe me, this world is a carcass; dogs only quarrel over it."

He received a visit from M. Olivier, Commissary-General of the Provisional Government. The great Republic had deigned to think of its captive. But it approached him not as a Paladin, chivalrously determined to redeem French honour, but as a suppliant, trembling at the magic of a name which, even in its collapse, was of ominous import to French dominion. He was asked what guarantees he could give to France that he would not appear again in Algeria.

"I have no other guarantee to give of my unchangeable resolution for the future," he replied, "but that which I have already given. If I had not wished to surrender I should not have been here. I came to you freely and voluntarily. This guarantee is worth all others." "Would you sign with your hand," pursued the delegate, "and will the chiefs who are around you sign with their hands, a document sworn to on the Koran, by which you solemnly declare that you will never appear again in Algeria, or mix yourselves up, directly or indirectly, in its affairs?" "Such a document I would sign with my eyes, if my hands were not sufficient." Abdel Kader was then asked to address a letter to the Provisional Government, enclosing a document to that effect. He penned and forwarded the following *précis :—*

"Praise be to the one God, whose empire alone is everlasting.

"To the upholders of the Republic which governs France, and who are, with regard to it, as the eyes and limbs are to the body.

"Sidi Olivier, your commissioner, has been to see me. He has informed me that the French, with one accord, have abolished royalty, and have decreed that their country shall henceforward be a Republic.

"I was rejoiced at the news, for I have read in books that such a form of government has for its object to root out injustice, and to prevent the strong from doing violence to the weak. You are generous men. You desire the good of all ; and your acts are expected to be dictated by the spirit of justice. God has appointed you to be the protectors of the unhappy and afflicted. I look to you, therefore, as my natural protectors. Remove the veil of grief which has been thrown over me. I seek justice at your hands.

"That which I have done not one of you can condemn. I defended my country and my religion as long as I could ; and I am persuaded that, as noble-minded men, you cannot but applaud me. When I was conquered—when it was impossible for me any longer to doubt that God, for inscrutable reasons, had withdrawn his support from me—I decided to withdraw from the world. It was then, when I could have found an asylum with perfect ease amongst the Berbers, or the tribes of the Sahara, that I consented to place myself in the hands of the French.

"I was convinced that when once they promised to do so, they would convey me to the country whither I declared it my wish to go. It was with this conviction that I selected France wherein to put my trust; for the word of France up to this day has been held to be inviolable. I demanded from General Lamoricière that I should be conveyed to Alexandria, without touching at Oran, or Algiers, or any port in France.

"To this demand he not only gave a verbal adhesion, but sent me a letter solemnly guaranteeing the fulfilment of my wish, signed with his name in French, and sealed with his Arabic seal. When this letter reached me, believing the word of the French was *one*, I gave myself up into his hands. At present this belief is shaken. Confirm me in it by giving me my liberty. You have accomplished a work which promises to confer happiness on all. Let me not be a solitary exception.

"Often have I said to myself, 'Had the French taken me prisoner in battle, they would have treated me well; for they are brave and generous, and know how to hold the balance between the conqueror and the conquered.' Well, I have not been made prisoner. I gave myself up of my own free will. Some of you may imagine that, regretting the step I took, I still harbour thoughts of returning to Algeria. That can never be. I may actually be numbered amongst the dead. My sole wish is to be allowed to go to Mecca and Medina, there to worship and adore the all-powerful God, until He calls me to Him.

"Receive my salutations.

"ABDEL KADER IBN MEHI-ED-DEEN.

"9 *Rebia il Oual,* 1264.

"*March,* 1848."

Within this letter was enclosed the document demanded at his hands. It ran as follows:—

"Praise be to the One God.

"I give you a sacred word which cannot be doubted.

"I declare that I will never henceforward excite troubles against the French, either in person, or by letters, or by any other means whatsoever.

"I make this oath before God, by Mohammed (praise and salutation be to him), by Abraham, Moses, and Jesus Christ; by the Pentateuch, the Gospel, and the Koran. I make this oath with my heart as well as with my hand and tongue.

"This oath is binding on me and on my companions, one hundred and more in number; on those who sign this document, and on those who sign it not, being unable to write.

"Salutation from ABDEL KADER IBN MEHI-ED-DEEN."

Abdel Kader felt assured that these documents, having been officially demanded, would prove the immediate prelude to his release. The dawn of each successive day was hailed as the harbinger of liberty. At last the anxiously expected answer arrived. It was opened with impatience. Its substance was, that "the Republic considered itself bound by no obligation to Abdel Kader, and that it took him as the previous Government had left him—a prisoner."

The bitter mockery pierced Abdel Kader to the heart. He sunk into the deepest despondency. Life was a burden to him, he declared. General Daumas approached him with words of consolation. "How can you be surprised," he exclaimed in reply, with mournful earnestness, "that my resignation should falter before the greatness of my calamity? My family, my followers, are in despair. My aged mother and the women of my household weep night and day, and no longer credit the hope I am obliged to hold out to them.

"What do I say? Not only the women, but the men, give way to lamentations. Their state is such, that I am persuaded if our captivity is much prolonged, many will die. And it is I who am the cause of all this misery! I alone persisted in surrendering to the French. None of them willingly consented to it. You have, indeed, made me a deceiver; and now they all reproach me for my confidence in you.

"Is there no tribunal in France especially charged to hear the cries and reclamations of the injured? Call together all your Ulemas, and I undertake to convince them of my rights. Ah! the Republic is far different from that Sultan who, having become deaf, was seen to weep; and being asked the cause of his tears, replied, 'I weep because I can no longer hear the complaints of the distressed and afflicted.'"

An order came for the removal of the prisoners to the Château of Pau. They arrived there April 20th, 1848. The authorities had been informed that English agents were in the neighbourhood seeking to facilitate Abdel Kader's escape. The windows of the château were barred with iron. Sentinels paced under them night and day.

Abdel Kader smiled inwardly at all these precautions. The season of suspense was over. He felt himself a prisoner for life, and he stoically reconciled himself to his fate. A severe self-control disciplined his hitherto tempestuous emotions. The magnanimity of his soul resumed its wonted ascendancy. In a man possessing the mental energy and resources of Abdel Kader, there could be no such feeling as that of solitude. But the outer world now pressed on him. He accepted its diversion as a duty rather than a pleasure. Crowds from all parts of France knocked at the portals of the château. Impelled by mingled feelings of curiosity, sympathy, and admiration, statesmen, diplomatists, and warriors, vied with each other in doing homage to the august prisoner in his misfortunes. Abdel Kader was obliged to hold levees, which sometimes lasted for hours.

All were charmed with the loftiness and originality of his observations, the delicacy of his allusions, the felicity of his compliments. Above all, they were astonished to find that, so far from upbraiding those who had been the cause of his severe trial, he seemed to take a pleasure in suggesting extenuating circumstances for their conduct, and in endeavouring to relieve them of the burden of their treason and their shame.

General Daumas was his constant attendant. The general impression respecting Abdel Kader may be gathered from the following letter, addressed by the General to Monseigneur

Dupuch, the Bishop of Algiers:—"You are going to see the illustrious prisoner of the Château of Pau. Oh! you will certainly not regret your journey. You have known Abdel Kader in his prosperity, at a time when, so to speak, all Algeria acknowledged his rule. Well, you will find him greater and more extraordinary in his adversity than he was in his prosperity. Still, as ever, he towers to the height of his position.

"You will find him mild, simple, affectionate, modest, resigned, never complaining; excusing his enemies—even those at whose hands he may yet have much to suffer—and never permitting evil to be spoken of them in his presence. Mussulmans and Christians alike, however justly he might complain of them, have found his forgiveness. He throws the conduct of the former on the force of circumstances. The safety and honour of the flag under which they fought explains that of the latter. In going to console such a noble, such an exalted character, you will add another work of sanctity to those by which your life is already distinguished."

The Christian bishop and the Arab chief had long been bound by ties of common fellowship in deeds of mercy and compassion; and Abdel Kader selected his magnanimous co-adjutor in the convention of Sidi Khalifa as the depository of his inmost thoughts and reflections. His correspondence with the bishop was constant and unremitting.

Latterly he wrote, "As you may have discovered in the mirrors of our conversation, I was not born to be a warrior. It seems to me I ought never to have been one for a single day. Yet I have borne arms all my life. Mysterious are the designs of Providence! It was only by a wholly unforeseen concourse of circumstances that I suddenly found myself thrown so completely out of the career pointed out to me by my birth, my education, and my predilection—a career which, as you well know, I ardently long to resume, and to which I never cease praying to God to allow me to return, now at the close of my laborious years."

A record of all the remarks made by Abdel Kader to his numerous visitors would require in themselves a volume. Not one left him without carrying away and treasuring up some charming efflorescence of his facile and comprehensive intellect. A distinguished advocate assured him of the sympathies of an influential statesman. "I believe there is a little fire of affection for me in his heart," replied Abdel Kader; "but do not let that prevent you from supplying it at times with fuel."

When grasping simultaneously the hand of a priest and that of an officer, he remarked, "I like such visits and such faces, because one knows you at the first glance. Yours is the double uniform of devoted souls and generous hearts."

To a numerous company he once said, "I see around me kind and amiable people, who are pleased to extol the few good qualities which I possess by the favour of Heaven; but I fear there is no real friend here to tell me of my defects, which are much more numerous."

" I am often afraid for you," said the Archbishop of Tours, "when I think of the rigour of our climate." "It is true your climate is cold, but the warmth of your reception makes me forget it," was the reply of Abdel Kader.

On receiving a colonel at the head of his staff, he said,

" I thank you, colonel, I am deeply touched by your visit, and that of your brave companions. You have fought me bravely in Africa, and vanquished me. I adore the designs of God. Your present visit shows me that you think that I also did my duty; but of that you are the best judges. Again I thank you. After all, without alluding to any in particular, there ought to be many an officer in the French army who should be grateful to me, since but for me many a colonel would be still a captain, and many a general a colonel."

To a statesman he thus generously expressed himself :— " I am not irritated at the previous delays in the execution of the convention between me and General de Lamoricière. I know well that in the actual position of France it would be indiscreet and importunate in me to press the matter too strongly. I only beg not to be overlooked too long."

A beautiful *bouquet* having been presented to him by some ladies, he addressed them in the following strain of Eastern compliment, " In looking at this, and inhaling the perfume of so many lovely flowers, I seem to see a symbol of your hearts, and to breathe their delicious odours."

The continued succession of visitors at last fatigued him. He begged that the hours of reception might be restricted. All beheld the serenity, the cheerfulness of his aspect with wonder and astonishment; but who could fathom the inward and silent sufferings of that ardent and impassioned soul, which had worn itself out to absolute exhaustion during fifteen years, in contending bravely for its country's independence; which had only consented to relinquish the sacred struggle in order to save the domestic hearth; and which now, far from both home and country, saw all those most dear to it gradually sinking under the slow and lingering agony of imprisonment and exile?

Still, as the illustrious captive sought to fortify his spirits by those religious exercises and consolations which had been his life-long strength and support, the waters of affliction rose around him. In vain he strove to propitiate Heaven by penitential abnegation, by the most rigorous fasts, by the most persevering prayers. A remorseless fate seemed as it were commissioned to hold him in its iron grasp. Death was almost daily ravishing from him the dearest objects of his love and solicitude.

Scarcely were his eyes dried from weeping over such of his faithful companions as had expired in his arms, than they were bent with feverish anxiety on those whom he still saw before him sinking under the complicated ravages of disease, melancholy, and despair. After having wept over a son, a daughter, a nephew of the brightest hopes, he trembled for his mother and mother-in-law, whose advanced age and infirmities seemed more especially to mark them out as the next victims.

But despite all these cruel trials, Abdel Kader maintained an unshaken equanimity of look and demeanour. His words never ceased to breathe the spirit of heroic resignation. A sympathising voice once reproached him for his pious austerities. "Why," he replied, with a melancholy smile, "why grudge me the consolation and hope of thus rendering my prayers less unworthy to Him to whom I pour them out from the bottom of my heart, and who yet, perhaps, one of these days, may answer them from his throne on

High?" With Job he seemed to exclaim, "Though He slay me, yet will I put my trust in Him."

Such saint-like simplicity of character, such humility, such almost feminine grace and gentleness, combined as they were in Abdel Kader with all the lion-like qualities which exalt and dignify the manly nature, composed a *beau-ideal* of moral and physical grandeur, which involuntarily extorted enthusiastic reverence and adoration. The extraordinary fascination which he exercised on all around him, whether resplendent with the flashing of thousands of sabres unsheathed around him at his command, or enveloped in a prison's gloom, . is attested by instances of devotion and attachment too numerous to be mentioned.

Abdel Kader had left Algeria for ever, but the magic spell of his name still remained, and it remains to this day. When some Arab chiefs, after the surrender of the Sultan, visited the stables of the French authorities at Mostaganem, the last person in the minds of the latter was probably Abdel Kader, of whose ominous presence they had been happily relieved. To their surprise they saw the Arab chiefs throwing themselves frantically on a splendid black stallion, kissing its neck, its shoulders, its very feet. It had been Abdel Kader's charger. " It has borne him! it has borne him!" was the repeated outburst of their irrepressible feelings, and with difficulty they were torn away.

When Kara Mohammed, Abdel Kader's equerry, and his inseparable companion in all his battles, dangers, and reverses, looked on a porter at the gates of the château still wearing the royal livery, he could not help exclaiming, "What! your master is in England and you here! We would cross mountains and seas to follow our master to the ends of the earth. In receiving his benefits we are bound to him for life and death."

Notwithstanding all Abdel Kader's efforts and exhortations, his followers gave way to a hopeless despondency. These sons of the desert, to whom the boundless plains of the Sahara had been a home and the distant horizon the only limit, languished and pined away in their novel and dreary abode. The iron had entered into their soul.

At last an order came for their release. The bearer of the news expected to be hailed with cries of joy and delight. "No, no!" they all with one accord exclaimed, "while *he* is a captive, none of us will separate our lot from his!"

"But your master is going to be removed to another fortress," was the answer, "where you will be even more strictly confined than at present."

"Never mind," was the general cry. "What signifies? We are willing to suffer more if necessary: but quit *him* in his misfortune we never will."

In the month of June, 1848, General de Lamoricière was appointed Minister of War. Abdel Kader now anticipated with certainty the near approach of his deliverance. The man who had pledged his word to him was in power. In the pressure of public affairs, however, Abdel Kader feared he might be overlooked. He hastened, therefore, to address the general a letter, in which he solemnly abjured him to vindicate his own honour, as well as the national honour of France. Days, weeks, months elapsed, and no answer was vouchsafed.

Abdel Kader maintained his usual imperturbability; but his Algerines became furious. They formed a conspiracy to fall on their guard, unarmed as they were, kill as many as they could, and taste in a desperate self-sacrifice the sweetness of revenge. "We thought not of escape," they afterwards avowed. "We wanted to die, that our blood might be an eternal shame to France, inasmuch as we should have been slain for reclaiming the execution of the promise made to our master." Abdel Kader, duly averted of this mad design, interposed in time to thwart it.

The Minister of War was also apprised of it. He dreaded a catastrophe. He sent an officer to the despairing and over-tortured captives, with an offer of freedom. It was then they returned the noble and sublime answer already recorded. On the 2nd November, 1848, they voluntarily followed their beloved master to the Château of Amboise.

An order had preceded them. Neither Abdel Kader nor any of his suite was to be allowed to have intercourse with persons from without. They were neither to be permitted to receive nor to write letters. The privilege of freely receiving visitors was to be taken from them. No applicant for an interview was to be granted his request without an especial permission from the Minister of War.

This order was signed "De Lamoricière!"

CHAPTER XXII.

1848—1853.

ALTHOUGH the republican Government of France had acquiesced in the perpetration of this glaring act of perfidy to Abdel Kader, the President of the Republic raised his voice in vindication of the cause of right and justice. On the 14th of January, 1849, twenty-four days after his election to the presidency, Louis Napoleon convened an extraordinary council to take the subject into consideration.

In the warmest terms he pleaded the prisoner's cause. He insisted on the voluntary surrender, the frank and noble reliance on French honour on the one hand, and the word plédged and the convention signed on the other. Such language, emanating from the heir of the illustrious captive of St. Helena, had more than the weight of a protest; it had in some respects the sanctity of a reminiscence. Though supported by Bugeaud and Changarnier, the President's views were overruled. The Minister of War, General Rulhière, refused to incur the responsibility of sanctioning the release of Abdel Kader, and successfully opposed such a step.

Animated by feelings of esteem and sympathy for his fallen adversary, Marshal Bugeaud now wrote Abdel Kader a letter suggesting a course which, while it would diminish the bitter sense of captivity, would assure him an easy and even enviable existence :—

" I would wish you to decide on adopting France as your country, and to ask the Government to make you a grant of property, with right of descent to your heirs. You would thus have a position equal to that of our most influential men, and be able to practise your religion, and bring up your children according to your wishes.

" I am aware such a prospect may have little in it to seduce you; but it is one which ought to weigh with you, for the future of your children, and the fate of the numerous persons who surround you. You see they are languishing and dying of *ennui*. Were they employed on a property belonging to you, their mode of life, on the contrary, would be pleasant and agreeable. The cultivation of the soil would amuse them; they might have the diversion of sporting. The pursuits of agriculture would daily offer them fresh subjects of interest; and nothing tends more to cheer the spirits than the sight of nature elaborated by man's own exertions.

" Such is the sincere advice I give you, dictated by the feelings of extraordinary interest which your misfortunes, and the great qualities with which you have been endowed by God, has raised within me."

Abdel Kader was inflexible. He steadily persisted in refusing to hear of any compromise; and he thus replied :—
" If all the treasures of the world were laid out before me, and it was proposed to put them in the balance with my liberty, I would choose my liberty. I demand neither grace nor favour. I demand the execution of the engagements which have been made with me.

" I demanded, as the condition of my surrender, the word of a Frenchman. A French general gave it me without restriction and without conditions. Another general, the King's son, confirmed it. France was thus bound to me as I to her. To desire to obliterate the past is now to desire an impossibility. I will not give you back your word. I will die with it to your eternal disgrace and dishonour; kings and people will then learn, from my example, what confidence is to be placed in the word of a Frenchman."

The question of Abdel Kader's liberation was now to all appearance postponed indefinitely. He himself ceased to allude to it. He found consolation in his books, his studies, and devotions. His hours were so strictly appropriated to their respective duties, that time passed lightly. He now occupied himself with literary composition.

Two works, one on the " Unity of the Godhead," another entitled " Hints for the Wise, Instruction for the Ignorant," were the fruits of his mental labours. The first-mentioned work is a collation and, at the same time, an able exposition of all the arguments which support and elucidate that vital doctrine of the Mohammedan faith. The latter is divided into three parts. The first part treats of the advantages of learning; the second, of religion and morality; the third, of the art of writing and general science.

Although Abdel Kader had permission to take exercise in the park which surrounded his prison, he never availed himself of the privilege. Indeed, he rarely left his apartment, except to repair to the room where his family and suite assembled for prayer. His medical man urged the necessity of out-door exercise. " No health," he replied, " can come to me within the bounds of a prison. What I want is the air of liberty; that alone can revive me."

Time creeped on. At last came a change as joyful as it was unexpected. Louis Napoleon, disgusted with the party jealousies which thwarted his measures, had appealed to the national sentiment. He showed himself to France. He visited the provinces. On arriving at Blois, he sent word to M. Boissonet, who commanded in the Château of Amboise, situated not far distant from that town, that it was his intention to pay Abdel Kader a visit.

The ultimate design of the Prince President in making this visit had been surmised by the general officers and ministers of state who were around him. St. Arnaud and others tendered him their counsels, and suggested caution. But the Prince was resolute. The necessity of vindicating the national honour, too long tarnished by breach of faith, prevailed in his mind over every other consideration. On the 16th of October, 1852, the Prince and his suite drove in carriage to the Château of Amboise.

On the way he had written out in pencil the following document :—

"ABDEL KADER,

" I am come to announce to you your liberty. You will be conducted to Broussa, in the Sultan's territory, as soon as the necessary arrangements can be made. The French Government will give you a pension worthy of your former rank.

" For a long time your captivity has caused me real distress. It constantly reminded me that the Government which preceded mine had not fulfilled its engagements towards an unfortunate enemy; and in my eyes a great nation is humiliated, when it so far mistrusts its own power as to break its promise. Generosity is always the best counsellor; and I am convinced that your residence in Turkey will in nowise affect the tranquillity of my possessions in Africa.

" Your religion, as well as mine, inculcates submission to the decree of Providence. Now, if France is supreme in Algeria, it is because God has so willed it; and the nation will never renounce the conquest. You have been the enemy of France, but I nevertheless am ready to do ample justice to your courage, your character, and your resignation in misfortune. I, consequently, feel it to be a point of honour to put an end to your imprisonment, and to entertain a complete reliance on your word."

Overpowered with gratitude, Abdel Kader poured forth his heartfelt thanks. His aged mother begged to be allowed to see the generous and noble-minded ruler, who had shed such joy and consolation through her household; and on being presented to Louis Napoleon, covered him with her benedictions. After hastily partaking of the " couscoussu," the national dish of Algeria, the Prince departed. As he disappeared in the distance, Abdel Kader turned to his followers and said, " Others have overthrown and imprisoned me, but Louis Napoleon alone has conquered me."

Abdel Kader was now desirous of doing homage to his deliverer in the capital. He obtained permission to go to Paris, and arrived there October 28th, 1852. A worthy reception had been arranged for him by order of the Prince.

A popular demonstration awaited him. Crowds thronged the streets through which he passed, and gazed at him with mingled pride and curiosity. The feelings of a warlike people were gratified by his presence; but respect for the great military renown of the Arab chief was the prevailing motive.

The very evening of his arrival, Abdel Kader was invited to visit the Grand Opera. He excused himself at first on account of fatigue; but, being told that the Prince was to be there, he consented to go. He was conducted to the box in which the Prince sat. Abdel Kader stooped to kiss hands, but the Prince, amidst loud applause, embraced him. Then, placing the ancient enemy of France by his side, he showed him the most marked attention.

An invitation was now given to Abdel Kader to visit the Prince President at the palace of St. Cloud; and thither, accordingly, he went on the 30th October, accompanied by his equerry Kara Mohammed, Ben Allal, nephew of his celebrated Khalifa Sidi Embarak, Sidi Kudoor, and a staff of French officers especially deputed to escort him. He arrived a few minutes before the time appointed for his audience. There was a clock in the waiting room, which he was told indicated the exact time of day at Mecca. Delighted with the incident, he set his own watch by the time of the Holy City of his faith. He found it was exactly the hour for afternoon prayer; and in the presence of all assembled he knelt down and prayed.

Shortly afterwards he was presented to the Prince President, who stood surrounded by his great officers of state. The ceremony over, Abdel Kader asked permission to say a few words. Leave having been granted, he thus expressed himself, not without considerable emotion.

"Highness, I am not accustomed to your usages. Perhaps I am about to commit a fault; but I wish to express my sentiments to you, and the exalted personages I see around me. Others have made promises which they have not fulfilled. Your Highness has fulfilled engagements which you had not contracted. Thanks to your generosity, I shall be enabled to go and live in a Mussulman country. Words vanish like the winds. Writing is durable. I offer your Highness this paper. It contains a written promise."

He then placed the following declaration in the Prince's hands :—

"Praise be to the One God!

"May God ever continue to protect and preserve our lord, Louis Napoleon, and guide and direct his judgment.

"He who presents himself to you is Abdel Kader, the son of Mehi-ed-deen. I come before your Highness to thank you for your bounties, and to gratify myself with a sight of your countenance. You are, in fact, dearer to me than any other friend, for you have conferred on me a benefit which exceeds my power of thanking you, but which is worthy of the nobleness of your character, and the splendour of your position. May God glorify you.

"You are of the number of those who neither make use-less protestations, nor deceive by falsehood. You have had confidence in me. You have not listened to those who mistrust me. You have given me liberty; and, without having made me any promises, you have fulfilled engage-ments which others made with me without fulfilling them.

"I come then to swear to you, by the covenant and promises of God, and by the promises of all the prophets and messengers, that I will never do anything contrary to the trust you have reposed in me, and that I will religiously keep this my oath never to return to Algeria. When God ordered me to arise, I arose. I employed gunpowder to the utmost extent of my means and ability. But when he ordered me to cease, I ceased. It was then that I abandoned power and surrendered.

"My religion and my honour alike ordain me to keep my oaths and to scorn deceit. I am a *shereef*, and no one shall ever accuse me of treachery. How, indeed, could that be possible to me after having received such great benefits at your hands? A benefit is a golden chain thrown over the neck of the noble-minded. I venture to hope that you will deign to think of me even when I am far away, and that you will place me on the list of your intimate friends; for although I may not equal them in their services, I at least equal them in their affection towards you. May God increase the love of those who love you, and strike terror into the hearts of your enemies."

To this solemn protestation Louis Napoleon replied,—

"Abdel Kader, I never mistrusted you. I had no need of this written paper which you so nobly offer me. I never demanded from you, as you know, either promise or oath. You have chosen, nevertheless, to draw up and deliver into my hands this document. I accept it. This spontaneous avowal of your sentiments and feelings proves to me that I was right in placing unlimited confidence in you."

When the audience was over, Abdel Kader was shown all

the apartments of the palace, and then taken to see the Prince's stud. He particularly admired a magnificent white Arab horse. "The horse is yours," said the Prince, who was present. "I hope it will make you forget that you have been so long without one. You must try it with me in the park to-morrow, at a review of cavalry, which I have ordered expressly in your honour."

Abdel Kader mounted his new steed the following day, and rode by the side of the Prince to the review. To a courteous inquiry from the latter as to the health of his aged mother, Abdel Kader replied with animation, "During my captivity my mother required a staff to bear the weight of her body, bent down with years; but since I am free, by your Highness's generosity, she has thrown off the weight of years and walks without support."

Abdel Kader was present at another grand review at Versailles. He dined with the Prince twice. All the ministers gave him grand entertainments, and he daily received visits from statesmen, generals, and men of science. He was mostly touched, however, by the visits of several officers who had formerly been his prisoners, and who had come to thank him for the kindness and attention they had received at his hands during their captivity.

Abdel Kader afterwards visited all the public edifices of Paris. On entering the church of the Madeleine, he said to the priest who accompanied him, "When I first began my struggle with the French I thought they were a people without religion. I found out my mistake. At all events, such churches as these would soon convince me of my error."

He then asked to be taken to the residence of his old

friend M. Dupuch, Bishop of Algiers. "Having consecrated my first visit to God," he said, "the next should be to the best of his servants."

Going through the Notre Dame, he stopped to examine all the marvels of art and relics which it contains, with an attention which, as coming from a Mussulman, surprised the by-standers. Its sculptures, its paintings, the mantle worn by Napoleon I. at his coronation, and the piece of the true cross given by Baldwin to Louis XII., all successively engaged his attention.

On arriving at the Hôtel des Invalides, the first request of Abdel Kader was, as usual, to be taken to the church. The temple where the Deity was worshipped was invariably the first place to which he directed his steps. He viewed with a soldier's interest and satisfaction the numerous flags with which it was adorned. Amongst them were some of his own standards. When his eye fell on them he gazed on them for a while in silence, and then quietly observed, "Those times are past. I wish to forget them. Let us always endeavour to live in the present."

At the tomb of Napoleon he again paused long. At length he spoke: "All that the genius of man and the wealth of the world could possibly do," he said, "would be merely to give this tomb a pale reflex of that greatness which filled the world with its glory." As he turned away he remarked, "I have now seen what was mortal of the great captain; but where is the place where his name is not still living?"

The hospital particularly struck him. The patients stood up as he passed by. One old soldier had even risen with pain and difficulty from his bed, as a mark of respect to the great warrior. Abdel Kader stopped before him, shook him by the hands, and made him the following address:—"How worthy it is of a great people thus to watch over the old age of its brave defenders, and to employ the best medical advice for the cure of wounds received in the country's defence! I have seen the tomb of Napoleon, and touched his sword; and I should leave this place completely happy were it not for the thought that there may be some here who have been disabled by me or mine. But I only defended my country; and the French, who are just and generous, will pardon me, and perhaps admit that I was an open and honest enemy, one not altogether unworthy of them."

The Museum of Artillery and the imperial printing establishment were the next objects of his inspection. The autographic press produced under his very eyes, to his intense astonishment, a facsimile of the document he had presented to the Prince. After minutely watching the process of printing, and the marvellous rapidity with which impressions were thrown off, he exclaimed, "Yesterday I saw the batteries of war—here I see the batteries of thought."

Abdel Kader had now a parting interview with Louis Napoleon. The Prince announced his intention of presenting him with a sword of honour. "But," he added, "I wish it to be worthy of you; and I regret that, notwithstanding the diligence of the workmen, I shall not be able to give it you before your departure for Broussa." The blade of this sword, which Abdel Kader afterwards received, is of the time of the Abassiades, who flourished at the commencement of the Mohammedan era. On it have been inscribed the words— "The Sultan Napoleon III. to the Emir Abdel Kader, son of Mehi-ed-deen." The next day Abdel Kader returned to Amboise.

On the 21st of November the French people were called upon to elect an emperor. Abdel Kader claimed the right of suffrage. By a singular coincidence, the day was the anniversary of that on which, twenty years before, he had himself been elected Sultan of the Arabs. His claim was admitted, and a ballot-box was made expressly for the occasion. In this box he deposited his own vote and those of twelve of his suite.

Abdel Kader returned to Paris to be present at the proclamation of the empire. He stood amidst the great officers of state and public functionaries who assembled at the Tuileries to offer the Emperor their congratulations. As soon as the latter perceived him he went up to him, shook him by the hands, and said, "You see your vote has brought me good luck." "Sire," replied Abdel Kader, "my vote is of no value but as it is the interpreter of my heart."

On the 11th of December, Abdel Kader, with his family and suite, left Amboise for the East. The same attention and hospitality which had been shown to him in Paris awaited him in all the provincial towns through which he passed. At Lyons, the Comte de Castellane gave him a splendid reception. A banquet was offered to him, and a review of the garrison held in his honour. When Abdel Kader approached the lines he was saluted with military honours. Delighted with this unexpected mark of respect, he turned to the noble marshal who rode by his side, and exclaimed, "The Emperor gave me liberty, but you have adorned her with garlands."

On the 21st of December, Abdel Kader embarked on board

the *Labrador* for his final destination. The steamer touched
at Sicily. He landed, and, attended by the governor, made
a tour in the interior. He ascended Etna. At his departure
he addressed a letter of thanks to that officer, in which he
thus records his impressions of what he had seen :—"We
have everywhere met with the traces of the various populations who have inhabited your island. The sight made us
reflect that God is indeed the Lord of the universe, and that
He gives the land to whom He wills. The mountain
of fire is truly one of the wonders of the world. On viewing
from its heights the highly cultivated and thickly populated
plains which spread out before us, we thought of the Arab
poet's lament on the evacuation of Sicily by the Saracens,
' The recollection of you, O plains of Sicily, from the heights
of Etna, makes my despair ! If my tears were not salt, they
should make rivers of water for this glorious island. An
inhabitant of Paradise only is fit to recount the wonders of ·
Sicily.' "

Abdel Kader arrived at Constantinople, January 7, 1853.
On landing he went directly to the grand mosque of Tophané,
filled with joy and gratitude at finding himself once more in
a temple of the Prophet. The French ambassador gave a
grand entertainment in his honour, to which the principal
personages of the Frank society were invited. This act of
hospitality closed the social relations of Abdel Kader with
the civilised world. During his passage through it, his worth,
his genius, his honour, had been magnanimously recognised
in one long ovation. He was now in a capital where
barbarism is harlequinised into a constrained semblance of
European civilisation.

He visited the Turkish ministers. They received him with ill-feigned demonstrations of civility and respect. Policy alone made them outwardly courteous. Such is the eradicable arrogance and self-sufficiency of the Turks, that they despise all races alike but their own. Utter strangers to noble sentiments, and scorning to admit the possibility of there being anything in the world more important than themselves, they regarded the attentions paid to Abdel Kader (despite his glorious struggles for their common faith) with jealousy and even derision. His fame oppressed them. An Arab hero was, in their minds, an incongruity, an impertinence.

CHAPTER XXIII

ABDEL KADER at length sailed from Constantinople for Broussa. The Pasha in that town had been ordered by the Turkish Government to place a carriage at his disposal, on landing. "What!" said the Turk, "an Arab ride in a carriage! Who ever heard of such a thing? Surely there are plenty of camels to be had. Why does not the man hire a camel? Is not a camel good enough for him?" The Turk was spared the indignity of supplying the Arab with a carriage, on account of the simple fact, that it was impossible to traverse the road from the landing-place to Broussa in any vehicle whatever; and of this fact, the Sublime Porte, at a distance of scarcely twenty miles, was profoundly ignorant.

Fortunately for Abdel Kader, though thrown amongst the Turks, he was in no way obliged to be dependent on them. The munificence of Louis Napoleon had largely provided for his wants. The Emperor had settled on him a pension for life of £4,000 a year. With Abdel Kader's habits, this income was more than a competence, it was superfluity. With such wealth he might have lived in princely state, and indulged in ostentation. But he was regulated by other principles.

At all times averse to self-gratification, Abdel Kader
looked upon this liberal allowance as a trust; and he considered that after deducting what was absolutely necessary
for his own expenses, he was bound to expend the remainder
for the benefit of others. His income now enabled him to
provide for the wants of many who had nobly refused to
separate themselves from his fortunes, and even to extend his
generosity to other quarters. Reserving barely a half for
himself and family, he disbursed the residue in salaries to his
most needy chiefs and dependents; in charities to the poor,
presents to the mosques, and other benevolent purposes. It
is to be remarked that out of his income he had also to
support his two brothers and their families.

So averse, indeed, was Abdel Kader to vain and trifling
expenditure of every sort, that the outlay generally devoted
by his co-religionists to rejoicings and festivities, at one of
their most important religious rites, was by him directed to
charitable ends. On the occasion of the circumcision of one
of his sons, the people of Broussa were surprised to see, in
place of the usual costly procession, with all its concomitants
of pomp and show—the cavalcade, the flags and the music—
a vast assemblage of the poor congregated in front of his
dwelling, and receiving from his own hands presents of bread,
and clothing, and money. Such was, in the eyes of Abdel
Kader, the best commemoration of the sacred rite.

The building which the Turkish Government had allotted
for his residence was an old dilapidated khan, in many parts
without a roof. With some difficulty he contrived to make
it habitable. The wildness and gloom of the old ruin were
terrible. But he bought a small farm in the neighbourhood,

to which he escaped at times to regale himself with a sight of the sun and to breathe the fresh air.

His days were passed, as usual, in the education of his children, in readings at the mosque, and in private study and meditation. Still he felt himself in a land of strangers. Few understood his language. Between the Turks and himself there was no possible sympathy, and there never could be. The Ulemas amongst them envied and disliked him for his superior learning. The Effendis, in their supercilious pride, scarcely vouchsafed to notice him. The public functionaries, gradually recovering from their dread of his widely-spread influence, smiled with inward repose and satisfaction, not unmingled with contempt, as they congratulated each other on the discovery that the great Arab hero was after all only a " derweesh."

Thus time wore on with him for nearly three years. He secretly longed for a change in his place of exile ; but he was diffident in asking for it. At last, the appalling earthquake which, in 1855, nearly laid all Broussa in ruins, afforded him a plea for opening the subject, and he hastened to avail himself of the circumstance. He obtained permission to go to France. He once more saw the Emperor, who graciously acceded to all his wishes. It was arranged that for the future his residence should be at Damascus.

Whilst Abdel Kader was in Paris, the news of the fall of Sebastopol arrived. He was asked to assist at the celebration of the *Te Deum* in Notre Dame ; and he was told that the Emperor would be flattered by his presence on the occasion.

Though prostrated by a recent severe illness, he consented to go. No small sensation was created amongst the vast throng which filled the cathedral, as Abdel Kader advanced up to the altar, leaning on the arm of a French marshal, and accompanied by other officers of rank. On leaving it he was loudly cheered.

The principal aide-de-camp of the Minister of War conducted him over the International Exhibition, which on the year of this visit made Paris the rendezvous of all the civilised world. After viewing all the varied productions which it contained, he paused for a long time in perfect astonishment at the marvellous elaborations of machinery which expanded in various compartments before his eyes. Then he suddenly exclaimed, "Surely this is the temple of reason and intelligence, animated by the breath of God."

After returning to Broussa, where he remained for a few weeks to arrange and settle his affairs, he finally embarked on board a French steamer, with his family and suite, amounting in all to more than one hundred persons, and reached Beyrout, November 24th, 1856; and from thence, after a short stay, he proceeded to Damascus.

Midway on his ascent of the Lebanon he was surprised to hear the sound of firing, as though a battle were raging close by. Presently he saw the heights and slopes covered with large bodies of men, keeping up a well-sustained roll of musketry; and then, a compact and splendidly attired cavalcade advancing to his encounter. The Druzes had assembled to give him a welcome.

Their chiefs, on approaching him, dismounted. He returned the compliment. They bowed before him with oriental prostrations, and kissed his hand. Then they begged him to do them the honour of reposing amongst them, if only for one night. He accepted their invitation, and found once more a hospitable Eastern home. His heart expanded. He was once more amongst the Arabs.

Long and closely did these mountain warriors question him as to his campaigns against the French. " If your fame," they said, " has so long raised our spirits and excited our admiration; if it has so long rejoiced our hearts to hear of you, how much more must we rejoice to see you !" On his leaving the Lebanon he was escorted by the Druzes to the frontiers of their territory. After thanking them for their courtesy and attention, Abdel Kader parted from them with the words, " God grant we may ever remain one !" and the Druzes replied, " God grant it ! May we soon meet again."

Another ovation, and on a larger scale, awaited Abdel Kader at Damascus. The whole Mohammedan population—men, women, and children—turned out to receive him. For more than a mile outside the gates the road was lined on either side with all ranks and degrees of persons dressed in holiday attire, who had come forth to feast their eyes by gazing on the renowned champion and hero of Islam. Preceded by a detachment of Turkish troops and a band of military music, Abdel Kader passed, almost like a conqueror, through the crowd, joyfully returning the unintermittent salaams with which he was greeted. No such Arab had entered Damascus since the days of Saladin.

The Sultan had ordered a serail to be placed at the disposal of Abdel Kader. Luckily for him, the khans were all already fully occupied. He only took up his residence in the abode prepared for him temporarily, and until he could select and purchase a house for himself. The Turkish authorities

x

paid no further attention to him. It was quite enough for them that they had to endure him. They could not lower his rank and position, for an arm was outstretched over him stronger than theirs; they could not undermine his influence, for his was an ascendancy that defied their malice; they looked upon him as a painful and unavoidable anomaly, and succumbed.

Visits and salutations of various kinds soon multiplied upon him. Ben Salem, his old and devoted Khalifa, and some hundreds of Algerines, who had already obtained permission to settle at Damascus, and who proudly swelled his suite as he entered the city, now thronged around him day and night, never sufficiently satisfied with the sight of their adored Sultan, from whom they had been so long separated. The great Arab Effendis offered him the most ardent demonstrations of respect.

But it was to the Ulemas and the lettered classes that Abdel Kader became the great centre of attraction. By virtue of his triple warrant, as descendant of the Prophet, Ulema, and leader of the Djehad, he was entitled to their profoundest reverence. They felt themselves bound to him not only by feelings of national sympathy, but of religious duty. Their experience of his superior learning, quickly obtained, made them anxious to profit by his instructions. They begged him to become their teacher. A theological class, consisting of upwards of sixty students, was formed. It held its daily sittings in the great mosque, and Abdel Kader presided over it with scrupulous punctuality. The Koran and the Hadeeth naturally formed the great staple of discussion; but unlike the ordinary teachers, whose utmost stretch of mental power only extended to worn-out remarks and commentaries on the sacred books, Abdel Kader astonished and delighted his disciples by choice quotations from the works of Plato and Aristotle, and occasionally even from authors of less repute, selected from his own library, which he had been carefully re-forming during his residence at Broussa.

The light which thus shed its rays over the literary world of the Mohammedans of Damascus, was of course accompanied by its attendant shadow of envy and detraction, fostered by offended vanities and obscured reputations. Such, on the whole, was the social position of Abdel Kader in Damascus, when events unexpectedly occurred to disturb for a moment the tranquil tenor of his life.

The Peace of Paris, concluded in 1856, filled the Turks with mingled sensations of exultation and mistrust: of exultation, because the peace had rescued them from an impending doom, and renewed their lease of political existence; of mistrust, because the deed of deliverance was saddled with a decree of death. Such a doom, it is true, depended on the realization of a theory; but that theory was, to them, of ominous importance. By eliciting from them the Hati Homayoom of 1856, the Christian Powers simply made the Turks put the knife to their own throats.

If that famous "Magna Charta for the Christians of the East," as it has been ridiculously styled by those who know nothing at all about the politics of the East, was to be strictly carried into execution, the relative position of Turks and Christians, as a body, throughout the Turkish empire, would in due course of time be completely reversed. The Turks have as yet escaped the stern necessity of giving themselves the fatal gash; and their kind and forbearing allies have for the moment refrained from pressing the completion of the sacrifice. Nevertheless, it behoves the Christian Powers, seriously and conscientiously, to reflect that, on the execution or non-execution of the Hati Homayoom, depends the gradual enfranchisement, or the continued bondage and degradation of Christianity, under Turkish rule.

When the Christian Powers signed a document giving the Turks an indefinite tenure of political existence, they virtually ratified the bond by which the latter have consigned some of the fairest provinces of the earth to irremediable depopulation, barrenness, and sterility. When they contented themselves with receiving in exchange an impossible programme of amalgamation, progress, and refinement, they not only stultified themselves, but betrayed the vital interests of humanity and civilisation.

If England, passively consenting to be bound down by traditions which took their rise in an age when the East, with all its glorious destinies, was universally ignored, chooses still to regard the maintenance of the Turkish empire as indispensable to the balance of power in Europe—as though, in the event of its abruption or collapse, national adjustments would become impossibilities, political arrangements fictions, and diplomatic treaties myths—if, with suicidal arm, she still persists in helping to lock up those rich, fertile, and widely extended regions, which, if that empire were to pass under Christian sway, would rapidly be opened up to her commercial enterprise, and would increase the demands upon her arts and manufactures ten, fifty, and a hundred fold; then let her, by all means, go on worshipping her "log of wood," and lavish in its support her money, her arms, and her men, thereby wasting and crippling her actual and prospective resources.

But if, awakened at length to a due sense of her dignity and of her best interests, to say nothing of her responsibilities to a Higher Power, England should resolve to abandon the fruitless and thankless task of attempting to mould, tutor, and reform a government which by its very nature must ever be a stumbling-block and an offence in the path of Eastern advancement—which is the fanatical and persecuting enemy of her faith, which laughs at her credulity, practises on her forbearance, and is a permanent obstruction to the full development of her wealth and greatness—then her policy will lie in a nut-shell. Let her leave the Turks to fight their own battles. Howsoever, wheresoever, and by whomsoever attacked, let her stand by an undisturbed spectator. Let her quietly see the game commenced. She will always be in time to cut in and play her own cards.

The Christians of Syria have ever been viewed by the Turks with gloomy jealousy. They are called "the Key to the Franks." The Turks imagine them to be ever ready to welcome and aid a Frank invading force; furnishing it with supplies, and in various ways initiating it into the land's capabilities and resources. Their increasing population, wealth, and prosperity, are to the Turks a perpetual source of exasperation, exciting in their breasts feelings of hatred and broodings of revenge.

These Christians had deluded themselves into the idea that the Hati Homayoom was to become a reality. They gloried in the prospects of civil, military, and political equality with their Mohammedan fellow-subjects which it held out to them. They craved to be permitted to enter the service of the State, and offered to serve in the army. They were told their services were not wanted. At the same time the information was vouchsafed to them that they were to be subjected to a yearly fine of ten shillings per head, in lieu of military service.

"What!"—they argued amongst themselves—"is this all that our friends and protectors, the great Christian Powers, have been able to procure from the Turks by the promulgation of the Hati Homayoom? Could they do no more than achieve mockery and derision for themselves, and for us an additional mark of inferiority and humiliation?" They could not believe it. The mistake, they were sure, would be rectified. They protested, and refused to pay the tax.

The Christians of the Lebanon soon after observed, with just alarm, the menacing attitude displayed towards them by the Druzes. They knew at once that the Turks were going to play their old game of letting loose these tribes against them. What had they to do? They armed themselves to the teeth; and they were right. The Turco-Druze compact was already completed. Such was the aspect of affairs between the Turks and the Rayahs in Syria in 1859.

The Turkish authorities in that province had duly reported the refractory conduct of the Christians, and the general tone of assumption evinced by them, to their superiors in Constantinople. In the instructions they received, they were emphatically told that the Christians must be "corrected." The expression seems trivial, but those to whom it was addressed perfectly well understood its cabalistic meaning.

As a Turkish sultan was once entering his kiosk, a handsome, comely-looking youth, the son of one of his viziers, attracted his notice. He approached him, patted him on the cheek, and stroked his chin. The lad, well knowing the feelings which prompted such a mark of attention, turned away from the caress with offensive abruptness. The Sultan looked towards the father, and sternly said, "Your son must be corrected." That same day the lad's head was cut off. He had been "corrected." In Eastern phraseology this is called "imperial correction."

In May, 1860, the civil war between the Druzes and Christians, so sedulously fostered and excited by the Turks, broke out. In little more than a month the Lebanon became a vast scene of slaughter and conflagration. In an evil hour the Christians, despite their better convictions, had allowed themselves to be deceived by the solemn protestations of Turkish pashas and colonels, who called upon God to witness that they were about to act as mediators.

They repaired by hundreds to the different Turkish garrisons planted over the mountain, hourly expecting the signal for peace. There, after having been politely requested to give up their arms, as a mark of confidence, they were crammed into open courts, or penned up in small chambers, according to the nature of the locality, and assured they were in perfect safety. And then, after a time, the Druzes and the Turkish troops fell on them, and massacred them all. They had been "corrected."

The Christians of Damascus were the next to be "corrected." Abdel Kader, entirely ignorant of the great Turco-Druze plot, had sent messages to some of his friends among the Druze Sheiks, at the commencement of the civil war in the Lebanon, calling upon them to exercise forbearance and moderation. He soon had occasion to turn his attention to events nearer home. Rumours were daily becoming more and more rife that the Mohammedans of the Pashalick of Damascus intended to rise on the Christians.

Abdel Kader was at first incredulous. But his Algerines came round him day by day, repeating to him the fearful gossip of the town. Many of them, who had been tampered with, were asked to join in the scheme. He now went to the Ulemas, and begged them to use their influence with the people to allay the feeling, and avert such a frightful cata-strophe. He wrote urgent letters in the same sense to the Ulemas of Homs and Hamah.

Having received information that some straggling parties of the Druzes were extending their ravages towards Damas-cus, he hastened to send the following collective letter to all their leading Sheiks :—

"To THE DRUZE SHEIKS IN MOUNT LEBANON, AND IN THE PLAINS AND MOUNTAINS OF THE HOURAN.

" We continually invoke for you eternal happiness, and continuation of prosperity.

" You are aware of our friendship for you, and our good-will towards all the servants of God. Hearken to what we say to you, and accept and be advised by our admonition. The Turkish Government, and all men, know your old enmity towards the Christians of Mount Lebanon, and you may imagine that the Government will not hold you wholly responsible for the war which is now raging between you and them. The Government may accept your excuses.

"But if you make offensive movements against a place with the inhabitants of which you have never before been at enmity, we fear such conduct would be the cause of a serious rupture between you and the Government. You know how anxious we are for your welfare and happiness, and that of all your countrymen at large. The wise, before taking a step, calculate the consequences.

"Some of your horsemen have already been pillaging in the environs of Damascus. Such proceedings are unworthy of a community distinguished for its good sense and wise policy. We repeat it, we are most anxious for your welfare, and are hurt at whatever reflects on your name.

"ABDEL KADER IBN MEHI-ED-DEEN.

"*May*, 1860."

Abdel Kader next proceeded to Achmet Pasha, the Governor, and stated his apprehensions. The Pasha told him that there was no occasion to be alarmed, and that all reports were mere idle rumours. A second and third time he went to the Governor and renewed his representations, but with little or no effect. At last the Pasha allowed a few arms to be distributed amongst Abdel Kader's followers, but without instructions under what circumstances they were to be used.

On the 9th of July, in the forenoon, Abdel Kader's Algerines came running in, in breathless haste, and told him the town had risen. Without a moment's delay he sallied forth, ordering his attendants to follow him. After a few turnings he met a furious mob in full career towards the Christian quarter. He drew up with his men in the centre of the street. The mob stopped short. A pause ensued. Abdel Kader harangued the rioters, expostulated with them, and endeavoured to convince them of the awfulness of the crime which they were about to commit. He implored them to desist and return.

"What!" they shouted, "you, the great slayer of Christians, are you come out to prevent us from slaying them in our turn? Away!"

"If I slew Christians," he shouted in reply, "it was in accordance with our law—Christians who had declared war against me, and were arrayed in arms against our faith."

"Away, away!" retorted the mobs, and the rioters rushed by. Within three hours the Christian quarter was a waving sheet of fire. The hot blast, fraught with the moans of the tortured and the shrieks of the defiled, rolled over the city like a gust from hell.

The Pasha had some days before made a pretence of affording protection to the Christians by stationing Turkish troops in their quarter. He now sent his soldiers orders to withdraw. They piled arms and plundered. But Abdel Kader hurried to the rescue. Altogether about 1,000 of his Algerines had by this time gathered round him. He patrolled the flaming streets. His men went from house to house, entering and crying out, " Christians, come forth! Do not fear us —we are Abdel Kader's men, and are here to save you! Come forth, come forth!"

At first, no voices responded. The unfortunate victims dreaded fresh treachery. By degrees, however, after repeated and earnest assurances, they gained confidence. Men, women, and children issued forth trembling and crawling from their hiding-places. They emerged from wells, from sinks, from gutters. As fast as they could be collected together, they were hurried off to Abdel Kader's abode, enclosed in long oblong squares, formed by the Algerines to protect them on the way from insult and attack.

Abdel Kader, who had more than once narrowly escaped suffocation, now returned to his house. He found it filled to overflowing. He induced his immediate neighbours to vacate their abodes in order to give shelter to the unhappy fugitives. But the tide kept pouring in, and still more space was wanted. As a last resource, he proposed to the Christians to send them for protection to the Turkish castle. But at this proposition a wild cry arose from all. The poor creatures fell on their knees, and with frantic gestures and agonising accents exclaimed, " O Abdel Kader, for God's sake do not send us to the Turks ! By your mother! by your wife ! by your children ! O Abdel Kader, save us from the Turks ! "

Abdel Kader endeavoured to reassure the supplicants and allay their fears. He pledged himself for their safety, and offered to accompany them to the citadel himself. Not a hair of their heads should be touched, he said, while he was alive. With sad misgivings and sinking hearts, the Christians at length consented to go. Abdel Kader headed the sad procession in person. His Algerines marched on its flanks and in its rear. It moved on rapidly. An unwonted gloom pervaded the great city. The bazaars were all deserted, and reverberated to the escort's tramp in sad funereal echoes. The castle, which lay nearly a mile off, was reached a little before sunset, and Abdel Kader gave over his charge. The Turks looked at him askance.

For several days his Algerines were constantly engaged in escorting fugitive Christians, in batches of twenty, fifty, and a hundred, to the same destination. As they were being hurried along, all exclaimed alike, "Do not leave us to the mercy of the Turks! Come back to us! Stay with us! The Turks will yet murder us!" Nor indeed were their fears unfounded.

On the third day, when the large quadrangle within the castle was crowded with the Christians, to the amount of some thousands, of all ranks, ages, and sexes, the Turks coolly divided the males from the females into two large bodies. The one was intended for massacre; the other was reserved for violation. They only awaited the arrival of the Druzes, whom they were hourly and anxiously expecting, to co-operate with them in the fiendish work.

But here, also, Abdel Kader had marred and circumvented their diabolical designs. He had heard of the approach of the Druzes. He had ridden out to meet them. He had fallen in with them at the village of Ashrafeeiy, in the outskirts of the city. There he had parleyed with their Sheiks, had reasoned with them, and by his personal influence, and his eloquent and persuasive arguments, had succeeded in turning them aside from their bloody errand.

For ten days he continued engaged in his arduous task. Once the mob approached his house, and demanded with frantic yells that the Christians within it should be delivered up to them. He drew his sword, and, accompanied by a strong body of his followers, at once went out to confront the yelling crowd. "Wretches!" he exclaimed, "is this the way you honour the Prophet? May his curse be upon you!

Shame on you, shame! You will yet live to repent. You think you may do as you like with the Christians; but the day of retribution will come. The Franks will yet turn your mosques into churches. Not a Christian will I give up. They are my brothers. Stand back, or I give my men the order to fire." The mob withdrew.

When he returned to his post it was to keep anxious watch by day, and sleepless vigil by night. He had a rug spread at his entrance door, and on this hard bed he snatched intervals of troubled rest. He never once retired. He felt that his personal presence was absolutely indispensable for the safety of all. The stream of fugitives was incessant. Every moment Abdel Kader was called up to give orders to form escorts, or to issue provisions to the thousands congregated under his roof.

The European Consuls, leaving their burning consulates behind them, had fled to him with their families on the first day. The British Consul alone, living in the Mohammedan quarter, had thought himself secure. But, as an additional security, he had sent to the Pasha, and requested that Turkish troops might be stationed at his house. A detachment of soldiers was accordingly dispatched for his protection.

Shortly after their arrival one of his cawasses came and told him to beware. He had overheard the conversation of the Turkish soldiers. They were talking of breaking into the consulate, and murdering every one within their reach. After a slight deliberation, it was decided that Abdel Kader was the only resource now left. To Abdel Kader, accordingly, a messenger was instantly sent, craving immediate assistance. To the surprise and astonishment of the Turkish soldiers,

seventeen Algerines suddenly appeared, and seemed to super-
sede them in their functions. The Turks were overawed.
Their bloody plot was frustrated ; and the safety of the British
Consul was secured. The interposition had been indeed both
timely and providential. In a few minutes more the Consul
with his staff and household would have been *massacred by
their Turkish guard !*

Though the great mass of the Christians had been forwarded
to the castle, the Consuls and many of the wealthier classes
remained partakers of Abdel Kader's hospitality for more
than a month. By degrees, however, this assemblage broke
up, moving off in successive parties, always escorted by
Algerines, to Beyrout.

Abdel Kader was at length enabled to repose. He had
rescued 15,000 souls belonging to the Eastern churches from
death, and worse than death, by his fearless courage, his
unwearied activity, and his catholic-minded zeal. All the
representatives of the Christian powers then residing in
Damascus, without one single exception, had owed their
lives to him. Strange and unparalleled destiny ! An Arab
had thrown his guardian ægis over the outraged majesty
of Europe. A descendant of the Prophet had sheltered and
protected the Spouse of Christ.

CHAPTER XXIV

THE Turkish authorities at Damascus, acting under the orders of Fuad Pasha, marked their sense of Abdel Kader's humane intervention in behalf of the Christians, by sending him an order that his Algerines should deliver up their arms. Abdel Kader resented the order as an insult, and protested. "Never," was his reply to this injunction, " will I submit to such an order, until Fuad Pasha has formally declared that I and my men have made a bad use of our weapons. In that case I will leave him to vindicate his conduct as best he can, with the European powers who have applauded my course of action."

Being powerfully supported from an influential quarter, Abdel Kader succeeded in averting the indignity which the Turks had deliberately and maliciously meditated against him. The spirit which had dictated Fuad Pasha, and the Turkish authorities in general, then became apparent. A general disarmament of the inhabitants of Damascus had been commenced, and about six hundred muskets had already been collected, when the above-mentioned order was sent to Abdel Kader. When they failed to obtain the arms of Abdel Kader and his suite, the Turks at once discontinued the general disarmament. The measure had evidently only been a pretext for the infliction of a humiliation on the defender of the Christians.

The Christian powers covered Abdel Kader with the most distinguished marks of their gratitude and admiration. Letters, presents, and orders came from every side. France sent the Grand Cordon of the Legion of Honour; Russia, the Grand Cross of the White Eagle; Prussia, the Grand Cross of the Black Eagle; Greece, the Grand Cross of the Saviour; Turkey, the Medjidié of the 1st class. England sent a double-barreled gun, beautifully inlaid with gold; America, a brace of pistols similarly inlaid. The Order of Freemasons in France sent him a magnificent star. All these gifts and decorations were accompanied by letters of thanks.

But not only in the Christian world had the conduct of Abdel Kader, in the midst of the hideous scenes enacted through the fell working of Turkish fanaticism, created a deep sensation and elicited tributes of praise and general rejoicing. In the Mohammedan world also, a profound feeling of astonishment and abhorrence had been excited at the vindictive daring, the blind fatuity, and the sanguinary anti-Christian malevolence of a Mohammedan power which, while pretending to be amenable to the higher instincts of European civilisation, could thus stimulate to deeds of atrocity, gratuitously barbarous, and not even sanctioned or countenanced by the most ferocious and exaggerated doctrines of the Koran itself.

This feeling found its most eloquent exponent in the illustrious hero of the Caucasus. Schamyl, from his place of exile in Russia, addressed the following letter to Abdel Kader:—

"To him who has made himself celebrated amongst all classes, high and low; who by his numerous and precious qualities stands distinguished from the rest of men; who put out the fire of discord before it had time to extend; who rooted up the tree of enmity, the fruit of which is, as it were, a head of Satan. Praise be to God, that He has clothed His servant with strength and faith! We would speak of the true and sincere friend, Abdel Kader the just. Salutation to you! May the palm tree of merit and honour be ever fruitful in your person!

"Be it known to you, when my ear was struck with that which is hateful to the sense of hearing, and repulsive to human nature—I allude to the events lately occurring in Damascus, between the Mussulmans and the Christians, in which the former displayed a conduct unworthy of the professors of Islamism, and which can only lead to every kind of excess—a film spread over my soul, and my face, usually tranquil and serene, became covered with the shade of sadness. I cried out to myself, 'Evil is on the earth and on the sea, by reason of man's wickedness and perversity.'

"I was astonished at the blindness of the functionaries who have plunged into such excesses, forgetful of the words of the Prophet, peace be upon him :—' *Whoever shall be unjust towards a tributary (a Christian), who shall do him a wrong, who shall lay on him any charge beyond his means, and finally, who shall deprive him of anything without his own consent, it is I who will be his accuser in the day of judgment.*' Oh, the sublime words! But when I was informed that you had covered the tributaries with the wings of kindness and compassion; that you had opposed yourself to the men who do contrary to the will of the Most High God, and that you had conquered the palm of victory in the amphitheatre of glory—a success which you have richly merited—I praised you, as the Most High God will praise you in that day, when fortune and children will avail but little. Truly, you have realised the word of the great Apostle whom the Most High God sent as a mark of pity for his creatures, and you have opposed a barrier to those who rejected his great example. May God preserve us from those who transgress His laws !

" Impatient to testify the admiration I feel for your conduct, I hasten to address you this letter, as a drop out of the reservoir of my sympathies.

" The unfortunate, who through the working of the decrees of the Great Master, has fallen into the hands of the infidels.

" SCHAMYL, the Exile."

To this sympathetic effusion Abdel Kader thus replied :—

" Praise be to God, the Master of worlds ! May God be propitious to our lord Mohammed and all his brother prophets and apostles.

" This comes from him who has great need of his all-abundant mercies, Abdel Kader, son of Mehi-ed-deen, il Hassany, and is addressed to his brother and friend in God, the glorious Schamyl. May God be favourable to us and you, at home and abroad ! May the peace and grace of God rest ever upon you !

" We have received your honourable letter, and your charming words have rejoiced our heart. That which you have heard about us, and which has given you such satisfaction, respecting our defence of the tributaries and the protection we gave them, both as regards their persons and their goods, according to our zeal and our means—all that, as you well know, is nothing but the fulfilment of the principles of our sacred law and of the dictates of humanity. Indeed, our law is the confirmation of all the best qualities, and embraces all virtues as a collar encircles the neck.

"Vice is condemned in all religions; and to allow oneself to be carried away by it is like taking a poisonous aliment into the stomach. Nevertheless, as the poet has said, 'Man, in certain moments of trial, has a bandage over his eyes, so that he calls that desirable which is just the reverse.' Truly it is a case to say, 'To God we belong and to Him we return.' When we think how few men of real religion there are, how small the number of defenders and champions of the truth—when one sees ignorant persons imagining that the principle of Islamism is hardness, severity, extravagance, and barbarity—it is time to repeat these words, 'Patience is lovely; in God let us trust.'

"We were informed, some time ago, that you had arrived near the Emperor of Russia; and that this prince, treating you in a manner worthy of you, had loaded you with civilities and covered you with honour. We were told, moreover, that you had asked for permission to visit the holy cities (Mecca and Medina); and we pray God that he may prosper your demand and accomplish your wishes.

"Indeed, the Emperor of Russia is one of the most distinguished of sovereigns. He is one of those who desire to see the record of their exalted deeds preserved in books. We hope, therefore, that his magnanimity will grant you your wishes without difficulty. It is thus that the Sultan Napoleon III. has acted towards us. He has performed things for us which could never have entered into the mind of man. After all, it is in God alone that we must place our hope. He only has a right to our homage.

"ABDEL KADER IBN MEHI-ED-DEEN IL HASSANY."

The tranquil current of Abdel Kader's life, momentarily ruffled, but scarcely interrupted, by the terrific episode which had broken in on his retirement, now resumed its wonted course. The simplicity, the scrupulous regularity, the exact and unvarying conscientiousness which guide and influence his actions, operate upon the thread of his existence with all the harmony of fixed laws.

He rises two hours before daybreak, and is engaged in prayer and religious meditation till sunrise, when he goes to the mosque. After spending half an hour there in public devotions, he returns to his house, snatches a hurried meal, and then studies in his library till mid-day. The muezzin's call now summons him again to the mosque, where his class is already assembled, awaiting his arrival. He takes his seat, opens the book fixed upon for discussion, and reads aloud, constantly interrupted by demands for those explanations which unlock the varied and accumulated stores of his troubled years of laborious study, investigation, and research. The sitting lasts for three hours.

Afternoon prayer finished, Abdel Kader returns home and spends an hour amongst his children—his eight sons—examining the progress they are making in their studies. Then he dines. At sunset he is again in the mosque, and instructs his class for one hour and a half. His professor's duties for the day are now over. A couple of hours are still on hand; they are spent in his library. He then retires to rest.

Abdel Kader is punctual in his charities. Every Friday the street leading to his house may be seen filled with the poor, who are gathered together for their appointed distribution of bread. The poor who die (if utterly without means), not merely in his own quarter, but throughout Damascus, are buried at his expense. Every case of destitution has only to be brought to his notice to be instantly relieved. He lays out regularly more than £20 a month in charitable donations.

Abdel Kader had long cherished in his heart the hope and desire of being able, sooner or later, to complete his round of religious duties by a crowning act of devotion. In the eyes of the devout Mussulman, no earthly rank or dignity is to be compared to that which carries with it the glorious distinction of entitling its bearer to be called " the Fellow of the Prophet."

To obtain this signal privilege, it is necessary to dwell continuously at Mecca or Medina for two years, or, at all events, to remain in the holy cities until two successive pilgrimages (Hadj) have arrived at and departed from those places. Abdel Kader now obtained the permission of his friend and benefactor, the Emperor Napoleon III., to prosecute his pious purpose. Being asked one day how he could bear to separate himself, at his age, for so long a time from his family, he replied, " It is true my family is dear to me, but God is dearer."

He left Damascus in January, 1863; and, after staying a

few weeks in Cairo, embarked for Djedda, and in due time reached Mecca. There he was received by the great body of Ulemas and Imams, who make that holy city their constant place of residence, with the most marked respect and consideration. The Shereef of Mecca ordered a couple of rooms, within the precincts of the Haram, to be placed at his disposal. He was overwhelmed by visitors. After ten days, he intimated that his period of reception was over. He begged to be left in undisturbed privacy and seclusion.

For the next twelve months he never quitted his hermit's cell, except to go to the great mosque. His whole time was given up to sacred studies, meditation, and prayer. The fervour of his religious abstraction was stimulated by the most rigorous self-denial. He only allowed himself four hours' sleep. He broke his fast but once in twenty-four hours, and then only to eat bread and olives. The severity and long continuance of this bodily and mental discipline told even on his iron frame. In the spring of 1864 he indulged in a short relaxation by going to Taif, a town delightfully situated in a mountainous region about fourteen hours from Mecca, and surrounded with flowing streams and delicious gardens.

Returning thence to Djedda he took ship, and in five days reached the port of Reis, six days' distance by land from Medina. The whole of the intervening districts between Mecca and Medina, spreading far into the interior, and down to the sea-coasts, are infested by a race of Arabs called the Arabs Hurb. These demi-savages are hideous to behold. They wear little or no clothing. Their skins resemble burnt and crackling parchment. Their thick, shaggy, black hair floats wildly

over their shoulders. They have few horses; but they themselves run like ostriches.

These Arab tribes are at perpetual war with the Turks.
No caravan dares to cross these dangerous tracts without
being strongly guarded. This duty devolves on Turkish
troops, who run the gauntlet with hearts failing them for
fear. They are generally attacked, mostly defeated, sometimes destroyed, the caravan reaching its destination naked
and penniless.

Amongst the Arabs Hurb the name of Abdel Kader had for
years been a household word. On hearing of his arrival at
Reis, their Sheiks sent him a deputation requesting permission for them to be allowed to come and offer him their salutations. He replied, that as they were at open enmity with
the Turkish Government, and as some Turkish officials were
accompanying him on his proposed journey inward, he begged
to be spared the distinction they would have offered him.
They acknowledged the delicacy of the dilemma, and did not
persist. For once, and solely for the sake of Abdel Kader,
they allowed the caravan from Reis to reach Medina without
the slightest molestation. The return caravan was attacked
and plundered, and the Turkish guard cut to pieces.

Abdel Kader remained at Medina for four months, resuming,
near the Prophet's tomb, the course of life he had practised
while at Mecca. The guardian of the sanctuary repeatedly
invited him to examine all the precious treasures it contained
—the votive offerings of diamonds and pearls and precious
stones, and gold and silver, sent by kings, princes, potentates,
and grandees, from all parts of the Mohammedan world. But
Abdel Kader refused even to look at the treasures. He

regarded them as a wasteful and useless prodigality, and a sinful misapplication of wealth, which might have been far better employed in works of general charity.

When the time for his departure arrived, the Arabs Hurb again pressed on him their services, and offered to escort him in perfect safety through the overland route of fourteen days to Mecca. He would have availed himself of their offer had not two Ulemas who were his travelling companions dreaded the fatigues of the journey; and not wishing to separate himself from his fellow-travellers, he was again obliged to decline these flattering marks of personal devotion and attachment. He returned to Reis, and reached Mecca by the way he had come, in time to be present at the rites and solemnities of the Beiram, for the second time. His object and his vow were thus accomplished. He now turned his face homewards, and in June, 1864, arrived at Alexandria.

Abdel Kader had just succeeded in achieving, after much toil and self-abnegation, the highest distinction to be attained in a religious profession pre-eminently dogmatic and exclusive. By a singular contrast, he now claimed to wear the badge of a society based and established on the principle of universal brotherhood. The Masonic body in Alexandria hastened to welcome the illustrious neophyte. The Lodge of the Pyramids was especially convoked for the occasion in the evening of the 18th of June. Abdel Kader was initiated into the mysteries; and to the privilege of being the "Fellow of the Prophet," added the more time-honoured privilege of being "a free and accepted Mason."

After staying a short time at Alexandria, in order to complete the requisite documents and arrange the necessary details which were to enable him to take possession of a large landed property, presented to him by the Viceroy of Egypt, he left for Syria, and reached Damascus towards the end of July, 1864. There, for the present, we leave this "great and complete man," pursuing that career which he considers to have been marked out for him by destiny. Of this career he himself has said, " It was pointed out to me by my birth, my education, and my predilection. It is one which I ardently long to resume, and to which I never cease praying to God to allow me to return, now at the close of my laborious years."

Though such, however, was the career which Abdel Kader had imagined for himself, an over-ruling Providence had ordained it otherwise. His career, as it stands before the public, is without a counterpart in the annals of great and extraordinary men, for its sudden and unexpected rise, for the strange variety of its phases, and the unlooked-for stages of its development. Never was there a career more completely typical of the riddle of human existence—never one which more completely illustrated the truth of the wise man's saying—" A man's goings are of the Lord ; how can a man then understand his way ? "

That career may now be recapitulated in a few brief sentences. A young Mohammedan Arab had devoted himself to the seclusion and religious exercises of the cloister. A crisis in his country's fate called him reluctantly from his retreat to the head of affairs. The seeds of his latent genius burst forth at once into full-blown maturity. He shone with unrivalled splendour as the preacher and leader of a Holy War against the encroachments of a Christian power. He kept the armies of this great power at bay for fifteen years, with forces immeasurably inferior, and only made available by the fiery enthusiasm with which he knew how to inspire them. Twice he compelled his enemy to grant him advantageous terms of peace, and to salute him with titles of sovereignty.

All the while, he was moulding and forming an internal administration, which, rapidly superseding the wildest anarchy and confusion, presented a pattern of order, regularity, and justice. He laid the foundation of a Mohammedan empire. In his own person he offered to his subjects a model of bravery, fortitude, activity, perseverance, piety, and zeal. He yielded at length to overwhelming numbers. He surrendered to his Christian foes, on the express condition that they should conduct him, in the full enjoyment of complete and unrestricted freedom, to some other Moslem soil.

His enemies treacherously conveyed him to their own land. Their Government threw him into hopeless and apparently life-long captivity. A prince whose genius, like his own, had sustained him with unfailing trust and confidence through adverse fortunes, overthrew that Government and arrived at supreme power. The magnanimity of that prince restored him to liberty.

Then, by a wonderful turn in the wheel of fortune, this brilliant and uncompromising champion of Islamism was seen to take a marked and foremost place in the Christian world. He became a member of many of its literary and scientific bodies, corresponded on terms of equality and friendship with its most illustrious potentates; and finally, near the close of his ostensible career, saw his breast covered with the martial emblems of that very faith which, at its commencement, he had drawn his sword to resist and to defy! Truly, such a career is without its parallel in history.

Those who have perused the preceding pages will have found many grounds for salutary reflection. In the example there laid before them they will have been profitably reminded of the utter short-sightedness and uncertainty of all human calculations. They will, at the same time, have been instructed, edified, and encouraged, by the striking proof which it affords that the only really strengthening and peace-giving motives of human action are, a practical and persevering sense of duty, and a humble, cheerful, submissive, and unswerving trust in God.

THE END.

VIRTUE AND CO., PRINTERS, CITY-ROAD, LONDON.

www.ingramcontent.com/pod-product-compliance
Lightning Source LLC
Chambersburg PA
CBHW021802110726
47902CB00006B/1614